"So what's *your* code name?"

Marnie met the faux-security-guard-turned-special-agent's gaze and continued, "I mean, I can hazard a few guesses, but none of them is worth uttering in polite society."

"I owe you an apology," he said in an amazingly courteous voice.

"Yeah, I'll say you do," she retorted before she could stop herself. "What brings on this sudden change of heart?" For such a supersecret, sophisticated organization, they sure seemed like a bunch of boneheads.

"We ran a check on your name," he said, "and we realized you are indeed who you say you are."

"Why didn't you run a check like that the minute I got here?" she demanded.

"We were convinced you were Lila trying to pull a fast one. We didn't have any reason to believe you were who you said you were."

Marnie nodded slowly. "Okay," she said. Even though she was still suspicious of the sudden turnaround. "So does this mean I can go home?" she asked hopefully.

He nodded. "I'll drive you myself...."

ELIZABETH BEVARLY

express male

HQN™

ISBN-13: 978-0-373-77277-3
ISBN-10:   0-373-77277-7

EXPRESS MALE

For the Robinson women.
All four generations.
We rock.

CHAPTER ONE

AN AWED SILENCE FELL over Carnegie Hall as Marnie Lundy strolled confidently across the stage in her elegant black formal, the flowing crepe whispering about her wrists and ankles with every step. The darkness of the auditorium hid the thousands of eyes she knew were fixed upon her, but she wavered not once. Smiling to herself, she recalled, as she always did when she took the stage, the old Bugs Bunny cartoon where the celebrated symphony conductor Leopold appeared amid hushed and reverent murmurs of "Leopold. Leopold. Leopold."

Tonight, however, there was no symphony. Tonight, there was no conductor. Because tonight, Marnie Lundy, concert pianist, would solo for thousands of her admirers. Tonight, the hushed and reverent murmurs were of "Marnie. Marnie. Marnie."

She threw back her head, shaking silvery blond hair over her shoulders, and seated herself gracefully on the bench. Her posture was impeccable, the piano was tuned to perfection and her knowledge of the music was complete. The gods were smiling, the planets were aligned and all was right in the universe. Lifting her hands to the keys, she gently stroked the ivory, filling her ears and her mind and her heart with the lovely, lilting strains of—

"Hey, lady, where's the bathroom?"

She squeezed her eyes shut tight, sighing with much eloquence as her fingers went still. "It's behind you," she said glumly. "Through ladies' hosiery and designer handbags, in men's sportswear. Next to the Tommy Bahama display."

"Thanks, toots."

When she opened her eyes, it was to see a stout, balding man in an ugly Hawaiian shirt and enormous pants waddling away in the direction into which she'd sent him. Instead of a darkened Carnegie Hall, she was seated in the middle of a brightly lit department store—Lauderdale's of Cleveland, to be precise—where Marnie Lundy appeared every Monday, Wednesday and Friday evening playing the piano. And where she appeared hawking overpriced underwear in the lingerie department other days. The black crepe formal was actually a straight, gray cotton skirt and light blue sweater set, and the silvery blond hair was really more of the dishwater variety. It *was* long enough to throw over her shoulders, though, if she wanted to. But that didn't happen often, since it was generally twisted into a loose knot atop her head, as it was now.

Alas, the thousands of adoring eyes Marnie had imagined worshipping her actually amounted to only eight, mostly indifferent ones: two on the face of a young mother seated on a sofa near the piano (the two on the baby to whom she was feeding a bottle were closed), two on the bored saleswoman in ladies' hosiery, two on a teenage girl who was clearly trying to decide if anyone would notice her tucking the Kate Spade wallet she was fingering into her jacket pocket and two on the face of the store manager, who really should have been keeping his eyes on the teenager in Kate Spade instead.

Fortunately, those final two eyes were approving of Marnie. Unfortunately, they were a little *too* approving. In spite of his name, Bob Troutman wasn't much of a catch. Not just because he was a greasy, revolting little fish-faced man—though, granted, that part was pretty off-putting. But also because he had a wife and four little Troutmans living with him at the bottom of whatever contaminated body of water he called his habitat. All told, it was enough to put Marnie off her lunch whenever she saw the guy. Which was why she always looked away whenever she caught him watching her. Like, for instance, now.

Dropping her gaze back to the piano keys, she repositioned her fingers and played the opening bars of "Stardust." In her Carnegie Hall fantasy, she would have flawlessly performed Chopin's *Polonaise* in A flat, but here at Lauderdale's, old standards were de rigueur, since so many of Lauderdale's shoppers were little old ladies who remembered when cotton briefs only cost ten cents a pair. And, boy, don't think Marnie didn't hear about *that* every day of the week, either.

Still, it was a decent job, as jobs went. The pay wasn't great, but it had flexible hours and gave her the time she needed for other pursuits, like writing her music and giving lessons to her young students. She'd never been one for setting the world on fire, Carnegie Hall fantasies notwithstanding. Having grown up as the only child of a widowed, never-again-married English professor father, hers had always been a quiet life, and that still suited her. Working for Lauderdale's enabled her to keep living that way.

Well, except when Bob Troutman's scaly bad self was on the prowl. On the swim. Whatever. But if he was the worst thing that ever happened in her life—and so far, hands down, he was—Marnie would die a happy, tranquil woman.

The music flowed from her fingertips for the three hours she was scheduled to play—interspersed, it went without saying, with periodic directions to the bathroom, the elevator and better dresses. At closing, she straightened up for whoever was scheduled to play in the morning, tidying with what a couple of the other pianists had called her obsessive-compulsive neatness. Well, could she help it if she liked the sheet music alphabetized? And then put in numerical order according to the year it was written? Things like that brought order to a troubled civilization. The world would be a better place if more people took a few minutes out of their day to alphabetize and put stuff in numerical order.

But Marnie had to take more than a few minutes that evening, because whoever had played over the weekend had really fouled things up. That was why, when she finally found her way to the employees' exit at the back of the store, there was no one left for her to walk out with. Not that Lauderdale's was in a bad part of town—on the contrary, this part of Cleveland was quite upscale—but no woman relished entering a dark, deserted parking lot alone. The presence of a few cars indicated there must still be a handful of people around somewhere, so she decided to wait.

Fifteen minutes later, she was growing impatient. She could see her car from where she stood, she reassured herself, right in the middle of the lot beneath a streetlight, with nothing parked near it. Pulling her keys from her purse, she jingled them merrily in defiance of the unwelcoming darkness.

There. Take that, *Mr. Bogeyman.*

But Mr. Bogeyman snapped back when she took her first step through the exit. The night was heavy and damp from rain earlier in the day, and even darker than usual thanks to thick clouds looming overhead. The streetlights dotting the parking lot radiated fat, milky halos of light that never quite reached the pavement, trapping moisture within. Something about the sight made Marnie feel trapped, too. A faint shudder of apprehension stole down her spine, and goose bumps rioted on her arms beneath the sleeve of her sweater.

How strange. She was one for neither whimsy nor portent, never succumbed to omens or premonitions or shudders down the spine and goose bumps under the sleeve. Whatever she was feeling now was unfounded and silly. Today had been like any other day. Tonight would be no different.

With her purse dangling from one bent elbow, she buttoned up her sweater against the cool April evening and squared her shoulders. This was silly, this unfounded aversion to nothing, and honestly, she'd walked through this door and into this parking lot hundreds of times without suffering so much as a stubbed toe, and I mean really, stop being so ridiculous. Marching forward with renewed purpose, she strode into the night. And she got almost all the way to her car before she felt a hand clamp down on her shoulder. Hard.

She cried out as she spun around.

Then halted at once when she saw that the hand was

attached to the arm of a tidy, wizened little man who was shorter even than she. And since Marnie stood no more than five-three on a good day—in one-inch heels—that was saying something. The man wore an aged brown suit, and his gray hair was slicked straight back from his face, though whether that was due to the damp air or some kind of hair goo favored by elderly men, she couldn't have said. His features gave him the appearance of being kind, sweet even, and he smiled benignly at her reaction.

"I'm so sorry," he said gently. "I didn't mean to frighten you."

Marnie smiled back, though the gesture was less a greeting than it was a reaction to profound relief. This guy probably didn't weigh much more than she did, and couldn't possibly be dangerous. Probably, he was a shopper who'd lost his way to his car and wanted help finding it. Certainly he wasn't menacing.

Until he said, "I'm so relieved to have found you, Lila. I was beginning to think they weren't going to send anyone. I was beginning to think they didn't even believe me."

That was when Marnie began to suspect that the guy, however unassuming, might just be a stark raving lunatic, and maybe it was something other than his car that he was looking for, and maybe it would be a good idea for her to throw up her hands and run screaming like a ninny in the other direction.

Not wanting to be an alarmist, however, she replied instead, "I beg your pardon?"

The man smiled his kindly smile again. "I wasn't expecting them to send *you*, though, Lila, since this is something one of the junior operatives could have handled. Still, using a department store for the exchange is quite ingenious. I just wish I'd had some warning. I couldn't believe it when I saw you working last night. One minute, I was looking for a birthday present for my daughter—she loves those big flannel pajamas, you see, especially the ones that have some kind of happy-hour motif. Though I myself kind of worry about her in that regard. She really does drink too much sometimes, and…" He blinked rapidly a few times in succession, as if he were confused—thank God, Marnie wasn't the only one—then asked, "Where was I?"

"Um, happy-hour pajamas?" she prodded. Though, really, he was someplace that Marnie would just as soon not visit. La-la land.

"No, before that," he said, tapping his head lightly, as if that might stimulate his brain. Good luck on that, Marnie thought.

"Oh, I remember now," he finally said. "One minute I was shopping for my daughter, and the next minute, I saw one of the most dangerous women in the world straightening underwear at Lauderdale's. Obviously, when I saw you, I knew you were waiting for me to make the exchange. Though it would have been nice if someone had told me you'd be here," he added in a chastising voice. But before Marnie could utter a word in response—not that she had any idea what to say—he hurried on, "Anyway, I stayed up all night last night getting my opus together, and I waited until closing time tonight to give it to you. I didn't want anything to interrupt us."

He spoke so quickly—and so strangely—that Marnie

was feeling dizzy by the time he paused for breath. What little sense she did make of his speech left her even more confused. Clearly, the man had mistaken her for someone else. Possibly, he was a tad delusional. Conceivably, he was quite mad. Suddenly, the parking lot seemed a lot more menacing than it had before. Suddenly, her aversion to leaving the store by herself didn't seem silly at all.

A quick glance around indicated she was still well and truly alone—alas—so it might serve well to just play along for a minute and pretend the guy was making sense. At least until she figured out how she could make the short sprint to her car without giving him enough time to whip out a carving knife.

"I beg your pardon?" she asked again.

The man's eyes went wide, and he covered his mouth with one hand in an uh-oh-what-have-I-done gesture. "Oh, of course," he said in a chastened voice. "I'm not supposed to call you Lila, am I?" He made a fist and gently tapped his forehead. "Silly me. I've been out of the service too long. And that little run-in with the KGB years ago didn't help." He smiled at Marnie again. "What name are you going by on your current assignment, dear?"

Current assignment? Marnie repeated to herself. Run-in with the KGB? Oh, yeah. Definitely delusional. "Uh…Marnie," she said without thinking. But that was probably okay, wasn't it? As long as she didn't give him her last name, she should be fine, right?

He nodded as if he understood completely. Well, that made one of them. "Marnie. Of course. Was it chosen by He Whose Name Nobody Dares Say?"

Oh, yeah. Definitely quite mad. "Um, actually, it was my father," she told him.

"Ah." The little man nodded in a way that made her think he knew something she didn't. She hated to think what. "I had no idea the two of you were related," he continued. "How did that get by me? That must have aided your quick climb up the professional ladder. Not to imply that your ruthlessness and intelligence and complete flouting of personal safety weren't also responsible," he hastened to add. "And it's a lovely name." He winked at her before adding, "Marnie."

"Thank you," she said. She tried to backtrack to the exact moment when her life had slipped into the surreal. In hindsight, it probably hadn't been a good idea to have that kielbasa from Hank's Franks at the mall food court for dinner. Just how long had it been on the rotisserie anyway? Maybe she should have risked the long line at Ruthie's Smoothies.

Not that a digestively generated hallucination was her biggest problem at the moment. Especially since her new bestest friend in the world—or, at least, Lila's bestest friend in the world, whoever she was—seemed to be getting excited about something. And gosh, Marnie *really* hated to think what.

"Although I must say, it's not just your high-ranking status that makes me surprised to see you in Cleveland. Last I heard, you were on a leave of absence in Las Vegas. And then there was that rumor about you having tried to kill—"

He stopped abruptly, his expression indicating he'd almost said something he would regret later. Funny, that, since Marnie was regretting it right now. He'd mistaken her for someone who'd try to kill someone else? That couldn't possibly be good, could it? Thankfully, he hurried on before she had a chance to think too much about that. Or experience a stark, raving panic attack.

"Well," he said, "let's just say I'm glad you're here. For a number of reasons."

"Um, look," she interjected as gently as she could, thinking it would probably be best if she didn't hear *any* of those reasons. "You've obviously mistaken me for someone else. My name isn't Lila. It's Marnie. I'm sorry I'm not who you're looking for, but…" She shrugged, the internationally recognized sign language for *Can't help you, fella.*

"Of course you're not who I'm looking for," he said. "I should have realized that right away."

Marnie would have breathed a sigh of relief, but the little man took a step closer, looked first one way, then the other, then leaned in very close, crowding her personal space way more than she liked.

"I didn't realize we were being watched," he whispered so softly she almost didn't hear. "I should have realized." He moved a hand to his mouth to mimic the locking of a lock and throwing away of the key. Very quietly, he promised, "From now on, I'll just call you Marnie, Lila. I won't call you Lila anymore, Marnie."

Since he was so close, Marnie took advantage of the opportunity to inhale a deep breath, to see if it might offer some clue as to what he had been drinking. Smoking. Sniffing. Absorbing subcutaneously. All of the above. But there was nary a hint of alcoholic, herbal or chemical enhancement about him. A touch of garlic, perhaps, but as far as she knew, garlic had never driven anyone around the bend like this.

He did that look-one-way-then-the-other thing again, then held up a fat manila envelope that had seen better days. It was stuffed about as full as it could be and still be closed, the flap torn and bent, the paper soiled and wrinkled. Two big rubber bands were wound around it, one vertically and one horizontally, as if he feared the envelope might give way and spill its contents any moment, something that seemed entirely possible. Then he smiled again.

"Here's my book," he said. "I finished it, just as I promised them I would."

Book? Marnie wanted to say. That was no book. It was just a big, dirty envelope full of papers. Why would he bring it to her? To Lila? To anyone? And just who was the "them" he was talking about?

"It's only a first draft, you understand," he hastened to add, "but it is my greatest opus."

Ooh, it was a book he'd *written*. Now Marnie *really* didn't want to have anything to do with it.

"Um, that's really nice, and I appreciate it," she said as politely as she could. She glanced around again, hoping *somebody* might have shown up by now. At this point, she'd even welcome the appearance of Bob Troutman. Well, probably. Maybe. Oh, okay, she could handle this little guy for a few minutes more. "But I'm probably not the best person to give it to," she added. "I'm not much good when it comes to literary criticism. I'm more of a music person."

"No, no," he insisted, his smile falling some. "You'll like this, no matter what. I assure you, it's a wonderful *opus*."

There was that word *opus* again. He really seemed to be attached to it. "Oh, I don't doubt that for a minute,"

Marnie assured the man. "But, honestly, I just don't think I'm qualified to—"

"It's the story of a powerful sorcerer," he interrupted in a singsongy, once-upon-a-time voice. "A sorcerer who has betrayed people, and who's been hiding from those people, hoping they won't find him."

"Um, sounds great," Marnie said flatly, not wanting to encourage him—especially since fantasy novels *really* weren't her thing. "But, really, I—"

"This book tells all about this *sorcerer,*" the man began again, emphasizing that last word meaningfully. Meaningful to him, anyway, since Marnie had no idea what he was talking about. "It tells things about the *sorcerer* no one knew before. And it tells about where the *sorcerer* has been hiding and what he's been up to. It tells about where he's going next. You'll like it, I promise." He winked at her again, a gesture that was beginning to creep her out. "It is my finest *opus,*" he said again.

Hoo-kay, Marnie thought. Whoever this guy was, he'd caught the express train from la-la land and hopped off at weirdsville. And now he was looking around for the platform for his connection to loonytown.

He shoved the envelope at her again, using both hands now. "Take it," he insisted. "Read it. Read my *opus* about the *sorcerer.*"

He was growing agitated now, and Marnie wasn't sure what crazy people did when they became agitated. Nor did she have any wish to find out. She wondered if she should just take the envelope from him and hope that would make him leave. Then she could return to Lauderdale's and alert mall security about the incident and go home.

"Um, okay," she said as she warily took the manuscript from him. "I'll read it tonight. How will that be?"

"It's just a first draft," he reminded her. "I have many notes, and will write more. When it's done, I'll bring it to you."

Oh, goody. "Well, that's…that's just fine," Marnie said, nodding. Hoping he fell for her fake smile. Hoping he went away soon. Hoping he didn't hack her to death with a carving knife on his way. "I'll, um, I'll really enjoy that."

He nodded, too, his own warm, benign smile so at odds with his stark, raving lunacy. "Thank you, Lila. Oops, I mean…Marnie." He winked again, and she tried not to flinch. "I know where to find you now," he added. As if she really needed for him to put that fine a point on it. "And I'll contact you again when the time is right."

Now there was something to look forward to. She held up the hefty manuscript. "I, um, I'll read this tonight," she said again, since he didn't get the hint the first time and leave.

"Good," he said. "Take good care of my opus. Marnie."

"I will," she told him. "I promise your opus is safe with me."

His smile went kind of sentimental and satisfied and serene at that, and his expression softened to the point where he looked almost lucid. Relief, Marnie realized. He looked profoundly relieved about something. As if by taking the manuscript from him, she had just freed him of a burden that had been almost too much for him to bear.

He leaned in close again and said quietly, "I knew not to believe what they were saying about you, Lila. I knew you could never do what they said you did. I trust you completely. I always have. And I'm so glad you're back. They need you."

Strangely, there was something about the way he said it, and the way he looked at her, that made Marnie feel honestly grateful for his trust. Something that made her want to promise him she would do anything for him in return. Suddenly, he didn't seem mad at all. In fact, he seemed quite sane, and quite sincere. Before she realized what she was doing, she reached out to touch his shoulder, the physical contact feeling surprisingly nice. Surprisingly comfortable. Surprisingly *comforting*. It was the oddest thing.

"I will take care of this," she told him as she held up the manuscript, "whatever it is." And she was astonished to discover that she meant exactly what she said. "You don't have to worry about it anymore, okay?"

He nodded and smiled again, then lifted a hand in farewell. "I'm glad it's with you…Marnie," he said. And without another word, he turned and walked away.

Marnie stood motionless in the middle of the deserted parking lot as she watched him go, mesmerized by his steady, purposeful stride. Not once did he look back, clearly content with how their exchange—whatever it had been about—had gone. She waited for him to approach one of the half-dozen cars still scattered in that direction, but he kept walking until he reached a hedgerow at the edge of the parking lot. She watched, amazed, as he pushed the branches of two bushes aside and stepped through them.

On the other side of that hedgerow was a park, she knew, which eventually spilled into woods. All the houses near the mall were in the other direction—and none was within comfortable walking distance for a man his age. She couldn't imagine where he was going.

Strange. Very strange.

She looked down at the thickly stuffed envelope in her hands and, for the first time, noticed writing on the outside of it. Nothing intelligible, mostly a bunch of doodles that didn't make sense. Turning it over, she saw the flap was fastened with one of those winding cotton cords that was whipped into a figure eight over and over again. Marnie told herself to go back into Lauderdale's and call mall security. Instead, she took the end of the string between thumb and forefinger and began to unwind it.

She was just freeing the final figure eight when she heard the scuff of a shoe over the asphalt behind her.

When she turned, she saw a man standing there who was much larger, much younger and much more menacing than the one who had just left. And where the first man's smile had been sentimental and satisfied and serene, this man's smile was feral and forbidding and frightening.

"Hello, Lila," he said. "You naughty girl, where have you been? Opus has been looking all over for you."

CHAPTER TWO

ACID HEAT SPLASHED through Marnie's belly at the man's words, spoken in a velvety voice she might have found appealing in another situation. His sophisticated good looks, too, she might have rather liked under other circumstances. A situation or circumstances like, oh…she didn't know…like maybe if she *wasn't* standing in the middle of a dark, deserted parking lot with her car still a good ten yards away. Like maybe if she *didn't* feel as if she'd slipped into the *Twilight Zone.* Like maybe if he *hadn't* come up out of nowhere like a deranged movie murderer. Like maybe if she *wasn't* a complete sissy about things like deserted parking lots and surreal life and deranged murderers.

Stuff like that.

But since Marnie was the proud owner of a sissiness that rivaled some of the greatest sissies in history, she wasn't much impressed by the man's good looks and velvety voice. Especially since he was calling her Lila, something that jerked her right back into that distorted—and soon to be sordid—reality, and, well, suffice it to say that her day just wasn't turning out to be anything like she had anticipated when she'd rolled out of bed that morning.

"And OPUS isn't the only one who's been looking for you, sweetheart," he added, the endearment dripping not with affection, but with what sounded very much like animosity. "I've been looking all over for you, too."

Too frightened now to even move, Marnie tried to at least mentally catalogue the man's features, so that she could give an accurate description to a police artist later. Providing, of course, she survived. Somehow, though, she didn't think she could ever forget his face, so arrestingly handsome was he, in spite of his malevolence. His dark auburn hair was groomed to perfection, his amber eyes reflected intelligence and, incongruously, good humor. His clothing was faultless and expensively tailored; dark trousers and a dark T-shirt beneath a jacket that was darker still. All the better to hide in the darkness with, my dear. Nevertheless, had Marnie seen him inside Lauderdale's instead of out here, she would have thought him a very attractive, wealthy businessman on the way home from happy hour. Out here, there was nothing happy about him. And she didn't even want to think about what kind of business he might be up to.

"I'm not Lila," she said before she even realized she'd intended to speak, amazed at how calm and level her voice was. "I seem to have one of those faces that resemble a lot of others. I'm not who you're looking for."

In response to her assurance, the man smiled and said, "Of course you're not. Your name is Marnie, right? This week, anyway. Of course, the last time I saw you, you were going by the delightful moniker of Tiffannee. With two *f*'s, two *n*'s and two *e*'s."

Oh, please, Marnie wanted to say. What kind of woman actually claimed such a name? "That wasn't me," she insisted politely. "I've only gone by the one name all my life."

But the man seemed to have stopped listening to her. Because his gaze was fixed on the battered manuscript she was hugging to her midsection, as if it were a magic shield that might shelter her from harm.

"Well, just give me what Philosopher gave you," he said, "and I'll forget all about that pesky episode in Indianapolis. Fair enough?"

Philosopher? Marnie wanted to ask. Indianapolis? What was he talking about? She hadn't been to Indianapolis for years. And what kind of name was Philosopher? Obviously the guy was talking about the little man who'd given Marnie the manuscript, but how did this guy know him? And if he knew him, then why hadn't he asked for the manuscript before Marnie ended up with it? And why had both men mistaken her for the same woman?

Just what was going on?

He brought his gaze back up to hers, his smile in place again, then extended his hand, palm out, in a request for the package. "Come on, Lila, hand it over."

Having no idea why she did it, Marnie clutched it more tightly to herself. Very slowly, she shook her head. "No."

He didn't seem surprised by her answer. Which was funny, because Marnie sure was. The smart thing would be to forget about protecting it, since she didn't know what it was anyway, and she certainly had no obligation to the strange—and she meant that in more than one sense of the word—man who had given it to her. She should just throw it as far as she could away from herself then bolt for the employee exit, and call mall security from the safety of the store. But something made her hesitate.

She remembered how the little man's face had gone all relieved and gratified when she'd promised him she would take good care of his opus. She recalled the way his entire body had seemed to shift, as if she'd just literally unburdened him of a weight too onerous to bear. She heard again the utter trust in his voice when he told her he was glad she was the one accepting the responsibility. Even though she knew it was nuts to feel obligated to him, she did. She'd made a promise to him. And for some reason, it seemed vitally important that she keep it.

"I'm sorry, but I'm not who you're looking for," she said more forcefully this time. She curled her fingers tightly around the envelope. "And this doesn't belong to you. It belongs to someone else, and I promised him I'd take good care of it."

Once again, the man seemed in no way surprised by her reply. "Of course," he said mildly. "It's much too valuable for you to allow it to fall into the wrong hands, isn't it? And whose hands could be more wrong than mine?"

"Look, mister, I don't even know you," Marnie said, biting back the fear that rose in her throat, and feeling uncharacteristically defiant. There was just something about the man that challenged her. Of course, that same thing that challenged her would probably be responsible for her being cut into little pieces and left at various landmarks around the city, too. For now, she tried not to think about that. "If you don't leave right this minute," she added, "I'll scream."

He chuckled. "Yes, well, the last time you screamed at

me, Lila, it was because I was giving you a spectacular orgasm during the best sex either of us ever had. You'll forgive me if I don't take your threat too seriously." He lifted a hand as if he intended to touch her, and Marnie instinctively, physically, recoiled. Smiling sadly, he dropped his hand again, and said in a voice that held both regret and resolution, "Pity things turned out the way they did, isn't it? We were extraordinary together."

Her eyes went wide at that, her stomach pitching at the implication. If he thought she was a woman he'd known intimately—or whatever it was that passed for intimacy with a man like him—then he wouldn't think twice about trying it again. *It* being a word for something she absolutely didn't want to think about.

Run away, she told herself. *Now, when he's not prepared for it. Run back to the store and hope someone's there.*

He seemed to read her mind, though, because before Marnie could even lift a foot from the ground, he lunged at her, grabbing her upper arms and hauling her against himself. His face barely an inch from hers, he said, "Give me the manuscript, Lila. I'd rather not hurt you if I can help it."

Marnie's heart was pounding now, her entire body going hot. Her brain lurched into action, but it rushed in so many directions at once, she couldn't hang on to a single thought. The man's fingers curled more tightly into her arms, hard enough that he was able to lift her partly off the ground. When she cried out at the pain, however, he eased his grip some, as if he really *didn't* want to hurt her.

But he did pull her forward even more and murmured, "Give it up, Lila. You know you want to. You know they haven't treated you as well as they should. And you know I treated you better than anyone has. Join me. You and I together would be invincible."

Dizzy now, and too terrified to speak, Marnie felt her eyes begin to flutter closed. She feared she would faint, that she wouldn't be able to fight back, and although she struggled to hold on, she had no idea what to do. Nothing like this had ever happened to her before. She was the product of the most normal upbringing, the most normal life. She had no enemies. She avoided confrontations. She was tolerant, decent, compassionate. She lived a quiet, uneventful life. She taught music to children. She donated money to the local animal shelter. She volunteered at the food bank two weekends a month. She was a good person. Why was this happening to her?

She would have given anything in that moment for a knight in shining armor to gallop up on his faithful steed and fell her attacker with an enchanted sword. But as a thirty-three-year-old single female well versed in the local dating scene, she knew Cleveland wasn't overrun by paladins these days.

But as if cued by her hopeful thoughts, a soft buzzing erupted out of nowhere, a sound Marnie recognized as one of the little golf carts the mall security guards used for their patrols. Until now, she'd thought the vehicles were kind of silly for law enforcement, even at an upscale mall. But when she glanced to her left and saw one circling the corner of the building just then, it looked very much like a white stallion indeed. And the uniformed guard behind the wheel could have easily passed for a gallant man-at-arms.

Ah. Just the paladin she was looking for.

Evidently making his nightly rounds, the security guard wasted no time coming to Marnie's rescue. No sooner had he stopped the golf cart than did he launch himself out of it, running at full tilt toward her assailant. Without even stopping to ask what was going on—not that it probably wasn't kind of obvious, a six-foot-plus man looming over a much smaller woman in a dark, deserted parking lot— the security guard hurtled herself at her accoster, who, likewise surprised, released Marnie and threw himself into the battle.

Everything happened very quickly after that. But even amid all the chaos and confusion, Marnie sensed something out of kilter. Both men, she noted, fought with a forcefulness and expertise that just didn't jibe with the common man. As she watched them brawl, she realized they weren't brawling at all. There was too much elegance of movement, too much definition in the blows, too much orchestration of the combat. It was almost as if she were watching a violent ballet, so graceful was the altercation. This was no garden-variety street fighting they were doing. This was something way outside the knowledge of the ordinary man.

They were well matched, though, however they had come by their learning, and for several long minutes continued their fight. Not sure what to do, Marnie stood where she was, still clutching the manuscript, marveling at the sight. If it looked like her assailant was going to win, she would make a run for it. But all signs were pointing toward her rescuer instead, who seemed to have a slight edge over the first man now. A moment later, his edge became dominance, until Marnie's assailant lay flat on his back on the asphalt.

Though not for long.

Because he scrambled quickly back up again, his nose bleeding, one cheek abraded and studied the security guard through slitted eyes. For a single, weighty moment, both men only eyed each other warily from six feet apart. Then Marnie's attacker smiled bitterly.

"I knew OPUS wouldn't be far," he muttered, "but I didn't think you'd be this close, not yet." Then, without further ado—or further adieu, for that matter—he turned and fled.

The security guard completed a half-dozen steps in the same direction, then must have had second thoughts about going after the guy. Smart man, Marnie thought. Who knew what kind of lunatic her assailant was? He might have even been armed. Best just to stay safe until they could make sense of what had happened. Not that Marnie thought for a moment that anything that had happened to her tonight would ever make sense.

After halting, the security guard watched her attacker flee until the other man was out of sight, his hands curled into fists at his side, as if he hated having to let his adversary go. Then he spun around to look at Marnie, pinning her in place with a ferocious gaze.

Wow. He was even better looking than her assailant. And as much as she hated to admit it, he kind of seemed more ominous, too.

Oh, stop it, she told herself. There was nothing ominous about this man. He'd just rescued her from danger. He might have even saved her life! Her nerves were just so raw from everything that had happened tonight that a scoop of butter brickle ice cream would have seemed ominous at that point.

Her rescuer was way too handsome to be anything but a good guy, with straight, dark blond hair falling over his forehead, and eyes so blue even the scant lamplight couldn't diminish their vividness. As he made his way toward her into better light, Marnie noted that they were a lucent pale blue, the color and clarity of a summer sky. In contrast to his soft eyes, however, the rest of his face was all dark planes and hard angles. High cheekbones were carved out above lean, tanned jaws. An elegant nose was chiseled above a full mouth that looked as if it had been wrought by an angry god. It occurred to Marnie then that his fierce features gave him the look of not a paladin, but a mercenary. Someone who only came to the rescue when he was being paid for performing the service.

It wasn't exactly a comforting realization.

Nevertheless, he was tall and strong and sturdy, easily topping six feet, his broad shoulders straining at the seams of his white shirt, his black uniform trousers hugging powerful thighs. He continued to stride toward Marnie until he came to a halt with barely a foot of distance separating them, a position that felt...

Well. To be honest, it felt kind of menacing in light of the episode she'd just escaped. She told herself it was only because her nerves were frazzled from all that had happened tonight. Her rescuer had a nasty scrape on his jaw and a split lip, and his shirt was filthy from having rolled around on the asphalt. Anyone would look menacing under such conditions.

Of course, that didn't explain why he was looking at Marnie as if she were his most hated enemy….

"Thank you," she told him, shaking off the impression almost literally. "I don't want to think about what might have happened if you hadn't shown up when you did."

His gaze was fixed entirely on her face, but he said not a word to acknowledge her gratitude. He seemed to be cataloguing her features, as if he were trying to figure out if he knew her from somewhere. But he didn't, she was sure, unless it was just in passing at the mall. She would have remembered a man like him. For a long, long time. And then she would have dreamed about him. A lot. Probably without clothes. On either of them.

"Um, I guess you need to fill out a report or something?" she asked when he remained silent. And when, you know, her thoughts started to get away from her. "I know this sort of thing doesn't happen often. I've worked at the mall for two years, and I've never heard about any woman being accosted in the parking lot."

Although he still didn't reply, his expression did at least change. A little. If possible, it became even more furious.

"Uh," Marnie tried again, "I mean, if you need me to answer any questions, I can." It wasn't like she had any plans for the evening, other than to go home, curl herself into a fetal position in the closet and weep with gratitude to still be alive.

"Or if you think it would be better to wait until tomorrow, that's okay, too," she added. "I could come to mall security on my morning break. Or you could come to Lauderdale's at your convenience. That's where I work, in the, uh—" Gee, she wasn't sure she wanted to be interviewed by this guy surrounded by women's underthings. "Well, maybe it would just be better for me to come to security. What time will you be in?"

Two things occurred to Marnie as she asked the question. Number one, that although she knew most of the mall security guards by name and all of them by sight, this guy wasn't one she recognized. And number two, his uniform didn't hug his physique so snugly because he was muscular and well-formed—though, granted, he was certainly muscular and well-formed. It was because the uniform was two sizes too small.

She dropped her gaze to the gold-tone name tag each of the security guards wore and saw that his said "Randy Fink." Which was funny, because he didn't seem like a Randy Fink at all. Who did seem like a Randy Fink was Randy Fink, a mall security guard who made regular rounds in Lauderdale's. Him, Marnie knew well. And he was indeed both randy and a fink. The man who stood before her now was neither. Well, not a fink anyway—she couldn't speak for the other. He wasn't Randy Fink, though, that was for sure.

Before she could say a word to point that out, her rescuer—such as he was—reached down to unsnap the holster of his gun. Marnie had always thought it a bit extreme for the mall to arm its security guards when the greatest enemy for most of them seemed to be the kielbasa at Hank's Franks. Now it scared her even more that the mall security guards went around armed.

He spoke then, finally, in a voice that was deep and smooth and even more velvety than her attacker's. The words he spoke, however, were just as puzzling. "Enough with the games, Lila." He fingered the handle of the gun that rose out of his holster. "I was hoping you'd come along peacefully, but now I'm not so sure. And I really don't want to have to do this the hard way."

Funnily enough, it didn't scare Marnie this time when a strange—and she meant that in more than one sense of the word—man called her by a name that wasn't her own. No, this time, it kind of ticked her off. Whoever this Lila was, she really got around. And her choice of men left *a lot* to be desired. Marnie was sick and tired of being confused with her.

She had infinitely better morals than Lila for one thing. Maybe she didn't attract a lot of men—or any lately—but the ones with whom she *had* been involved had *not* carried weapons, or engaged in fisticuffs, or threatened women, or slunk around in dark parking lots. She did have some standards. Which, now that she thought about it, might explain why she hadn't attracted a lot of men—or any lately.

But that was beside the point.

The point was… Hmm. Well, she seemed to have forgotten the point. Anyway, it was better to live one's life alone than to be involved with guys like the ones Lila dated. So there.

"I am *not* Lila," she said adamantly for the third time, to the third man, that night. "I don't know who Lila is, and I don't know why you guys keep thinking I'm her. But lemme tell ya something. If I *were* her? First thing I'd do is torch my little black book and start over again. Because the men that woman attracts are just plain *odd*."

The faux Randy Fink continued to gaze at Marnie in the

same way he had before—as if he weren't buying any of it. And he remained silent in light of her remarks.

She sighed heavily. "What do you want?" she asked calmly. Because so far tonight, she'd experienced, let's see…fear, panic, confusion, terror, relief, happiness—oh, all right and a little lust for a minute there when she got that first good look at her rescuer—bewilderment, anger and sarcasm. Yep, calmness was about the only emotion she *hadn't* felt tonight. And she figured she might as well just get them all over with, so she could go back to the beginning and begin once more with fear, since she figured fear was what she probably ought to be feeling again.

Faux Randy's eyes narrowed at her question. "You know what I want, Lila."

"No, I don't, actually," Marnie told him. "The first guy I met tonight wanted to give me this stupid manuscript. The second guy wanted to take it away from me. You seem to want to shoot me. At this point, I have no idea what to expect. So I'm asking you again. What do you want?"

Faux Randy settled his whole hand on the butt of his gun. Uh-oh. She'd been joking about that. Still, he did seem to be weighing the prospect of shooting her against the prospect of answering her question, so maybe there was still hope for a good outcome. Or, at the very least, an outcome that didn't involve gunfire.

"First," he said, "I want to know where you've been for the past five months."

Well, that was easy enough to answer. In a vague, I'm-not-giving-out-my-address-to-strange-in-more-than-one-sense-of-the-word-men kind of way.

"I've been here," she said.

Maybe if she could keep him talking long enough, a real security guard would come along. Not that she trusted a single person on the entire planet at this point. Except maybe Bob Troutman, who, she knew, would be a slimy little git no matter the circumstances. Which currently made Bob Troutman the only human being on the planet Marnie would trust at this point. And of all the things that were going to keep her awake tonight, that one had to be the most troubling.

"Where's here?" Faux Randy asked.

"Cleveland," Marnie said. "Ohio. I was born and raised here. Save five years in Columbus to go to college, I've always lived here."

"Right," he replied in a way that indicated he believed not a word of what she said. "So I guess we *are* going to have to do this the hard way." And with that, he did pull his weapon, and he pointed it right at Marnie's heart.

Okay, cycling back to fear again.

"Look, this is nuts," she said. She tried to hold up her hands, but thanks to the manuscript, could raise one only to shoulder height. Still, she turned both hands palm out. "I don't understand any of what's happened tonight, and all I want is to be left alone. If it's the manuscript you want, take it. But please, just leave me out of it."

"Oh, it's definitely the manuscript I want," he told her. "And I definitely will take it. But you know full well there's something else I want. And I'm going to take it, too."

"What more could you possibly want?" Marnie asked.

"You, Lila," the man said without hesitation. "I want you."

CHAPTER THREE

AT HEARING THE ROUGHLY uttered declaration, every one of those emotions went zinging right through Marnie again. Even lust, briefly, which said a lot about her so-called standards. But instead of going back to square one this time—fear—she put on the brakes at calmness. In spite of the gravity of her situation, she sensed something about this man that prevented her from feeling true fear.

She had no idea why, but her instincts told her he wasn't going to hurt her unless she badly provoked him, and she'd always been a strong believer in instincts. The way she saw it, human instinct had survived from caveman times, even when the overhanging forehead and unibrow had evolved into much nicer lines. Well, for people other than Bob Troutman, she meant. There had to be a reason for that. Other than that Bob Troutman was a Neanderthal, she meant. So she'd learned long ago to trust her instincts, and her instincts had never let her down.

The man released the safety on his weapon with a deft flick of his thumb and sharpened his aim.

Of course, there was a first time for everything.

"Please," she said, spreading her fingers in entreaty. "There's got to be some way to get this all straightened out without anyone getting hurt. Please," she said again, even more solicitously this time.

"Give me the manuscript," the man said. "Hold it out with one hand, very slowly. And don't try anything funny, Lila. Because I *will* shoot you if I have to."

Marnie did as he asked, keeping one hand airborne as she gripped the envelope with the other and very carefully extended it toward him. Cautiously, he accepted it from her, his gaze never leaving hers, as if it was more important for him to watch her eyes than it was to watch her hands.

"Which car is the one you've been driving?" he asked as he tucked the envelope under one arm, still holding the gun steady. Still not removing his eyes from hers.

She found the phrasing of the question peculiar. He hadn't asked which car was hers, but which one she'd been driving. As if he assumed she didn't own the car but was only using it. Still, if he was saying anything at all about her car, it was only because he intended to use it. And that couldn't be a good thing. Unless he used it by himself. Which was probably asking too much.

Marnie closed her eyes, surrendering to the inevitable. "The one behind me is mine," she said. "The yellow Volkswagen Beetle."

"Turn around, and walk slowly toward it," the man told her, "keeping your hands where I can see them at all times."

"Oh, please," Marnie said, unable to help herself. "You can't possibly think I'm any threat to you."

He laughed out loud at that. "Oh, sure. You're harmless, Lila. Everyone knows that. Like that guy in Zagreb. The one you put in a coma a few years ago? The one who's still in a coma? He'd definitely agree that you're as gentle as a lamb."

Yeah, Marnie thought, this Lila for sure needed to hang out with some different people. Not to mention find some new hobbies.

"Turn around," he said again, his voice steely now. "And walk to your car. And don't try anything funny."

Oh, gosh, no. She wouldn't try anything funny. That would be *so* inappropriate in a situation like this.

She did as he asked, making her way carefully to her car with both arms awkwardly extended, constantly aware of his eyes—and his gun—on her back. When she arrived at the driver's-side door, however, she remembered she'd dropped her keys when the second man grabbed her. She started to say something about that when she heard the merry *chirp-chirp* of the key fob unlocking the doors. Braving a look over her shoulder, she saw faux Randy standing a few feet away, her keys in his hand. Evidently he'd seen them on the ground and scooped them up, but she sure couldn't have said when. He had to have moved awfully silently and awfully quickly to do that.

Gee, color her suspicious, but if he kept this up, she was going to start thinking he wasn't a mall security guard at all.

"Get in," he said. "Put your hands on the steering wheel and keep them there."

She did as he instructed, then watched as he rounded the front of her car, his eyes never leaving hers. He honestly seemed to be afraid that she might overpower him. Either this Lila really was a very dangerous woman, or faux Randy was the lamest excuse for a man in the world. As much as Marnie wanted to cling to that second theory, she figured the first one was more accurate. Which meant three men tonight had mistaken her for a very dangerous woman. Her. Marnie Lundy. Who shrieked at the sight of an unexpected dust bunny.

The tiny car shrank to microscopic when faux Randy folded his big frame into the passenger seat, accomplishing the feat with a swiftness and economy of movement that belied his size, his gun never straying from Marnie's midsection. Once inside, he slammed the door shut and thumbed the locks into place, then dangled her keys from his fingers. When she reached for them, he snatched them back. Her gaze flew to his in silent question.

"I'm going to tell you where to drive," he said. "And you're going to follow my directions. You will not exceed the speed limit. You will not swerve off the road. You will not try to attract the attention of another driver. If you do, you'll be sorry."

"Where are you taking me?" she asked.

Fear was creeping back in again, now that she realized just how little chance there was for escape. She was well and truly alone with him, helpless against him. She might be able to run once they reached their destination, but unless she could outwit him, there was no way she could get away. He was bigger, stronger, faster than she. He had clearly been trained for things she would never be able to master. He could easily overpower her. If he wanted to.

"How much gas do you have?" he asked.

"I filled up on the way to work," she told him reluctantly. And damn her for not being one of those people who could drive a car until it was down to fumes. She couldn't let the tank get below half before she started worrying.

"We shouldn't have any problems then."

Oh, yeah, speak for yourself, why don't you? Aloud, she only asked, "Where are you taking me?"

He studied her in silence for a moment, as if he were trying to decide how much to tell her. "It's one of the few places we have that you don't know about," he finally said. "And it's not far from where we are right now."

He extended the keys toward her again, and Marnie reached for them gingerly. Although he allowed her to wrap her fingers around them this time, he still didn't release them.

"Now what?" she asked.

"Buckle your seat belt," he told her. "We wouldn't want anything to happen to you, would we?"

She managed to refrain from rolling her eyes but did as he said, reassuring herself that she wasn't following his instructions this time because she would have buckled up anyway. Nyah, nyah, nyah. Only then did he relinquish her keys. He lowered the gun so it couldn't be seen by other drivers, but pressed it against her thigh. She guessed that that was because, if she tried anything, he could shoot her in the leg, disabling her without killing her. That would prevent her from crashing the car, and make it possible for him to escape with his own life—if not hers.

As she went to insert the key into the ignition, she realized her purse, a whimsical little Mary Frances number decorated with buttons and ribbons and lace in varying shades of blue—she'd spent way too much on it, even with her store discount, but she hadn't been able to resist—was still swinging from her elbow. She turned and straightened her arm to let it slide down over her wrist, only to have her wrist seized by her companion, who gripped it with firm fingers.

"Problem, Lila?" he asked as he jerked her hand back up between both their bodies.

"I just wanted to put my purse in the backseat," she said.

He smiled grimly. "I'll do it for you."

"Thank you," she bit out.

"But not before seeing what you have inside."

Of course.

Still pressing the gun against her thigh, he released her wrist, and Marnie held her arm still as he guided the purse carefully over her hand. She winced as she watched him manhandle it, turning it over and over in his big brawny fist, having not a care for any of the intricate detailing. Watching him treat the ultrafeminine accessory so carelessly hammered home how little trouble he would have mistreating her, too.

"How the hell do you open this thing?" he demanded.

"That beaded flower on the side facing away from you has a snap beneath it," she told him.

He found the part she was talking about and unfastened it, but his big hand barely fit inside the little purse, so he turned it upside down and emptied the contents into his lap. One by one, he inspected each item before replacing it, starting with the tube of lipstick, then the tin of mints, then her hanky and so on. He was methodical and dispassionate in his task, even handled her emergency tampon with complete indifference. He saved her leather card case for last, flipping it open to extract one-handed her Visa card, her AAA card, her health insurance card and her driver's license, studying each in turn.

"These are excellent forgeries," he told her. "If I didn't know better, I'd swear they were the real thing." He glanced up to look at her. "But we weren't the ones who made them. Who did?"

Marnie inhaled a deep breath and released it slowly. "Well, that first came from the bank when I opened my Visa account. The second came from triple-A. That third was from my insurer and the fourth is from the Ohio DMV."

He narrowed his eyes at her. "Very funny."

"Wasn't meant to be," she said. "They're not forgeries."

Without returning the cards to the case, he dropped all of them into her purse and snapped it shut. "Start the car," he said as he tossed it into the back without bothering to see where it landed.

Damn men, anyway, Marnie thought as she watched him do it. They had no clue as to the importance of the ideal accessory.

"Which way am I supposed to go?" she asked when the little car purred to life.

"Use the mall's north exit," he told her.

His directions after that were clipped, concise and to the point. After ten minutes of driving, they were out of the Cleveland suburbs. Another fifteen, and they were crossing the county line, headed west on Interstate 90 toward any number of small towns that doubled as weekend retreats on Lake Erie. Obviously "not far" was a relative term to him, because it was nearly another hour before they finally reached their destination. During that time, he spoke scarcely a word to her—not that Marnie was all that fired up to get to know him better—and she kept her own thoughts to herself. But when he finally instructed her to pull the car to a halt, throw it into Park and cut the engine, she saw that they had arrived at—

Oh. An isolated cabin in the woods. Why had she not seen this coming from a mile away?

"Get out," he told her. Then he repeated what seemed to be his mantra. "And keep your hands where I can see them."

Yeah, yeah, yeah.

Marnie waited for the fear to roar up again, but she felt only resolve now. Exiting the car, she inhaled the pungent aroma of fresh evergreen, and through a break in the trees, she could just make out the glitter of moonlight on water. But not Lake Erie. They'd left the interstate for a county road some miles back and headed east, away from the lake. This must be a small tributary that fed into it. Had she been arriving here for a weekend getaway, she would have been charmed by her surroundings. In the moonlit darkness, she saw that the cottage was of the faux-rustic variety—perfect for a guy like faux Randy—built to look like a log cabin but obviously fairly new. It was enchanting, really.

How comforting to realize she'd enjoy such a cozy atmosphere during the last hours of her life.

Marnie still didn't know what to do. She could try to run, but she didn't relish the idea of being in the woods alone at night. Who knew how far it was to another cabin, or if there even was another cabin nearby? Besides, her captor would probably tackle her—or shoot her—before she even made it to the tree line. She didn't want to go inside the house, since that would make escape even more difficult if not downright impossible, but there might be something inside she could use for a weapon....

The matter was taken out of her hands when faux Randy circled the front of the car and wrapped the fingers of his free hand around her upper arm. "Walk," he said, jabbing the barrel of his gun into her ribs.

Well, okay. If he insisted.

He had the manuscript tucked beneath his arm as he guided her forward. Marnie made it up the three stairs of the front porch without tripping, but her entire body was racked with trembling by the time they reached the front door. Something cold and slimy had settled in the pit of her stomach, and she wanted to throw up. Faux Randy released her arm long enough to fish a new set of keys out of his trouser pocket, but his grip on the gun never wavered as he unlocked the front door and pushed it open. He dragged her over the threshold behind him and shut the door again, turning a single dead bolt with an ominous thump before flipping a wall switch to turn on the lights.

In stark contrast to the ugliness of her situation, the cabin itself was quite pleasant. Amber light radiated from a single lamp in the corner, warming pine-paneled walls that housed pencil sketches of the wilderness. The furniture was big and boxy, looking hand hewn of more pine, and upholstered with blankets of Native American design. The floor was dotted with wool rugs of a similar pattern, the hardwood beneath them gleaming. A large creek stone fireplace took up most of one wall, shelves crammed full of books taking up the rest of it. Opposite her was a row of windows that looked out onto darkness, but which doubtless offered a magnificent view of the woods or water during the day. The whole place was tidy and spotless, as if it had just recently been cleaned. Had she not been here as a prisoner, Marnie would have found it charming.

"That way," her captor said, tilting his head toward a doorway that led to a darkened room.

She swallowed with some difficulty, but walked carefully in that direction. Her captor, naturally, followed close behind.

"There's a light switch on the wall to your left," he told her. "Turn it on."

Again, she did as she was instructed, her heart sinking when she saw the room was, as she had feared, a bedroom. Again, the decor was cozy and warm, the pine walls and floor continuing into this room from the other, the pencil sketches replaced by watercolor renditions of lake and sky. She felt his hand on her back, his fingers splaying wide between her shoulder blades and she instinctively jerked away. But he caught her easily, circling her upper arm with strong fingers. He tugged her back toward himself and propelled both their bodies forward, kicking the bedroom door closed behind them. He pushed her again, toward the bed, and nausea rolled into her belly.

Her mind raced to recall every self-defense trick she'd ever read in *Glamour* magazine and could only remember two: Jab him in the eyes with your keys or stomp on his instep with your spike heel. But he'd taken her keys from her and she wasn't going to do much damage with a pair of knockoff Birkenstocks. Even scratching him would be impossible. She had been a nail-biter since childhood.

When he was undressing, she told herself, that was when she'd make her move. When his pants were down around his ankles, she'd run. Or she'd grab Mr. Happy and make him very unhappy indeed. Something. Anything. The moment his guard was down, she would figure out how best to hurt him. And then she would run like hell.

Little by little, they drew nearer the bed, with him behind her, slowly urging her forward. Closer now… closer…three more steps…two…almost there…one more step…

He walked right past the bed, heading toward another room off the bedroom.

Oh. Well that kind of threw off her plan of attack. Now what?

He instructed her to flip on that light, too, and when she did, Marnie saw a bathroom like any other, except that there was more pine instead of tile, and no bathtub. In place of one was an incongruously modern-looking shower stall in the corner, covered on two sides with frosted glass.

"Get in the shower," he told her.

Oooh. He was one of those weirdos who had an obsession with cleanliness. That could work for her, she thought. It could. If she could just… If she could just… Well. If she could just get her brain to stop jumping around long enough for her to make sense of it.

"I really don't think I need a shower right now," she said. "I took one this morning, and honestly, if I could just wash my face, that would really be all I—"

He interrupted her by uttering a long, exasperated sound. He followed it with a very perturbed, "Just get in the damned shower, Lila."

She narrowed her eyes at him as understanding began

to dawn. Like a good, solid blow to the back of the head. "You mean, get in it with my clothes *on?*"

He actually had the nerve to roll his eyes and look at her as if she were an idiot. "Get. In. The. Shower. Now."

She made a face at him. "Oh. Kay." Just for that, she *would* leave her clothes on.

A half-dozen steps brought her to the shower door, which she carefully pulled open. Inside, she saw…a shower stall. Clean. Dry. Empty. On one shelf was lined up an assortment of toiletries, no two brands the same. Someone must be a coupon shopper. Marnie knew that because she never had the same brands in her house, either. There wasn't a shower smell to the stall, though, neither soapy nor mildewy, and she found that odd. It didn't even smell of disinfectant, as if it had just been cleaned. It didn't smell like anything.

She was about to turn around, to ask faux Randy what she was supposed to do next, but he was climbing into the shower stall right behind her, something that made the words get stuck in her throat. She opened her mouth to scream—well, it was as good a reaction as any—but he reached beyond her, pointing what she thought was her car-key fob at the soap holder.

Okay, now that was just plain weird.

Weirder still was the fact that one of the plastic shower walls suddenly went sliding to the left, revealing a cubby on the other side. The walls of the cubby were lined with metal, something that looked like brushed aluminum, and when she looked to the left, she saw a flight of stairs heading down. She closed her eyes for a second then opened them. Nope, it was definitely not a hallucination.

Sometimes a shower stall wasn't a shower stall. What this one was, though…

"Go on," faux Randy said from behind her.

"Go where?" she asked.

"Down the stairs."

She was going to jokingly ask him if that was where he kept his torture chamber, but was afraid it might not be a joke at all. He must have sensed she was about to refuse—and she was—because she felt the gun press into her back again. She sighed and stepped cautiously into the metal cubby and looked down the stairs. There were about fifty or sixty of them, emptying into a well-lit hallway below. Whatever was down there, faux Randy hadn't built it by himself. It was too perfect a construction for it to have been completed without some kind of sophisticated technology.

"What's down there?" Marnie asked, really, really hoping he didn't reply, *My torture chamber.*

"Lots of people who have been looking for you," he said.

"Lots of people?" she echoed, puzzled. That actually might be good. Unless they were all like faux Randy.

He nodded. "Lots of people. And lucky you, Lila. One or two of them *might* even be happy to see you."

CHAPTER FOUR

NOAH TENNANT TUCKED Philosopher's manuscript under one arm and pressed the gun more insistently into Lila's back. He honestly wasn't sure which of the two was the bigger prize. Hell, he'd been *that* close to collaring Sorcerer tonight, too, and had only let the other man escape after making the split-second decision that Lila was worth more. Had Noah run after Sorcerer, she would have disappeared back into the netherworld where she'd been living undetected for the past five months. And they couldn't have that.

Sorcerer had a habit of popping up again from time to time. Not so Lila. When she dug in, she stayed there. Noah had decided to seize the moment and grab her now, because he might not have another chance. Frankly, he was surprised she hadn't used that split second to make her own escape. Or, even more characteristic of her, clean his clock and *then* make her escape. Lila Moreau could do a lot of damage in a split second. Nobody knew that better than Noah.

Still, had he succeeded in bringing in her, the manuscript *and* Sorcerer, he would have been promoted to the position of All Powerful Emperor of Everything Without Exception So There. And that would have looked great on a résumé.

"I'm not Lila," Lila said. Again. "There's been some terrible mixup somewhere. My name is Marnie. Marnie Lundy." She'd said that several times tonight, too. Though how she could honestly think Noah would ever believe *that* was beyond him.

"Walk, *Lila*," he said emphatically, "and keep your hands where I can see them."

He jabbed the gun into her waist again to urge her down the stairs, not hard enough to hurt her, but hard enough to let her know he was willing to pull the trigger if she tried anything stupid. And he was, dammit. She'd pissed him off plenty in the past, but never like this. What the hell kind of game was she playing? She knew better than to try and pass herself off as someone else to anyone in OPUS, especially Noah. Hell, OPUS had created her. And Noah had been her senior agent at one point. He'd been more than that for one night, but that was something he did his best not to think about these days. Bad enough it had happened in the first place.

When he'd received the intel last night that she was in the middle of Lauderdale's department store hanging up underwear, Noah's first impulse had been to send every agent they had to bring her in right then. He couldn't imagine what could possibly be going on at that store to have attracted her attention enough to not just bring her out of hiding, but put herself on display. Then he'd reminded himself that Lila was efficient and expeditious when carrying out an assignment—whether it was one OPUS gave her or not—and he made himself wait. And watch. Now that Philosopher had passed her the manuscript, it all made sense. But having Sorcerer, a rogue agent they'd been hunting for years, show up within moments of the transfer...

Well. Suffice it to say it looked like all the rumors about Lila going rogue, too, were true. But Noah was willing to give her the benefit of the doubt. For now. There weren't many in the Office for Political Unity and Security who were willing to do that.

With a heavy sigh that could have meant anything, she lowered one foot cautiously to the first stair. Step by step, she descended with her arms kept at shoulder height, Noah never allowing more than an inch of space to separate her and his gun. At the bottom, she hesitated, even though there was only one direction into which they might travel—forward. Before them was a long hallway dotted on both sides by metal doors all the way down. The two of them appeared to be alone, but dozens of people worked in the facility around the clock. Just because the day came to an end didn't mean an OPUS workday ended. The Office for Political Unity and Security never slept.

"Walk," Noah said again.

She moved forward slowly, her arms still held out by her head. It was good that she was being so cooperative, but he had no idea why she was being so cooperative. He'd seen Lila take out ten men twice her size in one evening. That she had accompanied him here without a fight was nothing short of astonishing.

As they made their way down the hall, the only discernible sounds were the soft hum of the air conditioner and Lila's shallow, uneven breathing. Her hands were trembling, and she stumbled more than once as they walked. If he didn't know better, Noah would have thought she was

genuinely terrified. Which was laughable, because Lila
Moreau wasn't afraid of anything. Least of all OPUS.

"Stop here," he said when they arrived at the door he
wanted. She did so without hesitation. Without a fight.
Without so much as a curse. "Turn the knob and go inside,"
he told her.

Again, she followed his instructions, leading them into
an empty interrogation room. Still training his gun on her,
Noah closed the door and thumbed a green button on the
wall, to announce their arrival. Within seconds, the door
opened again and another agent entered the room.

Noah nodded once at the man in acknowledgment, who
nodded silently back in reply. His dark eyes widened, and
his shaggy black eyebrows shot high when he noted the
extent of Noah's injuries, until he obviously remembered
it was Lila Noah had just brought in. Noah didn't bother
to tell the man it was Sorcerer, not she, who'd inflicted the
damage. No reason for the other man to let down his guard.

By now she had retreated to the opposite corner of the
room. She stood with her back pressed against the place
where the two walls met, hugging herself tight, as if she
were trying to hold herself together. Her eyes, an incredible aquamarine that Noah had never seen on any human
being but her, were wide with what looked like fear—
yeah, right—and her entire body seemed to be shaking
now.

For the first time, he noted her attire; the slim gray
skirt, the pale blue top and sweater. Her hair, darker blond
than it had been the last time he saw her, was wound atop
her head in a loose bun, except for a few stray pieces that
had fallen free, probably during her scuffle with Sorcerer.

She wore no makeup, and her legs were bare, her feet encased in chunky, ugly shoes. It was a remarkably bland getup, worn obviously because she didn't want to attract attention. Noah had seen her outfitted in everything from black camouflage to designer evening gowns to perform her job. But never had he seen her try to carry off a persona like this. Mild. Unobtrusive. Compliant. It didn't suit her at all.

"Good to have you back, She-Wolf," said the second man, an agent whose code name was Zorba, thanks to his Mediterranean heritage. "Though it would have been better if you'd come in on your own, instead of having to be dragged back."

Lila's expression changed at the man's use of her code name, a slip Noah noticed with some satisfaction. Maybe she was finally going to give up the lame pretense, and then they could start talking in earnest about why she'd taken off, where she'd been and what the hell she'd been doing while she was gone and prior to her disappearance.

"She-Wolf?" she echoed, her voice edged with irritation. "I thought you people were convinced I was this Lila person. What's with the She-Wolf? What kind of name is that?"

Noah almost smiled. Oh, yeah. Lila was about to reveal herself. Even backed against the wall—literally—she could still snarl.

Zorba looked at Noah. "Gonna be a long night, I see."

"Don't sell yourself short, Zorba," Noah said, not taking his eyes off Lila. "If anyone can make her crack, you can."

Her eyes went wide at that, and he smiled with satisfaction. She'd been out of the game too long if she was re-

. vealing herself that easily. Then again, this was probably all part of *her* game. Since she kept insisting she was someone else, she had to pretend to be scared of what was happening to her. Smart agent. Excellent actress.

"Go ahead and get started without me," he told Zorba. "I need to get cleaned up and find something to eat. I'm starving. You hungry?" he asked Lila.

She didn't seem to know what to make of the offer. After a small hesitation, she said softly, "A little."

"Too bad," he told her. "You'll get nothing until you tell us what we want to hear."

And without awaiting a reply—or a dagger in his back, which was the most likely response from Lila Moreau— he left the room.

"NOW, LET'S TRY this again, Lila, starting five months ago. We know you went to the Nesbitt estate to make contact with your partner after knocking Romeo unconscious and taking his clothes. But that was the last time anyone saw you. Where did you go after that?"

Noah bit back a growl at hearing Zorba ask the question *again*. Four hours after bringing Lila to the OPUS interrogation facility, she was still insisting she was someone named Marnie Lundy who'd grown up in Cleveland and held down two jobs, one for the department store where he'd picked her up tonight and one teaching piano to schoolchildren.

He'd actually laughed out loud at that. The only reason Lila would get near a kid would be to have it for breakfast. And the only way she'd get near a piano would be to cut the wire for garroting someone later. Not that OPUS had ever called on her to be an assassin. But she sure as hell had all the right moves and qualities to make a good one.

During a break in the interrogation, when Noah and Zorba had stepped out of the room, the other man had suggested they bring in an OPUS shrink, on the outside chance—the *way* outside chance—that Lila really had gone off the deep end this time. She'd been out in the cold for five months, all alone, without any of her usual tools or contacts to help her. She'd lost her mother just prior to her disappearance, and although Noah knew there was no love lost between the two women, the death of a parent could still have a powerful impact on a person. Lila's past was troubled—to put it mildly—her background unstable—ditto. Throw all of that into a pot and it made for a toxic stew that might undo anyone. Even Lila Moreau.

Reluctantly, Noah had called in not just a shrink, but also his superior officer from OPUS headquarters in Washington, D.C. Although Noah headed up the Ohio unit, there were interstate implications with this, and he felt obligated to alert the big guns to what was going on. Especially the biggest gun of all, He Whose Name Nobody Dared Say—mostly because nobody knew what it was. After all, he was the one Lila had reportedly tried to kill.

Now, both No-Name and the shrink had arrived and been briefed on what was going on. The psychiatrist, a middle-aged woman with salt-and-pepper hair cropped short, code name Gestalt, had joined Noah and Zorba in the interrogation room, and He Whose Name Nobody Dared Say was watching from another room on the closed-circuit TV.

"My name isn't Lila," Lila said wearily for what felt like the hundredth time.

She was sitting with her arms crossed on the table, her forehead resting on the top one. She was clearly exhausted, and they'd allowed her no food or drink, nor breaks of any kind, since her arrival. Anyone else would have rolled over by now. But not Lila.

"My name is Marnie Lundy," she said again. "I live at 207 Mockingbird Lane in Cleveland, Ohio. I was born and raised in Cleveland. I'm thirty-three years old. I graduated from Moore High School in 1991, and from Ohio State University with a B.A. in music in 1995. I earned my master's in music from OSU in 1996. My work record has been varied and eclectic since then, but I now work at Lauderdale's Department Store, and I teach piano to kids after school and on weekends." She lifted her head and met each of her inquisitors' gazes in turn. "I don't know who you people are or why you're keeping me here. But I swear, if it's at all within my power to do so, once this is over, I will hunt down every one of you like dogs and call you Rover."

Well, at least she'd been honest about her age, Noah thought. And maybe the part about hunting them all down like dogs. Except that she'd do a lot more than call them names once she found them.

"Perhaps you should let me ask a few questions." The comment came from Gestalt. "I'd like to speak to Ms. Lundy alone for a bit."

Noah was about to decline, but one look from the psychiatrist stopped him. Fine. If she wanted to call Lila Ms. Lundy, hell, who was Noah to stop her? It wasn't like he and Zorba had had any luck all night. And they could watch from the closed-circuit TV, too.

"All right," he said. "Zorba and I will go for coffee. And I think they put out some doughnuts, too," he added, looking at Lila. "Anybody else want anything? Except you, I mean?"

If looks could kill, Noah would have been atomic fallout about then.

"We'll be fine," Gestalt told him. "Ms. Lundy…Marnie," she said, softening her voice, "and I will have a nice little chat, I hope."

Whatever, Noah thought.

He and Zorba left the room, locking the door behind them, just in case Lila decided to ditch the compliant, complacent role and return to her old badass self. Then they strode to the next room to join their boss. Also present was Noah's secretary, Ellie Chandler, a slim brunette on the tall side wearing a dark suit similar to the ones the men favored. Only instead of a necktie, she'd closed the collar with an understated bit of jewelry.

Normally, Noah wouldn't include his secretary in something like this. But Ellie was ninety percent finished with the instruction and training required to become an agent, and he did his best to include her in things that might be helpful to her education. He was confident she would be an excellent agent. He was, after all, the one who had recommended her to the program.

"All set for your first field assignment?" he asked her now.

It was a rhetorical question. She'd be going undercover in three days, so she'd damned well better be ready. Not to mention she'd made clear her desire to become a field agent on the first day she'd been assigned to his office. The fact that it would only be a training assignment, and therefore not particularly dangerous, didn't seem to make any difference to her at this point. He just hoped her enthusiasm didn't ebb when she discovered the particulars of what her assignment would involve.

"I am *so* ready for it," she told him. "Bring it on."

"Funny you should say that," he replied. "Because I just so happen to have the dossier with me. You can take it home with you after we're finished here and start going over it. Since you're working tonight, take tomorrow at home. Get a few hours of sleep before you dive in. You need to be fresh when you review everything."

She looked slightly disappointed to be taking a day away from the office, and Noah tried to curb yet another grin. Honestly, if even half of his agents were as gung ho as Ellie, OPUS would have ensured world peace ages ago.

The room in which they had all gathered was outfitted more comfortably than the interrogation room, but was by no means luxurious. In addition to a metal table and chairs, there was a long couch and two upholstered chairs. Along one wall was a kitchenette of sorts, with sink and refrigerator and countertops—upon which whattayaknow, were some doughnuts—and a coffeemaker.

That last was coughing out the final drops of a fresh brew, so Noah made his way over and removed the pot, filling a white ceramic mug. Over the speakers, he could hear Gestalt's voice as she spoke to Lila, a low, indulgent, monotonous tone clearly meant to be soothing. It put Noah's teeth on edge. He moved to stand next to the others, his attention fixed on the television. His boss, too, a man of indeterminate age and average everything else, had his attention focused entirely on the TV screen.

Gestalt had seated herself at the end of the table kitty-corner to Lila, a less adversarial position than Noah and Zorba had held sitting across from her. She'd removed her jacket and hung it over the back of the chair to further her image as relaxed and less administrative. Lila leaned back in her chair with her hands in her lap, eyeing the other woman warily, just as she had Noah and Zorba. But she didn't seem to reek quite as much contempt for Gestalt. Yet.

"Do you mind if I call you Marnie?" Gestalt said.

Lila's response was an irritated sound, followed by a weary, "No. It would be nice to hear my name. I just wish you were calling me that because you believe I am who I say I am and not just to humor me."

"I do believe you."

"Then why aren't you doing something to see that I'm released?"

"Because it's not up to me to make that decision."

"Who *are* you people?" Lila demanded. She sounded genuinely confused, which Noah knew she wasn't, and genuinely angry, which he was sure she was.

Gestalt smiled in the way a kindergarten teacher might smile at a new pupil. "We work for a branch of the U.S. government called the Office for Political Unity and Security."

"I've never heard of you," Lila muttered.

"That's because we're a small, top-secret organization," Gestalt told her, clearly unconcerned about revealing information she shouldn't be revealing to anyone outside the organization, since Lila wasn't outside the organization, no matter how much she insisted she was. "We don't want anyone to hear about us, so few people have."

"Are you law enforcement or what?" Lila asked.

"We fall under the domain of Homeland Security, and we have many functions," Gestalt said. "Essentially, OPUS tackles anything or anyone that poses a threat to national security, be they domestic or international. We are both collectors of information and enforcers of the law. Right now, much of our focus is on finding two people. One man, one woman."

"Let me guess," Lila said. "The woman is this Lila person."

"Lila Moreau," Gestalt said. "She works for us. Her code name in the organization is She-Wolf."

"Code name?" Lila echoed dubiously. A nervous-sounding chuckle escaped her. "You people actually have code names?"

"We do."

"Gosh, do you have a secret handshake and decoder rings, too?"

Gestalt smiled that benign smile again. "No secret handshakes," she said.

Lila hesitated a telling beat, narrowing her eyes before saying, "So then you do have decoder rings."

In response to that, Gestalt removed what looked like a college ring from her right ring finger and laid it on the table between herself and Lila.

Lila looked at it blankly, then back at Gestalt. "You have *got* to be kidding me."

"It has a laser in it, too," Gestalt told her. "And a camera.

And a microphone. And a global-positioning device. And a few other little features that are too hush-hush for me to share with a civilian like you." She reached for the ring and put it on again. "But I could break into the Bank of Switzerland and take out half the United Arab Emirates with it if I wanted to."

"Unbelievable," Lila said, even though she owned a ring exactly like it. Just as Noah did. Just as every agent did. "So what makes you people think I'm this Lila Moreau slash She-Wolf person?"

"Well, you do look very much like her."

Ha, Noah thought. She looked exactly like Lila. Same face, same height, same build, same mannerisms. Because she was Lila. Yeah, her hair was a little darker and she'd dropped a few pounds, but he'd know Lila anywhere.

"What's she done to make her such a priority with your organization?" Lila asked.

"She's an agent with top-secret clearance, and she disappeared five months ago without a trace."

"How do you know she's not dead?"

"We don't know that. But it would be unlikely. She's quite a good agent. Arguably our best."

No argument here, Noah thought. At least, Lila *had* been their best agent, up until the time she vanished. Unfortunately, there was so much innuendo and rumor surrounding her disappearance that he wasn't sure what to think now.

The official word was that Lila had taken a short leave of absence in the middle of an assignment to return to her hometown of Las Vegas because her mother was terminally ill and near death. Within a few weeks of her arrival in Vegas, her mother died, so Lila had asked for a little more time to sort through her mother's effects and settle the woman's estate. Well, as much estate as a woman could leave behind when she'd spent her adult life as a showgirl and hooker and had no family besides the illegitimate daughter who'd left home at age sixteen and never returned.

After that, things got a little murky. Last November, Noah, like everyone at his level and higher, had received a report that She-Wolf had returned to Washington and, while being debriefed by He Whose Name Nobody Dared Say, had gone nuts and tried to murder him. Then she'd disappeared.

This, Noah had trouble believing. At one time or another, everyone in OPUS had wanted to murder He Whose Name Nobody Dared Say. But everyone in OPUS, especially someone as smart as Lila, knew that to even attempt such a thing would be suicide. Plus, Lila wasn't one to lose control and go nuts. She never let her emotions overrule her. She was the coolest, at times the most emotion*less* person Noah knew.

So, like many in OPUS, he'd had his doubts about the reliability—he hesitated to use the word *veracity*—of the report. It wouldn't be the first time the big muckety-mucks in D.C. had inflated—or created—a story to suit their own needs. Still he'd had no choice but to follow protocol and treat Lila as an enemy of the organization.

Watching her now, he couldn't quite figure out *what* she was. She certainly wasn't cooperating with them. But she didn't seem to be a threat, either. So Noah would reserve judgment and observe.

"If she's your best agent," Lila said to Gestalt, "and if

you think I'm her, then why are you treating me like a criminal? For that matter, if I'm her, why wouldn't I come along peacefully and cooperate with you? Why would I keep insisting I'm someone else?"

"Well, there were some…circumstances…surrounding her disappearance," Gestalt said. "Circumstances that are a bit unclear."

Lila was silent for a moment, clearly digesting the information. Then she said, "Meaning she either screwed something up really badly, or else she's turned to the dark side."

Gestalt smiled again. "Let's just say there are a few questions we'd like to ask her. A few things we need for her to clear up. But let's talk about you, Marnie. I want to hear more about you right now."

For the next half hour, Gestalt quizzed Lila on her pho-ny-baloney Marnie Lundy persona, asking questions that ranged from her childhood illnesses to her high-school social life to her experiences as a teaching assistant at Ohio State. Had he not known better, Noah would have sworn Lila really was some woman named Marnie Lundy. Not once did she stop to think before responding, and not once did she waver from her story. Even when Gestalt tried to trip her up, Lila always made perfect sense.

But that was Lila. She had a gift for changing herself into whatever she needed to be. When she took on the identity of someone else, she didn't just pass herself off as that individual. She *became* that individual. Mind, body and soul. The fact that this time the identity was one she'd assigned to herself instead of being assigned it by OPUS didn't change that.

At the end of Gestalt's questioning, she left Lila alone and returned to the room where Noah and the others were waiting. Much to his surprise, her expression when she entered was one of philosophical acceptance.

"You think she's telling the truth?" he asked incredulously.

"I think she's telling the truth as she sees it, yes," Gestalt told them. "I think She-Wolf genuinely believes that she's Marnie Lundy."

"What?" Noah barked.

"She's delusional," Gestalt said. "Something happened to her that's made her block out her actual identity and assume the identity of a fictional person who lives a life completely different from the one she's used to. A quiet, uneventful, *safe* life," she added meaningfully. "She's even given that fictional person her initials, albeit reversed. Lila Moreau. Marnie Lundy. But I'm quite convinced that right now, She-Wolf firmly believes she's who she says she is."

"So what are we supposed to do?" Noah asked. He still wasn't sure he believed Gestalt's analysis, but he couldn't offer a better explanation himself.

The psychologist sighed heavily. "There are a number of ways we can deal with it, but most of those take time, and I gather you don't have much of that to spare."

"You got that right," Noah told her. "Sorcerer has resurfaced, and She-Wolf's made contact. Hell, Philosopher's turned up again after being missing for three years, and She-Wolf has made contact with him, too. I never thought we'd see him again. If we're going to nail Sorcerer and find out what Philosopher knows, not to mention discover what Lila learned over the last five months, we need her."

"Then we need a quick fix," Gestalt translated. "And I have an idea. It's unconventional, and normally not what I would do in such a situation, but…"

"What?" Noah asked. "I'll try anything."

"Then try playing along with her," Gestalt told him. Though she clearly still had some reservations about what she was saying. "Go in there and tell her you ran her name through the databases and found out Marnie Lundy really exists, and that everything she's said tonight has been corroborated, and we're so sorry for detaining her and now she's free to go."

"Oh, yeah, right," Noah muttered. "Like I really believe there's a Marnie Lundy out there in the world who looks exactly like Lila Moreau and just happened to have her path cross with both Philosopher and Sorcerer in one night."

"You don't have to believe it," Gestalt said. "Just make her think you do. She was specific about her background and home life and jobs. She has a firm grip on her delusion. So expose that delusion for the fantasy it really is. Prove to her that all of what she's told us is completely false. Once she's forced to confront the fact that there is no reality to support her convictions, she may—and I do mean *may*—come out of it."

"How do I do that?" Noah asked.

"Take her to the address she insists is hers. See if it really exists. And if it does, go inside and see what you find. Ask her questions. Try to trip her up. Do the same thing with her workplace."

"You didn't have much luck tripping her up," Noah pointed out.

"Here, I have no choice but to accept that what she says is true. Out there, you'll have more opportunities to force her to accept the *un*reality of the world she's created for herself. I'm betting she won't be able to prove much of what she told us tonight. And I'm betting it will happen fairly quickly."

"And then she'll go back to being Lila again?" Noah asked dubiously.

"Maybe," Gestalt told him. "Of course, she might be propelled into an even worse state than she's in now." Her gaze shifted from Noah to No-Name, then back to Noah again. "But I don't think something like that is really a concern for OPUS, is it?"

Noah clamped his jaw shut tight. Gestalt was right. OPUS never put the human condition before national security. They couldn't afford to. National security was job one. Even more important than the health and well-being of one of their top agents.

"It's worth a try," No-Name said without hesitation. "We need to know where She-Wolf's been and what she's discovered. At this point, she may be our only hope for bringing in Sorcerer."

And they needed to bring Lila up on charges for trying to take out the big guy, too, Noah thought. If indeed she had tried to take out the big guy. The big guy was acting awfully calm for a man whose alleged would-be murderer was on the other side of the wall.

"All right," Noah said, ignoring the sudden bad taste in his mouth. "I'll do it. I'll take her home and see what happens."

He looked at the TV screen again and saw that Lila had

laid her head back on her arms on the table. She was completely motionless. He didn't think he'd ever seen her in such a state. Even when she slept, she moved constantly. He remembered that much, and more—too much more—about her.

He shifted his attention to Gestalt. "This better work," he muttered. "And it better work fast. I need She-Wolf back."

CHAPTER FIVE

IN HER DREAM, Marnie was playing the *Polonaise* in an empty Carnegie Hall, her passion and love for the music swelling inside her, flowing out through her fingertips and into the cavernous room. As she completed the final stanza, she dropped her head and let her hands fall from the keys into her lap. But when solitary applause erupted, she snapped her head up again.

Not an empty auditorium after all. A lone, tuxedoed gentleman sat center stage in the front row, his crisp white shirt and tie a direct contrast to the black cut of his jacket and trousers. His dark-blond hair was swept straight back from his face, giving more prominence to his blue, blue eyes, his finely sculpted cheekbones, his full, sexy mouth. Marnie's own lips parted in surprise at seeing him and her heart hammered hard in her chest. But she said nothing.

He stood silently, moved fluidly to the end of the stage where steps appeared, climbed them with clear intention. She remained seated on the bench as he approached from stage right, her mouth going dry at the sight of him, her pulse racing faster with every step he took. Her dream self remembered now that he had attended all her performances, always seated in the same place, watching her with a hazy half smile playing about his lips. He always seemed to enjoy the music—or something—but not once had he applauded with the rest of the audience. Only tonight, when he was alone.

Now he strode toward her with that same half smile curving the corners of his mouth. When he drew close enough, he reached for her and Marnie stood, hooking her fingers over his, thinking he meant to walk her off the stage. But he twined their fingers more tightly together and kept coming toward her, pulling her to himself, sweeping her into his arms and covering her mouth with his, completely and with utter possession.

She gasped as her head jerked off her arm. She felt the cool metal table beneath her hand, blinked at the bright light overhead. She'd dozed off, she realized. She'd been dreaming. But when she turned her head toward the door, she saw the man from the empty auditorium standing there, as if he'd exited her dream with her. Instead of a tuxedo, he wore the dark suit in which she'd last seen him. And instead of the slicked-back, Rudolph Valentino hairstyle, his dark-blond tresses were dry. But they were creased and untidy, as if he'd been running his fingers restlessly through them. The swelling had gone down on his lip some, and the abrasion on his face had faded to a less angry red smudged by a faint bruise. In spite of the injuries, his was still a very compelling face.

How long had she been asleep? she wondered, pushing the thought away. What time was it? When she looked at her watch, she saw that nearly seven and a half hours had passed since her shift had ended at Lauderdale's. Would that she had dreamed everything that had happened since then, she'd be waking up in her own bed this morning, readying herself for another day's work.

Straightening in her chair, she met faux Randy's gaze and asked, "So what's *your* code name? I mean, I have a few I could use for you, but none of them is worth uttering in polite society. Then again, the society I've experienced tonight has been anything but polite."

"I owe you an apology, Ms. Lundy," he said, addressing her by her real name. And in an amazingly courteous voice, too. She wasn't sure which surprised her more.

"Yeah, I'll say you do," she retorted before she could stop herself. Reminding herself that snarkiness wasn't going to get her home any faster, she gentled her tone some before adding, "What brings on this sudden change of heart?"

He left the door open as he approached the table, something he hadn't done all night. "We ran a check on your name," he said, "and we realized you are indeed who you say you are. Marnie Lundy of 207 Mockingbird Lane in Cleveland, Ohio, and that you've been an employee of Lauderdale's for two years, just as you said."

"Well, why the hell didn't you run a check like that the minute I got here?" she demanded.

"I'm sorry," he apologized. "We were convinced you were Lila Moreau trying to pull a fast one. We didn't have any reason to believe you were who you said you were. So we didn't see the point."

"And what made you change your mind?" she asked, still skeptical. For such a supersecret sophisticated organization, they sure did seem like a bunch of boneheads.

"The woman who spoke to you a little while ago was a

psychiatrist we brought in to examine you when we thought you were Lila. After speaking with you at length, she realized—and assured us—that you're neither crazy, nor pretending and that you are precisely who you claim to be."

Marnie nodded slowly. "Okay," she said. Even though she was still suspicious of the sudden turnaround. "So does this mean I can go home?" she asked hopefully.

He nodded. "I'll drive you myself."

His offer, too, surprised her. "That won't be necessary," she assured him.

"Do you remember how you got here?"

"Um, no," she admitted.

"And you haven't had any sleep tonight," he pointed out.

Well, except for that one little nap with the weird dream about ol' blue eyes there kissing her, which, now that she thought about it, was really a nightmare, except for the fact that it had actually been kind of nice….

She sighed. She really did need to get out and date more if she was thinking a dream kiss from a virtual stranger who'd abducted and terrified her was kind of nice. Even Lila probably didn't have anyone like that in her little black book.

"You haven't had any sleep, either," she said.

"I can go without it. Something tells me you can't."

Yeah, like the fact that he'd walked in on her fast asleep. She hoped she hadn't been drooling. Or making those soft murmuring sounds of satisfaction out loud that she'd been making in her dream when he kissed her.

"So when can we go?" she asked.

"Any time you're ready," he told her, surprising her again.

"But don't you have to…"

"What?"

"Debrief me or something?"

She remembered after asking the question that she was indeed wearing briefs, a realization that made her hope "debrief" really was the word spy types used in such situations, and not just in movies and on TV. Otherwise, things could get a little embarrassing.

When he smiled at her the way he did, she had a feeling he was thinking about the same kind of debriefing she was. Which was bad, because she wasn't thinking about the movie and TV kind of debriefing just then. He really was very handsome. Even if he was a big jerk.

"I don't need to debrief you, Ms. Lundy," he said.

Ah, well. Story of her life.

She realized then that although he knew her by not one but *two* names—even if one of them was wrong—she didn't know even one of his. And, gosh, a girl always wanted to know the name of the man who abducted her and made her life hell for a night. So she asked, "What's your name?"

His smile fell some at that. "Why? Are you planning to write a letter of complaint about me?"

"And send it where?" she asked. "I don't know anything about you guys except for your being under Homeland Security." Which led her to another thought. "The woman who spoke to me said your organization is top secret and no one's supposed to know about you. Aren't you afraid that by letting me go home, I'll spend the day on the phone alerting the media to my experience and your existence?"

"They won't believe you," he said with complete conviction. "Except for the media outlets who publish stories about alien Elvises and women who marry Bigfoot, and we've already been written up by them dozens of times. Those stories just reinforce how we can't possibly exist anywhere outside someone's delusion. Besides, if we find out you're talking about us, we have ways of making you stop."

Her blood went cold at the matter-of-fact way he said that. "Are you threatening me?"

"Yeah."

"With what?"

He chuckled at her expression. "Don't worry, we won't kill you or make you disappear. But you'll find out what all the ruckus is about identity theft. We'll ruin your credit and tie up your finances and create debt for you where you never had it before. We'll make you lose your job and your home and everything else we can think of. It's not a good idea to piss off Uncle Sam."

Unbelievable, she thought. But, alas, totally believable.

"I won't say a word to anyone," she vowed.

"Good."

"So then you won't mind telling me your name," she added, not sure why it was so important for her to know.

He hesitated for a moment, then, "Noah Tennant," he told her. "Code name Sinatra."

Of course, she thought. With those eyes, what else would his code name be?

"Now if you're ready to go," he said, "we can leave anytime."

"I'm ready now," she told him. Actually, she was ready seven and a half hours ago. "But before we leave…?" she added, her voice trailing off before finishing the question.

"Yes?"

"Could you tell me if there's a ladies' room nearby?"

THE EASTERN SKY was stained with orange and gold by the time Lila directed Noah to an older section of Cleveland and a neighborhood of tidy homes built between the two world wars. The driveway into which she told him to turn belonged to a red-brick bungalow whose porch spanned the front of the house, and whose broad front windows sported window boxes awaiting spring planting. Terra-cotta pots, likewise empty of flowers this time of year, lined the concrete shelf wrapping the porch and a white wicker swing hung at one end. A quartet of hanging Boston ferns dotted the front, suggesting the owner had been impatient for *something* to grow, and yellow bug lamps glowed on each side of the front door.

Noah wondered who lived here and why Lila was pretending it was her. She could no more nurture plants—or feel comfortable in such a blatantly cozy house—than he could. He hoped she didn't try to go inside. It would be difficult to explain the situation to the owners.

"Thanks for driving me home," she said from the passenger seat as he dropped her car keys into her hand. "You're sure you have a ride coming?"

"I'm sure they're right behind us," he lied.

"Well…thanks again," she said, reaching for the door handle. "I appreciate it."

She sounded exhausted, which he was certain she was after being interrogated all night, and glad to be home, which he was certain she was not, since this couldn't possibly be her home. Nor could she be happy to be anywhere in his vicinity. He wondered how much longer it would take her to crack.

"I'll follow you in," he offered. "Make sure everything's okay."

She looked vaguely alarmed by his offer. Which she naturally would be. If he followed her in, she'd have to admit she didn't live here. And she wouldn't be able to run away if he stayed too close.

"That's okay," she said as she pushed open the door. "I'll be fine. It's a safe neighborhood. And I should know, since I grew up in this house."

Noah smiled indulgently. Of course she'd grown up in this house. It just screamed ruthless agent Lila Moreau. "Humor me," he said. "I feel bad about what we put you through tonight, and I want to make sure you get all the way home safely."

Still looking wary, she said, "All right."

Her easy acquiescence put him on alert, and he quickly scrambled out of the car before she had a chance to escape. But instead of running, she made her way up the front walk, flipping through her keys until she found the one she wanted. Without hesitation, she strode up the stairs, shoved the key into the lock of the front door and twisted it.

To Noah's amazement, the door swung open and Lila went in, turning to wait for him before closing it behind them both. Two cats—one black, one with orange stripes— came running to greet her, both skidding to a halt when they saw Noah.

"It's all right," she cooed to the cats, dropping down to a crouch. "He won't hurt you. And I'm sure he was sincere when he told me how bad he feels for being so mean to me tonight."

That last was spoken half over her shoulder, and Noah almost smiled. Even delusional—if indeed that was what she was—the true Lila kept creeping out.

Her word was evidently good enough for the cats, because both scurried forward again, bumping their heads into her knees, her hands, her hips. They obviously knew her well and were quite enamored of her. And she was clearly attached to them, laughing as she scrubbed them behind their ears and murmuring soothing words to explain her overnight absence.

Noah's mouth dropped open in amazement at witnessing the scene. Lila purring to cats? Lila showing affection? What the hell was going on? Just what had she been doing for the past five months?

He drove his gaze around the room, taking in the furnishings that were as snug and pleasant, and as pre-World War II, as the house itself. An overstuffed flowered sofa and chair took up much of the right half of the living room, a white fireplace beyond it bisecting two sets of floor-to-ceiling bookshelves crammed full of books. The mantelpiece played host to crystal candlesticks and cut-glass bowls, an antique clock and framed photographs whose subjects were indeterminate from this distance. Some were black-and-white, appearing to be quite old.

To the left of the furnishings, French doors opened into what appeared to be a dining room, though Noah could only see part of it from where he stood—an expanse of wall covered in old-looking wallpaper of dogwood blossoms, the corner of a lace-covered table, the end of a china cabinet filled with enough china to make Martha Stewart look like a slacker.

Scanning to the left side of the living room, he saw a baby grand piano sitting in front of a big bay window whose window seat was upholstered by a different kind of floral fabric from the sofa. Artfully scattered throw pillows covered one end, while sheet music was stacked neatly at the other. A feminine-looking briefcase sat on the floor near the piano, and sheets of lined paper, some filled with handwritten music—were stacked on the bench.

Directly in front of him was a long hallway, the hardwood floor, like the floors of the living room, covered by a worn floral rug. But where the walls in the living room were the dark blue of a twilit sky, the walls of the hallway turned to butter yellow. Taking a few steps to the left, Noah saw that the hall walls were also covered on both sides by scores of framed photographs.

Whoever lived in this house seemed to have a long history here. And whoever lived here was obviously very comfortable living here. He looked at Lila again. She was standing now, laughing at the cats who were still twining around her ankles. And somehow, she looked perfectly at home.

No, Noah told himself. *No way.*

"So you grew up in this house?" he asked carefully.

She looked up at him with a puzzled expression. "Lived here my whole life," she told him. "Except for my time at OSU. My father had retired by the time I graduated, and he was getting on in years, so I moved back home with him to live."

"And you're a music teacher?" he asked, remembering how adamant she had been about that.

"For my livelihood, I am," she said. "And I work at Lauderdale's to bring in a little extra. My real love is songwriting and composing. I haven't sold anything yet, but I haven't been pursuing publication for very long."

Noah nodded slowly, his mind working fast. Maybe what Gestalt said was true. Maybe Lila really did believe she was this Marnie Lundy person. Maybe she'd believed it for the past five months. She appeared to have been living in this house for some time, and the cats obviously knew her well. When he got back to OPUS, he'd run a check on the name Marnie Lundy and see what came up. See if maybe she just appeared out of thin air five months ago.

What could have happened to Lila to drive her over the edge this way? he wondered. It must have been something heinous to have messed with someone as strong—and as dangerous—as she was.

"This house reminds me of the one where I grew up," he said.

"Really?"

No, not really. He'd grown up in the lap of luxury. His parents had employed servants who lived in bigger houses than this. "Yeah," he lied. "Except I spent my childhood in Cincinnati." That much, at least, was true.

"That's a wonderful city," she said. "I have a good friend from college who lives down there and we still try to get together once a month, either here or there."

Of course she did, Noah thought, marveling at just how deeply a person could clinically delude herself.

"Do you mind if I have a look around?" he asked. "It would almost be like revisiting my childhood."

She smiled at that. "Go ahead. I have to feed Edith and Henry."

He narrowed his eyes. "You named your cats Edith and Henry?"

"Actually, my father did. After Edith Wharton and Henry James. He was a professor of literature, specializing in the Gilded Age."

Of course he was, Noah thought. Naturally Lila, who was the offspring of a showgirl hooker and didn't even know the identity of her father, would create such a fantasy father when she was losing her mind. It made perfect sense.

"Well, I wouldn't want to keep Edith and Henry from their dinner. Breakfast," he quickly corrected himself when he remembered what time it was.

Lila took off through the dining room with the cats running alongside her, and Noah headed into the hallway to check out the gallery of photographs. Most of them were old black-and-whites of people he didn't recognize. But others, not quite as old, made his stomach go tight.

Lila. As a girl. As a teenager. In this very house. In one shot, she was wearing a graduation cap and gown, even though Noah knew for a fact—or, at least, had thought he knew for a fact—that she never formally graduated from high school. But she didn't look old enough to be in college in the photo. And there was a man standing beside her, bearded, bespectacled, old enough to be her father—maybe even her grandfather—with one arm slung proudly over her shoulder.

In another shot, an adolescent Lila was blowing out the candles on a birthday cake that said *Happy 13th Birth-*

day...somebody. Noah couldn't make out the name from the camera angle. In another photograph, she was elementary-school aged, standing in the backyard with the garden hose arcing water above her, wringing wet and laughing. In yet another, she looked to be in middle school, wearing a full-length gown with a corsage on her wrist, a dark-suited boy the same age standing awkwardly beside her.

And then another, much more recent photo of Lila, at a time when she should have been working for OPUS. Instead, she was sitting on the piano bench not a dozen steps from where Noah stood, a Christmas tree behind her, a glass of what looked like eggnog in her hand and fake reindeer antlers lit with red and green lights on her head. Not at all the sort of whimsy in which Lila would indulge.

Panic rose in Noah's chest, and he strode back into the living room, to the photographs on the mantelpiece, hoping they offered more insight. But his gaze strayed instead to the bookcase, falling on a row of high-school yearbooks. Hastily, he jerked down the one closest to him, dated 1987. He did some quick mental math. Lila would have been a freshman, so he opened it to look for that class. His attention went instead to the plethora of handwriting on the inside cover, dozens of different signatures, all looking like teenaged writing, all messages inscribed to "Marnie."

Heat splashed through his belly. Shoving pages to the left, he found the freshman class and looked not for Moreau, but for Lundy. Sure enough, Marnie was there, looking just like Lila would have looked when she was in ninth grade. Except that, knowing what he did of Lila's life when she was that age, her expression would have been sullen, angry and scared. Marnie Lundy fairly beamed from the page, an obviously happy, well-adjusted kid.

Noah pulled down the next yearbook and found Marnie Lundy as a sophomore, and the inside covers once again obscured by good wishes from what seemed to be the entire class. The next two yearbooks held more of the same.

"Agent Tennant, what are you doing?"

Noah spun around at the question and saw Lila—no, Marnie, he made himself admit—framed by her dining-room doors, staring at him as if she were very, very sorry she had allowed him into her house.

"I'm sorry," he apologized. And then he laughed anxiously. Boy, was that an understatement. "I mean…" He faltered, studying her again. She was Lila. But…not. She looked like her, sounded like her, even moved like her. But she wasn't her.

"You're not Lila," he said, knowing the declaration must sound ridiculous to her. "You really are Marnie Lundy."

"I know that," she said, her voice edged with impatience. "That's what I've been telling you all night. I thought you realized it. I thought that was why you let me come home."

He shook his head. "I didn't realize it until this minute," he told her. "I thought I was humoring a delusional agent who would break under the pressure of having to confront her delusion."

"You thought I was crazy Lila?" she translated.

He expelled a single, humorless chuckle. "Yeah. Instead, I find that you're…"

She settled her hands on her hips, shifting her weight to one foot, and glared at him. It was a gesture he'd seen Lila perform too many times to count. But it wasn't Lila doing it this time.

Then another thought struck him. He and Zorba and Gestalt had told this woman all kinds of things tonight about OPUS, convinced that they were telling Lila things she already knew. Marnie Lundy knew some pretty sensitive stuff about the organization and Lila's disappearance. She knew Noah's name. She knew his code name. She'd seen their operation, if only from a limited standpoint. If she tried very hard, she might even be able to retrace her steps to the cabin in the woods.

"I'm what?" she demanded.

But Noah honestly had no idea what to say. Except maybe, "You're not the woman I'm looking for."

IT WAS MIDMORNING before Marnie's head finally stopped feeling fuzzy over everything that had happened in the past twelve hours. In the meantime, Noah Tennant had requested and inspected as many of her personal documents as she could pull from her filing cabinet, from the deed to her house to her and her father's wills to the checking account on which she had written thousands of checks over the past ten years. He hadn't said much as he'd reviewed the documents, had only asked questions that she'd done her best to answer. But two interrogations in such a short span of time had left her feeling a tad raw emotionally, and coupled with the lack of sleep, she was growing more than a little irritable. Even a steady stream of herbal tea hadn't been enough to soothe her. On the other hand, the coffee she'd fed to Agent Tennant had only seemed to sharpen his mind, something else that kind of ticked her off.

How could he look so cool and collected—and dammit, so handsome—when she felt like a world-class frump with only one half-functioning brain cell? And why, of all the things that should or could have been circling through her head at the moment, was it his voice of a few hours ago she kept hearing?

You're not the woman I've been looking for.

Story of my life, she thought as she watched him on the other side of her dining-room table, studying her social security card again. She was never the woman men were looking for. Not in the long run. She was always too… something…for them. Too serious. Too dedicated. Too quiet. Too old-fashioned. Too focused. Too straitlaced. Too stuffy.

Not a single charge was true. Yes, she was all of those things from time to time. But never to a point where that was *all* she was. And she was other things, too, things men just couldn't seem to see. She could be fun when the situation called for it. She *could.* And she could be witty and adventurous and outrageous, too. Really. She could. Honest. She'd just never met any men who made her want to be those things, that was all. The men she met were always too…something…for her, too.

"We'll still have to run a check on you," Agent Tennant said now, not looking up from her social security card. She'd noticed he'd come back to that little scrap of cardboard several times, as if something about it still bothered him. "There's a lot I can learn about you from our sources that I can't from all this." He gestured toward the piles of paper records fanned out across the table.

Marnie narrowed her eyes at him. "Are you telling me you know more about me than I know myself?"

He was smiling when he looked up at her, but there was nothing happy in the expression. "Well, not at the moment. But by day's end…"

She shook her head. "Unbelievable," she said for a second time since meeting him. But again, unfortunately, it was easy to believe.

He studied her in silence for a moment longer, then picked up her birth certificate. It, like her social security card, had seemed to interest him more than anything else she'd presented for his examination.

"This is just a photocopy," he said. "Do you have the original?"

She couldn't see what difference it would make, but told him, "No. I don't remember ever seeing an original, to be honest. I only needed the copy for school registrations and such. I imagine it's packed away somewhere with my baby effects."

"According to this," Agent Tennant said, his attention falling to the document again, "You were born May first, nineteen seventy-two, to Elliott and Lucie Lundy."

He glanced up again, and again, Marnie was struck by how very blue his eyes were. That, of course, made her notice again how handsome he was, and for some weird reason, she found herself wondering if he was married. Of its own volition, her gaze fell to the hand that was holding her birth certificate—his left. No ring. No tan line or indentation, either. Still, some married people didn't bother with them. Then she reminded herself it was none of her business if Agent Tennant was married. More to the point, she further reminded herself, she didn't care.

So why did she need to be reminded of that?

"You mentioned your father passed away," he said, pulling her back to the matter at hand. Which was *not* his hand, she assured herself. "Is your mother still alive?"

"No. She died when I was a month old," she told him. "In a car accident. I have no memory of her, and my father never remarried."

For a long moment, Agent Tennant said nothing. Then, "May first, nineteen-seventy-two," he repeated. But softly, this time, and with some distraction, as if he were thinking about something else when he said it.

She couldn't imagine why he'd find her date of birth so worthy of consideration, but he said nothing more and stayed quiet so long, Marnie began to feel a little uncomfortable.

Then she realized it wasn't his silence making her uncomfortable—it was the intent way he was studying her face. He seemed to be most interested in her eyes, however, pinning his gaze there for a long time. Long enough to make heat swamp her entire system. Again.

"I need to borrow this for a little while," he stated—not asked—as he held up her birth certificate. "I'll get it back to you this afternoon. This evening at the latest." He looked down at the papers on the table again and plucked her social security card from the assortment. "I'll need this, too."

"Okay," she agreed reluctantly. Not that she got the feeling that she had much choice. "But why do you need them?"

"I can't say for sure just yet," he told her. "But I think, Ms. Lundy, that you and I both are going to be surprised by what I learn."

Oh, Marnie didn't like the sound of that *at all*. "I have to work tonight at Lauderdale's," she told him. "And I have students to teach this afternoon."

"Tomorrow then," he said. "We should talk then. Are you free in the morning?"

She nodded. "But I have to work at the store in the evening."

He took a step backward, into her living room. But he continued to look at her face, as if he wasn't able to look at anything else. "I apologize again for the inconvenience of last night."

"Inconvenience," she repeated blandly. "It was a lot more than that. You scared the hell out of me."

He made a face that indicated he was genuinely sorry, and continued to watch her eyes. "I apologize for that, too."

A shudder of heat wound through her at the relentlessness of his gaze. The way he was looking at her then… Hungry. That was the only way she could think to describe him. Like a man who'd been starved and neglected for years and had just stumbled upon a banquet.

He kept walking until he was at her front door, his attention divided between her birth certificate, her social security card and her. Marnie seemed to finally win out over the paper documents, however—and my, but wasn't *that* a huge compliment, being more important than paper?—because he stuffed the former into his inside jacket pocket and studied her face again. Or, rather, she couldn't help thinking, her eyes. But she couldn't shake the feeling that he was seeing something—or someone—else.

"I'll be back in the morning," he said. "Around nine okay?"

"Fine."

"We can talk more then."

Marnie wanted to ask about what, since he seemed to already know, but decided maybe she wasn't all that fired up to hear. There was still a chance, however small, that this was nothing but a bad dream. By tomorrow morning, she might wake up to discover Agent Noah Tennant didn't exist anywhere outside her feverish imagination, so whatever he had to tell her didn't, either.

And maybe, she thought further, she'd also wake up tomorrow to discover that an asteroid the size of Lithuania had crashed into Ohio, making this whole episode—not to mention Cleveland—moot.

Without a further word, Agent Tennant opened the front door and passed through it, closing it with a soft click behind him. Marnie moved to the big bay window to watch him make his way toward the plain black sedan he'd called to have someone bring to the house earlier. But he didn't immediately start the car when he slipped behind the wheel, and instead pressed some buttons on his cell phone and put it to his ear. As he spoke to whoever answered at the other end, he studied both her birth certificate and social security card again, clearly reading off the information on each.

At one point, he glanced up to see Marnie looking at him out the window, and he stopped talking, as if he were afraid she might be able to discern what he was saying.

Then, obviously realizing that was impossible, he began to speak again to whomever he had called. But he continued to watch Marnie watching him, and for several long moments, neither of them looked away. Finally, though, after ending the connection, he lifted a hand in farewell. Then he started the car and maneuvered it out of the driveway, and made his way down the street.

Not once did he look back.

CHAPTER SIX

ELLIE CHANDLER SAT cross-legged on her living room floor with an oversize mug of coffee in one hand and a sealed OPUS file in the other. She'd shed her suit and heels in favor of baggy brown cargo pants, a waffle-weave Henley the color of red wine and slouchy socks; her dark auburn hair had been shifted from the sophisticated French twist she wore to work to the loose ponytail she favored for home. Like a good agent—even though she wasn't one yet—she'd followed Noah's instructions and gotten a few hours of sleep before looking at the file, so now the noonday sun tumbled raucously through the window. Her belly was full of Krispy Kreme jelly-filleds, the coffeepot was full and she was about to embark on her first field assignment for OPUS.

Oh, yeah. Life was *so* good.

The sleek white envelope, Staples style #4673, if she knew her office paraphernalia—and it went without saying that she did—had nary a smudge nor crease to be seen, a testament to how seriously her boss took the job. Even more seriously than Ellie did, which was pretty hard to believe, since she took the job more seriously than anything. Noah never left the office before she did, and she generally never left her desk before six. She'd stay later, but she was always finished with her work by then, and if she got started on the next day's too soon, she'd run out of things to do by lunchtime. Maybe someday, if she was very lucky, she'd be as overworked as her boss. Because she had her sights set on going straight to the top.

Someday, some way, Ellie Chandler intended to be She Whose Name Nobody Dared Say.

Hey, it wasn't like she had anything better to do. The alternative to working late was going out to hang with friends, then home to unwind. Enjoy a glass of wine. Read a book. Watch a movie. Take a long, luxurious bubble bath. Who needed that kind of crap in their life?

4A wasn't just the number on the front door of her apartment. It was her personality type, too. She hated sitting around waiting for things to happen, craved a life of adventure and excitement. She wanted to meet the world head-on, on her own terms. Hell, she wanted to change the world to suit her own terms. She hated nonperformers, didn't suffer fools, couldn't tolerate idleness. To Ellie, a day without work was a day wasted. She was smart, ambitious, driven. She was the perfect candidate for OPUS field agent.

She was only days away from undertaking her first assignment to prove that. Oh, she'd still be under supervision while completing it, and would have to submit regular reports to Noah. And it wouldn't be anything major for a first-timer, she knew. But it *would* be exciting. Finally, she'd have a job—no, a calling—with purpose. Finally, she'd have something in her life that was important. Finally, she'd have something that would *be* her life.

Unable to tolerate the suspense any longer, she set her mug on the coffee table and turned her attention to the dossier. The back flap was closed by an official OPUS seal, under which she ran her thumb to carefully separate it from the paper. With a soft whoosh of sound, it pulled away, and she withdrew the contents of the envelope, placing the stack of papers on the floor in front of her as if they were a holy epistle. A brief note from Noah lay on top. It said:

Ellie,
    Congratulations on earning your first field assignment. The enclosed material is pretty self-explanatory, but I'm sure you'll have some questions after you read everything, so don't hesitate to call me. I know you'll make us proud.
Noah

Well, duh. Of course she'd make them proud. She'd been born for this job. It was coded into her DNA.

She set aside the letter and took a deep breath, then began to read hungrily over the first few pages. But by the second paragraph, dread had coated her stomach like rancid fish oil. By page three, she felt as though she was going to throw up. And not just because she realized she'd be remaining in Cleveland for the duration of her assignment when she'd been hoping to go overseas—or, at the very least, Pennsylvania. But because the target of the investigation was also the object of her desire.

Daniel Beck. The boy next door.

Literally. Ever since Daniel had moved into 4C a year ago, Ellie had been lusting after him. Unfortunately, he'd never offered any indication he was interested in her the same way. Though not because he was gay, since she'd seen him in the company of enough women—and she'd heard enough feminine moaning erupting from his bedroom, which abutted her own—to make her realize it wasn't her gender that put him off. It was her specifically.

No surprise, really, since the women she always saw with him were, to a tart, tarts. Heavy on makeup, light on clothing. A surplus of breasts, a deficit of brains. Most likely to put out. Least likely to move in. Daniel Beck was a good guy who liked bad girls. And men who walked on the wild side always took their time going around the block.

So Ellie had tried to be philosophical and remain just friends with him. They shared the occasional evening together when neither had a date, which was most often Ellie's condition, not Daniel's. Or they went to the action flicks together that his usual dates didn't enjoy. Or when Daniel couldn't find an extra hand for poker with the boys, he knew Ellie was always up for it. Just like he knew he was always welcome in her home, the same way she knew she was always welcome in his.

Well, except for when that feminine moaning was erupting from his bedroom. But he'd make the same allowance for her, she was sure. Problem was, there hadn't been any masculine moaning coming from her apartment for a while. Certainly not since Daniel moved in next door. Except for that time the super let himself in to investigate the source of a leak when he thought she wasn't home, and Ellie coldcocked him before realizing who he was.

So whenever she was with Daniel, she just tried not to

notice how his thick black hair made her want to run her fingers through it and how his chocolate-brown eyes made her want to melt in his mouth *and* his hands. She'd tried not to pay attention to the way his T-shirts hugged his finely sculpted biceps and strained against his broad chest with such loving familiarity. She'd made every effort not to daydream about how his big hands might feel skimming over her naked body. And she'd done her best not to ogle his chiseled rump whenever she happened to be walking down the stairs behind him. For the most part, she'd been successful.

Well, except for how she kept noticing his hair, eyes, mouth, hands, biceps, chest, abdomen and rump. And except for how she'd not really been able to keep her feelings for him friendly at all. Other than that, though, everything was fine.

Until she moved aside another page in the dossier to find a color eight-by-ten glossy of Daniel staring back at her.

It was a photo she recognized, too, taken from his employee ID for ChemiTech, the company where he worked as a research chemist. Which was another thing Ellie liked about him. He was a total brainiac, something that also made her marvel at the women he pursued. How such an intelligent man could be so stupid to overlook what was right under his nose in favor of throwaway sex was beyond her. Especially when Ellie was perfectly willing to give him all the throwaway sex he could want.

Damn. Here we go again. She waited for the kaleidoscopic mental images of his hair, eyes, mouth, hands, biceps, chest, abdomen and rump to pass, then looked down at his photo again.

Daniel Beck was the only guy in the world who was handsome enough that his work ID could pass for a sample from a modeling portfolio. Those dark eyes gazed back at her with a spark of mischief she knew was an integral part of his personality. His unruly, overly long hair curled carelessly over his ears, and his full mouth was curved into just a hint of a smile. He looked playful and charming and sweet. Something twisted painfully in her chest as she looked at him. Hell, he *was* playful and charming and sweet.

He couldn't possibly be selling government secrets to terrorists.

But when she turned another page, she was hit by a wall of incriminating evidence. ChemiTech held a lot of government contracts, many of them pretty hush-hush. Now, leaks of top-secret information were streaming from the department where Daniel worked, and they'd begun almost immediately after his employment at the company began. The information that had been sold overseas had all come either from projects Daniel was working on, or ones to which he could easily gain access. There had been two suspicious deposits made to his bank account in the past nine months, one for twenty thousand dollars, and one for fifteen thousand dollars. The money had then been immediately withdrawn, and there was no trace of where it went.

Of course, there were others, too, in that department, working on those projects, who had access to the additional files—though no one else's financial records reflected sudden substantial income. OPUS had narrowed their search to five potential suspects. Daniel was third on that list. The primary suspect was the very man who had brought Daniel to work at ChemiTech, his mentor and former professor, Dr. Sebastian Baird, who had begun working for the company less than a year before Daniel.

Ellie's stomach roiled with nausea as she read the rest of the file. OPUS had collected a lot of background information on each of the suspects, and there were a number of discrepancies in what OPUS had uncovered about Daniel and what he'd told her about himself. He'd said he grew up in Santa Barbara, California, when in fact he hadn't moved there until he went to college. He'd actually been born and raised in Apache Junction, Arizona. He'd told Ellie he was a starter for his high-school basketball team and had been elected homecoming king for the girls' basketball team, mostly because he'd dated the girls' team in its entirety. He'd also told her he'd lettered in track in college. But according to OPUS's findings, he'd only been a standout in the Chemistry and Latin clubs in high school, and had been ostracized by the more popular students. In college, his biggest claim to fame was patenting a new synthetic fiber.

In fact, according to OPUS's files, Daniel Beck carried all the characteristics of the very sort of person who would commit the very type of crime of which he was suspected. He'd been an involuntary outsider at school, smarter than just about everyone else and had had few friends, none of them close. Likewise damning was the fact that he'd been in counseling for a while as a teenager, to treat his unmanageable anger.

The picture OPUS painted of him was in no way similar to the guy Ellie had come to know and...like very much.

Daniel Beck was probably the least angry person of her acquaintance. He had lots of friends, and even more girl-friends. There was no freaking way she could see him being the kind of person who would sell out his country, sell out himself.

But then, she didn't think there was any freaking way he could be a liar, either.

She sighed heavily as she turned another page in the dossier. No wonder Noah had told her she'd have questions after she went over everything. The problem now was that she didn't think Noah would be able to answer them. No, only Daniel Beck could do that. And Ellie couldn't think of a single way to ask them that wouldn't make him sus-picious of her right from the start.

At least her cover would be convincing. Naturally Ellie hadn't told Daniel about her training to become an OPUS agent, since no one was allowed to know where she worked or what she did for a living. To explain her unavailability on Mondays, Wednesdays and Fridays for her spy training, she'd told everyone she'd returned to college to earn her MBA because she wanted to climb the corporate ladder. But she hadn't even been able to tell anyone she worked as a secretary for OPUS, since the general public wasn't supposed to know the organization existed. As far as anyone outside OPUS was concerned, Ellie was an accountant for an agency that did government auditing, which was the cover for Ohio's OPUS office in reality. She'd be reporting to ChemiTech in that persona to perform a standard auditing of the records for every government contract ChemiTech had been awarded, something that should look to Daniel like a happy coincidence and nothing else.

Hiding what she did for a living and covering up her spy training were only small lies, she assured herself. And they didn't affect her friendship with Daniel. Besides, she'd never expressly said she was going for her master of business administration. She'd been thinking of MBA in terms of Most Buff Agent. And she for sure could be that. She worked out every morning.

She thumbed through the rest of the dossier and tried to sort through her myriad feelings. This was a plum assignment, not at all the sort of thing that generally went to a trainee, which was probably another reason Noah had told her she'd have questions. Ellie had been assigned to it expressly because of her connection to Daniel—her cover would just be that much more convincing. If she wrapped this up quickly and efficiently—which, of course, she would—she'd shoot right to the top of the list for future plum assignments.

But would she be abusing Daniel's friendship and betraying his trust if she investigated him for wrongdoing without his knowledge? Then again, if she wanted to rise to the higher echelons of OPUS—and yeah, baby, she did—she couldn't let little things like abuse of a friendship or betrayal of trust stop her.

Wow. Her first big rite of passage as an agent. And she wasn't even an agent yet.

Bottom line, she thought, OPUS wanted her to complete an assignment. Period. And Ellie, like the premier OPUS agent she intended to be, would complete it to its fullest extent. She just hoped that doing so wouldn't wreck the lives of two people who had become very important to her—herself and Daniel Beck.

IT WAS DARK by the time Daniel Beck climbed the fourth flight of stairs in his apartment building at the end of another long day. But then, it was almost always dark outside by the time he called it a day. Even in the summer, when darkness didn't come until very late, he was often holed up in his lab working on some project till after hours.

Unless, of course, it was the weekend. Weekends he was doing something else till after hours. Weekends were when he made damned sure he enjoyed the things he earned as a hardworking man in contemporary American society. Which, interestingly, were the same things he'd been denied as a geeky teenager and even geekier college student in not-too-long-ago American society: a social life and smokin' sex. On account of he hadn't had anything remotely resembling a social life—or sex of *any* kind— until he'd been out of college for more than a year. Therefore, he had a lot of making up—and making out—to do. Frankly, so deprived had Daniel been as a young man, there were times when he thought he'd never get caught up. Which actually suited him fine, because it meant he had a lifetime ahead of him that was full of smokin' sex.

The jingling of his keys as he fumbled for the one to his front door were a fitting accompaniment to the clinking of the biker jacket he was entitled to wear because, unlike many wearers of such garments, he actually *owned* a motorcycle. It was a welcome change from the fifteen-year-old, four-door Chevette he'd had to drive throughout high school and college, something that had contributed significantly to his social-life-and-sex-lacking geekdom during that time.

But he wasn't that geek anymore, and he would never

be that geek again. He had a bitchin' Harley now, not a Chevette. He had his own cool bachelor digs, not his parents' basement. He'd gone through a most excellent second puberty in college that had cleared up his skin, pushed him past six-two in height and enabled him to bench-press his own body weight. And he had made the most of all three developments. Now, he dated the most luscious babes, and not nobody, who had been his constant female companion in youth.

As if conjured by the thought, just as Daniel was inserting his key into his front door lock, the front door to the apartment next to his flew open to reveal Ellie Chandler standing on the other side. He grinned when he saw her.

"Hey, Ellie to the rescue," he said, withdrawing his key again. "You can take me to dinner."

Instead of the smile he'd been expecting, her eyes widened in what looked very much like panic. Immediately, Daniel glanced back over his shoulder, to see if someone was about to jump him, but the hallway was empty. When he turned to look at Ellie again, the panic on her face has morphed into something else, but she still didn't look like her usual self.

"You okay?" he asked. "You look like you don't feel too good."

"Uh…" she replied eloquently.

"Ellie?" he tried again. "Is something wrong?"

"Um…" she said.

Alarm bells began to rattle inside Daniel's brain. Ellie at a loss for words? Something pretty horrible must have happened to cause that. "What is it? What's happened?"

"Ah…rough day," she finally said. But the words came

out rushed and breathy, as if she were just pulling them off the top of her head. "Really, really rough day."

He regarded her curiously. Something was going on, and she didn't want to tell him what it was. Which was weird, because the two of them talked about everything. It was one of the things Daniel liked so much about Ellie. He could talk to her as easily as he could one of the guys. So he asked, "You want to talk about it?"

"No," she said adamantly, her eyes going wide.

"Might help."

She shook her head quickly. "No. Trust me. It wouldn't."

"Then let me take you to dinner," he offered. "We haven't had Indian for a while, and I've been craving some lamb vindaloo. But you have to buy. I'm busted till my next paycheck."

She hesitated before replying, as if she were giving serious thought to her answer. Then she smiled. Not her usual Ellie smile, the one that lit up her whole face, but she at least seemed to relax a bit. As if to reinforce that, she took a couple of steps toward him and came to a halt.

"How can you always be so broke?" she asked. "I thought research chemists made pretty decent money."

"Not this one," he said. "I'm too low on the food chain at ChemiTech right now."

She nodded slowly and studied him with the same kind of consideration she might give to an upholstery selection. "All right," she finally agreed. "I'll buy you dinner tonight. I was just headed out to get something myself. But *you're* buying dinner next time."

He smiled. "As long as you eat light."

She smiled back. "You already know I eat like a horse."

"Perfect. You'll be happy to make do with oatmeal."

They kidded each other all the way to a diner near their apartment building, and Daniel's concern for Ellie gradually ebbed. Whatever had happened today, she seemed to be less bothered by it now. And if she did want to talk about it at some point, he'd be there to listen.

The diner was virtually deserted when they entered, thanks to it being well past the usual dinner hour. Two men seated at the counter looked like they were on their way to a bowling tournament, and a young couple in a back booth looked like they were all ready for bed—though not necessarily to sleep. Either the place had gone totally retro in recent years, or it hadn't changed one iota from the time it opened in the early 1950s. Judging by the cracks in the plastic seating and the scars on the Formica tabletops and the patched linoleum, Daniel had always suspected it was the latter.

"I did get some good news today," Ellie said as she slid across the cracked plastic seating of the booth.

"Yeah? What?" Daniel asked.

She plucked a laminated menu from the napkin holder and began to inspect it very carefully, even though the two of them had eaten here often enough that she should have had the thing memorized by now. Hell, Daniel already knew he wanted the tuna melt and a Heineken.

"I'm going to be working at ChemiTech for a couple of weeks," she said, finally looking up to eye him in a way that made him feel a little edgy for no reason he could name. "Auditing the books on a couple of projects you guys are doing for Uncle Sam. So you better not be funneling off any cash or selling government secrets."

He grinned at that. "Excellent. You can buy me lunch for the next few days, too. That ought to reassure you I'm not funneling off any cash."

"Maybe you could sell some government secrets and earn a few extra dollars," she suggested.

He laughed outright at that. "Yeah, right. Good one, Ellie. I don't even like to share my findings with my co-workers most of the time. No way would I let an enemy of the people in on what I'm doing. We research chemists are a competitive bunch, ya know."

She studied him in silence for a moment more, then went back to studying the menu.

"So, almost finished with the master's," he said, knowing Ellie's classwork for that was winding down. "That means you can kiss your junior accountant job goodbye and go for the big money. Be Madame CEO of Big Money Ellie, Incorporated, someday. Then maybe you won't have any more rough days at work like today. And then you can buy me dinner and lunch every day. So do I get an invitation to the graduation ceremony?"

"I'm not going through the ceremony," she replied, still looking at the menu instead of him. "I mean, I'm almost thirty years old, so it's not like it's some major rite of passage. And my parents aren't all that keen to schlep back to the States for something like that."

"I guess Hong Kong is a pretty fair haul," he agreed. "Though I still don't see why they had to retire on the other side of the world, when their only kid lives here."

"My mom always wanted to live someplace exotic," she

said by way of an explanation. "I still see them a couple times a year."

"Well, *I'd* come to the ceremony to see you get your degree," he told her. "I think it's great you're moving up in the world. You've worked hard enough for it. And I know you'll do a great job at whatever you put your mind to."

When she glanced up at him this time, she looked a little more like her usual self. She smiled tentatively and closed the menu, slipping it back behind the napkin holder. "That's nice of you to say all that, Daniel. I appreciate it."

He smiled back. "Hey, what are friends for?"

She nodded, and her smile brightened some more, until she definitely looked like her old self. "Yeah. If you can't count on your friends, then you have no business being friends with them, right?"

"Right."

"And friends wouldn't tell each other stuff that isn't true, would they?"

Not sure where that one came from—and not especially wanting to answer it—Daniel hedged. "Well, not about anything important, that's for sure."

The sudden turn of conversation put him on edge. Okay, so he hadn't always been honest with Ellie about everything. He'd always spoken the truth when it came to stuff that mattered. And it wasn't only Ellie he hadn't been honest with when it came to certain aspects of his life. There were some things that happened to a guy—and some things a guy had done—that he didn't much feel like sharing. None of those things had anything to do with his friendship with Ellie. They were just things he wasn't especially proud of and would rather others didn't know. So he changed the subject again.

"When do you start at ChemiTech?"

She hesitated before answering, as if she wasn't ready to change the subject. Then, "Thursday morning," she told him. "How far away from the records room are you? That's where I'll be working most of the time."

"A few floors and corridors. Maybe a five-minute walk."

"You get down that way often?"

He shook his head. "Only when I'm returning files for Sebastian that he's checked out. I don't really need to reference stuff myself." He pointed to his head. "I keep it all up here."

"Lucky you've got such a big head," she said with a grin.

He narrowed his eyes at her. "Takes one to know one."

"Ooh, what a comeback. However will I top that? Wait, I know. I'll say, 'Nanner nanner boo-boo.' Your turn."

He was about to respond with an eloquent *I know you are, but what am I?* when a waitress approached their table to take their orders, and after she left, Ellie began speaking again.

"So what's Sebastian working on now? Is it something you're working on, too?"

"There's one project the two of us are on together, and I'm filing regular reports to him on a couple that I'm doing myself. One or two others where we're both part of a larger team. Why?"

She shrugged. "Just curious. You never really talk too much about what you do at ChemiTech. And I know you and Sebastian are pretty tight."

"It's pretty boring stuff to anyone who isn't a chemist."

"Maybe."

"You never talk much about your job, either," he pointed out.

She smiled. "That's because it's pretty boring stuff to anyone who isn't an accountant. Hey, will you give me the grand tour after I start work Thursday? Show me where you work and what kind of stuff you do?"

"Why?" he asked, genuinely puzzled. He and Ellie hardly ever talked about their jobs. There were too many other interesting things to talk about instead. And his job *would* seem boring to anyone else. Just like her job sounded boring to him.

"I'm suddenly curious," she told him. "I think it would be fun to see where you work and what you do."

"Okay," he said. "But just a quick one. And only surface stuff. A lot of what we work on is government contracts we're not allowed to talk about. But you already know that if you're coming to audit the place. Security's pretty tight on any given day. That's why no visitors are allowed. They won't even let school kids come through on field trips."

"Oh, right," she said. "Like I'd even know a government secret if it bit me on the ass. And even if I did, who would I tell?"

"I never said you'd tell anyone," he said, finding the remark odd. "I'm just telling you why the tour has to be short."

That look was back on her face again, Daniel noticed. The one that just didn't seem quite…right. Like maybe she knew something he didn't know. Though whether it was about herself, or about him, or about them, he couldn't imagine.

Something had for sure happened to her today, though, that much was certain. And she wasn't telling him about it. Which was a definite first. Ellie was the only woman on the planet Daniel liked talking to, the only woman he really *could* talk to. With other women, it was all just fluff and flirting. He and Ellie could and did talk about everything. Openly. Freely. Without fear of reprisal or criticism or ridicule.

Until now. There was something going on with her that she wasn't telling him. And he didn't like to think about that. Because it could only mean one of two things: One, whatever had happened was so terrible, she couldn't talk about it to anyone. Or, two, she was afraid he might respond to whatever it was with reprisal or criticism or ridicule. Either way, it boiled down to a lack of trust on her part. And Daniel didn't want to lose that. Losing Ellie's trust meant losing Ellie's friendship. And that was the last thing in the world he could afford to lose.

CHAPTER SEVEN

TRUE TO HIS WORD, Agent Tennant returned to Marnie's house at precisely nine Wednesday morning when she was enjoying her second cup of coffee on the porch swing and miring herself in denial that her life hadn't become a big, reeking pile of offal. Since she'd gotten almost no sleep for a second night in a row, she'd dressed to complement the circles under her eyes, in a pair of softly worn blue jeans and a lavender turtleneck sweater, her hair gathered at her nape in a loose braid.

When he unfolded himself from the same nondescript black sedan he'd driven away in the day before, she saw that he was wearing nondescript black sunglasses and was dressed in what looked like the same nondescript black suit he'd had on then. Briefly, she wondered if he'd even gone home since yesterday morning. Then she noticed that his necktie today was a discreet dark blue, and she recalled the one from the day before being a discreet dark red. She envisioned him standing in front of an open closet filled with wall-to-wall black suits and white dress shirts, and one of those rotating tie holders containing two ties, turning with a laconical hum while he decided what mood he was in that day.

The blandness of his wardrobe belied the rest of him, however. Marnie had to bite back a sigh as she watched him make his way up the front walk to her porch. He had some way of walking, she'd grant him that, all hips and swagger and purposeful stride. His entire body seemed to get into the action, his long arms swaying, his broad shoulders rolling, his brawny hands flexing, his powerful thighs scissoring, his…

Well. Suffice it to say Marnie just liked the way he walked, that was all. She sipped her coffee and battled an uncharacteristic wave of nervousness—where was that coming from?—as he strode up the steps, and somehow she kept her focus trained on his face.

"Good morning," he said as he removed his sunglasses and tucked them into the breast pocket of his jacket.

"Good morning," she echoed. Knowing it was a lie. And she could tell by the look on his face that he'd been lying when he greeted her, too. Whatever news he had, it wasn't going to be good.

For a moment, he said nothing more, only studied her much as he had yesterday, as if he were taking a thorough inventory of her with those incredibly blue eyes that made her insides turn to warm pudding. Finally, "You and I need to…talk," he said.

She wasn't sure she liked the way he'd said *talk*. Because he made the word *talk* sound more like *discuss something that's going to stuff your life even deeper into the garbage disposal and give it another good whirl.*

"Talk?" she repeated.

Only then did she notice he was carrying a manila envelope in one hand—well, it hadn't been moving when he walked, so what was the point in noticing it?—and it seemed to be pretty full. Not the way the curious little man in the parking lot had stuffed his manila envelope to near bursting, but Marnie was beginning to experience a fear of manila that bordered on psychosis. Manilaphobia. That must be what she had.

"Talk," he reiterated in that same ominous way.

"About what?"

He inhaled a deep breath, as if needing the extra oxygen for what he was about to say. Marnie's heart plummeted. "I get the impression, Ms. Lundy, that you're made of pretty stern stuff, so I'd like to dispense with the niceties and just say what I have to say. Will that be all right?"

Marnie had always thought she was made of pretty stern stuff, too, and she'd never been one for niceties, either. Until that moment. But suddenly, she felt like a quivering mass of goo, and she had the strangest urge to go inside and bake some petits fours and make a pot of tea and serve it all on doilies. Nevertheless, she said, "All right."

Agent Tennant flipped open the flap of the envelope and reached inside. "Ms. Lundy," he began.

"Marnie," she corrected him. "If you're about to tell me something that's going to shatter my world, you might as well call me by my first name."

"Marnie, then," he said. Thereby confirming that he was indeed about to flick the switch over the sink.

She closed her eyes.

"You weren't born in Cleveland," he told her.

She snapped her eyes open. "I beg your pardon?"

"You weren't born in Cleveland," he said again. "You were born in Las Vegas, Nevada."

"What?" she exclaimed, the word coming out louder than she had intended. She gentled her tone some as she continued. "No, I wasn't. You saw my birth certificate. I was born right here in Cleveland."

"No. You weren't," he told her. "Your father lied to you about that, Marnie. He lied to you about a lot of things."

He might as well have slapped her, so acute was her response to what he said. She'd always felt so confident in the knowledge that she and her father had been able to speak frankly about everything. She'd always found comfort in having a parent who was completely honest with her. Now she closed her eyes as she waited to hear the rest of what Agent Tennant had to say.

"You didn't move to Cleveland until you were almost a year old," he continued. "And you came here from Pittsburgh, Pennsylvania—where you still have some extended family, by the way—which was where you moved when you were three months old, immediately after leaving Las Vegas."

She was shaking her head before he finished. No. He was wrong. She had no family besides her father. Her father had told her that. Why would he lie about such a thing, when he'd spent his life being such a strong family for her?

"No," she said aloud, opening her eyes. "That's impossible. My birth certificate says… My father *told* me—"

"And your mother's name wasn't Lucie Lundy," he interrupted.

"No," she said again. "You're wrong. That can't be true." Then another thought struck her. Oh, God. Oh, no. No, please. He couldn't possibly be telling her… "My father," she managed to say. "I mean, he *was* my father. You're not going to tell me he—" She halted before finishing because she simply could not bring herself to doubt her paternity. The thought that the man she'd grown up loving as her father wasn't the man who'd deserved that love was too terrible to bear.

"Your father was Elliott Lundy," Agent Tennant said gently.

She expelled a long sigh of relief, not realizing until she did so that she had been holding her breath.

"But he lied to you about a lot of other things."

Oh, God...

Tennant withdrew a piece of paper from the envelope and, without asking for her okay, joined her on the swing. Automatically, she scooted all the way to one side to allow him room. And, automatically, she pulled her legs up before her, scrunching her entire body into a ball, as if that might protect her from whatever else he had to say.

He extended the paper toward her. "This is a copy of your actual birth certificate that was faxed to us yesterday," he said. "The original is on its way via courier to our Cleveland office. It should be here this afternoon."

Reluctantly, Marnie glanced down at the document without touching it, noting what looked like a state seal but was different from the one on her Ohio birth certificate. But she couldn't discern much else, because the words were too blurry. Must be a lousy copy. Then she felt dampness on her cheeks and realized the words weren't blurry because of the lousy quality of the printing. It was because of the lousy quality of her emotions.

"My mother," she managed to say as she swiped away

the uncharacteristic tears. Honestly, she almost never cried. "If she wasn't Lucie Lundy, then who was she?"

"Her name was Susan Townsend," Tennant said.

Marnie shook her head slowly. "I've never heard of her."

"Maybe not. But you've heard of her other daughter."

"Her other daughter?" Marnie echoed. "What are you talking about? I don't have a sister. That proves this woman isn't my mother."

Agent Tennant hesitated for a moment before saying, "Susan Townsend had another daughter besides you who eventually became Lila Moreau."

"What?" Marnie exclaimed. Confusion swamped her, making her head feel like it was full of cobwebs.

"Lila Moreau is your sister," he said again.

"What?"

"Your twin sister."

"What?"

"Your identical twin sister."

"What?"

"Look down here," he told her, pointing his finger at one area of the birth certificate. "Where it says 'multiple birth.' The box for twin is checked. And up here," he added, moving his finger to the top of the page, "is where your parents' names are listed. And here's your name," he added, indicating the first line.

Marnie directed her gaze to that part of the document and saw that what he had told her was true. Her father was identified as Elliott Cameron Lundy. Her mother was Susan Gloria Townsend. And Marnie was, as she had always been—

"Marnie Catherine Lundy," Agent Tennant read when he saw where her gaze had settled. "Your sister is Lisa Ann Townsend."

Now Marnie was really confused. "But you said my sister was Lila Moreau."

"That's the name OPUS gave her when she became an agent. No one keeps their real name when they become active as agents in order to protect their identity and the identities of their loved ones."

"Then your name isn't really Noah Tennant?" she asked.

And of all the questions that should be plaguing Marnie at the moment, why was that the one she asked?

"No, my name is Noah Tennant," he said. "But I'm not an agent anymore. When I was, I went by a different name."

"So Lisa Townsend became Lila Moreau," Marnie said.

Agent Tennant nodded.

"And she's my twin sister," Marnie added, the words sounding strange—and feeling stranger—on her tongue. "I don't understand. Why would my father not tell me the truth about my mother or where I was born? Why would he not tell me I have relatives in Pittsburgh? And why on earth would he not tell me I had…I mean, *have*…a…"

She couldn't say it again. She couldn't say the word *sister.* Ironically, the more real it became, the less she was able to put voice to it. Marnie had spent her entire life as the only child of a widowed father. The sudden discovery that she had a sister out there somewhere…that she'd had a sister out there her entire life…a sister who looked exactly like her, no less, without her knowing about any of it… It was just too much to take in.

"What did your father tell you about your mother?" Agent Tennant asked.

Oh, God, where to begin? Marnie wondered. Lucie Lundy, according to her father, would have been as close to perfect as she could be as a mother, had she lived long enough to be one to Marnie. A woman so wonderful, so ideal, that her father never met another who came close, and had remained single until his death.

"He always made her sound so romantic whenever he talked about her," she began. "He said he met her when he was doing a fellowship at Oxford. But she was French. She moved to England to go to college. Her father was a doctor in France, but her parents died when she was young. Dad said she was just incredibly kind, sweet, decent... He always said how just plain *good* she was."

She smiled as she continued. "He used to love to tell this story about how he and another guy, a lawyer named Sydney, were both in love with her, but she chose my father to marry. Apparently a lot of guys were in love with my mom, but my dad was the one who won her."

When she looked at Agent Tennant again, his expression was troubled, as if she'd just told him something alarming.

"What?" she asked. "What's wrong?"

He arched his dark blond brows philosophically. "Well, I'm just thinking your father's description of your mother sounds a lot like a character in a book I read."

Now Marnie felt a little alarmed, too. "What book?"

"*A Tale of Two Cities.* Your father's description of your mother makes her sound like Lucie Manette."

A sliver of cold slid down her spine at hearing the

literary analysis. Her father, the English professor, had loved books so much that Marnie had sometimes wondered if he didn't live more of his life inside them than outside them. So often, he would compare one of life's little setbacks to some episode from a classic novel. So often, he'd describe people or situations as Shakespearean or Byronic or Orwellian or—

Dickensian.

Agent Tennant added, "And your father did for you what Lucie's mother did for her, telling you your mother was dead when she really wasn't. The same way Lucie's mother told Lucie her father was dead, to avoid telling her the truth about him having disappeared into the Bastille. Not that your mother went into the Bastille, but… Knowing what I do of Lila's mother, I wouldn't be surprised if she hadn't been on the wrong side of the bars at some point."

Something cold and hard had settled in Marnie's stomach, and two fat tears tumbled down her cheeks before she could stop them. She reached for the birth certificate, reading over all the information recorded there. Her name, birth date, time of birth, weight, length, eye and hair color were all identical to the information on her Ohio birth certificate. She told herself not to believe anything Agent Tennant was telling her, that the Nevada document was the fake. Who knew what these people were capable of?

But why would a supersecret government organization create a bogus birth certificate for a woman who lived in the Cleveland suburbs and played the piano in a department store?

"And your social security number, Marnie," he continued as if he could read her thoughts and see her doubt.

"What about it?" she asked, her voice sounding as if it were coming from a very long distance away. "Is it bogus, too?"

"No, it's the real thing," he said.

She opened her eyes again, to see him extending the card toward her. "But the first three numbers are known as area numbers and refer to geographical locations. They're assigned according to the address provided by the applicant on the application for the social security number. Ohio applicants are always given a first number of either two or three. Always. Nevada residents are always assigned a first number of five. Always. Your social security number starts with—"

"A five," she finished for him.

"That means your father applied for your social security card while he—and you—were living in Nevada. And your number is very, very close to Lila's in chronology, meaning they were processed at roughly the same time."

Marnie's focus ricocheted from her social security card to her Nevada birth certificate and back again, too many thoughts pounding in her head for her to make sense of any of them. Except one. Her father had lied to her. And he'd kept *a lot* of important information from her.

"None of this makes sense," she said as she ran her fingers over the information on the Nevada certificate, as if touching it might make her feel she was part of it. "Where would my father have gotten a forged birth certificate for me? And why? Why didn't he tell me about my mother and my sister and that I was born somewhere else? What could he have possibly been protecting me from?"

Because that had to be the reason he had done what he

did, Marnie decided. Her father had loved her more than anything. She knew it not just because he told her that virtually every day, but by the way he'd treated her. He had adored her. Just as she had adored him. They'd been two of a kind. A team. A family. Bonded in more ways than most people ever knew. He'd never lied to her about *anything*. She'd always been so certain of that. Until now.

"We may never know the answer to those questions," Tennant said. "But he must have had his reasons."

We, she echoed to herself. As if Tennant had a vested interest in this. Then she remembered that he did, in a way.

"Do you have my... Do you have Lila's birth certificate, too?" she asked.

"I have three, actually," he told her as he selected a trio of documents from the bottomless envelope. "First, we have a bogus copy, like yours, except that the only false information is the fact that hers was a multiple birth. According to this one, she wasn't a twin, either. Then we have the original that says she is. And then we have a different falsified one that not only excludes mention of a twin birth, but also contains a phony name on the line for father. And the forger for that one was OPUS."

"Why would OPUS falsify Lila's birth certificate?" she asked. "That really doesn't make sense. Unless it was part of some undercover thing for her." And then another question erupted in her brain. "Does she know about me?"

Tennant's expression by now was so flat, Marnie had no idea what he was thinking. But of all the questions, she'd just asked, the only answer he gave her was, "Yeah, let's say it was for some undercover thing, all right? And let's leave it at that."

"But—"

"Let's leave it at that, Marnie," he said again, more adamantly.

Although leaving it was the last thing she wanted, another look at Tennant's expression told her it would be best to do so. For now. He passed her the copy of Lila's original birth certificate, and Marnie saw that it contained the same information as hers, except that Lisa...Lila...her sister...had been born eleven minutes later than she, and weighed three ounces less.

"A little sister," she said out loud, stumbling over the words. "I have a little sister."

And then, like a truckload of bogus documents, an even more staggering realization hit her. "Is my mother still alive?"

She snapped her attention up to Agent Tennant's face again, but her momentary happiness evaporated when she saw his expression.

"I'm sorry, no. She passed away six months ago."

Only six months. Marnie had been so close to knowing her mother.

No, she told herself. Not to knowing her mother. To meeting a stranger. Susan Townsend felt no more like her mother than Lucie Lundy had been. So, in a way, Marnie had no mother at all. Not even the lovely fantasy her father had created for her.

"Agent Tennant," she began softly.

"Noah," he corrected her. "Please. Call me Noah. I did, after all, just shatter your world."

He smiled with what she supposed was meant to be compassion, but it somehow looked like pity instead. Clearly, he was a man who didn't have a lot of experience with compassion. Still, she was grateful for his attempt, if not much comforted by it.

When she felt herself falling, deeper and deeper into the blue, blue depths of his eyes, she looked at her lap again. "Noah," she said. But, for some reason, calling him by his first name felt even more awkward than calling him Agent Tennant. "I won't say I appreciate you bringing all this to my attention, because, quite frankly, I would have rather spent the rest of my life in ignorance of it."

"Would you?"

She glanced up again, and her voice a lot steadier than she felt as she stated, "Yes. I would."

She told herself she was being honest. Truth be told, however, she really couldn't say how she felt at the moment. It was too much to have dumped in her lap in one sitting. Too much to consider. Too much to respond to. Too much to feel. It might be months before she could get a handle on any of it. It might be never.

"But I'm not sure why you've brought it to my attention," she continued. "I mean, you could have come back here this morning and returned my social security card and my phony birth certificate and told me 'Yep, you're Marnie Lundy all right, sorry to have bothered you,' and then left me alone feeling vaguely threatened by financial retaliation if I ever told anyone about you. Instead, you've turned my life upside down and made me feel threatened in a different way. In spite of your occupation, you seem like a nice man. I don't know why you'd do something like this."

As she spoke, his expression never wavered from what it had been since he sat down: mild concern, however manufactured it may have been. But as she uttered that final sentiment, suddenly, somehow, he looked as if he cared too much.

"I didn't mean to make you feel threatened," he said. "In any way. But you're right. There is a reason I've told you all this."

Marnie said nothing, but found herself holding her breath as she waited for him to elaborate.

"As we told you last night, Lila Moreau is the best agent we have, and she disappeared five months ago under unusual circumstances, in the middle of an assignment. We have no idea where she is, or why she hasn't surfaced before now, especially in light of the fact that…"

"What?" Marnie said when his voice trailed off.

He expelled an uncomfortable sound, then revealed, "Especially in light of the fact that she knows about your existence."

"But you just said—"

"I misled you."

"You mean you lied to me," she corrected him. And Marnie was getting awfully tired of being lied to.

"I needed to see how you would react to all this before I told you the truth."

"Why?"

"Because we're worried something may have happened to Lila. Something bad. Considering who she is, with the contacts she has at her fingertips, once she discovered your existence, it shouldn't have taken her any time at all to find you. The fact that she hasn't come forward to contact you concerns us."

Marnie would bet good money that wasn't the only thing that had them concerned.

"And now that I've reacted?" she said. "What made you decide to tell me this?"

"You're keeping yourself together pretty well in light of having learned some things this morning that—"

"Shattered my world?" she supplied helpfully.

"That could make a substantial difference in your life," he amended. "It isn't every day a person learns that her origins aren't what she's been led to believe for thirty-three years by the person she trusted most in the world."

Marnie lifted her chin a defensive inch. "Like you said, I'm made of pretty stern stuff." Of course, that quivering-mass-of-goo thing was right there at the fringes of her brain again.

"You are," he agreed. "Even having known you a short time, I can see you have all the qualities that make a good OPUS agent. Which leads me to what I'm trying to say," he continued. "We at OPUS would like to offer you a job."

CHAPTER EIGHT

NOAH WATCHED AN ARRAY of emotions parade across Marnie's face—first confusion, then amusement, then recognition, then disbelief, finally arriving at horror. Yep, that about covered his own reaction to his superior's instructions of the previous evening. Followed by two hours of trying to talk the other man out of what he wanted to do.

Two guesses who'd won that argument.

"A job?" she echoed in obvious disbelief.

Noah nodded.

"But I already have two jobs. I don't think I have time for a third. Not to mention—and I think this may have escaped your notice—I'm in no way qualified for the position of top-secret crime fighter."

"We can rectify that," he told her. Okay, lied to her. Details, details.

She looked at him blankly. "I see. And how would you change me from a mild-mannered music teacher into a kick-butt spy?"

Noah put everything he had into making his next statement sound in every way confident and in no way ridiculous. "By putting you through an intensive, two-week training session."

Man, had that sounded in no way confident and in every way ridiculous.

Marnie seemed to think so, too, because she stared at him as if he'd just smacked her across the face with a big, wet fish. She emitted a little sputtering sound of apprehension. Then she looked like maybe she was about to throw up.

"An intensive training session," she repeated doubtfully.

He nodded.

"For two weeks."

He nodded again, ignoring the feeling in his stomach that made him want to throw up, too. "We're certain we can teach you everything you'd need to know in two weeks' time," he said, hoping she couldn't detect his uncertainty.

"Everything I'd need to know for what?"

"To pass yourself off as Lila Moreau for as long as it takes to draw out Adrian Padgett, aka Sorcerer, so we can apprehend him."

She looked at Noah the same way she might look at a meteorite that had just crashed through her living-room ceiling. "The man you rescued me from the other night," she said. "You want to use me as bait to catch him."

Noah nodded. "Only this time, we'll be ready for him."

Her eyebrows shot up at that. "Will you?"

"Yes."

"He got away the last time you tried to catch him."

Noah didn't bother mentioning that Sorcerer had gotten away from them a lot more often than that. Instead he said, "That's because I didn't go after him. I thought you were the bigger prize." Then he realized what he'd said, and hastily corrected himself. "I mean, I thought *Lila* was the bigger prize."

She nodded with something akin to resignation, muttered what sounded like "Story of my life," and looked at the other side of the porch.

"We could really use your help," he said, adopting his most solicitous voice. Then, what the hell, he decided to play the patriotic card. "The whole country could use your help."

She did look back at him then, but it was to treat him to an expression that said silently, *Oh, please. How stupid do you think I am?* So he decided to go back to not underestimating her and laying out the facts straight, since, hey, that had worked so well before.

"Three times he's eluded us, Marnie. Lila's the only person who's been able to maintain contact with him. He approached you at the mall because he thinks you're Lila. He will almost certainly try to contact you again."

"He tried to assault me that night," she reminded him. "I don't want to think about what might have happened if you hadn't shown up when you did."

Noah didn't want to think about that, either. But Marnie needed to understand exactly what was what. "He thinks you're Lila," he repeated. "And he may come looking for you again."

That got her attention in a way nothing else had this morning.

"Do you think he knows where I live?"

"You're not that hard to find," Noah told her. "Especially for a man like him."

"He wanted more than information from Lila the other night," she said. "He indicated that the two of them had been…"

"What?" Noah asked, thinking maybe Marnie had been privy to something the rest of them hadn't.

She glanced at the other side of the porch again. "Something he said made clear he thought he and I had had...sexual relations," she finally revealed.

This was news to Noah. But not surprising. "What did he say?"

A bright spot of pink blossomed on Marnie's cheek. She was blushing, he marveled. He couldn't remember the last time he'd seen anyone blush. Over anything.

"I'd rather not repeat it," she said. "Just know that Mr. Padgett and your agent have been intimate. To put it politely."

Noah nodded philosophically. Using sex to extract information from a target or a source wasn't exactly something OPUS condoned, but neither did they rule it out if the agent engaging in the practice—regardless of gender—thought sex might produce results. Agents were generally left to their own discretion when it came to that. And OPUS always turned a blind eye.

"If Lila slept with Sorcerer," he said, "it was only because she thought she could glean information from him."

Still not looking at Noah, Marnie said, "Yes, well, bartering my sexuality isn't something I want to learn to do. Especially not from you people in an intensive, two-week training session."

"We'd never ask or expect—" He halted, trying a different tack. "Look, Marnie, I won't lie to you. What we're asking you to do is dangerous. Sorcerer is unpredictable. But you would be shadowed every second and every step by someone in our organization. You wouldn't be taking him on alone."

"Agent Tennant," she said.

"Noah," he corrected her.

"Noah," she amended. But she didn't seem comfortable with the familiarity. "I appreciate the enormity of what your organization is facing right now. But I couldn't do what you're asking me to do, even if you trained me for two years."

"How can you be so sure?" he asked. "Marnie, I've watched you over the past couple of days. Most people would have fallen apart during what you went through at our facility. Hell, even before that. You were approached by three strange men and endangered by two. Then you were thrown into a situation you couldn't understand that must have felt just as threatening. But you never backed down once. You never even bent. And after everything I've told you today about your past and yourself, you're rock steady right now."

"Only on the outside," she said.

"No," he disagreed. "I can't imagine what's going through your head right now after all this, but I *can* see that you're rock steady there, too. You have a lot to think about, but that's the point. You'll think about it, not react blindly to it. And ultimately, you'll accept what you have to accept. You're the sort of person who takes the punches she can't duck, but hits back hard when she has to. You can do this. At least long enough for us to catch Sorcerer."

She sighed heavily. "Then maybe I just don't want to do it."

"But—"

"Agent Tennant," she said, using the more formal address in spite of his invitation to use his first name, "I have a good life, one that I enjoy very much. It's quiet. It's peaceful. It's stable. It's secure. Or, at least, it was until the other night. I *like* it that way. I don't want to invite chaos into it. And doing what you want me to do would be inviting in a lot more than that. Now if you'll excuse me, I think I've had enough turbulence for one day." She emitted a nervous chuckle of apprehension. "In fact, thanks to you, I've had enough turbulence over the last few days to last me the rest of my life."

"Marnie, I—"

She stood abruptly before he could finish and turned to face him. "Thank you for returning my things, Agent Tennant. And I appreciate your telling me about my sister. I have a lot to think about. So I hope you'll forgive me if I say goodbye to you now and return to what's left of my regularly scheduled life."

And without a further word—or a backward glance, for that matter—she strode to her front door, opened it and passed through it, closing it securely behind her. Noah wouldn't say she slammed it exactly… Oh, hell. Yes, she did. Then she punctuated the action with a sound that was both symbolic and unmistakable: the thrusting of a dead bolt firmly into place.

BY BEDTIME Wednesday night, there was no longer any doubt in Marnie's mind that she had crashed through the guardrail on the highway of life, careened into the river of the netherworld and was now firmly and finally on the voyage of the damned.

So far this week, she'd been mistaken for a very dangerous woman, manhandled by an international criminal, kidnapped by a spy, discovered that her origins and her family weren't what she'd been led to believe her entire life and suffered through little Skylar McNamara playing not "The Tiresome Woodpecker," as Marnie had assigned to her, but "Great Balls of Fire," which her father had taught her instead. And it was only Wednesday. Good God, what else was going to happen this week?

And, oh, *dammit,* why had she just invited all kinds of worst-case scenarios into it by saying that?

Of all the weirdness that had occurred over the past few days, though, the weirdest had to be how thoughts of Noah Tennant kept intruding into her brain. Thoughts about how handsome he was. About the velvety timbre of his voice and the poetry of his body's movement. About his offer of a job. About how she might actually be kind of interested in learning how to barter her sexuality in two weeks' time— or less—if the instructor in the course was Noah Tennant.

Oh, she really did have to start getting out more.

She'd even taken his business card, which she'd found stuck in her doorjamb Wednesday afternoon—and on the back of which he had scrawled what he identified as his home phone number—and put it in her lingerie drawer along with her most treasured bits of ephemera: the sixteenth birthday card from her father, her high-school commencement program announcing her as salutatorian, her invitation to her friend Megan's wedding, the birth announcement of her godchild Sam. What could have possibly compelled her to put it there? And why was it there still?

Now, as she readied herself for bed that evening, she was, inescapably, thinking about Noah again. The man had even invaded her dreams at night. And in those dreams, the poetry of his body's movement had taken on a whole 'nother meaning. Mostly because his body hadn't been wearing many clothes in some of her dreams about him. Okay, *any* clothes in some of her dreams about him. Okay, in a *lot* of her dreams about him.

Oh, all right, in *all* of her dreams about him.

Truly, she did need to get out more.

After soaking away the day's travails in a bubble bath— and also drinking away the day's travails with a glass of very nice pinot noir—Marnie donned her favorite pajama bottoms decorated with whimsical blue moons and bright yellow stars, and slipped on an oversize yellow, man-style nightshirt. Then she went to the kitchen to pour herself another glass of very nice pinot noir.

At midnight, she was sitting up in bed, noting that she had been reading the same page of a new book for twenty minutes straight and was nowhere close to feeling sleepy. She glanced at the empty wineglass on her nightstand and considered the pros and cons of a third glass. Pro, it might make her pass out into a blissful oblivion where Noah Tennant was nowhere to be found, or, if he was, he would be fully clothed for a change. Which, on second thought, might be a con, at least where the part about being clothed came in. A bigger con would be that she'd have to spend her hour-long Thursday afternoon lesson with Tad "Mad Man" Merriweather hungover.

Blissful oblivion with no Noah Tennant. Mad Man Merriweather with a hangover.

Well, there was no contest. Mad Man Merriweather couldn't possibly be any worse that he already was, even with a hangover. Unless, of course, Mad Man was the one with the hangover. But since he was only six, that wasn't likely. Then again, if he was, it would explain a lot.

Collecting her glass, Marnie headed to the kitchen. She had uncorked the bottle and was about to tip it over the glass she'd set on the countertop when, without warning, one steely arm wrapped around her throat while an iron-gripped hand forced her free arm behind her back. Both bottle and glass went crashing to the floor, the latter smashing into a cluster of jagged pieces around her bare feet, the former spilling what was left of its contents into a ruddy river that streamed through and around the shattered fragments of the glass.

Instinctively, she hooked her pouring hand over the elbow at her throat, pulling with all her might to ease the pressure, not that she thought for a moment it would do any good. Surprisingly, the arm loosened enough to allow her to gasp for breath. The one pinning her hand behind her back, however, tensed, sparking a sharp pain that shot from her shoulder blade to her wrist.

When she cried out, the man eased his hold on her a bit more, enough that the pain was quelled, but not enough that she was able to move anything but her free hand, which she tightened even more over his elbow. Although she couldn't see him, she knew it was the man who had accosted her in the mall parking lot Monday night. Adrian Padgett, she recalled Noah saying earlier when he'd shattered her world. Adrian smelled tonight the way he had then, a sophisticated fragrance of spice and sea spray and expensive male that was more appropriate for a champagne-sipping, tuxedo-clad bon vivant than a slimy little scumbag on the lam from the heat.

"What do you want?" she asked, surprised by the calmness of her voice when her insides were screaming in terror.

"I assume you gave the manuscript to OPUS," he said.

"I did," she assured him. "Which means there's nothing here for you."

The hand at her back moved in a way she could only describe as a fond caress. Ew. "Well, now, Lila, I wouldn't say that," he murmured.

Her stomach exploded with heat at the way he purred the words, with such eerie fondness and familiarity. "There's nothing here that I will freely give you," she amended. "You should leave. Now."

He chuckled softly. "You know your hostessing skills could use some work. But that's okay. I know you've been away from polite society for a while. In fact, I know you were never a part of polite society to begin with. It's just one of the many things we have in common."

"I don't have the manuscript," she said again, trying to steer his thoughts away from any kind of bizarre romantic intentions he might have for Lila. "Please leave."

He sighed with something akin to disappointment. "I hope you realize that your turning over the manuscript could potentially create problems for both of us. *If* OPUS can decrypt it. And *if* it makes any sense when they do. Philosopher is nothing these days if not stark raving mad."

Philosopher. A name Marnie recalled from that night. The little man's code name, she deduced.

"Unfortunately, it isn't just toys he has in his attic," Adrian continued. "It's government secrets. Should the poor man say the wrong thing in the wrong company... Well, one can hope, can't one? No wonder OPUS wants him back as desperately as they wanted that manuscript. So since you've already given away the thing I want most," he added, "then I'll just have to settle for..." Without warning, he spun her around to face him, gripping both of her upper arms with strong fingers. "You," he finished with a smile.

Strangely, it wasn't a menacing smile. In fact, it was almost an...affectionate smile? Oh, surely not, Marnie told herself. No way could a man like him feel something like affection.

How unfair that such a demon could have the face of an angel, all sharp curves and soft angles, as if sculpted by the hands of a cozening god. His dark auburn hair was thick and silky, and his clear amber eyes reflected intelligence and, ironically, good humor. He was a good foot taller than Marnie's five-two, with broad shoulders and large hands that could easily—she tried not to think about it—crush her. It would be foolish to fight him. But she cinched herself up to do it all the same.

"I'm not Lila Moreau," she said, again surprised at the evenness of her voice. Would that her emotions disguised themselves as well. "My name is Marnie Lundy. I can prove it to you. Look at the personal papers I keep in the desk in my spare room. Look at my high-school yearbooks on the bookshelf by the fireplace." Hey, they had convinced Noah. Adrian Padgett was the same sort of man, just operating on the other side of the law.

"I've already looked at them," he said. "I went through your wallet and had a look at your calendar, too. And I did quite a thorough investigation of your computer."

Her stomach recoiled at the realization that he had been in her home when she wasn't there, going through her things so indiscriminately. "When?" she asked, her voice barely a whisper.

"Tonight," he said with a smile. "While you were in the bathtub, and then while you were in your bedroom reading."

Her stomach pitched even more. He'd been in her home long enough to do all that without her knowing it? How could he be here moving around without her hearing him, or without giving her a creepy feeling? How had he gotten in? She was meticulous about keeping her house secure, even living in a safe neighborhood. A single woman living alone couldn't afford not to be. She even dead-bolted her basement door after every use.

Then another thought struck her. If he'd already looked at all those things, then he knew she wasn't who he was looking for. So why was he still here?

"Your computer, predictably, didn't contain anything of interest," Padgett said, "but its records and your personal papers and possessions are all excellent forgeries. I have to hand it to OPUS. They're always so inventive when it comes to these things. I mean putting all the music downloads on your PC and creating all the phony purchases from musicwarehouse.com was genius. And the high-school yearbooks? So many signatures! They must have had everyone in their Credentials Department sign some bogus sentiment to class darling Marnie Lundy."

Well, she wouldn't exactly have called herself the class darling…

"What I can't figure out," he continued, "is why they've gone to so much trouble to create this boring, mousy suburban piano teacher persona—"

Hey! She wouldn't call herself that, either.

"—for someone with your capabilities, Lila. How can you be effective on an assignment playing such a bland role? And what is the assignment, anyway? I thought it was getting the manuscript from Philosopher, but you've still been showing up for work at the department store this week. And you could have grabbed him Monday when you had the chance. He'd be a pushover for you. But you didn't."

"I'm not Lila Moreau," Marnie told him. Again. "Look, you think you know so much, how come you don't know what OPUS does about me and Lila?"

His expression turned brutal, and the fingers on her arms tightened enough to hurt. "OPUS knows nothing about you that I don't already know," he assured her.

So. There was something that could ruffle the man, after all. The suggestion that OPUS was better at what they did than he was.

Marnie didn't so much as flinch at his implied threat. On the contrary, something inside her bulked up and dug in deeper. She was tired of being the victim. Tired of re-treating. Tired of people bringing disorder and insecurity into the life she tried to keep so orderly and secure. Enough was enough.

"OPUS knows I'm Marnie Lundy and that Lila Moreau is my twin sister. They know that we were separated at birth and grew up in different parts of the country unaware of each other's existence. They know we are *not* the same people and that I can't help them. And *they* won't be bothering me again."

Padgett started laughing before she even finished talking. "Twins separated at birth? Are you serious? That's what they told you to say? Leave it to OPUS to turn someone like Lila Moreau into a tragic cliché."

"What will it take to convince you I'm not the woman you're looking for?" she asked.

"There's nothing that will convince me of that," he said. "I know you, Lila. I've been intimate with you in more ways than one. You revealed things about yourself when you were with me that you probably didn't even realize you were revealing. I *know* you, sweetheart," he said again, more adamantly. "Don't even try to make me think you're someone else."

Several things clicked into place for Marnie in that moment. One, that Adrian Padgett had truly convinced himself she was Lila, and no amount of denying it would dissuade him. Two, he wasn't going to leave her alone until she gave him what he wanted—whatever that was. Three, he'd been able to find her at Lauderdale's and at home, and he had no trouble violating the safety of either environment. Four, she had no one but herself to rely on for protection. Five, considering points three and four, she was in a heap of trouble where Adrian Padgett was concerned.

"Fine," she said, injecting a coolness into her voice she was nowhere close to feeling, and hoping she wasn't making a terrible mistake in doing what she was about to do. "You know who I am. My cover is blown. I should have known better than to try and fool someone who is so much like me."

A flicker of wariness shadowed his eyes for the briefest of moments, then was gone. "Yes," he said, his voice edged with caution, "you should have known better."

"And you're right," she told him, praying to every available god that she could bluff her way out of this before the quivering-goo thing started up in her head again. "I gave Philosopher's manuscript to OPUS. So you can't have it. But you can't have me, either," she added forcefully. "So I ask you again. What do you want?"

He studied her in silence for a long time, his grip on her arms neither loosening nor tightening. Finally, slowly, he released her. "Maybe I'd just like to open another bottle of wine and chat with you for a little while." He lifted one hand to her face, and Marnie managed to not recoil when he stroked his fingertip lightly along her cheekbone. "I've missed you, Lila," he said softly, sounding almost wistful. "I still think about you, even after all this time. There was something there with you that I haven't experienced with other women. I'd like to experience it again."

Marnie closed her eyes, hoping he would interpret it as something other than the mind-numbing terror it actually was. "I never think about you," she said, slipping into what she hoped was a convincing Lila persona. "I experienced nothing with you that I haven't experienced with a dozen other men."

What a laugh. She wasn't sure she'd even *dated* a dozen men. She opened her eyes and met his gaze levelly. "I don't want to see you anymore. You're not welcome here. Ever. Now leave."

To her astonishment, he dropped both hands to his side and took a few steps in retreat. "For such a successful undercover operative, Lila, you're a terrible liar."

Which, Marnie thought, should have gone a long way toward convincing him she wasn't who he kept thinking she was. Men. They only saw what they wanted to see.

"Or maybe it's just that you're a terrible liar when it comes to me. Because you adore me," he added with complete conviction. "The same way I adore you."

"I want you out of my house," she reiterated. "And I never want to see you in it again."

He smiled. "You are not the owner of this house, Lila. It's an artfully created fantasy complete with bogus mortgage to go along with the bogus will of the bogus father who bogusly left it to you after his bogus death two bogus years ago."

Her fingers curled into fists at hearing him so casually dismiss her father's life and death, but she kept her hands firmly at her sides.

"But it is late. And you're clearly not in the same mood you were the last time I saw you. Put it down to working too many jobs at once."

Naturally. Because it could have nothing to do with the fact that he was such a staggering lunatic, could it?

"Overwork can kill anyone's libido," he said. "But I know you have a weekend off. And you only have that odious little Merriweather miscreant to contend with for lessons tomorrow afternoon. Of course, he won't do anything to improve your mood, will he?"

How could he possibly know all that? Marnie wondered, feeling sick all over again. Just how easy was it to delve into someone's life these days?

"Still," he continued, "by Saturday evening, you should be feeling rested and relaxed and ready for…oh, just about anything, if I recall. You were even more insatiable than I was that night. So I'll just come back Saturday. How will that be?"

"Fine," Marnie forced herself to say. "Saturday evening. I'll be expecting you. Bring a good pinot noir when you come, will you?" she added, dipping her head toward the mess on her kitchen floor. "You owe me one."

He grinned. "Now that's the Lila I know and love. Saturday evening. Pinot noir. I'll see you then."

With that, he spun around, strode to the back door and through it, and disappeared into the night beyond. Marnie picked her way through the broken glass and puddles of wine and followed far enough to lock the door behind him. For all the good it would do. Then she collapsed onto the floor as if every bone in her body had completely dissolved.

She wanted to throw up, pass out, cry, scream and throw something. Instead, she crawled to the other side of the room, gripped the countertop to pull herself up, and fumbled with the telephone receiver until she could hold it in a reasonably steady hand.

Adrian Padgett was convinced she was Lila Moreau. He had said he was coming back. Marnie wasn't sure she believed him on either count. But there was one thing of which she was absolutely certain.

She wasn't going to face him a second time alone.

CHAPTER NINE

BRIGHT AND EARLY Thursday morning, Ellie Chandler made herself comfortable in the records room of Chemi-Tech, Inc. and went to work on her bogus government auditing job. She looked anything but bogus, however, in her carefully chosen attire of plum-colored suit that was just a *tad* too snug, the skirt of which was just a *tad* too short and the jacket of which was just a *tad* too plunging. With it, she wore smoky stockings and three-inch black patent heels and a jet-beaded choker that was only a little tarty. Her hair she'd left unbound, mostly, pulling only the front sections back into a black barrette, to reveal her tri-ple-pierced ears, each of which sported a trio of black hoops in varying sizes.

Well, she didn't want to give accountants a bad name, did she? Not to mention she figured the boys in the science club might be more likely to talk to the new girl if she was a little on the naughty side without being too slutty. Ellie didn't want to give any of them heart attacks. But she did want them to give her information. And judging by some of the looks she'd seen thrown her way as she'd been directed to the records room, that wasn't going to be a problem at all.

In spite of its scientifically and technologically advanced work, the company still had a considerable chunk of its records on paper, so Ellie had to pull some of the files on which she was allegedly working the old-fashioned way. Every now and then, she returned to her desk to bend over it, jotting down notes on her yellow legal pad, in case anyone who came in was actually looking at what she was doing instead of at her ass. She couldn't afford to have any suspicious eyes falling upon her while she was completing her assignment. Unless, you know, they were falling on her ass.

She figured she'd need two days to implant herself convincingly into the ChemiTech landscape, then she could start nosing around in the more private areas of the company. Naturally, she intended to use Daniel to further her credibility, and had already arranged to meet him for lunch that day, just so everyone would see them together and realize she was legit.

Or, at least, that she *seemed* legit.

OPUS hadn't given her a specific deadline for when they needed her final report, but she intended to be the fastest, most thorough, most brilliant trainee the program had ever spawned, so she didn't want to waste a single moment. Therefore, even her lunch breaks would count toward cementing her assignment.

At noon on the dot, just as he had promised, Daniel arrived in the records room to escort her to the company cafeteria. He looked adorable, she couldn't help thinking as he threaded his way through the files toward her desk. His dark hair was rumpled, as if he'd spent much of the morning running his fingers through it in frustration, and his white mad scientist coat was flapping open over blue jeans, black hightop sneakers and a T-shirt that read "I Take No Guff From These Swine."

His black glasses had slipped low on his nose, giving him an air of absentminded professorishness that Ellie found strangely appealing, but when he caught sight of her he stopped dead in his tracks and straightened them. Then he studied her body, from the top of her head to the tips of her toes and back again, in a way that made her feel like he'd run his long middle finger up and down the length of her instead. When he started walking again, his pace was much slower, as if he weren't quite sure he knew how to greet her.

That made two of them, since Ellie never knew whether to keep pretending he had no effect on her, or say to hell with it, throw herself into his arms and shove her tongue down his throat.

Decisions, decisions…

"Hi," he said when he finally came to a stop in front of her. He did that up-and-down thing again and said, "You look…um, different. I don't think I've ever seen you in that suit before. In fact, I don't think I've ever seen your legs before."

She did her best to ignore the shudder of heat that rocketed through her when he looked at her the way he did. Unfortunately, it shot straight to a place that in no way needed heating. Not in a building full of geekboys, anyway.

"They were in my Wheaties this morning," she said. "I was supposed to get a poster of Mia Hamm. Imagine my surprise."

He said nothing for a moment, just continued to stare

at her face, until finally something shook him out of his preoccupation. Or whatever it was.

"No," he said. "I mean, yes. I mean… What was the question?"

Okay, so maybe he was still a little preoccupied. Or whatever it was. Ellie chuckled, hoping she didn't sound as nervous as she suddenly felt. Something had shifted between them in the past couple of minutes, but for the life of her, she couldn't say what. Daniel was just looking at her…differently. Like the other guys at ChemiTech had looked at her today. As if they wanted to get to know her—and her legs—better. *Much* better.

"Come on," she said, assuring herself she was only imagining the sudden breathless quality her voice seemed to have adopted. She was never breathless around men. Not even Daniel. She was too sure of herself for such inanity. "You're buying me lunch, remember? This place better be good," she added as she slipped her arm through his. "I'm tied into it for lunch for the next two weeks. What's with the Nobody-leaves-the-premises-during-the-day rule, anyway? I mean, what's so bad about sneaking off to Sonic for a coconut-cream pie shake or something?"

"It's hell on the cholesterol levels," Daniel said as he led her to the door. "And we can't have scientists dropping dead from heart attacks right and left. Training for our people is massively expensive. Even one coconut-cream pie shake could cost the taxpayers millions."

"Mmm."

"It's a security precaution, Ellie," he said patiently. "Which you should already know, since you're auditing us on Uncle Sam's dime."

"Yeah, but only to make sure you guys aren't ripping Uncle off. I'm not running a security check," she told him, mentally crossing her fingers to negate the lie.

This time he was the one to chuckle. "Yeah, I can just see that. Ellie Chandler, CPA, suddenly becomes Pamela Anderson in *VIP*. That's a good one."

Ellie bristled at the comment. Not only was her job light years ahead of Pamela Anderson's TV gig, but Ellie did hers for real. Who did Daniel think he was to overlook her potential for ass-kicking? For all he knew, CPA stood for Can Punt Ass. Yeah, she'd punt his ass to Abu Dhabi and back if he kept this up.

"What? You don't think I'd look good packing a piece?" she asked. It was a rhetorical question, naturally. She *was* packing a piece. And she looked *fabulous*.

He smiled. "I can't see you getting within a hundred feet of a gun. You'd shoot your eye out."

"Mmm." What she wouldn't give to be able to tell him she could shoot the eye out of the pyramid on the back of a dollar bill from fifty feet away.

It occurred to Ellie then that this assignment might be tougher than she thought. Not because she didn't think she could complete it without a hitch, because she could. And not because she was investigating Daniel, either, since after much consideration, she'd concluded OPUS was wrong about him, and her job now was to find the real culprit. There *was,* however, going to be a problem she hadn't anticipated.

She'd prepared herself for the possibility that seeing so much more of him than usual might make it more difficult to battle her feelings for him. She'd prepared herself for the possibility that it might even distract her from her task. What she hadn't expected was that there might be something else she had to fight that was even more powerful than her feelings for him. Something heinous and overpowering, and completely beyond her control.

Her pride.

She already knew Daniel didn't view her as a sexy thang. But now he was telling her she'd never be the very thing she was. And that kind of pissed her off.

Let it go, she told herself. If he thought she couldn't be what she was, then it meant she was exceptionally good at being what she was. She was *supposed* to be Ellie Chandler, CPA—Can't Punt Anything. As far as he was concerned, she didn't think she could be Pamela Anderson, either.

"Okay, so I'm no threat to security specialists around the world," she said. "There is, I'm sure, at least one piece of pie in that cafeteria that should be terrified of me right now."

Daniel laughed. "Now that I believe. But you're buying."

"I am not."

"You are so."

"Am not."

"Are so."

Ellie sighed. It was going to be a long assignment. "Am not…"

AFTER RECORDING the last of his findings on the day's research, Daniel launched himself into a full-body stretch and made his way to his locker, where he secured everything good and tight. He remembered as he spun the combination on his locker one last time that he had checked out some files that morning before Ellie arrived at work, and he needed to return them before going home. So he gathered them up and headed that way, knowing Ellie would, by now, be gone.

Not that he was avoiding her. No way. The only reason he hadn't seen her since lunch the day before was because he'd had to work so much. Yeah, that was it. It had nothing to do with the fact that he hadn't been able to keep his eyes off her during lunch. To the point where he'd wanted to make her his lunch. It wasn't because Ellie had suddenly turned into such a…such a…such a…

Well, whatever she had turned into, she was *not* a babe, luscious or otherwise. From the day Daniel had moved in next door to the girl, he'd thought of her as, well, the girl next door. Literally and figuratively. She was just too cute and too nice and too sweet to be anything else. And way too smart and easy to talk to to be a babe.

At least, she had been until yesterday. When he'd seen her in the records room, standing with her weight shifted onto one foot, her hip thrust outward, her legs encased in black stockings, wearing those mile-high heels… At first he hadn't even realized it was her. He'd thought—hoped— ChemiTech had hired a new file babe…uh, file clerk…that he'd have to check out immediately. His hopes, among other things, had risen when his gaze had drifted upward, over the *excellent* curve of her ass in that tight skirt, and the even more *excellent* curve of her breasts pushing against the tight jacket. The long fall of silky hair had only made his hopes, among other things, lift higher still.

Then she'd glanced up, and Daniel had realized the babe was in fact the girl next door, and he'd had trouble jibing the two together. What was really weird was that even after realizing it was Ellie he was ogling, not someone with bedable potential, his hopes, among other things, hadn't diminished any. In fact, one thing in particular had sort of gotten even more enthusiastic.

Not that that was why he'd suddenly had to work through lunch instead of spending it with Ellie. Hell, no. He'd just been busier than usual today, that was all. It wasn't because the entire time they'd been having lunch yesterday, he'd felt really weird.

The elevator pinged its arrival on the third floor, and Daniel sorted through some of the files as he approached the records room. Automatically—and not thinking about Ellie's ass *at all,* honest—he punched the proper series of numbers on the security keypad and pushed the door open, reaching for the light switch inside. He halted before flipping it on, however, because something in the dark room, in the farthermost corner, caught his eye. He looked in that direction and saw nothing but darkness. Still, he'd been certain there was something there when he first opened the door. A faint light where there shouldn't be one. Not unless the records room was being haunted by a ghost.

Or not unless security was being breached by an intruder.

Nah, he immediately told himself, laughing silently at his own stupidity. No way could security be breached in this building. It was tougher to get into than Fort Knox because some of the projects they were developing were worth a hell of a lot more than government gold. If someone was skulking around in the dark in the records room, it was someone who'd stayed late at work to rig up a prank set to go off the next morning.

The scientists at ChemiTech were big on the practical jokes. Not a week went by that some poor sucker didn't fall for a prank set up by someone else. Research chemists were a competitive bunch, each trying to be the first to make the big breakthrough that would change A) health-care as we know it, B) warfare as we know it, or C) women's wear as we know it, since those were the big three industries in this country. As a result, there was more than a little professional jealousy involved. Playing jokes on each other was a safe way to take out one's aggression toward or allay one's envy for another person. By besting another scientist in making him or her fall for a joke, it was a way of saying, *Nyah, nyah, nyah, nyah, nyah. I'm smarter than you are. Sucker.*

He wondered who this week's target was and who was setting up the poor sap. Hell, it hadn't been that long ago that Pulaski over in R & D had tripped up Daniel for an entire afternoon by putting the boron where the sulfur should have been. Funny guy. Even Daniel had had to laugh when he realized why the protozoans kept dying.

Instead of turning on the light, he stepped silently into the records room and closed the door behind himself, thinking maybe he could surprise whoever was back there and black-mail them into giving him a piece of the action. He picked his way carefully through the darkened rows of file cabinets, keeping both his ear tuned to any hint of movement and his body between his quarry and the exit. Only when he was certain he had his target cornered did he finally speak.

"Whatever you're up to, I want in. Especially if you're going to take out that new guy in radiology. I hate that ass-hole."

Much to his surprise, a familiar feminine voice piped up out of the darkness. "Daniel?"

"Ellie?" Who could she be trying to stick it to? She'd only been working here two days.

A spray of light erupted, and there stood Ellie, an arm's length away with a tiny penlight clutched in her hand with her keys dangling from the other end of it.

"What are you doing here?" he asked. "After hours? In the dark?"

"Uh…trying to finish my work," she said. "After hours. In the dark. Lucky I've got a flashlight on my keychain, huh?"

Something in Daniel went on alert. There was just a strange vibe coming from Ellie. "What's wrong with the lights?"

"They went off about an hour ago." She threw him a puzzled look. Well, kind of puzzled. Something in her expression was a little…off. "What?" she added. "Isn't the whole building dark?"

Daniel shook his head. "No. The rest of the building is fine."

"Really?" she asked, looking incredulous now. Well, kind of incredulous. There was still something in her expression that was a little…off. "I figured the electricity must have gone out in the whole building."

"The electricity never goes out," he said. "We have generators. If there's a power failure, they automatically kick on. The lights might flicker during the changeover, but they don't go out. Ever. And they didn't even flicker tonight."

"Well, then there's a short circuit in this room or something," she said.

The hairs on the back of Daniel's neck shot straight to attention. There was just something about Ellie that was...wrong. "I got in using the keypad with no problem," he told her. "If the power was out in here, that keypad wouldn't have worked."

"Well, something is wrong," she insisted.

Yeah, she had that right.

He dropped his gaze to the penlight in her hand, then lower, to where the jacket of her dark-red suit cinched in at her waist and then flared out again over curvy hips he'd never noticed before. Well, not before yesterday, anyway. Then his attention wandered lower still, over the brief red skirt and the slender legs. Who would have guessed a woman Ellie's size would have such long legs? His gaze traveled up again, to where the collar of her jacket dipped low enough to reveal a little of the dusky valley between her breasts. Strangely, though, none of those things really held his attention. What really held his attention was the fat file folder she had tucked beneath her arm.

Not sure why he wanted or needed to know, he asked, "What do you have there?"

Her eyes widened just the tiniest bit, in a way a casual observer might not have even noticed. But Daniel wasn't a casual observer. He was Ellie's friend. He knew her better than he knew just about anyone. Or, at least, he thought he had. Before she'd started dressing in a way that was meant to distract a man, should he stumble upon her in a darkened room doing something she shouldn't be doing.

"It's the last of the files I need to put back," she said. And Daniel was certain he wasn't imagining it now. She definitely sounded edgy and anxious. And that wasn't like Ellie at all. "Then I'm, you know, going home. But, hey, now that you're here, why don't we go out for a beer, huh? It's been a while since we did something like that."

He wasn't sure how he knew, but she was lying about the file. What he didn't know was why. "Ellie, what are you doing here?" he asked again.

"I'm working," she told him.

"No, you're not. You're up to something. And if you don't do some 'splainin' pretty quick, I'm going to think that whatever it is, it's no good."

She said nothing for a moment, only looked at Daniel in a way that made him think she was running through a million rehearsed lines she had stored in her head, trying to find one that might work. Ultimately, she ended up muttering a ripe expletive, one he'd never heard her use before, and she repeated it a half-dozen times. And hearing such a filthy word coming out of the mouth of someone as cute and sweet and nice as Ellie Chandler was frankly shocking. And offensive. And obscene.

And unbelievably, outrageously erotic.

"Dammit," she snapped when she was through. "Only two days into the job and I've already blown it."

Daniel narrowed his eyes at her. "Something tells me we're not talking about auditing for Uncle Sam. So what the hell is going on?"

ELLIE SETTLED more comfortably into the booth at Java Jerome's, blew on the oversize latte to cool it and avoided Daniel's gaze. She couldn't believe what she'd done. Two days into her field assignment, and she'd already blown it. Caught red-handed by the one person she hadn't even worried about misleading, a person she was supposed to be investigating, for God's sake. Some kick-ass spy she was turning out to be. So much for moving to the head of the class. She'd be lucky if they let her be a bathroom monitor after this.

"Come on, Ellie, what the hell is going on? What were you doing in the records room tonight?"

It was perhaps the tenth time Daniel had asked that since they'd left ChemiTech, and she still didn't know what to tell him. According to Spying 101, Espionage for Dumbass Spies, having been caught doing something she shouldn't by a suspect, Ellie was supposed to render him helpless and hold him hostage until her assignment was completed. As appealing as the idea of having Daniel tied spread-eagle to her bed was, however, she knew she had to be honest with him.

So she told him truthfully, "I was working."

"Ellie…"

"I was," she insisted. "Just not for ChemiTech."

"Who then? Some rival company? Is someone paying you to steal our secrets?"

She gaped at him. Did he really think she was capable of something so shallow and selfish? Something so lacking in morals? That made her sound like the women he dated. So why the hell wasn't he asking her out?

"Is that why you've got the new look?" he asked when she didn't reply.

He'd noticed her new look? Her tarty new look? Before Ellie could stop it, an extremely unprofessional ripple of pleasure wound through her. "What new look?" she hedged. Fished. Whatever.

He rolled his eyes. "Oh, please. The short skirt? The tight jacket? The fondle-me hair? You're dressed like… like…like…"

"Like Pamela Anderson in *VIP?*" she suggested helpfully.

"Like bait," he said.

So much for fishing. There was nothing like being compared to chum to make a woman feel sexy. Add to it the fact that not only did he think she was shallow and selfish and amoral, but he was noticing the tarty way she'd been dressing, yet he *still* hadn't asked her out, and Ellie was left wondering just what the hell a girl had to do to get Daniel Beck's attention. Other than break into his place of employment. At this rate, she'd be showing him her piece next. Uh, her gun, she meant. Her weapon. Though, all modesty aside, her piece *was* nice enough to use as a weapon. Certainly it would complement Daniel's gun. He had a nice piece, too.

Enough! she scolded herself. Man, she really wasn't fit to be an agent if she strayed from the course this easily and thoroughly. She had opened her mouth to begin explaining—not that she had any idea how to go about doing that—when Daniel started talking again.

"That file you had tonight was for one of my projects. I'm not going to ask you again, Ellie. What. The hell. Is going. On."

Her conscience warred with her obligations to OPUS. But a bigger battle was waging between her head and her heart. In spite of the evidence to suggest Daniel was up to something, Ellie just couldn't bring herself to believe he was the leak at ChemiTech. Whatever money had gone into his bank account, he hadn't used it for himself. He still drove his ratty old motorcycle, and he still couldn't afford his own lunch. Yeah, he probably dropped some decent cash on dates with his bimbos, but none of them were the type to require major upkeep. And if Daniel had lied to her about his past, then he must have had a good reason for doing so.

"Can I ask you a personal question?" she said.

He arched his dark eyebrows at that. "I thought I was the one who was supposed to be asking questions."

She eyed him back just as seriously as he was considering her. "If you answer my questions honestly, then I'll answer yours honestly. Deal?"

"Fair enough," he said.

"Why did you lie to me about growing up in Santa Barbara?"

His mouth dropped open in response to the question. "What makes you think I lied about that?"

"Just answer my question honestly. I know you didn't move there until you started college at UC. So why did you lie about where you grew up?"

He blew out an exasperated sound and lowered his eyes into his espresso double shot. "I didn't want you— or anyone else—to know about where I came from," he said. "Apache Junction doesn't exactly have a reputation for being the most glamorous place on the planet."

"Neither does Detroit, where I grew up. I still love the place."

"Yeah, I know. And it's not that I hate Apache Junction," he added. "I don't. I hate the person I was when I lived there."

"And what kind of person was that?" Ellie asked softly.

"A total loser," he said without hesitation. "I was a complete geek in high school. And even before that. I had no friends, no social life, no dates."

"No basketball letter?"

He blew out a joyless chuckle. "The only letters I got were the ones the school counselor sent home to my parents, expressing her concern over my…how did she put it? My 'sullen and dissociative personality.'"

"Sounds serious."

He shook his head. "I was fifteen. Who isn't sullen and dissociative at that age?"

"Peter Pan?" Ellie supplied helpfully. "The Olsen twins?"

"Yeah, and look how they turned out."

"Well, let's see," she said, ticking off her reply on her fingers. "Peter can fly, has never worked a day in his life and foists his sewing off on Wendy. The Olsens are cultural icons worth a gazillion dollars who will never have to work again if they don't want to." She lifted her hands up over her head and added, "Let's hear it for the perky and sociative!"

He managed a chuckle for that. "You were a perky and sociative fifteen-year-old, weren't you?"

"Well, not as perky and sociative as most, but…" She sighed. "Can I ask you another personal question and will you answer it honestly?"

He nodded. "What the hell," he muttered. "If I can't be honest with you, I'm not much of a friend, am I?"

Something twisted painfully inside her at that. He was right, of course. Which was exactly why she planned to tell him the truth about herself, too, as soon as she had the answers she wanted—needed—from him.

"Why were there two large deposits, one for fifteen thousand and one for twenty thousand, made to your bank account in the last year, and where did the money go when you withdrew it?"

His eyes went wide at that, and his mouth dropped open. If he was faking his surprise, he deserved an Academy Award. "What the hell are you talking about? I haven't made any deposits like that to my account. And I sure as hell haven't withdrawn that much. If I found thirty-five thousand dollars in my account, I'd be in Cancún."

Ellie wasn't sure why, but she believed him. It certainly wouldn't be the first time someone had parked hot money in a legitimate account for a day or two to muck up the money trail. Any good hacker could remove it again without evidence of its ever having been there in the first place, leaving the owner of the account entirely in the dark.

"I believe you," she said.

"So does that mean I get to ask my questions now?" he said.

She nodded.

"How do you know about all this stuff?"

"It's my job to know," she told him.

"Accountants don't know stuff like this. Okay, maybe the banking, but not the Apache Junction. How did you find out where I grew up? I've never told anyone that since I left there. And my family all live somewhere else now. I haven't been there for about ten years."

"I'm not an accountant," Ellie said.

"So you lied to me, too," he replied quietly.

"I had no choice," she told him. "What I do for a living is top secret. My parents don't even know about it, and they used to work for the same organization."

"And that organization would be…what?" he asked. "CIA? FBI? KGB?" When she hesitated, he added, "C'mon, Ellie. I'd appreciate an answer ASAP. Or is it SOP to remain on the QT about your job? You trying to mind your p's and q's, like you promised on your CV? I'd like an answer. PDQ. OK?"

She blew out an exasperated sound. "FU, Daniel," she muttered. She gentled her voice, gentled herself, as she added, "I work for OPUS. The Office for Political Unity and Security. And I haven't been working on my MBA at night. I've been attending training to become an agent. Now that the class work is over, I've been given my first training assignment in the field. It's supposed to prove that I'm ready for the job and can execute my duties flawlessly. If I can find out who's selling information from Chemi-Tech to the terrorists, I'll be a shoo-in for the next opening."

"Whoa, whoa, whoa," Daniel said. "Someone at ChemiTech is selling info to *terrorists?*"

Ellie nodded.

"Are you sure?"

She nodded again. "And OPUS intends to find out who."

"OPUS," Daniel repeated. "I've never heard of it."

"Good. You're not supposed to have heard of it. We're small, but can be vicious if challenged."

"Like a Chihuahua?" he asked.

"Like a heat-seeking missile," she corrected him.

He actually smiled at that. Not that it was a happy smile, necessarily. More like a sarcastic one. But he said nothing, only waited for her to finish. So Ellie was careful about what she said.

"Someone in your department is leaking top-secret information from government files to a group of terrorists overseas," she said. "Information that will enable them to produce some very dangerous weaponry that could then be turned back on us."

Gee, on second thought, maybe she hadn't been all that careful there. That was pretty revealing stuff. Even more revealing was Daniel's reaction to what she said.

"It's Truman," he told her. "Buzz Truman. That prick. I've had a bad feeling about him since the day I started working at ChemiTech."

"Why?" Ellie asked. Since Harold "Buzz" Truman was number five on her list of suspects.

Daniel looked at her as if she were too dense to live. "Because he's a prick," he reiterated.

Ellie bit the inside of her jaw. "Um, Daniel? Lots of guys are pricks. That doesn't mean they're selling government secrets."

"Yeah, but you don't know Truman," he told her. "He takes prickocity to a new level. He's like King of the Pricks."

"I think I dated him," she said, trying to lighten the mood. Or at least Daniel's convictions, since Truman was their least likely suspect. "But his name wasn't Buzz Truman then."

"I'm serious, Ellie. He's your guy."

"Well, he is on my list of suspects," she confessed.

And belatedly realized she shouldn't have. She was just too used to talking to Daniel. Used to sharing everything with him. It was too easy to reveal the particulars of her assignment. Which was all the more reason she shouldn't be telling him any of this.

Daniel's eyes widened at her admission, and he jumped all over it. "You have a list? Who else is on it?"

Ellie was shaking her head before he even finished asking. "That's classified," she said. "No way am I going to tell you that. I never even should have mentioned that Truman is on there."

He hesitated only a moment before asking, "Am I on it?"

She met his gaze levelly. "I can't tell you that."

But instead of being angry about his possible inclusion, Daniel seemed to find the prospect exciting. "I must be," he answered with a smile that could only be described as delighted, "if you know all that stuff about me. You had to have learned it from them. Do I have a file with your organization?" He sobered some at that. "A file with all kinds of personal information that's nobody's business but my own? What else do you know about me that I haven't told you?"

She squirmed in her seat, hoping he wouldn't notice her discomfort. Naturally, he did.

"Oh, great," he muttered. "This is just great. Nothing is private anymore. Just because I happen to work with the King of the Pricks, I'm suddenly a suspect for a major crime, which makes it perfectly legal for people to pry into my background. So what else do you know, Ellie?"

She sighed heavily. "It's not important, Daniel."

"It was enough to make you suspect me, wasn't it?"

She had to be honest with him. "Only for a little while. Deep down, I knew—I know—you're innocent of any wrongdoing."

"And how do you know that, Ellie?" he asked.

She met his gaze levelly again. "I trust you."

He nodded. Slowly, but with satisfaction. "Good. Then you won't mind me tagging along on your assignment, will you?"

CHAPTER TEN

EVEN AFTER such an emphatic dismissal on Wednesday, Noah hadn't been able to shake the feeling that he'd hear from Marnie Lundy again. He just hadn't expected it to be in the form of a frantic phone call in the middle of the night to tell him Sorcerer had broken into her house, very nearly assaulted her and planned to return Saturday with a lovely pinot noir. Now, as he sat in her living room Saturday afternoon, unpacking listening devices and recording equipment and other such paraphernalia for the night ahead, he found himself feeling an uncharacteristic concern for her welfare.

Not that it was uncharacteristic for him to be concerned about the welfare of the people who worked for him. But this was different from the concern he normally felt for the welfare of his people. And it was too much like the concern he'd felt for the welfare of one person in particular. Lila Moreau. Code name, She-Wolf. Who had, for one night anyway, been a whole lot more to Noah than a subordinate.

All these years, he'd tried to tell himself that any feelings he'd had for Lila had been temporary, unrealistic and born of extreme circumstances. They'd had sex. Once.

In a temporary, unrealistic, extreme situation. And although he'd briefly wondered after that night if maybe his feelings for her went beyond temporary, unrealistic and extreme, in the long run, he'd come to the conclusion that it was ridiculous to expect himself *or* Lila to fall in love—with *anyone*. And he'd stopped thinking about her. About that one incident. About that one night.

Since meeting Marnie, however, he'd caught himself thinking about Lila again. About that one incident. About that one night. He'd caught himself thinking about them a lot. He told himself it was understandable, inescapable, even, because Marnie looked exactly like Lila. It was inevitable that being with her would rouse all kinds of memories in him about her sister. And yet…

And yet.

He glanced up at Marnie now, seated on her sofa on the other side of the room, pretending she had no idea there was a government agent in her house getting ready to monitor her life. Really, she wasn't like Lila at all. Lila would never wear the tidy beige trousers and pale-pink sweater Marnie was wearing—not unless she was going undercover as the Invisible Woman. Lila would never coil her lush blond hair into what looked like a tennis ball affixed to the back of her head. Lila would never go without some kind of cosmetic enhancement, nor would she sit perched prim and proper with her legs decorously crossed at the ankles. And Lila sure as hell would never be quiet, apprehensive or demure.

And yet…

Noah wasn't convinced Marnie was any of those things, either. As prim and decorous as her exterior was, there was a fire in her eyes very much like her sister's. Some of her mannerisms, too, especially those that illustrated exasperation or impatience, were like Lila's. She was clearly intelligent like her sister. Sturdy, like her sister. Courageous. Strong—at least emotionally. In so many ways identical. In so many ways…not. And Noah just wasn't sure where his feelings for Lila ended and his feelings for Marnie began. Did he even have feelings for Marnie? Was it possible, knowing her such a short time?

"I'm sorry for making you work on a weekend," she said suddenly. Her voice, too, was and wasn't like Lila's. The resonance was identical, but Lila would never sound that uncertain. "I really didn't expect you to stake out my house this way. I mean, I thought…" She turned to look at him, and when she caught him staring at her, hastily glanced away again.

"What?" he asked as he went back to his task. In addition to the surveillance equipment, Noah had brought two agents with him, both posted in an empty house that was for sale halfway down the block. But where they were dressed like weekend suburbanites, he, in anticipation of lurking in the shadows later, wore basic black. Black trousers, long-sleeved black T-shirt, black shoes.

He heard Marnie sigh before she started speaking again, a sound that was both anxious and resigned. "I thought they'd…I don't know…stash me in a safe house somewhere or something and then assign someone to lie in wait here tonight for when Padgett came back. An agent or operative or whatever." She looked at him again, and again glanced away. "I didn't know they'd want me to be here. Or that they'd send you to do it."

Normally they would have assigned a field agent to

surveil her home, and Noah hadn't been out in the field for nearly a decade. But he hadn't trusted even a seasoned field agent with this assignment. Or, more specifically, he hadn't trusted anyone with Marnie's safety. He only trusted himself for that.

She'd been scarily cool Wednesday night when she'd recounted the episode with Sorcerer, but there had been an unmistakable edge of terror in her voice. To be on the safe side, Noah had immediately assigned an agent to watch the house 24/7, and he'd assigned himself to be on duty tonight, on the outside chance that Sorcerer made good on his promise to come back.

Noah's instincts told him Sorcerer wouldn't show. Yeah, the guy was driven by his libido even more than the average man, and if he thought Marnie was Lila—and if he and Lila had indeed had relations—she would certainly be a temptation. But Noah doubted even Sorcerer would risk capture for the sake of a one-night stand. Probably. Even if that one-night stand was with someone like Lila. Probably. Nevertheless, Noah intended to camp out here until morning, just in case Sorcerer was dumber than he looked.

"Agent Tennant?" Marnie asked.

"Noah," he automatically corrected her.

"Noah," she said more softly.

When she said nothing further, he looked up again to find her studying him as closely as he'd studied her a moment ago. "What?"

"Just what kind of woman is my sister?" she asked. "The way you people talk, she's one of the most danger-ous women in the world."

He went back to his task as he replied, "That's because she's one of the most dangerous women in the world."

"Has she…killed anyone?"

"Only with a quelling look."

"She just sounds so cool and calculated."

"She is cool and calculated," Noah told her. "When she's working. She's also tough and resilient. And dedicated and industrious. And honest and trustworthy. Not to mention funny as hell."

"You forgot thrifty and cheerful and kind," Marnie said with a smile.

"That, too," he assured her. Well, thrifty, at least. And, okay, she could be cheerful and kind, too. When she wanted something.

Marnie's smile fell some. "She uses sex to get information from men and for God knows what else."

Noah didn't bother denying it. "Yes. She does. But, really, Marnie, a lot of people use sex to get things they want. It's not necessarily a barometer of character. To some people, having sex is no more momentous an event than brushing their teeth."

"But what kind of life did she have, to make her that way? I mean, I could never use sex for—"

She stopped abruptly before finishing, dropping her gaze into her lap as two bright spots of red appeared on her cheeks, just as they had the last time the two of them had spoken. It was yet another way Marnie and her sister differed from each other. Lila was completely comfortable with her own sexuality while Marnie clearly was…not.

He'd really been hoping to avoid the topic of Lila today, and not just because he didn't want to think any more about her than he had to. But it wasn't fair that he knew so much about her sister and Marnie knew so little. So he gave her a few basics to get started.

"Lila grew up in Vegas with your mother, who was working as a showgirl at one of the bigger casinos when she met your father." Which was actually glossing over the truth, since it wasn't long after the girls' births that Susan Townsend lost her job and ultimately ended up in a club of rather low caliber. At that point, she stopped being a showgirl and became a stripper. And, unfortunately, a prostitute when times were especially lean.

But Marnie's jaw dropped at even the cleaned-up version of her mother's status. "My father had an affair with a Vegas showgirl? Are you serious?"

Noah bit back a smile. "You sound surprised."

"Of course I'm surprised. I mean, why was my father even in Vegas? The only time he ever traveled, it was for research or speaking engagements or conferences. And I can't see the Modern Language Association or the Henry James Society putting Vegas at the top of their must-see lists."

"Vegas is one of those cities a lot of people feel like they have to see at least once. Maybe your father just wanted to expand his horizons."

"Well, he expanded a hell of a lot more than that, didn't he?"

Immediately after she spoke the words, she slapped a hand over her mouth and blushed even more furiously than before. "Oh, my God," she mumbled from behind it. "I can't believe I said that. I am so sorry."

But Noah only smiled. Oh, yeah. She and Lila were becoming more alike with every passing minute.

She dropped her hand back into her lap and continued. "So Lila grew up where? In a casino?"

"A trailer," Noah said.

"A trailer," she echoed flatly.

"Susan Townsend didn't make a lot of money, Marnie. She and Lila went without a lot of the time."

"I wonder if my father ever sent money? He should have. He could have. He made a decent living."

"I don't know," Noah said truthfully. "But I do know Lila didn't have the greatest life growing up. Her mother drank. She had boyfriends who weren't exactly Mr. Right. Lila left home at sixteen and didn't see her mother again until she got sick, seven months ago. Lila spent some time on the streets before finding her way to a homeless shelter. She finished high school from there, and then put herself through college with three jobs and a handful of scholarships. She was recruited by OPUS before she even graduated."

What Noah didn't add was that that was less because of Lila's exceptional intelligence and more because she was exactly the kind of operative OPUS loved best. Angry. Bitter. Used to taking care of herself. No family or loved ones to speak of. Those were the kinds of people OPUS knew they could mold into fearless, risk-taking spies. And Lila had exceeded their wildest dreams.

"Her childhood and adolescence was very different from yours. She never had the opportunities or choices you had. But there's nothing you could have done to change that. For all we know, there was nothing your father could have done, either."

Marnie gazed at him in silence for a moment, as if there

was something else she wanted to ask him but wasn't sure how to say it. Ultimately, she went with, "You sound like you know her very well."

Noah's back went up at that, but he made himself answer honestly. Well, kind of honestly. "I was her immediate superior for a few years. She and her partner had to answer to me on all of their assignments."

"So you and she only had a professional relationship?"

Noah told himself he would be within his rights to ignore the question, or answer with a half truth, or even evade it with a lie. But he found, much to his surprise, that he was reluctant to lie to Marnie. So he only said, "There were times when, no, it wasn't entirely professional. But whatever happened, it's done. I haven't even seen your sister for a long time."

Marnie eyed him for another silent moment, then she slowly nodded her head. He wasn't sure if she believed him or not. And really, it didn't matter. Whatever had happened between him and Lila was none of her business. And it had no bearing on the here and now.

"Lila's a good person, Marnie," Noah assured her. "Maybe not the most conventional. And maybe not what you're used to. But you and she have a lot in common that way. You're a good person, too."

Those bright spots of color were back in her cheeks again, and he felt strangely gratified that he was responsible for putting them there. "Thank you," she said softly.

"You're welcome," he replied. "So let's focus on keeping you safe. Hopefully, Lila will turn up soon, and Sorcerer will be behind bars and then you and your sister can get caught up in person."

She nodded. "I'd like that. Especially the part about Adrian Padgett being behind bars. Only I think I'd rather have him in front of a steamroller. With me at the wheel." She met his gaze again, and this time her expression was steely. "He knows where I live, and where I work, and he could show up at either place anytime. I have students, Noah, who are children. I will not put them at risk."

"You canceled your lessons, though, right?"

She nodded. "For the entire week. And I've told Lauderdale's I need time off. I told everyone I had a family situation that's made me go out of state. But I can only buy myself so much time. And I don't want to be looking over my shoulder for the rest of my life." Her eyebrows arrowed downward in the first sign of fear she'd shown since his arrival. "Do you really think he's that dangerous?"

Noah wished he could lie to her. Wished he could reassure her that she was perfectly safe. But the truth was, he wasn't sure of that at all. "At this point, I honestly don't know what he's capable of. And in my opinion, Marnie, that makes him more dangerous than anything."

BY TEN-THIRTY, Marnie was a bundle of raw nerves. Anxiety hummed through her body, fairly vibrating her skin, and a silent scream hovered at the back of her throat. If something didn't happen soon, she was going to explode. At this point, she almost wished Adrian Padgett would show up with another half nelson.

Noah, wired for sound, had been comfortably parked in the closet of her spare room since six—well, as comfortable as he *could* make himself in a closet—and she hadn't heard so much as a floorboard creak since. For all she knew, he was sound asleep and she was fairly certain she'd never get a wink of sleep again. Not while Adrian Padgett was skulking about, thinking she was Lila Moreau.

Though she might as well be Lila at the moment, looking the way she did. Marnie had waited until after Noah made himself scarce to change her clothes. Because she was pretending to be Lila, and because Lila was supposed to be welcoming Adrian Padgett with open arms—among other body parts—Marnie had done her best to dress appropriately. Not that there was anything appropriate about the way she was dressed. Naturally, she'd had to go out and buy something yesterday because—go figure—there were no pieces in her wardrobe that screamed "Dangerous kick-ass spy with nothing even vaguely resembling morals."

So now she sat on her window seat—deliberately silhouetted by the lace curtains, just in case Padgett was out there watching—dressed in a snug, low-cut red sweater and skintight black leather pants. She'd loosed her hair from its usual tidy bun, so the dark blond tresses cascaded over her shoulders to nearly the middle of her back. She wore makeup, too, which was something she normally never did, including Midnight Confession eyeliner and Ravenous Red lipstick, both of which she'd taken pains to apply just like the model on the cover of a likewise newly purchased *Cosmopolitan,* a magazine she had bought exactly one time before, in a moment of weakness in the grocery store checkout, when she'd suddenly been overcome by a burning need to know the *Four—Yes Four!—Levels of Male Bliss and How To Take Your Guy Through the Roof!*

Unable to tolerate the tension twisting her insides, she made her way to the kitchen and plucked a full-bodied burgundy from the pantry and uncorked it. Emily Post would have been horrified by the way Marnie filled the biggest damned wineglass she could find to the brim and slugged back half of it immediately, but then Emily wasn't sitting around in leather pants waiting to be manhandled by an international criminal while some guy in the other room listened in.

Boy, had life changed for Marnie in the past week.

She drained the glass and refilled it, a nervous giggle escaping when she saw the crimson crescent of lipstick staining one side of the glass. It just looked so…dangerous. So lacking in morals. She couldn't believe she was the one who'd left it there. She dropped her gaze to the deep V-neck of the sweater that revealed her—actually surprisingly decent for a mousy piano teacher—cleavage, something she'd never put on display before, and she noted how her long hair curved under her breasts. Then her gaze traveled lower still, to the way the black pants hugged her thighs and calves, ending in spike-heel shoes, also a new acquisition.

Boy, had life changed for Marnie in the last week.

The depth charge of burgundy rocketed through her body, heating parts of her with enough velocity to send her straight to the moon. She remembered then that she hadn't eaten anything since breakfast because her stomach had been knotted with fear all day. When she lifted the glass to her mouth again, it was to sip the wine more carefully, but the quick initial injection…ah, she meant *ingestion,* of course…had done what it was supposed to do—calmed her nerves to the point where at least her hands weren't shaking anymore. Now if she could just get her thoughts to stop jumping around, too…

She enjoyed a few more small sips, refilled them—and then refilled a few more she hadn't taken yet—corked the bottle again and returned to the living room. Still no sign of Padgett. Still no sign of Noah. Not that she was surprised by that latter. He'd made it clear he would remain invisible until morning, should Padgett decide to show up later than the assigned hour. Like, say, in the middle of the night, when Marnie was fast asleep—or, say, passed out from wine—and completely vulnerable.

She wondered how Noah could stay awake all night. She barely made it past the ten-o'clock news. She hardly even stayed up to welcome in the New Year anymore. No way would she be coherent enough to catch a bad guy if she went to sleep past her bedtime.

Oh, good. That was getting her week—and life—back to where it needed to be. Realizing what a boring existence she had. Gosh, she felt so much better now.

The self-pity ebbed quickly, though, flowing away as easily as the wine that purled through her system. She smiled at the warm, fuzzy sensations that took over, and lifted the glass to her mouth for another sip. It was going on eleven, she noted with a glance at the mantel clock. Surely if Padgett was going to show, he would have by now. He'd probably only told Marnie he was coming back to make her sweat. Or, rather, to make Lila sweat. Not that it didn't sound like he'd already made Lila sweat. *A lot.*

Another nervous giggle erupted, and Marnie slapped her hand over her mouth to keep it from turning into hysterical laughter. The body sure did have strange ways of coping with stress. Crying when one was happy. Laughing when one was terrified. She slugged back another big gulp of wine. There was nothing humorous about being terrified. Uh-uh. Nothing funny about putting oneself in danger. No sir. Nosiree. Nosiree-bob. Nosiree-bobaroonie. Nosiree-bobaroonie-rama-lama-ding-dong.

Marnie began to giggle again, and since it hadn't worked to cover her mouth with her hand before, this time, to stop it, she took another hit…uh, she meant *sip*…of wine. And then, when another giggle erupted, she took another hit. Sip. Whatever. Then another. Then one more, just to be sure.

Then she went to look for Noah.

Well, why the hell should she drink alone, when she had a perfectly nice man lurking in a closet who planned to stay the night?

She detoured through the kitchen to retrieve the bottle of wine and a second glass, then crossed the hallway to her spare room. It was still furnished with her father's Queen Anne bedroom furniture, but Marnie had updated it a bit with a new terra-cotta matelasse spread and prints of flowering herbs and spices on the sage-colored walls. Pale yellow light spilled from a small lamp on the nightstand, giving the room a buttery glow that matched nicely the warm, buttery sensations winding through Marnie. She crossed to the closet and pulled the door toward herself, blocking what little light there was, but leaving enough to see Noah. He'd shoved the clothes to one side, then seated himself on the floor in the corner and his attention was utterly fixed on some sophisticated spy apparatus he held in his hand. He hadn't even noticed her arrival.

It was amazing, she thought as she watched him, how they could fit so much advanced technology into such a little piece of equipment. She wondered what the little miracle of science allowed him to do. Was he reading a file about Padgett? Reviewing some big plan about how to stop him? Or was he—

Her mouth dropped open when she recognized what he was holding and realized what he was doing. Grimacing, she leaned in closer to be sure. Yep, that was a Game Boy, all right. And he was playing Pokémon. Honestly. How dare he? How could he be doing that? It was unbelievable. It was reprehensible. It was irresponsible.

How could he possibly be battling Tate and Liza with a level twenty-seven Sandslash?

"Are you nuts?" she said. "You're never gonna make it to the Pokémon League like that."

He started at the sound of her voice, the Game Boy jumping from his fingers. He fumbled to retrieve it, held it firm in both hands, then began thumbing both the A button and the direction button again. "Do you *mind?*" he snapped. "I'm battling."

She shook her head, pushed the door open wider, then squeezed inside the closet and folded herself into a sitting position beside him. "Not for long," she said. "Tate and Liza are gonna kick your butt if that's the best Pokémon you have."

Still frantically manipulating the buttons, his attention focused entirely on the small screen, he said, "Dammit! Sandslash fainted."

She tried not to sound too smug when she said, "Toldja."

He growled something unintelligible under his breath. "Well, what would you suggest?"

"What else have you got besides Sandslash?" she asked.

He thumbed the appropriate buttons, then turned the screen toward her. She shook her head in disgust. "You've assembled an amazingly bad team. It's way too heavy on water types."

"It's my first time playing."

She sighed. "Novice. Level up your Swampert," she told him. "To at least thirty-six. His mudshot should be pretty good then. And find yourself a good electric type, for God's sake. You're gonna need it."

He turned the Game Boy back to himself and thumbed the buttons again, saving his game before switching it off. Then he turned to look at Marnie. Without the pale glow of the game, and with the scant bedroom lamp blocked by the open door, they were seated amid nothing but shadows. "What are you doing in here?"

She held up the hand clutching the empty wineglass and half-empty wine bottle. "It's happy hour."

"No it isn't. It's past happy hour."

"Not in Maui, it's not," she reasoned. "In Maui, happy hour is just starting. In fact, we have a lot of catching up to do."

"We're not in Maui."

She smiled as she set her glass down on the floor beside herself and went to work wrestling the cork out of the bottle. "Have a glass of this Château Lafitte. Drink it really fast. You'll be in Maui in no time."

She heard him chuckle, and the soft sound sent a ripple of pleasure winnowing through her. Oh, wow. That felt really *good.*

"Something tells me you've already made the transpacific flight yourself."

She handed him his newly poured wine, then lifted her other hand to show him her—wow, it was almost empty again; when did that happen?—wineglass. "Weather is beautiful. Wish you were here."

"You really should try to keep your wits about you," he said, not taking the glass, but eyeing it with something akin to longing. "Sorcerer could still show up."

"Not if he doesn't want his clock cleaned, he won't."

She extended the glass toward him again, but he shook his head. "One of us needs to stay sober."

Marnie did sober then. Some. Which only made her lift her glass to her lips again for another healthy sip. "Do you really think he still might show up tonight?"

"I don't want to assume anything where Sorcerer is concerned."

She sighed resolutely. "Well, will you at least come out and keep me company? I'm never going to get to sleep tonight."

And *boy,* did that come out sounding a lot different from what she'd intended it to mean.

Noah was kind enough, or sober enough—or maybe obtuse enough—not to notice. He shook his head. "If he's watching the house he'd see two bodies moving behind the curtains."

And *boy,* did that come out sounding a lot different from what he'd probably intended it to mean.

"Then I'll stay in here with you," she said, settling in. "This night's going to go on forever."

And *boy,* did that come out sounding—

Oh, never mind.

"So how do you know so much about Pokémon and Game Boy?" he asked as she drained her glass and set it aside to sip from his. Well, *he* wasn't going to drink it. And it was Château Lafitte. Duh.

"One of my students insisted I take his old one when he graduated to a new model. He left the game in it for me." She shrugged. "Sometimes I'm too distracted to read or play the piano. It takes my mind off of things."

Even in the darkness of the closet, she could see the flash of his grin. "Same here. Only it was my nephew who gave me his. And I hear ya on the distraction."

"So you have at least one nephew," she said. "That indicates that you also have at least one sibling."

"Two, actually," he told her. "Both brothers. Both younger."

"And parents?"

"I have two of those, as well. Both older."

She smiled, warming to the subject, much like the wine had warmed her insides. Too much of her insides, now that she thought about it. And too warm. Usually wine didn't make her warm *there.* Especially as warm as it was right now. But for some reason, sitting here in a confined, secluded place, wearing skintight leather pants and a cleavage-revealing sweater, all alone in the dark with a *very* attractive man who was so close that their arms brushed against each other and their thighs kept touch—

Oooooooh. That was why she was feeling warm *there.*

"And you grew up in a house like this one," she continued, pushing aside thoughts of warmness in places where it shouldn't be. Well, *trying* to push those thoughts away. For some reason, they just didn't want to budge. And neither did the warmth. In fact, the more she tried not to think about being warm in those places where she shouldn't be warm, the warmer those shouldn't-be-warm places got, until, honestly, she was getting so warm she just wanted to peel off the leather pants and discard the low-cut sweater and—

"Actually, that's not true."

Not true? Of course it was true. The way Marnie was beginning to feel, it wasn't just the leather pants and low-cut sweater that were going to disappear, either. It was going to be all of her clothes. And then all of Noah's clothes. And then the bedclothes. And then—

"I only said that about growing up in a house like this because I needed an excuse to nose around."

Oooooooh. Right. They'd been talking about…something else. Marnie couldn't remember what.

"The house I grew up in was much, ah, newer, than this one."

Right. Houses. Families. They'd been talking about that kind of stuff. *Not* being naked. She had to be careful not to get those things confused again. It could be embarrassing.

"So did you grow up in cleavage…Cleveland?" she hastily corrected herself.

But again, Noah was polite enough—or clueless enough—not to mention her blunder. "No, I told the truth about that part. I grew up in Cincinnati. Lived in a lot of places after I left home to attend college, then was happy to be transferred back to Ohio two years ago."

"And does your family still live down there?" she asked, wincing at the double entendre. Of course, Noah hadn't been privy to her thoughts, so he couldn't know what other *down there* she'd been thinking about recently.

"One brother does with his family. That's the nephew who gave me the Game Boy. He has a daughter, too. My parents live in Florida now that they're retired, and my other brother lives in Seattle with his wife and kids. But I have a lot of family here in Cleveland, too."

Marnie shook her head. She couldn't imagine having such a large immediate family. She didn't even have any extended family to speak of. Well, except for the ones in Pittsburgh Noah had mentioned. The ones she'd been trying not to think about, because it just reminded her that her father had lied to her her entire life. She lifted the glass to her mouth for another swallow and tried not to think about them again. Soon, she promised herself. After all this stuff with Adrian Padgett was settled. Then she'd find out more about them and maybe even go meet them. First things first.

"So when you were growing up," she said, "did you do the family vacations every summer? Boy Scouts and soccer and all that?"

"Why do you ask?"

She shrugged, trying to look as if she was just making conversation, when in fact she was desperate to hear all about what it was like to have the sort of family she'd so badly wanted herself when she was a kid. "Just making conversation."

"For the most part," he said. "My dad was big on camping, so we did a lot of outdoorsy stuff. Though five of us in one tent, with two dogs, wasn't always conducive to good family relations."

She smiled. "I would have loved that. It was always just me and my dad when I was growing up. We did take occasional trips, but it was usually to some place of great literary significance. Mark Twain's Missouri. William Faulkner's Mississippi. That kind of thing."

"Sounds…interesting."

This time Marnie was the one to chuckle. He was so polite. "But it's hard to meet boys when you spend most of your spring break in Key West touring Hemingway's house."

"Still, sounds like it was a nice way to grow up."

She nodded, letting memory after memory wash over her. Her father teaching her how to eat crabs in Baltimore. She and her father marveling at the beauty of a Nantucket sunset. The two of them meandering through the National Gallery in Washington, D.C., while her father told her stories about some of the famous faces they saw.

"Yeah," she said softly. "It was a nice way to grow up."

She wondered about Lila then, and what her growing-up years must have been like. And she thought, too, about how close she had come to having Lila's life herself. How had their parents decided which twin to take? she wondered. Had they flipped a coin? Said eeny-meeny-miney-moe? Picked a number between one and ten? Only sheer dumb luck had landed Marnie in a cozy suburban home with her father while dumping Lila in a trailer park with an alcoholic mother.

"It could have been me," she said softly.

"What could have been you?" Noah asked.

"Lila," she said. "I could have been the one who was raised the way she was, and she could have been the one raised by my father, here in this house." She looked at Noah, even though she could barely see him in the dark. "If that had happened, would I have turned out the way she did? Would she be like me? Would I be out there risking my life and having indiscriminate sex, and would she be here teaching music to children? It just occurred to me how different my life could have been if my father had picked Lila instead of me."

Noah said nothing, only looked back at her through the darkness. But then, what was there for him to say? Marnie had been speaking in hypothetical terms. Even if the questions themselves weren't really hypothetical at all. The situation could have easily been reversed. She might never have known the life she lived, had her father chosen Lila instead of her, or had her mother chosen her instead of Lila. And now, through a different kind of sheer dumb luck, Marnie's life had, in a sense, become Lila's. Because Adrian Padgett thought that was who she was. And that wasn't going to change unless Lila showed up, or Padgett went down.

"He's not going to leave me alone, is he?" she said, putting voice to her worst fear in the hopes that it might rob it of some of its power. But speaking it aloud only made it sound more powerful, more real. More scary. She turned to look at Noah. "As long as he thinks I'm Lila, he's going to be watching me. Waiting for an opportunity to…"

She couldn't bring herself to finish the sentence. Noah had told her the man was unpredictable. But Marnie had seen enough of Padgett to know he was a man who, when he wanted something, did whatever he had to to get it.

"Marnie," Noah began. But he never finished whatever he intended to say. Probably, she thought, because he couldn't offer any words of encouragement. He knew even better than she how dangerous Adrian Padgett was.

"I can't stay in this house," she said. "He knows where I live. He could come back anytime. He could be watching right now, knowing you're here and there are others outside, and he could just be waiting to watch you all slip away. Then, while I'm sleeping…" *As if I* could *sleep,* she thought dismally to herself. "While I'm sleeping, he could… He could… He could…" She exhaled a shaky breath. "He could do anything he wanted."

"That's not going to happen," Noah said.

"How do you know? He's already been here once. He could come back anytime."

"We need for you to stay at the house," Noah told her. "For the very reason you just cited. If he thinks you're Lila, eventually, he's going to come back here looking for you." She sensed more than saw him turn to face her. "But you won't be alone when that happens. I promise you that. If I have to be here myself, 24/7, I will be. Because we *will* catch Sorcerer this time, Marnie. I promise."

CHAPTER ELEVEN

WHY HAD HE promised her? Noah wondered as the first rays of sunlight crept through the window blinds in Marnie's spare bedroom Saturday morning. She'd scooted herself out hours ago to go to bed, but he'd stayed put until dawn, lest Sorcerer return to make good on his threat, just as he'd also promised her he would do. Because Noah always kept his promises. Always. That was why he so seldom made them. But he'd made more than one to Marnie Lundy last night. And now he would have to see them all through to the end. He felt obligated to do that for her.

He, Noah Tennant, felt obligated to someone. Somewhere in hell, someone with horns must be passing out parkas and lift tickets. He closed his eyes and leaned his head back against the wall, battling the fatigue that wound through him. And he wondered how many more promises he would make to Marnie before their time together drew to an end.

His head snapped forward again when he realized how he'd phrased that thought. He and Marnie weren't spending time together, he told himself. He'd just been doing his job when she happened to stumble onto the scene and become a part of it. And he should be happy that there *would* be an end to their…their whatever it was they had. Their liaison.

No, that wasn't what they had, he hastily corrected himself. That sounded too…too French. What they had was a partnership.

No, not that, either. *Partner* had too romantic a connotation these days. They had a working relationship.

No, not that, either. They did *not* have a relationship, working or otherwise. In fact, they didn't have anything that ended in a *ship*. Unless it was a luxury liner headed for Tahiti. And even then, they'd probably be in separate cabins.

Probably, Noah repeated to himself as he watched the sun seeping through the blinds melt from pink to yellow. A telling word, that *probably.* Especially when it crept into his thoughts the way it did just then. Because by virtue of having that *probably* in the mix, it indicated that some part of him rather liked the idea of spending time with Marnie Lundy outside a working situation. Like on a luxury liner. In a small cabin. Headed to the other side of the world where no one could bother them.

He told himself he shouldn't be surprised by that. She was an attractive woman—beautiful even, if you were the sort of man who went for wholesome elegance and classic good looks. Noah, however, was normally more attracted to the dark, exotic, mysterious types who didn't waste a lot of time talking. Marnie Lundy fit none of those descriptions. She was…comfortable. For some reason, that was the first word that popped into Noah's head. Easy to talk to, good-natured, warm. She made him smile. Reminded him that there was more to his life than getting the job done. Made him want to do things like take a slow boat to Tahiti.

Not to mention she reminded him of Lila.

He blew out an irritated breath. He'd already admitted to himself that he liked Marnie Lundy. He liked her a lot. He might have even asked her out, had they met under different circumstances—like, oh, say, he had the time for a social life and she wasn't living in fear for her own life. He just wished he knew if he was drawn to her because she was Marnie Lundy, the comfortable, classic beauty, or because she reminded him of Lila Moreau, the dark, exotic mystery.

Didn't matter, he told himself as he stretched out his legs and maneuvered himself to standing. He wasn't in any position at the moment to be attracted to anyone. Or, at least, in a position to *act* on that attraction. He supposed he couldn't help it if he found a woman attractive. And interesting. And luxury-cruisable. After all, it had been…how long since his last sexual encounter? He did some mental math: carry the one, make the seven an eight…multiply by pi…add the square root of sixty-two…do the hokeypokey and turn yourself around… When he saw the final number, he immediately erased the blackboard. No way could it have been *that* long ago. Hell, no wonder he was booking mental cruises with women he had no business getting attached to.

But attached to Marnie he was becoming, he realized as he exited her spare room to follow the luscious aroma of brewing coffee. What could he say? He liked courageous women, too.

He liked them even more when he entered the kitchen to find Marnie pouring coffee into two generous mugs. Though, surprisingly, it wasn't the coffee that made him feel that way. No, it was the picture of her standing in profile, dressed in baggy pajama bottoms that were spattered with cartoon penguins and a big, man-style shirt whose tail fell to mid-thigh, with thick woolen socks on her feet. Her hair was unbound, half of it cascading down to the middle of her back, the other half falling forward over the shoulder farthest away from him. The pale morning sun streamed through a nearby window, threading that loose fall with gold and silver, leavening her creamy skin with a rosy glow.

God help him, the moment Noah saw her there, his cock sprang to life, stirring against his boxers as if it were knocking on a door and saying, *Hey, lemme outta here. I wanna see, too.* And the pounding became even more insistent when Marnie glanced up from her task and smiled at him, and murmured a soft, "Good morning." By the time she crossed the kitchen to hand him a cup of the fragrant brew, his johnson was trying to crawl through the window and get a good look for himself.

"Ah, thanks," Noah said as he accepted the cup from her, shifting his weight to one foot in an effort to alleviate some of the pressure and hoping like hell she didn't notice what was going down down there. Hoping like hell something *would* go down down there.

"Did you get any sleep?" she asked.

She'd told him to make use of the bed if he wanted, that, despite her fears, there was probably little chance Sorcerer would come to her in the middle of the night. But Noah hadn't been as convinced as she and had continued his vigil. He could grab a few hours when he got home, and that would do him until nightfall tonight. His body had grown accustomed to his strange hours while he'd been a field agent, and had never quite slipped back to what normal daytime and nighttime hours were. As a result, he could almost turn on and off his consciousness like a lightswitch.

"I was fine without it," he said. "I'll get caught up later today."

"Do you want some breakfast?" she asked. "I'm not a big breakfast eater, but there's some yogur—"

She must have realized that yogurt was an affront to men everywhere and bit her lip to keep herself from finishing the offer. Noah's attention flew instantly to her mouth, and damned if Mr. Happy didn't become Mr. Joyful in that second.

"I mean, um…" she amended. "There's bread for toast."

"Coffee's all I need right now."

But Mr. Joyful took exception to that and began knocking on Noah's fly again, as if he were saying, *Hey, buddy, I got your needs right here.*

After giving Mr. Joyful a stern mental talking-to, Noah asked, "Were *you* able to get any sleep last night?"

"A little," she said. "I think it's going to be a while before I can feel completely comfortable in this house again."

Yet another reason for Noah to loathe Sorcerer. He'd made a perfectly nice woman like Marnie feel edgy in the home that housed all her happy memories.

She sipped her coffee thoughtfully and said, "Do you think—" But her question was cut short by the ringing of the telephone on the counter behind her. "One of my students, probably," she said as she reached for the receiver and murmured a breezy hello.

Instantly, Noah knew it wasn't a student. Because her

face went ashen, the hand holding the coffee cup began to tremble and the smile that had brightened her face fled. And for that last, if nothing else, Noah thought, Sorcerer was going to pay. To rob someone of her happiness and security was pretty heinous. To make sport of it, the way Sorcerer surely was, was just sick.

Noah made a motion with his hand for Marnie to share the phone, then leaned forward and pressed his head against hers so that he could hear, too. Strangely, though, it wasn't Sorcerer's voice at the other end of the line that captured his attention. It was the way Marnie smelled. Something sweet and floral, like powder or fabric softener. It shouldn't have been arousing. But for some reason, Noah found it sexy as hell.

"I'm sorry I couldn't come over last night," the man at the other end of the line—who definitely sounded like Sorcerer—said. "I had a little problem in Cincinnati that needed my immediate attention, and I didn't get back to Cleveland until just this minute. In fact, I'm still in my car, calling from the cell. I was hoping you'd be awake by now."

Marnie turned frightened eyes on Noah, pleading for some guidance on how to handle this. He nodded silently his encouragement for her to continue.

"Well, of course I'm awake," she said, only the shadow of a tremor muddying her words. "I never went to bed," she added, sounding a little steadier. "I waited up for you all night."

A satisfied masculine chuckle oozed out of the telephone. "Well, aren't you sweet? Keep flattering me, and you're going to make my...head...swell."

Somehow Noah refrained from rolling his eyes. The

guy was shooting straight to the top of the Most Wanted List, and that was the best he could do? Noah knew thirteen-year-olds who used better sexual innuendos. He was about to coach Marnie on a fitting comeback, but before he had the chance, she was doing it herself.

"Why don't you come over right now and I'll see what I can do about your…condition."

Noah's eyebrows shot up at that. Not just in response to the innuendo part, but in response to the low, throaty way Marnie had delivered it. Damn, she sounded sexy. He looked at her again and noticed that her cheeks were flushed and her pupils had expanded and an irregular pulse thrummed at the base of her throat. She was terrified, he thought. Yet she still managed to hold everything together and wasn't backing down an inch.

"You're too good to me," Sorcerer said in his own low, throaty voice. Though this one made Noah's flesh crawl. "But as much as I'd like to come over there right now and do all those wonderfully wicked things you and I did before, I have some appointments this morning that I absolutely must keep."

"But it's Sunday," Marnie said, somehow injecting a pout into the complaint.

"Alas," Sorcerer replied, "in my line of work, there are no weekends. No vacations. No personal days."

Yeah, Noah thought. 'Cause scumbags were scumbags, twenty-four hours a day.

"I'll come over tonight," Sorcerer said. "With an entire case of pinot noir. And a few…toys."

Somehow, Noah didn't think he was talking about Barbie and her pal Skipper.

"I remember how much you liked them last time," Sorcerer continued. "Especially the one with the leather straps. Remember?"

Noah saw Marnie's eyes flutter closed at that, but she rallied herself and said with surprising conviction, "I loved that one. I can't wait to do it again."

There was another low murmur of laughter at the other end of the line. "Excellent," Sorcerer said. "Look for me at nine tonight. And, Lila," he added before signing off.

"Yes, Adrian?"

"Wear something…interesting for me."

He ended the connection just as the telephone slipped out of Marnie's hand and went crashing to the floor. Noah waited for her to follow it, but she gripped the edge of the kitchen countertop with both hands, inhaled a deep breath and slowly, very slowly, released it.

Noah might have expected her to say a lot of things just then, few of them in any way polite. Once again, however, Marnie Lundy surprised him.

"I need to go shopping," she said. "My wardrobe doesn't provide for…interesting."

As NOAH CAUGHT some sleep in her spare room, Marnie shopped for something…interesting…while shadowed by two OPUS agents she never saw. And she did her best to hold herself together, even though she felt like crumpling into a heap of something even more interesting and staying there. Just hearing Padgett's voice again had roused all the fear that had filled her the night of their first encounter, to the point where she didn't think she'd ever feel safe anywhere again.

Actually, that wasn't quite true, she immediately amended as she approached her car with her purchases, which were in one teeny-tiny bag that shouldn't have been able to hold an entire outfit. She hadn't been quite as frightened this morning when she was talking to Padgett as she had been the night she met him. She told herself it was because he hadn't been there in person, so he'd been less of a threat. But somehow, she knew it was really because Noah had been with her. That was why she'd been able to sleep last night, too. The knowledge of his presence in her house had made her feel more secure. And not just because he was an OPUS agent equipped to deal with any danger Padgett might present. But because he was Noah Tennant, a man she trusted.

She'd been grateful when he'd offered to stay another day and night in the face of Padgett's promise to return, instead of assigning the job to someone else. She couldn't see herself feeling safe with anyone else. Mainly because she didn't trust anyone else. It was just too bad Noah couldn't stay in her house forever. She was beginning to think that was the only way she'd ever feel safe again.

Oh, who was she kidding? she thought as she tossed her tiny bag onto the passenger seat of her car and folded herself inside. That wasn't the only reason she was wishing Noah Tennant would hang around. He was the first man she'd met in ages who'd stirred feelings inside her she'd almost forgotten she had. Warm feelings. Woman feelings. Romantic feelings. Sexy feelings. And the fact that she was able to feel those things in light of the way her life had been turned upside down only made them that much more significant. That much stronger. That much more demanding.

Why couldn't she have met him under other circumstances? Normal circumstances. Circumstances that would have allowed them to get to know each other better and provided them with an opportunity to see if the attraction—or whatever it was—rising between them might turn into something more.

Because there *was* an attraction—or something—rising between them. Marnie could sense Noah's interest in her by the way he looked at her sometimes, and by the way he spoke to her, and she was certainly interested in him. Something had changed in the closet last night as they'd shared snippets of themselves and their lives with each other. In the kitchen that morning, before Padgett's call, there had been…something…going on between the two of them. Something that thrummed. Something that sizzled. Something that demanded acknowledgement. And she couldn't help wondering what might have happened if that phone had never rung.

But was Noah's interest in her generated by Marnie and who she was? Or was it because she reminded him of another woman who had interested him once upon a time? She just wished she knew. If only they had more time to spend together in a normal situation. If only her life wasn't such a jumble of confusion. If only he didn't view her as a part of his job.

If only, if only, if only.

Even though parts of last night *had* felt almost like a normal situation, it hadn't been normal at all. Noah hadn't come to her house to have dinner so that they could become better acquainted. He'd been there because Marnie was living in fear of an intruder. An intruder into her home. An intruder into her life. An intruder into her peace of mind. And until that intruder was captured, she wasn't going to enjoy any of those things again.

Not unless Noah was with her.

She told herself the reason she felt that way was because he was the only rock-solid thing in a life that had become filled with uncertainty. But she knew it wasn't just that. There was something about him that had compelled her since the moment she met him. Even when he'd been interrogating her, there had been something there that had touched her deeply enough inside that she'd had that sexy concert-hall dream about him. And having spent more time with him in a less adversarial role, she'd discovered she actually liked Noah Tennant.

She liked him a lot.

She just didn't know what to do about it. Men like Noah didn't come along in a woman's life very often. In fact, men like Noah rarely showed up at all. Unfortunately, what had brought him into her life would probably be the thing that drove him right back out again. And Marnie didn't want to think about how she would feel when that happened. Because there was already a part of her that never wanted to let Noah Tennant go.

NOAH WATCHED Marnie pace from one side of her living room to the other and did his best to curb his irritation. Strangely, what irritated him most wasn't the fact that Sorcerer had once again been a no-show and was again playing both of them for fools. No, what irritated him most was the fact that he hadn't spent more than five minutes in a row tonight thinking about the assignment.

Because the moment Marnie had stepped out of her bedroom dressed like…like…like…like *that,* he'd been too preoccupied by thoughts of…of…of…of…tasting her.

She may have never met her twin sister, but she'd pegged Lila's fashion sense to the last detail. *Interesting* was a seriously deficient word for the bright turquoise leather miniskirt and skimpy gold-sequined halter top that left her back entirely bare, save the trio of delicate ties that held the garment on. And the gold, three-inch spike heels she wore with the outfit were likewise in keeping with Lila's choice of attire. Add to it the dark eye shadow and lipstick that Marnie had applied to her features, and Noah would have sworn the woman pacing so restlessly was none other than Lila Moreau.

"I cannot believe I've been stood up again," she said as she made her way from the fireplace to the piano. "How dare he? This goes beyond insulting."

Were the situation not so precarious, Noah might have laughed. Mild-mannered Marnie Lundy, frustrated with being stood up by a menace to society she wished would leave her alone. Unfortunately, there was nothing funny about it. On the contrary, it only reinforced just how volatile Sorcerer was, just how unpredictable, just how dangerous. They really couldn't know when or where he would strike again. Or even *if* he would strike again. And he would continue to terrorize Marnie with a game of cat and mouse in the meantime.

"It may be time to start thinking about putting you in a safe house for a while," Noah said as she passed by him again. And as he did his best—honest he did—to keep his focus anchored above her shoulders. Inevitably, though, it slipped down instead to that expanse of creamy, naked back and the elegant curves of her hips.

She stopped abruptly before completing her usual circuit and turned to face him. "Safe house?" she echoed, sounding in no way pleased by the suggestion.

Noah nodded. And somehow made his eyes stay above her shoulders. "We can't know what Sorcerer is going to do next, and I can't keep watching your house this way. But until we find Lila or Sorcerer, he's going to continue to be a threat to you. A safe house will at least give you more security than you have here at home."

She blew out an exasperated sound and made her way to the sofa, collapsing onto the opposite cushion, much too close for Noah's comfort. Because as she landed, the loose neckline of her top shifted a little to the left, revealing the top swell of one breast.

"I'll think about it," she said. "But I really hate the thought of leaving my house."

"It's not safe for you here, Marnie," Noah told her. And didn't look at her breast. Honest.

"I know," she agreed. But she said nothing more about it.

They were sitting close enough that Noah could inhale the scent of her, an intoxicating aroma of the red wine she'd consumed to steady her nerves and the even more intoxicating aroma of Marnie. It was a contradictory combination of flowers and spices that was somehow not contradictory at all. In fact, it was damned nice. It made him want to lean in closer to enjoy it even more. Then, while he was leaning in closer, maybe he could run his tongue along her throat to see if she tasted as good as she smelled.

Though why stop there, when he could taste her jaw, too. And then her cheek. And her mouth. And her neck. Then lower, tasting her round, luscious—

He realized he was staring at that brief expanse of naked breast again, and he jerked his eyes back up to her face… only to find her watching him and having seen where his attention lay. But instead of looking angry and offended, Marnie looked…aroused? Oh, surely not. Surely that was just wishful thinking on his part.

No, not wishful, he immediately denied. The last thing he should be wishing for was Marnie. But when neither of them glanced away, and when her eyes grew darker and her mouth opened the slightest bit, as if she were silently requesting a kiss, he realized he'd gone beyond wishing for Marnie and right into wanting her.

So what else could he do but jump up abruptly and say, "Is there any more coffee?"

She looked confused for a moment—which, by God, made two of them—then nodded. "I think so. And coffee sounds, um, good."

Without thinking, Noah extended his hand to help her up, and automatically, Marnie took it. Her palm was soft and warm as it glided over his, stirring something deep inside him, low in his torso where he hadn't felt anything stirring for a very long time. He tugged her to standing, but must have pulled too hard, because she stumbled forward on her very high heels, landing against him with a soft nudge.

For a moment, neither of them moved. Marnie's head was tilted down toward his chest, so Noah couldn't see her face. He felt her, though. In lots of places. Her hand was still joined with his, and the fingers of the other were curled over his shoulder, where she'd grabbed him to catch herself. Beneath his other hand, he felt the swell of one hip, where he must have inadvertently caught her to steady her. Her respiration was a little off, and her breasts pushed against his chest with every rapid breath she took. Her belly, too, was pressed against his, as were her hips and thighs. But it was her heartbeat he noticed most. Because it hammered against his chest even more rapidly and raggedly than his own was pounding.

She began to push herself backward, away from him, mumbling an apology and something about too much wine. But her retreat didn't come quickly enough to prevent the sizzle of heat that shot straight to Noah's groin. Nor the keen hunger that erupted inside him to touch her more intimately. The second she moved away from him, he experienced a sense of loss, as if she'd reached inside him and plucked out something he needed to make him happy. And the only way he knew to get it back would be to have Marnie in his arms again, her body pressed against his from shoulder to calf, a place where she suddenly, strangely, seemed to belong.

That feeling, that *need,* was only compounded when he watched her bend over to collect the empty wineglasses from the table. The exquisite bow of her backside encased in the tight leather skirt beckoned to him, made him want to reach out and cup his hands over the lush curves or press his pelvis against hers. He'd never noticed what a great ass she had. But then, she'd never been wearing anything like…like…like *that,* had she?

His agitation—among other things—grew when she

straightened and turned to face him, because his eyes were drawn immediately to where the skimpy gold top had shifted, plunging even lower than before over truly spectacular breasts. Not because they were large—though they sure as hell weren't small—but because they were perfectly formed, high and round…and almost half revealed by the deep V of her neckline. Again, Noah battled the urge to reach out and touch her, and was shocked by his own lack of restraint. He'd never experienced such an immediate, profound response to a woman, had never had to curb an impulse to take what wasn't his.

He forced his gaze upward, to Marnie's face, but that part of her aroused him even more than the rest of her did. Because her mouth was full and ripe and red, her lips parted slightly, as if she were having trouble breathing…or wanted very much to be kissed. Her eyes were darker than he'd ever seen them, and at first he thought it was because of the addition of cosmetics. Then he realized her pupils had expanded, as if she were seeing Noah, too, for the first time, and trying to catalogue everything about him. In that moment, she just looked so beautiful and so sexy and so sensual and so arousing and so…

Without even realizing he was doing it, Noah took one small step forward, closing what little distance lay between them. He lifted a hand toward her face, wanting to touch her to see if she felt as hot as she looked. But he halted himself before his fingers made contact, knowing it would be a huge mistake. He was about to congratulate himself on his willpower when Marnie, without even paying attention to what she was doing, put both the wine bottle and glasses back onto the table, then closed her fingers over his.

Without hesitation, she pulled his hand forward to place it on her cheek, where he'd wanted so desperately to put it himself. She closed her eyes the moment his palm skimmed her jaw, flattening her own palm over the back of his hand to hold it there. Her lips parted again, but this time a sound escaped from inside her, a low, sensual, needy sigh that ripped through Noah and shredded what little hold he still had on his good judgment.

The next thing he knew, his mouth was on hers, though which of them had instigated the kiss, he honestly couldn't have said. He only knew that a line had been crossed, so there was no reason he had to retreat to his side just yet, in for a penny, in for a pound, you only live once, nice guys finish last, winner take all and every other cliché he could think of to justify doing what he knew better than to do.

She tasted even better than she smelled, a mix of potent spirits, forbidden pleasure and luscious woman. It was almost more than Noah could bear, and certainly more than he could resist. But then, why resist, when both of them clearly wanted the same thing? And wanted it so badly, too…

With a groan of surrender, he tangled his fingers in the hair at her nape, reveling in the rush of silk that tumbled over the back of his hand and forearm. Cupping his palm over the curve of her skull, he tilted her head to one side and slanted his mouth more insistently over hers, filling her mouth with his tongue. He couldn't seem to get enough of her, couldn't quite get her body where he wanted it to be, so he roped his arm around her waist and jerked her forward, harder against himself. She gasped at the action, but crowded herself into him, threading the fingers of one hand through his hair, as the other twisted in the fabric of his shirt.

For long moments, they warred over possession of the kiss. Ultimately, Noah won. Marnie's body went slack against him, and she wrapped her arms around his neck to keep herself from falling. He dropped both hands to her waist in an effort to help, then felt their bodies shifting. He didn't realize what was happening until he was flat on his back on the sofa, with Marnie lying alongside and on top of him. This time she was the one thrusting her tongue into his mouth.

Oh. Okay. So much for winning possession of the kiss. Or anything else. Funny, though, how he didn't mind relinquishing control at all….

Driven by instinct now, he moved his hands up over her back, reveling in the feel of the warm, naked flesh beneath his fingers. Up and down, around and back again his hands explored, over the subtle swells of her shoulder blades, down the slender column of her spine, along each delicate rib. When the ties of her top became a hindrance, he deftly freed each and pushed the garment away. Then he moved a hand between their bodies, upward, over the lower curve of her bare breast. She gasped when he did that, too. So he captured her mouth with his own and took command of the embrace again, pushing his fingers up over her breast and holding her completely in his hand.

She was so soft, so warm, so incredibly, unbearably sexy. She smelled of red wine, rare spices, rich blossoms. She was curved where he was angled, soft where he was hard, smooth where he was rough. And it had been so long, too long, since Noah had touched a woman this way. He'd forgotten how easily—and how thoroughly—he could lose himself to sex. Had forgotten how hypnotic and narcotic and erotic it could be. And he wanted to remember. All of it. He wanted to remember all night.

For long moments, he only kissed her and cradled her breast in one hand, palming her warm flesh, raking his thumb over the ripened peak, loving the way she arched her entire body into his with every stroke of his fingers. He felt her hands on him, too, frantically pulling his shirttail from his trousers, opening over his bare skin, running up and down his arms, molding his shoulders, cupping his jaw, tangling in his hair. He felt other things, too, inside—heat and need and want and desire unlike anything he had felt before. And when he moved the hand on her back lower, tugging the zipper of her skirt down, down, down, something began to hum in his belly like a wild, tempestuous thing.

Then he realized the vibration in his belly wasn't the result of a tempest, but technology. His pager, set on vibrate, was going off, and it was just enough to jerk him back to the reality he realized now he never should have left. Gently but firmly he pushed Marnie away and stood, turning his back on her in an effort to collect his frantic thoughts and quell his ragged breathing.

"That…" he began. But the word got stuck in his throat, so he cleared it and tried again. "That, uh, shouldn't have happened," he finally got out.

But his words belied his feelings when he turned to look at Marnie, lying on her sofa with her top held carelessly to her torso, revealing the lower and side swells of her breasts. Because not only was he thinking that it should, too, have happened, but also what the hell was the matter with him, stopping it now? She did nothing to cover herself or straighten her clothing; nor did she utter a word, either of censure or of solicitation. She only lay there watching him, her eyes never leaving his, her silky hair fanning out around her face, her lips parted and swollen and wet. One arm was thrown above her head while the other pressed her top in place and her chest rose and fell with her own rapid respiration.

Before Noah could stop himself, he was on the sofa beside her again. He hooked an arm over her body and anchored his hand above her head beside her own, then began to lean over her again. His mouth hovered a breath above hers, but just as he was about to close the distance, his cell phone began to vibrate, too.

"Dammit," he snapped, pushing himself up again.

This time he made himself move into the dining room, where he wouldn't be able to see, smell, hear, touch or taste Marnie. He plucked his cell phone from the clip at his back and flipped it open. "What?" he barked into it.

Silence greeted him from the other side, and he wanted to kill whoever had had the temerity to dial a wrong number at a time like this. Then a woman's voice said tentatively, "Sinatra? That you?"

Noah closed his eyes. Oh, yeah. He was working with other people on this assignment, wasn't he? People with whom he was supposed to check in regularly. Like, for instance… He glanced at his watch. Dammit. Fifteen minutes ago. Just how long had he and Marnie been doing the horizontal rumba?

"Holland," he replied, using the other agent's code name. "Yeah, what is it?"

She hesitated. "Well, sir, when none of us heard

anything from you at the check-in time, we started to get a little concerned. And then when you didn't answer your pager right away, we—"

"Everything is fine," he interrupted. "I just, um…I didn't realize what time it was."

There was another pregnant pause on the other end of the line. Probably because senior OPUS supervisors never said things like "I didn't realize what time it was." That was tantamount to saying "I'm an idiot." Even the greenest agents out of training knew what the hell time it was at any given time. But then, considering what Noah had been doing to make him lose track of time, he supposed he was lucky he was even able to string two sentences together.

"How are things out there?" he asked Holland, steering the topic away from his own stupidity.

"Quiet," she said. "This neighborhood makes the one where Beaver Cleaver lived look like Party Town. Even the dogs are too polite to bark. If Sorcerer's around, he's been bored to death by now."

Noah sighed, a mixture of fatigue and frustration and dread churning in his stomach. "Just try to keep your eyes open until morning, all right?"

"Yes, sir."

But he could tell from her tone of voice that she didn't relish the idea of spending the rest of the night in Marnie's neck. Ah, in Marnie's neck of the woods, he meant. He snapped his phone shut, stuck it back in the holder at his waist and berated himself most brutally.

What the hell had happened? He hadn't just crossed a line in there with Marnie. He'd damned well erased it. What he'd done was inexcusable. Reprehensible. Unfathomable.

So why were his instincts screaming at him to go back in there and start doing it again? Only this time, finish what he started.

As he tucked his shirt back into his trousers, he noticed it was unbuttoned down to the middle of his torso. But he couldn't remember if Marnie had done it or he had. Never in his life had Noah lost control like that with a woman. Or anything else. He didn't lose control. Ever. Even when lives were at stake and the balance of world power was threatened, he could always hold on to his emotions, his thoughts, his actions. With Marnie, though…

He inhaled another deep breath and released it slowly, then dragged his fingers through his hair to tame it. With Marnie, he had no control, he realized. And he couldn't figure out why.

By the time he returned to her living room, she had risen from the sofa and put herself back together as well as she could manage. She still looked sexy as hell, her hair a riot of manhandled silk, her lips red and swollen, her breasts thrusting against the fabric of her top, her hips round and ripe beneath the leather skirt. Noah forced himself to look past her, at the semi-opaque lace curtains behind her that could very well have been insufficient for hiding what was going on in her house. *Dammit.*

"That shouldn't have happened," he told her again.

"So you said," she replied softly. "Just before you were about to let it happen again."

He closed his eyes. "I made a mistake."

Man, what a night. First Noah had told an agent he lost track of the time, then he admitted making a mistake. Worse, he *had* lost track of the time and made a mistake.

Next thing he knew, he'd be revealing the top-secret OPUS chili recipe, and then the world would *really* go to hell in a handbasket.

When he opened his eyes again, Marnie was still looking at him with an unflinching expression, so similar to one he'd seen often from Lila. From Marnie, though, the look affected him even more profoundly. Because somehow, there was more at stake with her than there had ever been with Lila.

He told himself that was because Marnie was a civilian, and he naturally felt a greater responsibility for her. Lila knew the job was dangerous when she took it. She'd been carefully trained to do the job well. She had weapons at her disposal, the most dangerous of which was Lila herself. Marnie had no idea what she'd gotten herself into with Sorcerer and was in no way prepared. It was only natural that Noah would have deeper feelings of…something…for her. He just wished he knew what the hell those feelings were.

"It won't happen again," he said. Though whether he was trying to convince Marnie or himself, he honestly didn't know.

She said nothing for a moment, only continued to stare at him in silence, her dark-blond eyebrows knitted downward. "Why did it happen just now?" she finally asked.

Good question, he thought. Too bad he didn't have a good answer to go with. "The two of us are involved in a strange situation, one where emotions are a bit strained and tension is running high."

Oh, good going, Noah, he derided himself. *Reduce it to*

a cliché. That'll definitely make her feel better. Ah, what the hell. He might as well admit the truth. To both of them.

"Look, Marnie, I'll be honest with you," he said. "I think you're very attractive." Okay, so that wasn't entirely honest, since he actually considered her to be unbelievably sexy. No need to reveal that much. He added, "And it's been a long time since I… Well. It's been a long time for me, that's all. Put it all together, and I guess I'm just a little…not myself," he finally finished lamely. "What I did was inexcusable, and I apologize."

"You weren't the only one who did something," she said. "And there's no need to apologize. Unless you're sorry it happened."

To attempt a response to that would be certain death. So Noah only repeated, "It won't happen again."

For a moment, he thought she was going to press the matter. She opened her mouth—that ripe, sexy, luscious mouth—to say something, then closed it again. Finally, slowly, she nodded. Once. Enough to let him know she agreed with his assurance. Not enough to convince him she believed what he'd said any more than he did.

"It would probably be best if we called it a night," he said, in spite of what he'd just told Holland. "If Sorcerer was going to show up, he would have by now. A safe house really would be the best bet, at least for now."

"Will you be at the safe house, too?" she asked.

And, God, he wished he knew why.

He shook his head. "No. But there will be two other agents there to keep an eye on things."

She said nothing for a moment, only continued to look at him as if she were weighing her options. Yet when she spoke again, he was in no way. prepared for what she had to say.

"I want to accept your offer of a job," she told him.

Certain he'd misunderstood, Noah said, "What?"

"I want to accept your offer of a job," she repeated, more forcefully this time. "The sooner I help you nail this bastard, Noah, the sooner I'll get my life back. I want the job," she reiterated. "When do I start?"

CHAPTER TWELVE

A WEEK AFTER TELLING Daniel the truth about her assignment, Ellie was ready to kick her own ass for ever telling Daniel the truth about her assignment. Because ever since their conversation in the coffee shop, he'd been convinced he was James Frigging Bond, and that Buzz Truman was the treacherous Dr. No. He'd even started making notes of all the reasons he was sure Truman was the leak, and Ellie was beginning to fear Daniel had even started poking around in the guy's business at work.

Barely a week into her first assignment, and she'd already violated rule number one of spy school, which was "Don't tell nobody nothin', dumbass." And also rule number two, which was "Don't let a suspect know he's a suspect, dumbass." And okay, also number three, which was "And whatever you do, don't let a suspect tag along on your assignment. Dumbass."

But Daniel had pretty much blackmailed her into doing just that. That night in the coffee shop, he'd told Ellie that if she didn't include him in the OPUS operation at ChemiTech, he'd go straight to the CEO and blab, stopping only long enough to tell Dr. Sebastian Baird to watch his back 'cause the feds had a file on him.

Which was something else that had ticked off Ellie. Somehow, over the course of the week, Daniel had correctly identified all five of the people on her list of suspects, simply by watching them all in action and forming opinions on their potential to be evildoers. And the four besides Truman, all of whose innocence he was supremely confident, like Sebastian and himself, he wanted to be cleared right away. It was Truman, he'd assured Ellie over and over again. It had to be. And who was better positioned to help her prove that than he himself, who'd worked at the company for years and had personal poop on all of the suspects, poop it would take OPUS months, maybe years, to learn by themselves.

Like she needed or wanted Daniel Beck's help with her training assignment. Dumbass…ah, she meant *kick-ass*…spies weren't supposed to *need* help. Especially not from civilians. Oh, sure, when she was finished with her training and was an officially recognized agent, she'd be partnered with another agent with whom she would complete all of her assignments. That was how OPUS worked. Agents were paired into teams where one of them went into the field to gather intel and feed it to the other, who then assessed and analyzed the information before passing it to the higher-ups.

But the whole point to this training assignment was to see where Ellie's expertise lay, whether she would be more valuable to OPUS as the member of the team out in the field gathering information, or the member who took the information and evaluated it. The former needed skills like stealth, deception and a complete flouting of personal safety, while the latter needed talents like intelligence, perception and an ability to recognize patterns and find connections in the data collected. Ellie already knew she was better suited to the field. But she still had to prove that. And there wasn't much proof in having been caught with her hand in the cookie file right out of the gate. There was even less proof in accepting the assistance of one of her suspects.

But every time she turned around, Daniel was trying to take charge of her assignment. He'd even won legitimate entrée into Truman's home via a Saturday afternoon house-warming party that Truman and his wife were hosting for all of Truman's co-workers, a little more than a week after Ellie and Daniel embarked on their—or rather *her*—assignment.

Originally, Daniel had told Ellie, he'd intended to return the RSVP with his own version of the abbreviation: Really Shan't, Vituperous Prick—honestly, sometimes his big brain wasn't all that sexy—but he'd never gotten around to it, so he called in a last-minute acceptance of the invitation, and asked if it would be all right for him to bring a date.

A *date*, she echoed derisively to herself as she got ready for the party. Not only was she no longer in charge of her own assignment, but she hadn't even been cast in the role of sidekick. She was just a prop that Daniel Beck, agent Double-Oh-*Fine* was using to further investigate his own suspicions.

But even *that* wasn't what was bothering Ellie the most at this point. What bothered her most was that she was finally going on a date with Daniel Beck, and it was nothing but a sham.

She blew out an exasperated breath as she awaited his arrival Saturday afternoon, steamed at herself for having her priorities so mixed up. She had a job to do, dammit. And she'd better start doing it quick.

She did her best to pretend their date was genuine, however—for the sake of the investigation, naturally—dressing for the party in a short denim skirt and a red, scoop-neck top that fell modestly off one shoulder, with flat black skimmers on her feet. Emma Peel aside, kick-ass spies rarely wore high heels, just in case they had to, you know, kick someone's ass. High heels could only poke someone's ass. And that just pissed off the bad guys even more. But since Ellie had been wearing her hair loose most days in her auditing-accountant attire—and since that would still be her cover at Truman's party—she left it loose today, letting it cascade past her shoulders, to nearly the middle of her back.

She was relieved when she opened the front door to Daniel's knock to see that he'd dressed a little more formally than usual, too. He still had on baggy cargo pants, these the color of a Hershey bar, but his usual T-shirt had been replaced by a creamy pin-striped button-down—though he hadn't bothered to tuck it in. He opened his mouth to speak, but it was his eyes that did the moving, traveling down Ellie's body and back up again in a way that made the strings of her heart do some serious zinging.

"I'm sorry, but I just can't get used to you with legs," he said by way of a greeting.

There was something in his voice that wasn't normally there when he was talking to her, and the warm humor in his eyes seemed to have heightened to something hotter and less frivolous than usual. Ellie told herself she was just imagining it, that wearing a short skirt wasn't enough to rouse such a reaction in him, since he'd seen women wearing a lot less than that, on a lot of other occasions. So she only muttered a soft thank-you and grabbed her purse to head out.

Daniel drove them in Ellie's car to the party, since short skirts didn't mix well with motorcycle seats, and, inescapably, his preferred topic of conversation was the assignment. No matter how many times she tried to change the subject—though *not* because she wanted to pretend this was a real date, since, of course, it wasn't, and she was just tired of talking about the assignment all the time and shouldn't be talking about it to him anyway—he managed to turn it back where he wanted. It wasn't until they pulled to a stop in front of Truman's house that he finally shut up. But then, Ellie wasn't sure what to say, either, when she got an eyeful of the place.

Except maybe "Holy cow."

She wouldn't exactly call the house a mansion, but neither was it a modest abode. The neighborhood was one of Cleveland's pricier ones, full of big, rambling old homes, lovingly refurbished, with enormous trees and crooked sidewalks. It was where the rich people used to live before the cow pasture McMansion explosion, and where the old money had stayed when the new money moved to the more ostentatious 'burbs. The Truman home was a three-story brick Victorian, complete with wrap-around porch and widow's walk, with lush landscaping and a cobbled walk and not a single thing that needed home improvement.

"Jeez, how much money does Truman make at Chemi-Tech, anyway?" Ellie asked.

"He can't possibly make enough to afford that," Daniel told her. "I mean, yeah, he's got seniority on me, so I'm sure he takes home more than I do, but not that much more."

"His wife must make a lot of money," Ellie ventured. "I wonder what she does for a living?"

"Or maybe the money comes from somewhere else," Daniel said ominously. "Like maybe from a group of terrorists overseas."

Ellie dropped her hand to the door release. "Only one way to find out," she said as she pushed the door open.

Daniel emerged from the driver's side and circled the front of the car to where Ellie was waiting for him, then surprised her by taking her hand in his and weaving their fingers together the way boyfriends and girlfriends had a tendency to do.

Her reaction must have shown in her face, because when she glanced up in confusion, Daniel smiled and said, "You're my date, remember? And I kinda have a rep at work that I need to maintain."

"What kind of rep?" she asked.

He lifted one shoulder and let it drop. "Let's just say I date well, all right?"

She narrowed her eyes at him. "Is that supposed to be a compliment for me or for you?"

His smile broadened. "Yes."

"So I have to spend the afternoon pretending to be besotted by you?" she asked. Not that it would be such a stretch for her to manage that, she had to admit.

"What do you mean pretend?" he asked. He feigned shock. "What? Are you saying you're *not* besotted with me?"

She toddled her head back and forth a few times. "Besotted, befuddled, bewildered…they're all pretty much the same thing, when you get right down to it."

"So then you *are* besotted with me," he concluded. But his voice was laced with something she could only liken to confusion, as if he wasn't quite sure whether or not she was kidding, and he didn't know where he stood with her, and he really wished he did.

Good, Ellie thought. If he was confused, then that made two of them. She wasn't sure lately where she stood with Daniel, either. Something had changed since the night he'd caught her in the records room. No, even before that. The first day she'd shown up for work at ChemiTech, when she'd turned around to find him ogling her. Daniel had never ogled her before. Not once. But he'd done it several times since that morning—looked at her in a way that made her think he was seeing someone else. Or maybe he was looking for someone else. Hoping for someone else?

Ellie just didn't know. But there was something there between them now that hadn't been there before, and for the life of her, she couldn't tell if it was good or bad.

Pushing her troubling thoughts to the back of her mind for now, she smiled at Daniel, deliberately didn't answer his question and turned to make her way up to the front door.

The game was afoot, she thought as Daniel lifted his fist to rap on the Trumans' front door. Ellie just wished she could figure out what game, exactly, they were playing, and who was making the rules.

THE MORE DANIEL SAW of Buzz Truman's house, the more convinced he became that Buzz was the one selling information to the bad guys. Not only had the place been restored to period perfection—work that had been done *before* Truman bought the house, Daniel had learned, so the place must have cost a small fortune—but it was chock-full of antiques and artwork that were probably worth even more than the house. And a short chat with Truman's wife Nicole revealed that she worked as a pre-school teacher, an occupation that had shown up on the "Most Lucrative Jobs in America" list a total of, um, never times.

Still, he supposed there could be some legitimate explanation for the flow of cash. Savvy investing, perhaps. Successful gambling. A bequest from a wealthy relative. Lottery win. It wasn't exactly unheard-of for people to suddenly come into large sums of money. But Truman, to Daniel's way of thinking, wasn't the brightest bulb on the Christmas tree, so he couldn't see the guy being some investment whiz or cardsharp. And a person was less likely to win the lottery than they were to be struck by lightning. On a sunny day in July. When it was snowing. Atomic dust. And, face it, the guy was too big a prick for *any* relative to want to leave him money. Daniel would have bequeathed his estate to Neo-Nazi Pedophiles for Satan before he'd let someone like Truman get his grubby hands on it.

An hour after his and Ellie's arrival, the party was in

full swing, with easily fifty people milling about inside and out. Nicole had hosted a few tours around the place at the beginning of the afternoon, and had made clear that anyone who wanted to look around anywhere was welcome to do so. Daniel figured you didn't get an actual invitation to pillage and plunder a suspect's house every day of the week, so he figured he and Ellie ought to take advantage of it. The minute the coast was clear—which was pretty much the minute Nicole Truman announced that food had been laid out in the kitchen—he wrapped his hand around Ellie's wrist and tugged her in the direction opposite the kitchen, where she was clearly headed.

"Hey!" she cried, pulling on her arm to free it. "What are—"

"Shh," Daniel hushed her in mid-objection. "We don't have much time."

"For what?" she asked.

He pointed at the ceiling overhead. "We need to get upstairs and check out Truman's home computer."

"What?" she exclaimed.

"*Sshhh,*" he hissed more adamantly. "Will you please keep it down? I'm trying to do a little spying here."

"But Nicole just put out the food. And I'm starving."

"You can eat later. There will be a line, anyway."

Although he wouldn't swear to it, Daniel thought Ellie's bottom lip thrust out the tiniest bit in response. Just enough to make her look like she was pouting, and just enough to make a jolt of something hot and frantic shoot through him when he realized he wanted to lean down and nibble it.

"But I heard someone say there are deviled eggs," she

told him. "I love deviled eggs. I want to get some before they're all gone."

Daniel threw her his most disgusted look. "You know, this country's in big trouble if the best spies they can produce can be tempted from the job by a little cooked albumen fancied up with mayonnaise and paprika."

This time Ellie frowned. But she did gingerly replace onto the stack the paper plate she'd been embracing like a holy grail. "Lead on," she muttered. Then, when they were out of earshot of the kitchen, she added quietly, "But *I'll* be the one checking out the computer. You can keep watch."

Oh, yeah, right, Daniel thought. Like that was really going to happen.

They milled around at the foot of the steps while another couple descended, then leisurely made their way up, as if they simply wanted to have a look around at the decorating job. Which, okay, Daniel had to admit, was very nice. The home office was the room farthest to the right in a long hallway/gallery on the second floor, an area that was thankfully deserted. With a couple of quick glances around, he saw that they were well and truly alone, so he tugged on Ellie's hand again to pull her along behind him. When they reached the office, they ducked inside, and as Ellie pushed the door closed a little—though not enough to rouse suspicion from anyone who might see it ajar, Daniel went immediately to the computer and booted it up.

"Hey," she exclaimed as she had in the kitchen, only more softly this time. "I'm supposed to be doing that. You're the lookout."

"Oops," he said to excuse his actions. And didn't offer to move or anything else.

Instead, he began plucking on the computer keys and guiding the mouse from one place to another, searching for he couldn't say what, but he'd know it when he saw it.

"Do you even know what you're doing?" Ellie asked from behind him. Close enough that he knew she'd left her post by the door.

"You're supposed to be keeping watch," he reminded her.

"No, I'm supposed to be hacking into that computer. *You're* supposed to be keeping watch."

"Oops," he said again by way of an explanation and continued to pound the keys. "Okay, here we go," he continued when his search returned something of interest. "There are some deep files hidden on this thing under Nicole's desktop, but they're locked tight. This could take a couple of minutes."

"Since when do you know how to hack into hidden and protected files?" she asked. Still close enough that he knew she wasn't watching the door as she was supposed to be.

Call him crazy, but Daniel was beginning to think Ellie wasn't even going to qualify for Hall Monitor by the time she finished her training assignment. "Since I discovered pictures of naked women on my old man's computer when I was nineteen," he told her. "Now leave me alone while I find my way in."

"And you plan to do that how? There will be passwords and God knows what else protecting those files."

"I know enough about Truman to figure out how he'd do it," Daniel said, knowing that was true. Hell, he worked side by side with the prick every day. "Gimme a couple of minutes. I bet I can even guess his password."

"Just a shot in the dark here, Daniel, but I'm going to guess it's *not* 'I'm a prick.'"

It took less than five minutes for Daniel to break into the files. He wasted no time reading them, simply pulled a memory stick from his pocket and stuck it into the proper drive and sucked every last piece of info he wanted out of Truman's computer and into the slender little device. Gotta love that modern technology, he thought as he removed both the memory stick and any evidence that he'd accessed the files. How the hell did anyone manage to steal secret information before the computer age?

The mind boggled.

When he stood and turned to leave, he discovered Ellie was *still* standing immediately behind him, where she had probably been standing the entire time, when she was supposed to be keeping an eye out at the door. How could she be so convinced she was suited to this spying business? Not that he was going to tell her she sucked, but she certainly didn't seem to take the proper precautions necessary for maintaining a low profile. Like, for instance, keeping an eye out. Hell, that was something Daniel had learned to do as a preschooler. He'd had to, the kind of home he came from.

But as he stood there in front of her, only scant inches away, he suddenly didn't mind so much that Ellie wasn't where she was supposed to be, way on the other side of the room. Now that he'd gotten what he came for—from Truman's computer, anyway—it was actually kind of nice to find her standing so close. He'd never really noticed how good she smelled, a mix of something sweet and spicy and earthy, just like Ellie herself. And he'd never noticed how her hair was less brown than it was something dark and fiery.

But the way the late-afternoon sun was streaming through the window just then, her hair was aflame with red and orange and gold. And her eyes. They were so huge, so dark, so full of everything that made her Ellie—kindness, wit, good humor, laughter. And something else, too. Something he'd never really noticed before, either. Passion. Not just for her job, and not just for her life, but for lots of other things, too. Things Daniel had never thought about in terms of Ellie.

Things he started to think about then.

Without realizing he'd decided to move it, his hand rose to her hair, aiming for one of the more golden highlights, which he wanted to touch to see if it was as warm as it looked. Her eyes went wide in surprise as he cupped his palm over the back of her head and dragged it slowly downward, over the long straight tresses that were silkier than he ever could have imagined. He liked her hair down. She should wear it that way more often. It would look especially nice streaming over the pillow on the opposite side of his bed, where she lay watching him in the aftermath of spectacular sex.

The mental image of just that exploded in Daniel's brain, and he immediately jerked back his hand. Not because it felt weird to be thinking of Ellie in sexual terms. But because it felt good to be thinking of her that way. Weirder still was the fact that thinking of her in sexual terms had encompassed her lying quietly beside him in the afterglow, and not with her bent naked on all fours with him pummeling her from behind, the way his sexual fantasies about women usually ran.

When she continued to watch him warily, silently, Daniel quickly swiped his hand over the front of his pants and said, "Dust bunny. You had a, um…a big glob of dust in your hair. Truman needs to pay his housekeeper more."

And then, without awaiting her reply, he took her hand in his again and steered her toward the door. Only this time, it wasn't because he wanted to guide Ellie in a specific direction. This time, it was just because he wanted to hold Ellie's hand.

CHAPTER THIRTEEN

THE NEAREST OPUS training center, Marnie discovered much to her surprise—and also her annoyance—was located in the same underground facility to which Noah had taken her that first night for the Spanish Inquisition. The training center was much deeper underground, however, reachable only by an elevator with no numbered buttons to indicate how far down she was going, though she was able to finish a cup of coffee on the way every morning. And do her nails. And figure her taxes. And read *War and Peace.* It opened onto a meandering warren of hallways and rooms, which, if one wasn't paying close attention to where one was going, one might never find one's way out again and stay lost forever. In fact, that was the first lesson Marnie learned about being a spy.

The next lesson she learned was that spy training was a lot more boring than she'd thought it would be. Leave it to the government to take a perfectly good Hollywood hyperbole like James Bond and reduce it to a classroom-and-textbook setting. Marnie had completed her first full week of "intensive training," and she *still* didn't know the difference between shaken and stirred. At this rate, she'd never get the Aston Martin with built-in machine guns and cappuccino maker.

On the up side, she was discovering that she had a facility for things she'd never known she had a facility for. Decryption, for example. She didn't know if it was her musical training, or having to decipher the handwriting of small children, or knowing how to compute a woman's cup size—perhaps it was a combination of all three—but she was a whiz at quickly identifying patterns in codes and deciphering them. She was also adept at changing her appearance and demeanor quickly and with just a few key items, which her instructor assured her had kept more than one operative alive in a dangerous situation.

Of course, Marnie had already known she was good at that—and she knew firsthand about that dangerous-situation business—because look how effective she'd been last weekend, when she'd slipped out of her usual mousy Marnie shell and into her Lila bombshell.

She still wasn't sure how she felt about the little, ah…interlude she had shared with Noah that night, even having had a week to think about it. Oh, she understood her own motivation for what had happened well enough— she'd been edgy from her nerves, mellow from the wine…and profoundly attracted to the man sitting so close to her on the sofa. But she wasn't sure she understood Noah's motivation. Certainly she'd been flattered by his claim that he found her attractive, too, and she sympathized with the whole it's-been-too-long thing, since that, too, had factored into her own impulses that night. And she agreed with him completely that what had happened wouldn't happen again. What was the point, since neither of them was in any position to pursue a romantic liaison?

But she couldn't stop thinking about the way he had

looked at her when she'd been dressed as Lila. The way he had responded to her when she was dressed as Lila. With such hunger and longing. With such need and desire. And she wondered again just what kind of relationship he'd had with Lila once upon a time. Had they been sexually involved? Had they been in love? Had *he* been in love? And had he only come on to Marnie the way he had because she looked so much like Lila? Was he still in love with her sister? Was her sister in love with him?

Marnie had only seen Noah a few times last week, but each time, he'd been cordial, unruffled, professional. In short, he had acted as if that night at her house had never happened. She told herself that was how she wanted him to act, and she'd done her best to act as if it had never happened, too.

But every time she saw him, all she could think about was the way he had kissed her and touched her that night. She remembered the heat and passion of his mouth on hers. She recalled the way he'd dragged his fingertips over her cheek and jaw, her throat and collarbone. She remembered the glide of his silky hair as it sifted between her fingers, the coarseness of his day-old beard beneath her palm, the warmth of his breath against her neck. She recalled the way he took possession of her breast, and how the raw coil of need that had erupted inside her had simmered beneath her skin until dawn.

And every time she remembered all that, God help her, she couldn't stand the thought of it never happening again. She wanted Noah. Badly. She didn't know if it was because she'd simply gone too long without the physical closeness of a man, or if there was something about him specifically that spoke to her. All she knew was that she couldn't stop thinking about what had happened. And she wished—oh, how she wished—it would happen again.

Today she would be seeing him again, this time in more than passing. Because she'd now completed the classroom part of her training, and week two heralded the ever popular and interactive hands-on segment. If it was Monday—and it was—Marnie must be going to the firing range.

Ooh, she got goose bumps just thinking about it. She and Noah, all alone in a sterile soundproof room, no chaperones save a target silhouette, wearing those sexy ear and eye protectors and strapping on weapons. Who needed a loaf of bread, a jug of wine and thou when you had all that?

She arrived at the range ten minutes early. At least, she hoped this was the range. All it said on the door was C-742, because even the departments in OPUS had code names. But even with decryption training, Marnie had never been sure if she was in the right place until she saw what was on the other side of a door. Which was why she was certain the infamous men's-washroom incident was going to be told and retold at every OPUS office Christmas party for years. Well, what could she say? She hadn't had her decryption training at that point. The memory still fresh, however, she warily pushed open the door to what she hoped was the firing range and found…

Yep. Looked like a firing range to her. Or, at least what the firing ranges on TV looked like. Had to give those creative consultants credit. They definitely earned their paychecks. She counted fully two dozen chutes for firing practice, each with a paper target at the far end. Most of the lights were off, save the entry where she stood, because the place was deserted. Noah had wanted to schedule the range before an eight-o'clock meeting, so it wasn't even seven now. And being a Monday, Marnie wouldn't be surprised if no one came in until after nine. She didn't care how much the OPUS drones insisted the facility ran 24/7. Monday morning was Monday morning. Spies had to hate that as much as everyone else did.

"Good morning."

She spun around at the sound of Noah's voice. Well, most spies were like everyone else. Noah Tennant wasn't like anyone.

As always, he was dressed in a dark, unobtrusive suit and white dress shirt, this time rounded out with a subtly patterned tie in red and sapphire. His tawny hair was perfectly combed, and when he drew nearer, she saw it was still damp in the back—she could smell a hint of his shampoo. Sandalwood. The same scent she'd inhaled from him that night at her house as she'd tried to consume him. The same scent she'd tried to recreate with a half-dozen different brands of sandalwood bubble bath since then, never coming close. Noah's scent was as distinctive as he was.

"Good morning," she replied.

"Awake enough to operate heavy machinery?"

She narrowed her eyes. "Just how heavy are you planning to get?"

He lifted one shoulder and let it drop. "Nothing major. Just the usual stuff. AK-47. Bazooka. Flamethrower. Rocket launcher. Things any good agent would have with him or her at all times."

"Very funny," she said. Just to be on the safe side, though, she added, "You're joking, right?"

"Tactical weaponry is no laughing matter, missy."

"Yeah, I guess it's all fun and games until someone loses a spy."

He laughed at that, his eyes widening in surprise. "So the lady can joke this early on a Monday. I'm impressed."

"Hold that thought," she said, smiling back. "See if you feel the same way after I've handled a rocket launcher or two without taking out the whole facility."

"I'm sure you'll be fine."

Just as he had been last week, today he was cordial, unruffled, professional. Even when it was just the two of them, he was going to pretend that night at her house had never happened. Even when it was just the two of them, he was going to act like there was nothing between the two of them other than a professional—and temporary—relationship.

But then, that *was* the only thing between the two of them, she reminded herself. For all she knew, Noah had moved past that night completely. If he thought about it at all, he probably only considered it in terms of how badly he'd done his job. Not with the fondness and wistfulness with which Marnie recalled it—too often—herself. She told herself to follow his example. To be a man about it, like he was. To view what had happened as an aberration that wouldn't happen again.

And then, she instructed herself, *forget about it.* The same way Noah had.

Thankfully, he really had been kidding about the major firepower, at least where this lesson was concerned.

Because the first thing he showed her was something called a MAC-10 pistol, the product, evidently, of some weird mechanical eugenics, in this case splicing the DNA of a tommy gun and a calculator. The result was a cold black chunk of metal Marnie didn't want to even get near. Noah, however, was perfectly at ease with it. And she couldn't help thinking how strange it was that a man who had touched her naked flesh with such tenderness could also cradle a weapon like that.

"You know what?" Marnie said when he held it out, presumably for her to actually hold it. "I don't like guns. I mean, I always suspected I didn't like guns, since I'd never actually been close to one. But now, being close to one? I realize I *really* don't like guns. Could I maybe see something in a taser instead? Size six and a half? Preferably blue?"

He made a face at her. "Come on, Marnie. It's harmless right now. It's not loaded, and the safety is on. Of course, I'll be showing you how to rectify both of those situations in this lesson, and then, well, yes, that sucker could potentially go off and take both your hands with it. But that's still a good ten, fifteen minutes away."

She gaped at him for a moment. "No, really," she said. "I think a taser would be much more my speed. Or, better yet, a slingshot. Or a butter knife. Wait, I know. How about a big rock I can throw like a girl while I run screaming like a ninny in the other direction? That would be perfect for me."

He sighed, a much put-upon sound, but did at least pull the weapon back toward himself. "What happened to the ferocious woman who stood up to Adrian Padgett? On two separate occasions?"

"I have no idea," Marnie replied, "since I've never met a ferocious woman who stood up to Adrian Padgett. I've only met a panicky woman who cowered in fear when faced with Adrian Padgett."

"Marnie, you can do this," Noah said. "I know you can. And so do you, or you never would have volunteered to take the job."

She could argue that she hadn't exactly volunteered, that Padgett's invasion into her life and then her home had left her with little choice. Instead, she said, "Look, I just don't think that particular gun is a good fit for me, that's all."

"When you're out there pretending to be Lila, you're going to need a weapon," Noah said. "And you're going to need to know how to use it. Lila loves the MAC-10."

"You told me I'd never be operating alone," she reminded him.

"You won't be," he assured her. "But there's going to be some distance between you and your backup. It isn't a likely scenario, but you need to be prepared for the possibility that there may be a time when you only have a second—or less—to defend yourself. That's when you're going to be happy to have a gun and know how to use it."

"I'll never be happy to have a gun," she told him with complete certainty.

"But you'll be prepared," he said.

It occurred to Marnie—too late—that maybe she really hadn't thought this thing through when she agreed to take the job. She'd only been thinking about making sure Adrian Padgett was caught and put away, so he couldn't terrify her anymore. She'd been thinking she'd dress up like Lila a few times to draw him out, then the real agents would swoop in and throw a net over him, and give her a pat on the back for a job well done. She hadn't been thinking that Padgett might get close enough again to hurt her. She hadn't thought about having to arm herself. She hadn't thought about putting herself in real danger. Not the way Noah was thinking about it.

"Something smaller?" she asked softly. "Something less menacing? That's just so…ugly."

He gave the gun a look of regret, then shrugged. "All right. I guess since you're not really an OPUS agent, you don't have to carry any of the standard-issue weapons."

"How do people conceal something like that, anyway?" she asked as he returned it to the locker from which he'd retrieved it. Especially someone like Lila, who seemed to do at least some of her undercover work, um, under the covers.

"You'd be surprised," he said as he reached for something else. "But we have guns to fit every mood," he said. "Not to worry."

Oh, finding a weapon to fit her mood wasn't what Marnie was worried about at all. No, what she was worried about was how she was going to pay the therapy bills after her OPUS job was over.

The gun Noah brought her this time was a small revolver that looked like something Nero Wolfe might have carried. She still didn't like guns, but at least this one didn't look like something favored by guys named Vinnie and Sal.

"It's a thirty-eight, not a six-and-a-half," he said as he extended it with the barrel aimed to the side. "But try it on anyway."

She eyed it warily, still reluctant to touch it.

"It's not loaded," he told her.

But it was still an instrument created to kill someone. Marnie preferred instruments created to make beautiful music. So she was understandably hesitant. Finally, she took the gun from him, her arm immediately falling in response to the surprisingly heavy weight of the thing.

"It will be even heavier when it's loaded," he said as she lifted the weapon again. "You should come to the range every morning this week to practice. The muscles in your shooting arm will hurt at first, even with a small firearm like that, so you'll need to get in a regular workout."

Wow. Never in her life had Marnie suspected she would someday have a shooting arm. What would be next? A decoder leg?

"Okay," she said cautiously. "Show me what to do."

He started with the basics, loading and unloading the revolver, which he made Marnie do a dozen times because her fingers kept trembling and fumbling with the pieces. When she finally managed to insert all six bullets in just over thirty seconds—a new record Noah told her, since even newbies in training for the first time could do it twice as fast—she strode to the nearest range to actually fire the damned thing.

"We forgot to turn on the lights," she said as she preceded him into a tiny room. It was barely big enough for one person to be comfortable shooting, let alone two.

Automatically, she spun around to look for a light switch, and ran face first—or, more accurately, chest first—into Noah, who had already entered and closed the door behind himself. He—likewise automatically, she was sure—caught her by the upper arms to steady her, but did nothing to move her away from him. Because there wasn't enough room in the confined space, she was sure. Though that didn't explain why he seemed to be curling his fingers more intimately over her arms and pulling her even closer....

"Noah," she said softly, splaying her free hand over his chest in a halfhearted—and, she had to admit, reluctant—effort to stop him. He did, but not before she felt her body pressing against his from chest to shin. She swallowed with some difficulty and added quietly, "One of us needs to turn on a light."

He shook his head. And still didn't release her. "The light's supposed to be dim," he said. "I want you to be able to aim in all situations."

"Wouldn't it be better for an amateur to start off with bright lights? All the better to see you with?"

"It's better with the lights low the first time. Trust me."

Funny, but she was beginning to think he was talking about something other than shooting. A gun, she meant. Or, at least, a mechanical one. "I, um, I never heard that before," she said.

"Trust me, Marnie."

He definitely seemed to be talking about something besides the weapon in her hand, but Marnie figured it probably wasn't a good idea to ask for clarification just then. Mostly because she was hoping for the sort of clarification he had assured her wouldn't happen again. So she nodded and turned around, focusing on the black silhouette of a paper man at the end of the range instead of the flesh-and-blood man who stood behind her. That became a tad more difficult, however, when the flesh-and-blood man behind her stepped close enough that his body was touching hers again, and the sandalwood scent of him surrounded her.

"Your first time," he said softly, "you want to take it slow and easy, and make sure you do it right. Notice everything. The way the weapon feels pressing against your palm, the weight and size and shape of it. Feel how the surface warms in your hand as you close your fingers over it. Grip it gently, but firmly."

Marnie's heart began to pound in her chest for some reason, and heat rushed through her body, warming parts of her that had nothing to do with the gun in her hand.

"Don't rush into anything the first time," Noah said softly from behind her. "Get to know the weapon intimately. As you let yourself get accustomed to the feel of it in your hand, think about how you're going to handle it, how much pressure you want to exert when you curl your finger over the trigger. Take your time touching it and investigating it the first time, Marnie. Take all the time you want."

A hot fist clenched her belly, squeezing tight. There was no way he could be talking about what he seemed to be talking about. Her errant thoughts just made his words sound sexual. Even erotic. The weapon he referred to was the weapon she held in her hand right now. Just because she was thinking about an entirely different kind of gun…

"The first time can be a little intimidating," he told her.

Whoa, yeah, she thought. It sure could. Especially with a man like him.

"That's why," he continued, "for the first time, you

should let go of all your inhibitions and claim the weapon with confidence."

Well, if he insisted…

"Get to know the weapon."

Here? Now? Was he serious?

"Take possession of the weapon."

Marnie's mouth went dry as he skimmed his fingers down the length of her arm to the hand that held the gun. Gently, he lifted it, guiding it upward, toward the target at the end of the range. She barely saw it, however, because her eyes fluttered shut the moment Noah's hand connected with hers. He must have felt it trembling, because he closed his fingers more insistently over hers as he extended both of their arms forward, then moved his other hand to her waist to help keep her body balanced.

At least, that was what she thought he was doing. Until the hand at her waist continued its forward motion, and his arm followed, roping completely over her midsection to pull her body back against his.

She felt him all along her then, his front pressed into her back from her shoulders to her thighs. At the small of her back, she felt the evidence of his arousal. Evidently, they *had* both been thinking about the same weapon during his instruction, and now she wanted nothing more than to carry through with everything he had told her to do. Instinctively, she moved her hips backward in response, something hot and frantic splashing in her belly when Noah's arm around her waist tightened, pulling her back even more. He growled something unintelligible under his breath and dipped his head to the curve of her neck, pressing his mouth to the skin above her collar. She sighed as she tipped her head to the left, to expose even more of her skin for him to taste.

He must have sensed she was about to drop the gun, because he closed his fingers over it, and she heard a soft metallic click she recognized as the safety being replaced. He set the weapon on the shelf in front of them and turned Marnie around to face him, capturing her mouth with his, covering her breast completely with one hand. He massaged her tender flesh as he thrust his tongue into her mouth, tasting her as intimately as he touched her. She opened one hand over his back and wedged the other between their bodies, cupping the part of him that swelled to even greater arousal.

The moment she touched him, he spun their bodies a quarter turn and pushed her against the wall, bracing his legs on both sides of her as he pressed himself harder against her hand. Marnie gasped at the ferocity of his response and his utter lack of inhibition, then realized it only mirrored her own. Because without even realizing what she was doing, she had dropped her other hand to his taut buttocks in an effort to push him harder into herself. As had happened the last time, they seemed to be warring for possession of the kiss. And as had happened the last time, neither seemed to care how long it would take to win. This time, however, they weren't battling in the privacy of her home. This time, anyone could walk in on them and see what was happening.

It was the only coherent thought that permeated her brain, and it only stayed long enough for her to consider the consequences of what would happen, should they be discovered. She managed to move both of her hands to his chest, and she managed to push hard enough to make him take a step backward, so that she was able to tear her mouth away from his. Immediately, he stepped forward again, cupping her shoulders with insistent fingers, dipping his head to hers.

Until she told him, "Noah, we can't do this here. Someone might come in and see us."

But even then, he didn't release her. He only gazed down into her eyes as if he couldn't quite understand what was going on. Marnie sympathized completely. She couldn't fathom her own behavior. Never in her life had she had such an intense response to a man. Noah Tennant had come at her from out of nowhere and turned her world, her emotions, her very self, upside down. And something told her she would never be quite the same—quite…right—again.

"I thought you said this wasn't going to happen again," she said softly, surprised she was able to manage the admonition, so badly did she want to succumb to it.

He continued to search her face, still looking confused. "Yeah, well… I stand corrected."

His heartbeat battered the hand she had splayed over the middle of his chest. "So what are we going to do about it?" she asked him.

His heart rate nearly doubled at that. "There's a hotel not far from here," he said.

She shook her head. "No. No hotel."

"Why not?"

Because if they went to a hotel for this, it would only be physical sex, and not… Not what she wanted. But she knew if she told him that, he'd refuse to go anywhere with her.

"Come to my house for dinner," she said. "Tonight."

Immediately, she sensed in him the very unease she had feared, and she knew by his expression she'd done something wrong. What, she couldn't imagine. But she suddenly worried he was about to reject her offer—and her.

The hands on her shoulders relaxed, and she feared he was about to push her away. Especially after he pulled her forward long enough to drop a soft, almost chaste kiss on her forehead.

But when he pulled back, his eyes were still dark with wanting. "How about we go out to eat?" he asked.

She shook her head again. She wanted Noah to herself tonight. All night. Somewhere private. Where there would be no interruptions, no second-guessing, no excuses to leave. She only told him, though, "I want you all to myself."

He smiled, and some of her uneasiness ebbed. "Then I'll bring dinner with me to your house," he said.

He was offering her a compromise. She didn't know how she knew that, but she did. He didn't want to come to her house at all, but he would, if she declined to cook for him. She supposed she understood. Cooking was such a homemakerish thing to do. And no way were the two of them looking to make a home together. She wasn't honestly sure what they *were* looking to do—something between physical sex and emotional commitment, evidently. If such a thing even existed.

In spite of her troubled thoughts, she said, "All right. You can bring dinner to my house tonight."

He nodded, but she could tell he still wasn't quite happy

with the arrangement. Then again, neither was she. So they were even. And in the long run, both of them would get what they ultimately wanted. To find some release for whatever was burning up the air between them.

"I'll see you tonight then," she said.

"I'll be there at seven."

Neither seemed to know what to say after that. The gun she was supposed to be learning how to use lay neglected on the shelf while the two of them continued to stare at each other, her hands opened on his chest, his roving idly up and down her arms.

"So what do we do in the meantime?" Marnie asked. "I mean, you're supposed to be teaching me how to shoot a gun."

He smiled at that, in a way that let her know he understood the double entendre. "Then I guess we better get started."

CHAPTER FOURTEEN

AT EXACTLY SEVEN O'CLOCK that evening, a soft rap sounded on Marnie's front door. Which she had no trouble hearing, since she was standing roughly two inches away from her front door when the rapping sounded, exactly where she had been standing for the past thirty minutes, trying to fend off hyperventilation and nausea.

She still couldn't believe she had invited Noah to her house tonight for the sole purpose of having sex with him. She'd never done such a thing in her life and was still questioning her sanity in having done it today. All right, yes, she was an adult woman with adult needs and desires, and she was attracted to an adult man who was perfectly willing to satisfy all of them. And yes, it was the twenty-first century and women had earned the right to have sex on their own timetable, under their own terms, with whomever they chose. That didn't make what was about to happen any less important. Or exciting. Or scary.

She inhaled a deep breath and checked her appearance as well as she could. She'd dressed in an effort to look sexy but not desperate, finally opting for a swingy circular skirt the color of tobacco and a clingy off-the-shoulder top in cream. To accessorize them, she'd added gold hoop earrings, a thin gold chain necklace and bracelet and brown flats. She knew flats didn't exactly scream rutting, relentless sex so much as they screamed *I've been working all day and, man, are my dogs tired,* but she'd had to make do. She'd done better, she hoped, with the black lacy panties and translucent black bra, both of which were held together—barely—by red velvet ribbon. Well, a girl had to have *some* sexy lingerie, didn't she? Even if she didn't wear it very often. Or, you know, ever.

She reached for the doorknob just as a second series of soft raps sounded, but hesitated long enough to quell the ripple of nerves winnowing through her belly. Telling herself she was as ready as she was every likely to be, Marnie took a deep breath and slowly pulled the front door open. She almost didn't recognize him at first, so accustomed had she become to seeing him in his nondescript black suits. Tonight, Noah was dressed in a way that was much more casual, and much sexier.

She wondered if he'd been digging through his closets and drawers all evening, too. Because if he had, and if she was even half as sexy as he was at the moment, then she was very sexy indeed.

His gently faded blue jeans were topped by a lightweight sweater the color of a winter forest with a shirt collar the same hue peeking out from beneath. Somehow the combination of indigo and forest brought a darker hue to his blue, blue eyes. The sun had disappeared into the trees on the other side of the street, staining the purpling sky with streaks of amber and ocher that somehow got tangled in his tawny hair, too. In one hand, he carried a bottle of wine—something red by the looks of it—and in the other, he held an oversize shopping bag emblazoned with the logo for an upscale, and very expensive, eatery presumably from his part of town.

She should be famished, she knew. But her appetite fled the moment her gaze connected with his and she saw the raw, unmitigated desire burning in his eyes. That was when her hunger took a turn toward something else. Wherein she became ravenous indeed.

"You, um, you look different," she said by way of a greeting. "I never would have pegged you as the blue jeans sort."

He lifted a shoulder, let it drop. "Consider it my rebellion to the prep school uniforms I always had to wear growing up."

"Ah," she said. Then, remembering she'd invited him here for rutting, relentless sex, which wasn't going to happen as long as he was out on her front porch—not without the police being called, anyway—she opened the door wider and said, "Come in."

He entered, but never took his eyes off her face as he strode past, turning his body until he was walking backward as he headed down the hallway toward her kitchen. So Marnie brushed past him to take the lead, not wanting him to trip and break a leg. That would ruin any chance they had for rutting, relentless sex. And she congratulated herself when, at the end of the hall, she made herself turn right into the kitchen instead of left into her bedroom. No easy feat, that, coming on the heels, as it did, of that rutting, relentless sex thing.

She'd set the table in the dining room for dinner—with her china, crystal and silver, no less—so Noah was able to place the bag and the wine on the kitchen table. Immediately, he began digging into the former to withdraw foam and paper cartons in several shapes and sizes, arranging them haphazardly as he went. There was no way the two of them could consume all that for one meal, and Marnie found herself wondering if he was planning to stay the week. If so, yay.

"Noah?" she said as he withdrew the last of their dinner and set it on the table, then began to fold up the big bag.

"Yeah?" he said, reaching for the wine.

But he looked up at her before he grabbed it, and his expression changed drastically. Evidently, he could tell what she had on her mind. Because one minute Marnie was leaning against her refrigerator door watching him, and the next, she was wrapped in his arms, his mouth slanted over hers. For a long time, he only kissed her, his hands skimming along her spine, curling over her nape, tangling in her hair, opening over her back. She lifted her own hands to his rough face, his smooth shoulders, his silky hair, savoring his different textures, relishing the heat and strength and barely caged power beneath her fingertips.

There was so much of him in that moment. He towered over her and surrounded her, seemed to touch her everywhere. Every time she inhaled, she consumed great gulps of his scent, and her mouth was filled with the taste of him. His heart pummeled against her own so fiercely she fancied she could hear its ragged thump-thump-thumping mixing with the rapid gasping of his breath.

Then she ceased to think at all. Because the hands he'd settled on her hips crept lower, inching over the curve of her fanny, curling over the lower swells to drive her body forward into his. Marnie responded instinctively, rubbing herself against him, sinuously, seductively, reveling in the growl of satisfaction he emitted in reply. He bunched the fabric of her skirt in both fists and began to pull it upward, and she felt the cool kiss of air on the backs of her legs with every new bit of flesh that was exposed. When he'd managed to jerk the garment all the way up, he drove his hands into her panties, cupping her bare flesh with confident fingers, dipping one into the sensitive cleft of her behind.

"Oh," she murmured against his mouth. "Oh, Noah…"

But he captured her lips again before she could say more. Not that she really wanted to say anything else, since she was much too consumed by the feel of him. And the taste of him. And the scent of him. And the sound of him. As he kissed her, he palmed and kneaded her flesh, pushing her against his ripening erection again and again, until she wedged a hand between their bodies to cup that part of him herself.

He growled his enthusiasm, moving his hips against her hand. He was so big, so hard, so much more than she had anticipated he would be. Eagerly, she unfastened the button at his waist and tugged down the zipper, tucking her hand inside his jeans, then his boxers, to cover him more intimately. Flesh to flesh, the way he was touching her. He sprang even more fully erect at the contact, his full head pressing into her palm, hot and velvety and smooth.

"Let's skip dinner," he murmured into her ear. "There's something else I'd rather eat."

She very nearly climaxed right there.

Instead, she somehow managed to whisper those three very important words: "Refrigerator. Reheat. Later."

Instead of following her instructions, Noah kissed her again, covering her mouth with his, thrusting his tongue inside, pushing her body against his own once more. Marnie let herself succumb for long moments before reminding herself that the sooner they stowed their meal, the sooner they could forget about it and move on to other, more insistent, appetites.

Tearing herself away from him, she jerked open the refrigerator door and began stuffing containers inside, not bothering to see where they landed. Then she closed the door and leaned back against it and said softly, "So. Where were we?"

His eyes darkened and he took a step toward her. Marnie's heart raced in anticipation of what he would do or say. But he only lifted a finger to her mouth and traced her lower lip with exquisite care. And he only said, "I believe you were about to invite me into your bedroom."

As if he needed an invitation.

They covered the distance in a half-dozen strides, but Marnie halted just inside her bedroom, trying to see it from Noah's point of view. She'd always thought it a comfortable room, but suddenly it seemed unbearably feminine, the sort of room that would make a man recoil in fear for his testosterone levels.

She'd left on the lamp by the bed—the frilly Victorian one with the silk, fringed shade—so the room was softly illuminated with buttery light. Flowered chintz curtains covered both windows now that darkness had fallen, their pattern reflected in the overstuffed parlor chair in the corner. She'd turned down the bed in preparation for the evening—well, what was the point in pretending?—but the crocheted coverlet seemed tidy in the extreme. A hooked rug with more flowers spanned the hardwood floor between the door and bed, and the cherrywood furnishings were decorated with scrollwork and—oh, dammit—even more flowers.

Noah ought to be fleeing for the front door any moment...

Instead, he entered the room behind her and slipped an arm around her waist, then pushed her hair aside and placed a soft kiss on her nape. Oh. Okay. So he obviously had enough testosterone to ward off even a room like this. That became obvious when he encircled her waist with his other arm and pulled her backward, because his arousal surged against her backside, something that sent heat rocketing through her entire body. When he buried his head in the curve where her neck joined her shoulder, Marnie arched backward, reaching behind herself to thread the fingers of both hands through his hair. The position left her vulnerable—which, of course had been her intention—and Noah took advantage of that vulnerability, moving his hands to her breasts.

First he gently kneaded her through the fabric of her top as he drew his mouth along the bare skin of her neck and shoulder. Then he dropped his hands to the hem of the garment and dragged it up, over her head. Then he cast it aside and unzipped her skirt, letting that slide down over her hips and legs. When it pooled around her ankles, Marnie stepped out of her shoes, too, and kicked everything aside, laughing softly when Noah starting kicking impatiently, too.

She turned to face him, waiting for the shyness she thought would overcome her at being half-dressed when he was still fully clothed. But when she saw the look on his face, she felt strangely empowered instead. His gaze raked over her from her face to her feet and back again, only his eyes seemed darker on the return trip than they had been before.

"Nice," he said. Though whether he was referring to her lingerie or what lay beneath it, Marnie couldn't have said. "Very, very nice."

Before she realized his intention, he had jerked off his sweater and began to unbutton his shirt, but she covered his hands with hers to stop him before he had the chance. "Let me do it," she said softly.

Immediately, he dropped his hands to his sides, and Marnie took her time slipping each button through its hole. When the last one was open, she tucked her hands beneath the shirt at his shoulders and pushed the garment off him, her heart pounding faster when she viewed the collection of muscle and sinew revealed beneath. He was spectacular, with broad shoulders and a sturdy torso that tapered into a lean waist. Tawny hair covered his chest from shoulder to shoulder, narrowing at his navel before disappearing into his unfastened jeans. His arousal was more than evident there, and Marnie's mouth went dry at the thought of the night ahead.

"You're not so bad yourself," she managed to whisper.

When he curled his fingers over her waist and kissed her again, she hooked her hands in the loose denim and pushed down, skimming it over his hips and thighs. And as she returned Noah's kisses, she danced him slowly backward, toward her bed. When his legs bumped against it, she cupped her hands over his shoulders and pushed down, making him sit on the edge of the mattress. She straddled his lap and roped one arm around his neck, covering his mouth with hers, tasting him as deeply as she could. Her other hand fell to his hardened cock, which she stroked leisurely, methodically as she kissed him. Noah cupped his hands under the lower curves of her fanny, caressing the sensitive flesh in time to the stroking of their tongues.

The combined touches and kisses aroused Marnie to the point of near-completion, so she abruptly ended the kissing and levered herself off Noah's lap. He opened his mouth to utter an objection, but halted when she kneeled before him and cupped her hands over his powerful thighs. Gently, she pushed his legs open, and with great care, she bent her head over him and drew him fully into her mouth.

Noah hissed his approval as she sucked him in deep, then sighed with pleasure when she released him enough to circle the head of his shaft with her tongue. She felt his fingers in her hair, sifting, threading, petting, heard his ragged respiration as she moved her mouth over him again and again and again. She tasted the erotic, musky strength of him against her tongue, felt the rapid pulsing of his blood beneath her fingertips. And in that moment, Marnie knew she had complete control of him.

So she made the most of it. Over and over, she sucked him deep into her mouth, then released him to treat him to the combined motions of her hand and her tongue. She loved the guttural sounds he emitted, the way his fingers convulsed in her hair, how his entire body succumbed to a few simple touches from her. Until he urged her away with the soft warning that if she didn't stop, there wouldn't be enough of him left to offer her the same courtesy.

She couldn't have that. She wanted as much of Noah tonight as he would give her. She wanted all of him, quite frankly. But she knew better than to ask. For a man like him, that would be asking too much. Still, she would take anything—anything—he had to offer her.

He wrapped both hands around her wrists and pulled her to standing, then stood to finish removing his clothes and roll on a condom he had fished from his pocket. Marnie undressed as he did, then stretched out on her side in bed to watch him, her entire body humming as she noted the elegant motion of every muscle. When he was naked, too, Noah joined her in bed, lying alongside her, draping his heavy leg over both of hers, throwing his arm across her breasts. He covered her mouth with his and thrust his tongue inside, and for long moments only kissed her and kissed her and kissed her. Then he dragged his open mouth over her cheek and her jaw, down her throat, over her collarbone to her breast.

There he lingered, flattening his tongue over her nipple before drawing it into his mouth, deeply and insistently, the way she had sucked him inside her own. He covered her other breast with his hand, catching her nipple between the V of his index and middle fingers, scissoring gently to generate even more heat inside her. She maneuvered one leg over his strong thigh and rubbed herself against his leg, her hot center demanding as much attention as the rest of her had received.

Noah seemed to understand, because after a few more maddening flicks of his tongue against the lower curve of her breast, he was moving downward again, tasting the dent of her navel and the skin beneath. Then lower still, pushing open her legs as he ducked his head between them, running his tongue over the hot, wet flesh of her sex without a second's hesitation.

It quickly became evident that he liked this part of sex very much. Because he licked and laved Marnie like a man possessed, devouring her with a fierceness that left her helpless to do anything but lie back and enjoy herself. He lapped leisurely with the flat of his tongue, then drew generous circles with the tip. He pushed his hands beneath her fanny and lifted her higher, driving his tongue into every fold of flesh, lingering at the sensitive little bud of her clitoris before diving lower, parting her with his thumbs so that he could penetrate her with his tongue. Over and over and over. Then he was using his finger to penetrate her, too, deeper now, slower, again and again and again.

With his hands in the action, an orgasm begin to shake her, starting low in her belly and shuddering outward. For long moments, her body quaked with her climax, until she cried out at its culmination and fairly melted into the sheets beneath her.

But before she'd even recovered, Noah launched himself inside her—deep, *deep* inside her. He lowered his body over hers, braced both elbows on the mattress on each side of her and thrust himself forward. Marnie bent her knees to facilitate his entrance, and he bucked his hips against her again. She cried out once more at the depth of his penetration, wrapping her fingers tight around his steely biceps. As he heaved himself forward, she circled his waist with her legs, pulling herself up to meet him.

Then he was crying out, too, thrusting one final time with enough force to lift Marnie off the mattress. For a long moment, they clung to each other, his body shuddering the way hers had before finally stilling as his climax ebbed. Then he was relaxing, falling to the bed beside her, one hand draped over her waist, the other arcing over her head.

And it was only in that moment that Marnie realized what a mistake she had made to invite Noah over tonight. Because she knew in that moment she would never make love to a man like him again. Worse, she would never *want* another man but him.

IT WAS NEARLY 2:00 a.m. by the time they finally ate dinner. Without bothering to reheat it. Sitting naked in Marnie's bed. She'd surprised Noah in a lot of ways tonight, but her complete lack of inhibition had been most surprising of all. He'd always been fairly adventurous in bed, had always thought there was no room for restrictions when it came to sex. But he hadn't met many women who felt the same way. Marnie had not only been audacious in her lovemaking, she'd even taken the lead at times. Which was something else that had surprised him. Usually, he liked to be in charge in the bedroom. With Marnie, he'd had no qualms at all about relinquishing control. Mostly because doing so had resulted in a mind-blowing—among other things—climax.

Within minutes of stowing the remains of their dinner in the fridge and opening a second bottle of wine, they were back in bed, feasting on each other for dessert. But this time afterward, they seemed to be at least a little satisfied, and for a long time, only lay in each other's arms, growing accustomed to each other's presence and trying to get a handle on whatever was happening between them.

As if Noah thought he'd ever get a handle on that.

Finally, Marnie pushed herself up on one elbow, settling one hand on his chest and anchoring her head with the other. Her silky hair tumbled over her naked shoulders and breasts, both concealing and revealing the even silkier skin beneath. He wished she would wear her hair like that all the time. Of course, that would necessitate her being naked all the time. Not that there was anything wrong with that....

He didn't think he'd ever seen a more beautiful woman. And he knew he'd never enjoyed more explosive, more potent sex. What was really strange was how comfortable he felt in Marnie's bed. Normally, once sex with a woman was over, Noah didn't like to hang around. That was the reason he preferred hotels instead of going to a woman's home. And he *never* brought a woman to his own house. Houses—homes—were too suggestive of permanence, of family, of intimacy. And Noah had never wanted any of those things with a woman.

Yet Marnie's house was the worst for all of them. She had deep roots here. Memories of her entire life with the only family she'd ever known. The house oozed love and affection and tenderness. Her girly-girl bedroom alone should have had him running screaming in horror, his hands cupped protectively over his manhood. Instead, he found himself wanting to pull her closer and cover their bodies with the bedclothes, and burrow there for days.

A ribbon of some strange, unfamiliar emotion unfurled

inside him, seeping into parts of him he hadn't even realized he could feel. His heart seemed to beat more slowly, and his blood seemed to flow more comfortably. Worry, fear, anxiety, all slipped away, to be replaced by well-being, fondness, affirmation. He finally recognized the feeling as satisfaction. Not the physical satisfaction a man felt after the completion of sex, but an almost unearthly, soul-deep satisfaction that all was right in the world.

Which was nuts. He knew better than anyone that the world was one seriously mucked up place. But here with Marnie, in her too-cozy bed, in her too-cozy bedroom, in her too-cozy house, he felt nothing in his life—or anyone else's—would ever go wrong again.

Until she said, in a sober voice, "I need to ask you a question."

Something about the way she said it made that agreeable ribbon inside him begin to curl up tight. He ignored the sensation as best he could and met her gaze. "All right."

"It's a very important question," she said.

He lifted a hand and touched it to her hair, letting it drape over his fingers before pushing it carefully back over her shoulder to completely reveal her naked breast. "Okay."

"It's a question I need for you to answer honestly," she added.

He skimmed the back of his knuckles along the line of the collarbone he had uncovered, then down over the top of her breast. "That sounds kind of ominous."

"Not ominous," she said. "Serious."

But there was a catch in her voice, and he knew she was

as affected by his seemingly careless touches as he was himself. He was trying to be serious, really he was. She was just so beautiful, so irresistible, he couldn't help himself. He turned his hand so that his palm was touching her and dragged it down more, over her nipple to the underside of her breast, which he caught in a gentle grip.

"Noah," she said on a half groan. "Please. I mean it. This is an important question."

Still cradling her soft flesh in his hand, he told her, "Then I guess you better ask it."

"And you'll answer honestly?"

He nodded.

"Promise?"

"I promise."

She'd settled her hand over the middle of his chest, her palm pressed to his flesh as if she were trying to gauge every heartbeat. She fixed her gaze on his, her eyebrows knitting downward. Very quietly, very somberly, she asked, "Were you and Lila lovers?"

"No," he replied immediately, honestly.

She closed her eyes, and expelled a long, lusty sigh of relief.

"But she and I had sex," he added, likewise honestly. If Marnie were any other woman, he could have lied to her effortlessly and without an ounce of remorse. But Marnie wasn't any other woman. That, if nothing else, had become clear tonight. And not only was Noah *unable* to lie to her, but he didn't *want* to lie to her. Which, he supposed, was the most surprising thing of all.

Her eyes snapped open, darkened by confusion. "But you said—"

"I said Lila and I weren't lovers," he repeated. "What happened between us had nothing to do with love. It just…happened."

She narrowed her eyes. "How many times?"

"Once," he replied, again quickly and honestly.

"A one-night stand?"

"It really wasn't even that," he said. And really, it hadn't been. It had just been…sex. A physical demonstration of profound relief that had come on the heels of a very dangerous situation. A way to work off an excess of adrenaline and rejoice in being alive. Had Lila been a man, Noah probably would have wrapped an arm around his shoulder and gone in search of a good bar fight with him. But because she was a woman—a very sexual woman, much like her sister—he'd put an arm around her shoulder and something else had happened instead.

Not that he wanted to dump the blame for that night on Lila, because he'd responded to her with equal need, equal hunger. But that was the point. It had been need and hunger. Physical need. Physical hunger. It hadn't been…anything else.

At least, he hadn't thought so at the time. But over the years since, there had been times when Noah wondered if maybe there had been more to it than he allowed himself to concede. There had been times when he'd seen Lila afterward when he'd felt…strange. About her. About himself. About what had happened. And he'd wondered if that strange feeling had been affection. Or something.

Eventually, though, he'd made himself stop thinking about it. He'd been promoted again and moved to Cleveland, and Lila had been assigned to report to someone else. It had been years since Noah had seen her. Years since he'd given her any thought. But since her disappearance five months ago, he'd found himself thinking about Lila a lot. Inescapably, those thoughts had included memories of that night. And inescapably, he'd begun to wonder again just what that night had been.

Seeing Marnie dressed like Lila, looking so much like her, had only confused him even more, since his response to her had been so quick and so profound. Because although she looked exactly like her sister, she wasn't like Lila at all. And Noah just wasn't sure if his response had been for Marnie or for Lila. Nor was he sure if it was just physical or…something else.

He'd hoped tonight might clear that up. Had hoped that by having sex with Marnie, he'd be able to identify the source of his response to her. Instead, he was more confused than ever.

"Will you tell me what happened?" she said, stirring him from his troubling thoughts.

He'd really hoped she wouldn't ask him that. He just wasn't sure he could explain that night in a way that would make any sense. Even if he understood it himself. If Marnie had known Lila, it would have been easier. But trying to explain Lila to someone who'd never met her was like trying to describe fire to a piece of wood. While the wood was on fire.

Then again, it probably wasn't Lila's motivation that night that Marnie most wanted to know about. And like so much else, Noah wasn't sure how to feel about that.

So, "Long story short," he began.

Marnie shook her head. "No. I want the long version."

Noah bristled at that. She was within her rights to ask about his relationship with Lila. She wasn't within her rights to have an answer that involved more than he wanted to give her. In spite of the heat the two of them had generated together, he and Marnie didn't have a personal relationship. They'd both known the reason for being here tonight was to have sex. Period. Neither was looking any further into the future than getting to work in the morning and being halfway coherent enough to do their jobs. Neither owed the other anything but physical gratification. Marnie had definitely given him that. And, all modesty aside, Noah knew he'd fulfilled his part of the bargain very well.

Dammit, he knew they should have gone to a hotel. By being in Marnie's house this way, she was assigning more to the experience than was actually there. What the two of them had had tonight was sex. Period. Just like what it had been between him and Lila.

As soon as the thought uncoiled in his head, though, Noah knew it wasn't true. What he and Marnie had done tonight was nothing like what had been between him and Lila. He felt different now from the way he had felt after having had sex with Lila. With her, there had been nothing immediately afterward except very pleasant physical exhaustion. With Marnie, there was…

He halted the thought right there. One problem at a time, he told himself. First things first.

"Long story short," he said again, more emphatically this time. "What happened between me and Lila only happened once. And it only happened because of an extreme situation that was never repeated. That's all that matters, Marnie. And it's all you need to know."

She studied him in silence for a long time, the hand that had been open over his heart slowly curling into a loose fist. Finally, softly, she asked, "What if the extreme situation *was* repeated?"

He looked at her blankly. "I don't understand. It wouldn't be repeated. Lila and I don't work together anymore."

His answer seemed to bother more than placate her, because her eyebrows arrowed downward even more and she removed her hand from his chest completely. "What if you and Lila *were* to work together again, and find yourselves in another extreme situation?"

"That won't ever happen, Marnie."

"But what if it did? Would the two of you react the same way?"

"What difference does it make?"

She uttered a soft sound in response to his question, one he couldn't for the life of him describe. He knew he wasn't giving her the answer she wanted, but she'd told him to be honest. And honestly? He couldn't predict the future. Besides, there was no future to predict. Not only was there little chance he and Lila would ever be working on an assignment together, never mind standing in the same room, but there was little chance he and Marnie would ever see each other again once this assignment was concluded.

And why, dammit, did the realization of that make him feel even edgier than her probing questions did?

"Look, Marnie, I—"

"No, it's all right, Noah. I understand."

Somehow, he doubted it. How could she understand what he was saying when he didn't understand much of it himself. "Do you?"

She nodded, but her expression indicated she felt something entirely different. She gripped the sheet in one hand and pulled it up over herself, hiding from view the delectable flesh Noah had been touching and tasting only moments ago. And that, he supposed, was the most telling response of all.

"It's late," she said softly. "And we both have to work in the morning. You should probably go."

He probably should. But he wanted to stay. Because somehow he knew that if he left now, there was little chance he would ever be back.

He told himself that was the way it should be. Reminded himself that was the way it always was. He and his partner had sex and then went to their corners. If it was good sex, they met for round two on a date that was mutually agreeable to them both, then went to their corners again. It was an arrangement that had always suited Noah in the past, even if he'd never had a partner who lasted more than four or five rounds. Sex, like boxing, wasn't a sport for the faint of heart.

His heart had always been able to take it. But Marnie's, he was beginning to realize, wasn't the pugilist that his own was.

"Yeah, you're right," he finally replied. "It is late. And we do have to be at work in a little while. Thanks for the reminder."

She uttered that soft little sound again, then, "Anytime."

Anytime, Noah repeated to himself as he pushed the covers away and swung his feet to the floor. Yeah, right. Such a short word, to be filled with so much.

CHAPTER FIFTEEN

"OKAY, ELLIE, TELL ME again why I have to sit out here twiddling my thumbs while you're inside having all the fun?"

Ellie bit back a growl as she turned from her place in the back of the van to look at Daniel, sitting in the driver's seat. Like her, he was dressed completely in black, but unlike her, he wasn't armed. At least, she didn't think he was armed. She was pretty sure she'd talked him into returning the automatic he'd purchased the day after he'd discovered who and what she really was. She never should have told him the truth about her job.

She bit back an exasperated growl. It was too late to start second-guessing herself now. What was done was done, and she'd just have to make the best of it. If Daniel wanted to tag along, she couldn't stop him. To a point. Yeah, he could drive the getaway car, she'd promised him, but that was it. Only *she* would be going into ChemiTech after hours, and only *she* would be in the physical line of fire, should anything go wrong. Bad enough she'd let him talk her into that party fiasco. Never mind that he may have been instrumental in furthering the investigation. Enough was enough. Starting now, the investigation was hers again. And hers alone.

And it would go perfectly, she assured herself further. As long as Daniel stayed out here where he belonged.

"You're not going to be twiddling your thumbs," she told him. "You're going to be listening to everything I do and say, and you're going to make sure it gets recorded back here." She jutted a thumb over her shoulder at the wall of sophisticated surveillance equipment behind her. "That's a very important part of the job. It's what half of OPUS agents do for a living." In addition to a million other things, she thought, but she wasn't about to tell Daniel any more about the workings of the organization than she already had.

"Yeah, right," he said. "I'm sure a lot of people who work for your agency get paid a ton of money to push a record button and peruse the latest issue of *Sports Illustrated* for the rest of the night."

Ellie gritted her teeth. "There's a little more to it than that. As it is, you're not actually trained to even push an OPUS record button, so consider yourself in perilous waters. You never know what's going to happen when you push a button in OPUS."

"Yeah," he agreed derisively. "A Diet Coke might come out instead of the Cherry Pepsi that you really wanted."

"Look, Daniel," Ellie said, her patience gone. "You're not even supposed to know what's going on. You're sure as hell not supposed to be a part of this. If the muckety-mucks at OPUS find out how far I've let this go, they'll not only jerk me from the program and blacklist me from ever going through agent training again, but they'll fire me from the job I *do* have. I could even face charges of treason."

His mouth dropped open. "What the hell was treasonous about you telling me what's going on?"

"It's a secret government assignment," she said, somehow managing to bite back the *dumbass* with which she wanted to punctuate the sentence. "And Uncle Sam doesn't like it when people tell his secrets, especially to those who have no stake in them."

"Well, I think that's nuts," he said. "I can be a huge help to you."

She closed her eyes. "Daniel…"

"Fine," he said tersely. "I'll stay out here and push the record button." He reached into the passenger seat for something as he added, "Luckily, I brought along the latest issue of *Sports Illustrated* to peruse while you're inside having all the fun."

"It's *not* fun," Ellie said, her teeth gritting again. "It's my job. And it's very dangerous work. The only thing that would make it *more* dangerous would be if you were in there with me."

"Just go do your very dangerous work, all right?" he said. "Wake me when you're ready to go home."

"Oh, for—" There was no reason to sit here like a couple of three-year-olds doing the am-not-are-too thing. She had very dangerous work to do. Daniel knew the drill. She'd briefed him before they left her apartment. The van belonged to OPUS but had been assigned to Ellie for the night. She'd shown Daniel how everything worked and, smart guy that he was, he'd caught on with no problem. Yeah, okay, so it pretty much amounted to pushing the record button. That was beside the point. The point was that Ellie should have kicked his dumbass when she had the chance.

Men.

She tucked the few items she'd need into the pockets of

her black trousers and slipped her weapon into its ankle holster. Then she mentally ticked off her breaking-and-entering to-do list. She hadn't wanted to risk working late again at her phony-baloney auditing job, since she'd already done that several times. She didn't want anyone taking too close a look at the daily check-in log and wondering why a lowly accountant was spending so much time going over the books. Best-case scenario, they'd think she was too incompetent to get her work done during regular hours and ask for someone else. Worst-case scenario, they'd think she was up to no good. Better just to leave at her regular time on occasion and, if necessary, slip back into the building after working hours, under cover of darkness.

Speaking of which.

With a final glance at Daniel, who had already begun perusing the magazine under what pale streetlight spilled through the windshield, Ellie silently opened the back door to the van and exited. They'd parked half a mile away from one of the back entrances of ChemiTech, so she covered the distance in a quick sprint, arriving barely winded. Daniel had filled her in on Sebastian Baird's habits and schedule—oh, all *right,* so he'd been sort of useful to have on board—so was a breath mint—so she knew Baird would be gone by now.

She checked her watch. Half-past ten. Daniel said Baird and several other of the ranking scientists consulted until nine tonight, which meant there had been plenty of time for all of them to vacate the premises. Hopefully, there would be few, if any, stragglers. Though Ellie had learned in her short time at ChemiTech that research scientists were prone to long hours, since some of them never wanted to do anything *but* research, she figured ten-thirty was pushing it for even the most dedicated. The building should be deserted save a dozen security guards, easily eluded, and a skeleton cleaning crew, easily deceived.

Ordinarily, the big brick building would be difficult to breach, so the security guards tended to be less-than-diligent in their nightly rounds. Talk about perusing your *Sports Illustrated.* But the gadgetry OPUS had at its fingertips—literally, Ellie thought as she withdrew a small metal device from her pocket—was anything but ordinary. With little effort, and even less time, she had the steel door open and the alarm disengaged.

In thirty minutes—probably less—everything would be back exactly the way it was supposed to be. And Ellie would have in her possession copies of some very confidential notes that were locked tight in Sebastian Baird's lower right-hand desk drawer.

Oh, all *right,* so Daniel had given her that information, too. And, yes, okay, he'd given her a key to Baird's office. Ellie would have found the notes *and* gotten into Baird's office just *fine,* thank you very much, even without Daniel's help. It just would have taken her a couple minutes longer, that was all.

She arrived at her destination with no trouble, let herself in and crossed to the desk on the other side of the room. Even in the dark, she could see that, like so many offices in ChemiTech, the place was a pigsty. Baird's office was bigger than most, thanks to his seniority and value to the company, but it was every bit as cluttered as the others. Security lights outside scattered some meager illumination through fat venetian blinds, striping the leather sofa beneath it that was burdened by boxes of files, textbooks, notebooks and computer discs. The desk held more of the same, along with haphazardly arranged items like a microscope, a telephone, a coffee mug and an iPod.

Ellie was careful to touch nothing more than she had to, then was meticulous about putting everything she did touch back in its proper place. She picked the lock on the drawer, collected the notes, used Baird's copier to copy them and returned the originals to their rightful place. Then she folded the copies and tucked them beneath the waistband of her pants at the small of her back.

She was making a quick survey of the room to double-check everything before leaving when the door suddenly opened and Daniel slipped through. He'd thrown on a white mad scientist coat over his black clothes, and he'd tucked a clipboard under one arm, presumably to look like he belonged in the building after hours. But his panicked expression was totally out of place. Likewise out of place was the flash of fear that singed Ellie's belly. Field agents did not know fear, singed or otherwise. She tamped it down and focused on Daniel instead.

"What the hell are you doing here?" she whispered.

"I forgot to tell you something," he whispered back.

"What?"

"Sebastian Baird is headed your way."

More than fear did more than flash in her belly at that. Ellie had to tamp down pure, clawing-at-the-back-of-her-throat terror. *"What?"*

"His car went right past the van, headed toward Chemi-Tech, so I hoofed it over here to tell you. I knew he and Howie—that's the security guard who does night duty at the front desk—would talk Cubs baseball for a good fifteen minutes, because they always do. But that was fifteen minutes ago," Daniel added ominously. "If Sebastian's coming to his office, and I'm sure he is, he'll be here any—"

The elevator chimed in the hallway outside.

"—minute."

"Oh, fu—"

Ellie never quite got the expletive out of her mouth, because Daniel suddenly lurched across the room and filled her mouth with his tongue instead. Then he swept an arm across the desk, knocking half of its contents to the floor. Keys were jingling on the other side of the office door, but Daniel pulled away from her to jerk her shirt from her pants, yank it over her head and the notes from her waistband and toss both to the floor. Then he went to work on unfastening his belt and the fly of his trousers.

Ellie's hands flew up over the bra that was as black as everything else she had on that night, and she started to object, "What the fu—"

But Daniel molded his mouth to hers again and pushed her back onto the desk, covering her body with his. She was about to roar an objection and then pop him in the eye, but something stopped her. Mostly the fireball of heat that exploded between her legs when she felt the full, ripening length of him pressed against her there. And also the torrent of pure, potent pleasure that flooded her when he covered her breast with his hand and squeezed hard.

Everything melted in that moment. Her body. Her thoughts. Her fears. Herself. There was a buzzing in her brain and a craving in her core that obscured anything else that might be happening. All she knew was that she was touching and being touched by Daniel the way she had always dreamed of touching and being touched by him. And all she felt was a passion and a hunger and a need for more.

As he filled her mouth with his tongue again, she dropped her hands to his waist and bunched up the fabric of his lab coat, until she could reach his shirt beneath. As she wrenched it free of his pants, she realized the latter garment was unfastened, so she tucked her hands inside, burrowing her fingers under the cotton of his briefs. As she cupped his bare ass in her palms, Daniel thrust his hips forward, his erection surging now against her belly. Ellie bucked her hips upward in demand, even knowing the gesture was futile when she was still dressed. She wanted Daniel inside her, *deep* inside her. Forget about foreplay or anything else. She wanted to be joined with him in the most primal, primitive way a man and a woman could be joined. And she wanted it *now*.

In response, he thrust his tongue deep into her mouth again and rubbed his body against hers, the hand on her breast squeezing hard again. There was nothing gentle or tentative about the way he touched her, as if his hunger for her was as inflamed as her own for him. Ellie groaned out loud as she hooked her legs over his, and met him thrust for thrust as he rocked his pelvis against hers. She moved a hand between their bodies, cupping her palm over the hard, heavy length of him, pressing the back of her hand against her own aching center. She stroked both Daniel and herself, once, twice, three times, four, driving them both deeper into their delirium. But she was jerked back to reality when a bright white light suddenly exploded overhead, and she realized it had nothing to do with an orgasm.

And also when a booming voice thundered, "Oh, for God's sake, Beck, not *again*."

Ellie tore her mouth from Daniel's and turned to look in the direction from which the voice had erupted, and found herself gazing at the very man she was supposed to be investigating. Dr. Sebastian Baird stood framed by his doorway, wrapped in one of those old geezer overcoats and carrying a dilapidated briefcase. Ellie knew he was nearing eighty, but he could have easily passed for a man in his early sixties. He was tall, over six feet, had a full head of steel-gray hair, a pale complexion and startling blue eyes.

Or maybe they were just startled blue eyes, Ellie quickly amended. After all, how often did you come to work after hours and find two people having sex on your desk?

"How many times have I told you not to use my office for your sexual liaisons with the new hires?"

Oh. Okay. So evidently this sort of thing happened to Sebastian Baird a lot.

"I'm sorry, Sebastian," she heard Daniel say from above her. "But I don't have an office of my own."

And only then did it truly gel, what had happened. In an effort to hide the fact that Ellie had broken into Baird's office, Daniel had manufactured a scene with which the scientist was clearly familiar: the young man he was mentoring had brought a girl to his office to experiment with a different kind of chemistry than what one usually found at ChemiTech. Obviously, this was the sort of thing Daniel did a lot, having sex with other employees after hours in

Baird's office. Ellie didn't know whether to be relieved or reviled. Daniel had prevented her from being caught red-handed—again. But he was an even bigger hound dog about casual sex than she'd realized.

Sebastian blew out a sound that was a mixture of disgust and resignation. "Well, until you have your own office, Beck, maybe you should try keeping it in your pants. At least while you're at work." He looked at Ellie, shaking his head in disapproval. "Sweetheart, if you want to sleep your way to the top in this company, you might want to think about starting a little higher on the ladder than this guy. He won't even clear off the sofa, which any moron knows is the more comfortable piece of furniture for this sort of thing."

Ellie bristled at that. Not that it was the first time she'd been talked down to by a man in a professional situation. Her irritation stemmed from the fact that Baird had so easily bought into a fictional scenario Daniel had created. Had she been alone in Baird's office when he returned just now, she wouldn't have had any way to explain her presence there. It was the second time she'd potentially botched the assignment, only to be bailed out by Daniel.

Worse than her irritation, however, was her disappointment. Not with herself—at least, not for failing to do her job as well as she should. Though certainly she was disappointed with herself about that. But she was even more so at the knowledge that Daniel had only kissed and groped her because he'd needed to create a cover, and not because he'd actually wanted to kiss and grope her. Unlike, evidently, dozens of women he worked with, who he seemed to bring to Baird's office for kissing and groping on a regular basis. Likewise disappointing was her realization that the kissing and groping would never happen again. Well, not with her. It would probably happen lots of times with other women working at ChemiTech.

And for God's sake, Ellie, she told herself, *why is that the thing that's bothering you the most right now?* She should have been infinitely more worried about jeopardizing the assignment. Instead, she was mooning over lost time with Daniel.

Baird shook his head at both of them, but instead of looking angry, he grinned in a way that made him look almost wistful. Like maybe he was recalling a similar event from his own past, when he'd been the one on his own mentor's desk with a co-worker after hours. "Look, I'll come back in thirty minutes, all right?" he said. "Will that give you two enough time to finish and straighten up and leave?"

God help her, Ellie's first reaction was to ask if they could have an hour instead. Or, better still, an entire weekend. Thankfully, Daniel answered before she had a chance.

"Make it an hour," he said.

The other man nodded. "I'll be in the lab."

And with that, he turned and exited his office, obviously unbothered by the fact that two people would be copulating on his desk for the next sixty minutes. He was even kind enough to turn off the lights before closing the door behind himself.

"Unbelieva—"

As had happened only moments ago, Ellie's comment

was cut off by the insertion of Daniel's tongue into her mouth. And just like that, she was once more lost to the frantic demand of her body, tangling her fingers in his hair, tasting him as deeply as he tasted her, wrapping one leg around his waist to propel her hips harder against his. The hand on her breast effortlessly flicked open the front closure of her bra, and then his hand was on her again, flesh to flesh this time, his heat seeping into her, inflaming her.

For long moments, they warred for possession of the embrace, each ceding only long enough to regroup before storming the gates again. By the time Ellie finally came to her senses—well, sort of—they were half-undressed and completely aroused. In spite of that, she managed to tear her mouth from his and flatten both hands on his chest, pushing him far enough away that she could say what needed to be said.

"Daniel, we can't do this. Not now. Not here."

For a minute, she didn't think he heard her, because his only reply was a few ragged breaths as he skimmed his hands along her rib cage. "Why not?" he finally panted. "Sebastian gave us his blessing."

"Because I'm working," she reminded him—and herself. "Or, at least, I'm supposed to be."

Through the darkness, she saw the flash of his grin. He raked his thumb slowly back and forth over her nipple until Ellie wanted to melt. "Consider this one of those killer government benefits you're always talking about," he told her.

Oh, he was much better than a government benefit. But this really wasn't the time or place for this. No matter how good it felt to be right here with him right now.

"Come on, Ellie," he said, his voice a coaxing purr. "You know you want to."

Truer words were never spoken. But, really…

He dipped his head to her breast, opening his mouth over her nipple now, sucking her deep inside. At the same time, he moved his other hand between her legs and stroked her through the damp fabric of her trousers, again and again and again. Ellie's eyes fluttered closed, and she groaned softly.

She shouldn't do this. She shouldn't. It was unprofessional. It was stupid. It was asking for trouble.

He stroked her again, harder.

Oh, it was *so good.* Maybe just a few minutes more…

Without even realizing she was doing it, she spread her legs, and Daniel cupped her completely in his palm. This time Ellie was the one to do the rubbing, lifting her hips from the desk and pushing herself against his hand. It was she, not Daniel, who unfastened the button at the waistband of her trousers and slid the zipper down. And it was she, not Daniel, who thrust her hand inside to touch. But Daniel helped, covering her hand with his from the outside to push it more insistently against her. He dictated the rhythm as he guided her fingers over herself, slow, then fast, then slow again. He was the one who, just when Ellie was about to come, halted the movement of their hands and pulled her to her feet. He was the one who jerked her trousers down over her hips and thighs. And he was the one who turned her around so that her back was facing him.

He pressed his naked chest to her naked back, aligning both of his arms against hers. She could feel the bumps and cords of muscle and sinew rising beneath his flesh from his shoulders to his wrists, so much more pronounced than her own. A ripple of something faintly like intimidation fluttered through her, and she realized she was aroused by the knowledge that he was so much stronger than she and could overpower her if he wanted to. He wove his fingers with hers and moved both their hands to the desk, then released her and flattened her palms against the cool, hard surface. Gripping her waist in both of his hands, he pulled the rest of her body toward himself, driving his hard shaft into her to the hilt.

Ellie sighed at the immediacy and totality of his possession. Never had she felt so full, so complete as she did in that moment. Again and again Daniel entered her that way, moving his hands forward, over her flat torso and along her rib cage, then down again. Eventually one hand moved up as the other moved down, the first cupping one breast while the other furrowed into the damp, sensitive folds of flesh between her legs. He nuzzled the soft skin where her neck joined her shoulder, rubbing his lips lightly over her sensitive skin before nipping her lightly with his teeth. She cried out at the sweet pleasure-pain that jolted her insides, then tilted her head to the side in a silent invitation for him to do it again.

For long moments, they coupled that way, Daniel's penetration slow and deep and thorough. Gradually, his movements became more demanding and less directed, until he was moving his hands to her waist again to take control. He opened one hand between her shoulder blades and urged her upper body downward, until she was bent at the waist over the desk. Then he gripped her hips in both hands and drove himself into her, deeper even, harder even, than he had been before.

Ellie's own orgasm began to swell inside her, a tight little ball of pleasure that slowly expanded. Larger and larger it grew, seeping into every inch of her, generating heat, demanding release. And then it was exploding, and Daniel was crying out behind her, spilling himself hotly inside her.

And then it was dark again. In the office, in Ellie. And she had no idea where to look for a light.

DANIEL WASN'T SURE how much time had passed since Sebastian had left him and Ellie alone, but he felt as though he'd been swimming in the Sea of HappyHappyJoyJoy for months before he finally beached himself in Port Climax. By the time he made his way to the Afterglow Beach Bar for a drink, however, he was alone, because Ellie had scrambled off the desk and was rooting around Sebastian's office, looking for something.

"I can't find my shirt," she said. "Where did you throw it?"

Daniel fumbled around blindly until he found the lamp at the corner of the desk, which had escaped his earlier clearing. Hey, if there was one thing he knew how to do, it was clear off Sebastian's desk in a way that allowed for maximum coitus and minimal loss of equipment. Hell, he'd done it often enough since coming to work here. With pale yellow light filling the room, he pulled his pants back up and threaded his belt through its loop. When he glanced up, he found himself staring at Ellie's half-naked ass, because her pants had dipped low as she bent over to scoop up her shirt. And all he could think was, *What the hell…?*

Of course, there were *way* too many ways to finish that question. Approximately eighty billion, in fact, since that was how many thoughts were ricocheting around in his head at the moment. And every last one of them was wrapped around what had just happened between him and Ellie. So Daniel picked the most concrete of the most immediate ones to speak aloud.

"What the hell is that on your ass?"

Ellie glanced over her shoulder as she jerked her pants over the body part in question. "What are you talking about?"

"Is that a tattoo?" he asked incredulously.

Ellie Chandler had a tattoo on her ass? The question was followed by a dozen more of a similar nature, the biggest of which was, it went without saying, *Ellie Chandler puts out?* That was followed closely by *Ellie Chandler will do it on a desk?* and *Ellie Chandler likes it from behind?* and *Ellie Chandler doesn't wear underwear?* and *Ellie Chandler pets her beaver?*

But of course, all of those questions paled in light of the big one Daniel was asking himself at the moment: *I just had sex with Ellie Chandler?* Rivaled only by: *And it was the smokin'est sex I've ever had?* Which was saying something, since Daniel Beck had had some pretty smokin' sex in his life. Hell, why bother if it wasn't smokin', you know?

"Yeah, it's a tattoo," she said as she thrust her arms through her shirt and pulled it over her head.

"Of what?" he asked.

"Nothing," she told him, her voice clipped.

"No, come on. I want to see it."

"No."

"Come on, Ellie. I saw a lot more than that a few minutes ago."

"No, you didn't. The lights were off." She punctuated the statement by switching off the desk lamp, so that they were once again thrown into darkness.

Okay, maybe Daniel wasn't the most clued-in guy in the world, but he was starting to sense some hostility. "Ellie?" he said softly. "What's wrong?"

Aside from the fact that he'd just had the smokin'est sex he'd ever had with a woman he'd never considered remotely smokin' or sexy.

"Nothing," she said in a voice that was even cooler than before.

"You don't sound like nothing's wrong."

Her response to that was silence.

Not once in the year Daniel had known her had Ellie ever seemed clipped and cool, the way she was now. On the contrary, she was about the nicest, warmest woman he'd ever met. Usually, he kept his distance from women like that because they were a waste of time. Nice, warm women were never interested in smokin'—and temporary—sex. Nice, warm women tended to want relationships. They wanted to get serious. They wanted to talk and share and, you know, relate about stuff. They wanted a lot more than Daniel was willing to give. So even though he'd thought Ellie was cute when he first met her, he'd realized within moments that he should steer clear of her. Because he'd realized within moments how nice and warm she was.

Of course, being next-door neighbors, he hadn't exactly

been able to avoid her. And in the weeks that followed his moving in, they'd struck up a friendship. But that was the point. It was a *friend*ship with a nice, warm woman. Not a *relationship* with one. So it was okay that they talked and shared and, you know, related about stuff.

So it was okay—and in no way unmanly—for Daniel to ask her, "Can we talk about what just happened?"

"No," she replied tersely. And, he had to admit, kind of manfully.

"Why not?"

"Because."

"Because why?"

"No."

"Are you going to keep answering every question I ask you with one word?"

"Yes."

"Ellie…"

He strode to the desk and turned the light back on again, just in time to see her tucking some folded papers into the waistband of her pants at the small of her back. Sebastian's notes. The reason she'd come here tonight. He'd forgotten about them after all that smokin' sex.

"We need to talk," he said, more adamantly this time.

She spun around to look at him, but her expression revealed no clue as to what she might be thinking. Her appearance, however, spoke volumes about what she'd been doing. Her nipples pushed through the fabric of her T-shirt, so agitated were they still. Her hair, which had been gathered at her nape in one of those plain Jane ponytails she liked to wear, was streaming around her shoulders, the clip that had held it having been flung only God knows where. Her mouth was red and swollen from the fierceness of their kisses and her neck flamed in all the places Daniel had nipped her.

He still wasn't sure what had come over him there. He'd never been one for rough sex. But something about the situation, about Ellie, had brought out the beast in him. What was weird—not to mention incredibly arousing—was how enthusiastically she'd responded. He probably had a few red places on his own neck, not to mention a few lines on his back where she'd scored him with her fingernails. He never would have suspected such a raging tigress lay beneath Ellie's nice, warm girl-next-door exterior.

"Talk," she said. Still with the one-word answers.

He nodded.

"About what happened."

Wow, three words. She was really starting to ramble.

"Daniel, I have a job to do."

Whoa, that was a good half-dozen words in one breath. Motormouth. Unfortunately, the words she spoke didn't cover any of the ground Daniel wanted to explore himself.

"You finished your job," he said. "You got Sebastian's notes. Now it's Miller Time. And we need to talk."

She was shaking her head before he even finished speaking. "This job is nowhere close to being finished," she told him. "I've got to find out who at ChemiTech is leaking classified information. After that, the *assignment* will be finished. But this is the kind of job where I'm never off the clock."

"No Miller Time?" he asked. "That sucks."

She hooked her hands on her hips—hips that had only

moments ago been bucking against his—and glared at him. "I'm serious, Daniel. People who work for OPUS don't just work for OPUS. We're on call all the time, ready to do whatever needs doing, wherever it needs doing, whenever it needs to be done."

"So then it's not a job, it's an adventure?" he asked.

"Stop trying to reduce what I do for a living to a slogan," she snarled. Actually snarled. Wow. That was even more arousing than the enthusiasm for rough sex. "Being an operative for OPUS isn't some nine-to-five occupation where, at the end of the day, I park my car in the garage and kick back with a beer. It's dangerous work. There's a reason agents work in the field alone."

"So they don't wind up humping like rabbits while they're on the clock?" he asked.

"Dammit, Daniel. Stop it."

"Stop what?"

"Stop trying to make light of what I do for a living!"

If Daniel hadn't known better, he would have thought he saw the sheen of tears in hers eyes. But what the hell would she have to cry about? She'd done her job well and had some smokin' sex at the same time. Any man would be proud of an accomplishment like that. Of course, Daniel also knew better—than just about anyone at the moment— that Ellie wasn't a man. She was a nice, warm woman. Who'd had some smokin' sex. Who would have guessed something like that was possible? Not Daniel, that was for damned sure.

And something else he wouldn't have thought possible had happened, too. He wanted to have smokin' sex with Ellie again. Lots and lots of times. In fact, he kind of didn't want to have sex with anyone *but* Ellie for a while. It had been that good. He even wanted to talk to her about how good it had been, and how he wanted it to happen again, lots and lots of times. But all she wanted to talk about, evidently, was doing her job.

He sighed deeply and took a few steps forward, sorting his words carefully before speaking. He wasn't trying to make light of what she did for a living. On the contrary, he respected her choice of occupation, and her passion for doing it, more than she knew. But what had just happened between the two of them was starting to feel kind of serious. And Daniel always reacted to things that were serious by making light of the situation. Obviously, that wasn't going to work this time. So he'd have to try a different tack.

He stopped walking while he was still out of swinging range and very softly he said, "Here's the thing, Ellie. This isn't what you do for a living. Not yet. And even if this does wind up being your job, you can't let it take over your life. Working isn't a living. Living is a living." He braved a few more steps forward, closing the distance between them. "But I don't think my view of your job is what's really bothering you right now, is it?"

She'd stopped looking at him as soon as he started talking, and the closer he'd moved to her, the more she had turned her head, until now she was practically looking over her shoulder. So Daniel reached out and cupped his palm over her jaw, gently urging her head back to where he could look her in the eye.

"Is it?" he asked again. "'Cause, see, that's why we need to talk."

She looked at him for a long time without speaking, her dark eyes fixed on his. Her lips were parted slightly, and it was all Daniel could do not to dip his head and kiss her. He already had another boner, one that was ready to party hard. Incredible. He never wanted a woman this much so quickly after having her. Usually, once he had sex with a woman, he lost interest in having sex with her again. The first time was always the best, and familiarity bred, if not contempt, then certainly indifference.

With Ellie, though, Daniel suspected the first time had only offered a taste of what was possible between them. Familiarity had bred a craving for more. He wondered how many times he'd have to have sex with her before he started losing interest. Strangely, he was pretty sure he already knew. And the answer both amazed and scared the hell out of him.

"No, *here's* the thing, Daniel," she said softly. "My job is more important to me than anything in the world. Anything. It's what I do. It's what I am. It's what I've always wanted to be. Maybe I'm not in the field for OPUS yet, but I will be. And it will be the most important thing in the world to me. Always. I was fully prepared for this assignment when they gave it to me. I don't need anyone's help to complete it."

"You needed me tonight," he said. And he hoped she realized he was talking about a lot more than the job. Judging by the way her expression changed, she did.

Which was why it felt like someone hit him with a brick when she replied, "No. I didn't."

Daniel ignored the hot nausea that singed his belly at her reply. Where the hell was that coming from? "If

I hadn't come in when I did to warn you Sebastian was on his way—"

"I would have managed just fine," she finished for him. "I don't need you, Daniel," she reiterated. "From now on, I work alone."

And since her work was her life, he interpreted, did that mean she wanted him out of that, too? The way she was looking at him now, he wondered why she'd ever let him in to begin with.

What the hell was going on? he wondered. A few hours ago, the two of them had shared dinner and conversation together the way they had a million times. Now, suddenly, they were at each other's throats. The only thing that had changed in the meantime was that they'd enjoyed an incredible sexual encounter that should have had them reaching for each other again. Instead, there was a divide between them he wasn't sure they'd ever be able to cross, never mind mend.

"Fine," he said through gritted teeth, because, at this point, he had no idea what else to say. "Work alone. See what it gets you."

"It'll get the job done," she snapped. "That's all that matters."

He nodded, clenching his jaw tight, pushing to the edge of his brain his fear that he was losing the best friend he had.

No, worse than that. He was losing Ellie.

CHAPTER SIXTEEN

MARNIE WASN'T SURE how she made it through the rest of her training. Though certainly the fact that Noah had made himself scarce helped. In fact, he made himself so scarce he was invisible, and her training was instead completed by a female instructor, code name Sugarplum. Though had Marnie been the one handing out code names that day, she would have awarded the woman with the moniker Metamucil.

Still, the woman imparted a lot of information and skill training that second week. Enough so that, by the end of it, Marnie felt fully prepared and totally confident in her ability to take on criminal mastermind and international wise guy Adrian Padgett.

Well, okay, she actually only felt that way after consuming an entire bottle of wine in dubious celebration Friday night. At least she hadn't been drinking to forget about Noah. She hadn't done that since Thursday night. Anyway, that was all beside the point. By the time Marnie concluded her training, she *was* better prepared to face Padgett than she'd been on her first encounter with him three weeks earlier. Of course, since she'd been a quivering mass of goo three weeks earlier, that wasn't saying much. Nevertheless, she *was* the best chance OPUS had to bring in Adrian Padgett.

And if that wasn't enough to make the flesh of every American citizen crawl, Marnie didn't know what was.

By the time she reported for duty the Monday morning of her third week in OPUS's thrall—or, rather, employment…she kept getting those two things confused—she pretty much had a handle on how she felt about Noah. Which was a good thing since she had to report to him. She'd had a week to think about what had happened, and she'd sorted through her response fairly well. First, she'd been shocked by what had happened between them. Then she'd found herself denying that there had been any significance to it. Then she'd done some bargaining in her head to ensure it never happened again. Then she'd felt guilty about it. Then she'd gotten angry about it. Then she'd gotten a little depressed about it. Finally, though, she'd just accepted what had happened and tried to—

Wait a minute. Those were the seven stages of grief.

Oh, right. They were perfect for what she felt.

She sighed with frustration as she waited for the elevator in the lobby of a different OPUS facility than the one where she'd completed her training, this one in downtown Cleveland. Though, mind you, *nowhere* on or in the building was there *anything* to indicate a superspy organization was housed here. And she finally admitted to herself that she still didn't know how she felt about Noah or what had happened, even having had a week to think about both. He'd never promised her anything other than a release for the sexual response they had to each other. And God knows he'd delivered that. She'd had a *very* nice, uh, release, at her house that night. Until she realized she wanted a lot more from Noah than a release. On the contrary, she wanted to be connected to him forever.

When an elevator opened, Marnie entered and pushed seven, having memorized the directions Noah gave her, just as a good spy should. It wasn't his fault she felt as lousy as she did. She just wished she knew what to do to stop feeling so lousy. As if she would never be truly happy again. As if her life was meaningless unless Noah was a part of it. As if she wasn't a whole person without him.

She knew it was ridiculous to feel that way. Before he entered her life, she'd been happy, productive, complete. She taught music to children. She volunteered for a number of good causes. She was an asset to society and contributed to other lives. She made a difference in the world, even if it wasn't on a large scale. She had joy. She had balance. She had stability. She had security.

But she didn't have love, she realized now. Not the kind of love that gives life the most meaning. The ceaseless, soul-deep, inalienable love shared by two people who know they're better together than they are alone.

And maybe, Marnie thought as the elevator slowed, that was the problem. She'd fallen in love with Noah Tennant. She didn't know when it had happened, or how, or why. She didn't know what it was in him that touched and spoke to something in her. She only knew that at some point, he had become…important to her. She felt more alive, more human when she was with him. On the few occasions he'd been in her home—especially that last one—her home had felt…better somehow. More comfortable. More…right.

She'd met him under extraordinary circumstances, and he was quite a remarkable man. But what Marnie felt for him was the most basic thing a human being could feel. Love. Pure and simple. Immutable and eternal.

The elevator doors opened on a soft whoosh of air. Okay. So she did have a handle on how she felt about Noah. Now she just had to figure out how to deal with it.

She stepped into the hallway barely seeing it, having no idea what to do about her newly discovered feelings. She would be meeting the man she loved—the man who didn't love her—in a matter of minutes, which didn't give her much time to dissect and analyze her epiphany. She wasn't even sure she was dressed appropriately for an epiphany. Then again, the salesclerk who had sold Marnie the black trouser suit and white blouse—and just when had she started dressing like a spy?—had assured her it was right for every business-related occasion.

But her epiphany wasn't business related. And it wasn't business she was worried about. Which told her exactly how far gone she was. She was less worried about the prospect of meeting Adrian Padgett face-to-face again, a man who frankly terrified her, than she was about seeing Noah. Then again, international criminals were just meaningless little grains of sand when weighed against the immeasurable ocean of true love.

Marnie bit back a groan. Please, for God's sake, someone shoot her, before she turned into a flaming Flavia greeting card.

Expelling another long sigh of frustration, she smoothed a hand over her spy suit and made her feet move forward. Fifth door on the right, she reminded herself.

With a brass nameplate affixed to it that read "Charles McAlistar, V.P. Public Relations." That would be the fabricated Charles McAlistar, pretend V.P. of nonexistent public relations for the phony corporation Universal Ventures, Inc., which was the front for the OPUS Cleveland field office. Of course, as far as Marnie was concerned, they could have called the dummy corporation Spies 'RNT Us and been every bit as convincing. But, hey, that was just her. She stole another moment to collect herself before entering, then turned the knob and walked inside.

A woman Marnie's age with dark brown hair and trendy, red-framed glasses smiled at her. "Can I help you?" she asked.

"I have an appointment with Mr. McAlistar," she recited from the script she'd been given. "Though I'm a bit early. I'm Denise Borden. Of Global Megatrends, Inc." She felt like adding, *We're a subsidiary of ACME, Inc., which manufactures products that are popular with coyotes.* Honestly. OPUS could really use some new copywriters.

"Mr. McAlistar is expecting you," Suzi Secretary said kindly, just as Marnie had known she would, since she was part of the script, too. And she was excellent at playing the mild-mannered role. Marnie never would have guessed Suzi was packing a bazooka under that desk, just in case someone—someone like, oh, say, Marnie—did stray from the script. "Go right in."

"Thank you," Marnie replied dutifully. And scriptfully. No way was she going to test that bazooka thing.

Although the script didn't call for it, she braved a quick, light rap of her knuckles on the door to Noah's office before entering, in case he needed a moment to prepare for their encounter, the way she did. But when she entered, she saw him hunched over his desk, writing something furiously on a pad of paper, so she concluded he hadn't even heard her come in. So much for his needing a moment.

It was the first time she'd seen him since he left her house in the middle of the night, the two of them uttering clipped goodbyes like strangers in a grocery-store line. She hadn't slept a wink afterward, and in the morning had stumbled bleary-eyed into the kitchen for coffee and opened the refrigerator to retrieve the half-and-half. But she hadn't been able to see it for the forest of foam cartons left over from dinner the night before. One by one, she'd extracted the containers, dumping them into a black plastic garbage bag, which she'd double-knotted and carried out to the curb.

And she tried not to think about how significant it was that the only mementos she had from her one true love were rotting in a landfill on the north side of town.

She closed the door behind herself with a soft click, a sound that finally made Noah look up. For a scant second, she thought she saw something in his eyes that engendered some small hope inside her that they might be able to—

But then it was gone, so quickly she knew she must have imagined it.

"Right on time," he said as she strode forward and folded herself into the chair in front of his desk. "Good to see you were listening during your training."

"Yeah, I was at the top of my class in spy school," she replied. "Valedictorian *and* salutatorian. And also homecoming queen. And calendar girl. And editor of the yearbook. Not to mention my own date to the prom."

And if she didn't shut up she was going to embarrass herself. Even more than she already had, she meant.

"Look, Noah," she hurried on. "I don't want to suggest that the last two weeks have been a waste of time, but how can you think I'll be effective when Adrian Padgett hasn't been spotted since that night he came to my house? How can you even be sure he's still around?"

It was a question that had plagued her for two weeks. Why had Adrian Padgett come to her house that one night, promised to come back and then never returned?

"He's still around," Noah said with utter confidence. "We've had people working on finding him since he showed up at your house, and one of them, a man named Joel Faraday, has identified an area where Sorcerer is most likely to be hiding out. We'll be sending you to D.C. first, so he can fill you in on the details, and then you'll be on your way to that area."

"Then how can you be sure Padgett still thinks I'm Lila?" she asked. "If he still thinks I'm her, and he wants to be with her, then why hasn't he come looking for me?"

Noah leaned back in his chair, looking totally relaxed, completely casual, utterly normal. Damn him. "There could be several reasons for that, actually. Maybe he's still not sure where your…or, rather, Lila's…allegiances lie, and he's worried you might try to bring him in again. Or he might think you reported his appearance to OPUS that night he came to your house, and now you're being watched too closely by other agents who might try to bring him in."

Marnie leaned back in her chair, too, hoping *she* looked totally relaxed, completely casual, utterly normal. And feeling none of those things. Damn her. "You don't sound like you think either of those possibilities is true," she said.

He grinned, and she tried to find some vague hint of what he might be feeling for her in the gesture. But there was nothing. He only looked like a man at work, describing a working situation with a co-worker. Which, she supposed, was all the hint she needed.

"That's because I don't think either of those possibilities is true," he told her.

"Then what do you think?"

"If I know Sorcerer," he said, "I'm betting it's because he wants *you* to come to *him*."

Oh, Marnie really didn't like the sound of that. "How am I supposed to go to him when I don't know where he is?"

"You're Lila Moreau, ace spy. You're supposed to be able to figure out where he is."

"No, I'm Marnie Lundy, B-list piano teacher in way over my head," she corrected him. "How the hell am I supposed to locate him?"

"You're not," Noah said. "It's only supposed to look like you're the one who found him. That's actually OPUS's responsibility. And, as I said, we're reasonably certain we've identified the area where you can find him."

Marnie's stomach knotted painfully. They knew where he was. And they were going to send her in to draw him out. "How did you find him?" she asked, hoping that the fear clawing at the back of her throat wasn't audible in her voice.

"Philosopher's manuscript was very helpful. While he was still working for OPUS, he kept meticulous notes about Sorcerer's comings and goings after he went over to the dark side. Joel Faraday looked over the information and was able to make some connections and identify patterns in Sorcerer's behavior. Coupled with some of the e-mails that we've intercepted between Sorcerer and other people he contacted online over the past year, we were able to narrow our search to a pretty specific area. Within that area, we've been able to identify a dozen or so establishments that would attract him. We figure if you start frequenting those, sooner or later, you'll find him."

Oh, God. It was actually going to happen, Marnie thought, panic pooling coldly in the pit of her stomach. She was really going to carry out an assignment. Put herself in the path of a dangerous man, on purpose, who had terrified her on two previous occasions. Her heart hammered in her chest, heat seeped through her body and she began to feel a little dizzy. She gripped the arms of her chair tightly and inhaled a deep breath, forcing down the fear and telling herself it would be okay.

It *would* be okay. She could do this. She would do this. Because it was the only way she could go back to living her life the way she'd lived it before. Before Adrian Padgett and Philosopher and Noah Tennant and OPUS had entered it.

She should be happy about that. She *was* happy about that. That was what she wanted, right? That was why she'd offered to help. So she could get her life back to normal. What was strange was that what had been normal in her life before didn't seem normal anymore. What seemed normal now was the life she'd been living for the past three weeks—which was nothing like the life she'd led before.

"You okay, Marnie?"

Noah's voice seemed to be coming from a million miles away, but she nodded her head in reply. "Yeah. I'm okay. I think it's just finally hitting me, what I have to do."

He hesitated a moment, his blue eyes fixed on her face. "You don't have to do anything you don't want to," he told her.

Marnie hesitated, too, before replying, unable to look away. "You said I'm your best chance."

"You are," he agreed.

"Then you need me."

"Yeah."

Though somehow, it suddenly seemed as if they were talking about something other than the assignment.

"I can do this, Noah."

"I know you can, Marnie. I'm just not sure—"

"What?"

He blew out an exasperated sound. "Nothing. It's not up to me."

That was what he thought. It was entirely up to him. Maybe not about whether or not Marnie should agree to take on the assignment. But it was definitely up to him what happened when she returned.

If she returned.

She closed her eyes and forced herself not to think about that. She would return. Sorcerer wasn't a killer. Then again, there were things he could do to her that might make her wish she was dead….

She opened her eyes again and met Noah's gaze levelly. "When do I leave?"

"We'll be fine-tuning the details tomorrow," he said. "Be ready to be on a plane to D.C. in thirty-six hours."

Thirty-six hours, she echoed to herself. She had a day and a half to prepare herself for travel to an unknown final destination and complete a job she'd never done before among strangers she wasn't even sure she could trust. And she'd be doing it without Noah.

"Where will I be going to look for Padgett?" she asked softly.

He studied her silently for a moment, his face completely lacking expression, and she would have given anything to know what he was thinking just then. But all he told her was, "You'll find out in D.C."

NOAH STUDIED Marnie on the other side of the desk, trying to gauge her emotions by the way she looked at him. But he could detect nothing of what she was feeling or thinking in that moment. He told himself that was good. That meant she'd been paying attention in spy school. She was probably at least panicky after everything he'd just told her—and was quite possibly terrified—but she didn't look anything other than mildly interested in what he'd just said.

Of course, it wasn't only her reaction to what he'd just said that he was really hoping to gauge. But he could detect nothing of what she might be feeling for him at the moment, either.

He told himself that was good, too, that he didn't want her to feel anything for him other than what she would feel for anyone with whom she happened to work. Going to her house had been a huge mistake. Their sexual liaison never should have happened. He should have known better. He was, in essence, her boss, at least temporarily. He should have realized anything else that might happen between them would be temporary, too. He should have controlled himself better. Should have stayed in charge. Should have played by the rules.

Yada. Yada. Yada.

It was the same pile of platitudes he'd been shoveling all week. And it still sounded like a heaping, reeking pile of—

Now Marnie was about to actually embark on the assignment for which they'd spent two weeks preparing her. An assignment that would have commanded at least six months of training for any other agent. And even then, OPUS would have been damned wary, putting a newbie on such a dangerous quest. Sorcerer had eluded their best people for years. Even Lila hadn't been able to bring him in. He was responsible for at least one death. He was ruthless. He was unpredictable. He was amoral. He didn't care about anyone but himself. And he would do anything—anything—to make sure he wasn't caught.

Sorcerer could crush Marnie. Either literally or figuratively. He could crush her. Noah knew that. And the knowledge was almost more than he could bear.

"I should go," she said, bringing him back to the matter at hand.

Already? he wanted to reply. He suddenly found himself making plans for the next thirty-six hours that had nothing to do with preparing Marnie for her assignment and everything to do with trying to talk her out of it, most of which, ironically—or something—was in no way verbal.

"I mean, if you don't need me for anything else," she added.

But he did need her. Just not in any capacity sanctioned by OPUS. And for something that had nothing to do with her assignment. Suddenly, Noah felt his own panic starting to rise. He hadn't let himself think about Marnie this week, except in terms of how that night at her house never should have happened. Because that was easy to think about, so obvious a mistake was it. Seeing her now, looking so beautiful, and remembering so many of their encounters before they'd had sex, he started thinking about other things, too. About her bravery that first night standing up to Sorcerer and to him. About her strength in remaining calm and steady in light of so many assaults on her secure life. About how she could joke about even the most serious things. About how she liked Game Boy, too. About the profoundly erotic way she made love. About how he'd felt…different since meeting her. Better. More human. Or something.

It was all too much to think about now. It might be too much to think about for a long time. But it occurred to Noah then that maybe he should think about it. Because maybe all that was way more important than anything else he had to think about right now.

"I'll get going," she said, smudging Noah's otherwise perfect mental paint job into a corner. "I have a lot to do before I leave, not the least of which is pack." She held up a hand when he opened his mouth, adding, "I know. Only take what I'll absolutely need. I learned that in one of my training sessions. Top of my class, remember?"

Actually, Noah had wanted to ask her if she had room in her suitcase for him. Good thing she'd interrupted.

"And I need to call my cat-sitter."

He could feed her cats.

"And stop the mail and paper."

He could collect her mail and paper. And drive by the house occasionally to make sure nothing was amiss. And roll her trash can down to the curb on garbage day. And mow her lawn when the grass got too long. And break into her house from time to time to make sure nothing was wrong…and perhaps go through her underwear drawer. Just to make sure nothing was missing.

"And I'll have to put my students and Lauderdale's on notice that I'll be out of town indefinitely. Looks like my little family situation out of town just got really big."

Indefinitely, Noah echoed to himself. Not a word he liked to hear used in a situation like this. Or in any terms that referred to Marnie's not being around. Indefinitely sounded way too definite. In fact, it sounded like forever. And although that, too, was a word he hadn't thought he'd ever want to associate with Marnie—or any woman—*forever* suddenly took on an entirely new meaning. An entirely new intention. An entirely new feeling.

Good God, what had gotten into him? He was a senior administrator for a government organization whose business was to protect the country from evildoers. Marnie Lundy had come to work for OPUS—and Noah—voluntarily. She'd been trained to do the job, and she'd been briefed on the potential dangers and risks. She was smart. She was brave. She was resourceful. She was ready.

So why wasn't Noah?

"So if there's nothing else?" she asked as she stood.

Oh, yeah, there was something else, Noah thought. There was too damned much else. So much that he couldn't even get a handle on one thing to make sense of it.

She must have taken his silence as assent, because she threw him one last glance—an expression on her face he couldn't begin to identify—and made her way to the door.

"Marnie," he said as she pulled it open.

She turned around and looked at him in silent question.

She was so beautiful. So determined. In that moment, Noah remembered the way she had looked and acted on every occasion he had seen her. No matter what was going on, no matter what she'd been dealing with, no matter how high her emotions had been running, no matter how much danger she had been in, she had always been beautiful. And always brave. And always smart.

She was a remarkable woman. And he might never see her again.

"I almost forgot," he said. "Once you're all official, OPUS gives you a new name. And a code name. Both of yours have come through. You'll receive your new ID and phony credentials once you're in D.C. After that, you'll be required to identify yourself by your bogus name in undercover scenarios and by your code name in professional circles."

She smiled at that. And, impossibly, looked even more beautiful, even more determined. "Really? I get to have a new identity? And a code name?"

Noah nodded and tried not to be so enamored.

"Well don't keep me in suspense," she said. "What are they?"

"Your new identity will be Amanda Bellamy."

She tilted her head to the side, as if she were giving that

some thought. Finally, she nodded slowly. "I can be an Amanda. So what's my code name?"

He grinned. "Chopin."

She grinned back. "Code name, Chopin. Now that I like very much."

Noah was glad to hear it, since he was the one who had suggested it. He liked it, too. He liked the woman wearing it even better. In fact...

"So no more Marnie Lundy," he continued before the thought—or whatever it was—could form. Though the idea of there being no more Marnie Lundy didn't exactly sit well with him, either. "Undercover, you'll be Amanda. With OPUS, you'll be Chopin."

"Thanks, Noah," she said. "I mean, thanks, Sinatra."

"You're welcome. Chopin."

She stepped through the door and closed it behind herself with a soft click. And just like that, she was gone.

No more Marnie Lundy, Noah repeated to himself as he stared at the closed door. But then, he suspected she hadn't been Marnie Lundy for a while now. Certainly not since her run-in with him. That had to have changed virtually everything for her, shaken her world from top to bottom and inside out. He'd been the one who told her the truth about her parents. He'd been the one to inform her of her sister's existence. He'd been responsible for her entrée into a world of espionage and danger. And it was he who had put her in the path of Sorcerer again.

It didn't matter that Marnie was smart and brave and resourceful and ready. It didn't matter that she had been trained in self-defense and with weaponry. It didn't matter that she had backup for her assignment. If anything happened to her—anything—it would be on Noah's shoulders. And if anything happened to her—anything—he would never forgive himself.

It was then that Noah realized he wasn't himself either, anymore, and hadn't been for some time. Not since meeting Marnie. She had changed virtually everything for him, too, had shaken *his* world from top to bottom and inside out. He felt things for her he'd never felt for anyone else. He worried about her the way he'd never worried for anyone else. He feared for her loss like he had never feared the loss of anything before. And it was all too new, too strange, too confusing for him to understand any of it.

Noah, too, had changed over the past few weeks. But unlike Marnie, he didn't have a new code name to mark the transition. No, he only had a heart full of feelings and fears he'd never had before. And he had no idea what to do with any of them.

As ALWAYS, by the time Noah left to go home, the building was virtually deserted save the security staff and cleaning crews. While Ellie was completing her training assignment, he had a temporary secretary, and like most temps—even OPUS temps—she didn't hang around any longer than she had to. Not that even Ellie worked as late as Noah did. But over the past couple of weeks, with Ellie's fill-in leaving so much earlier than Ellie did herself, it had been hammered home daily just how much time he spent at work.

Too much time, he'd begun to think. Then he'd remind himself he had the kind of job that demanded a lot of overtime. Not to mention the rest of his co-workers had personal, social and family obligations. Noah had…

He sighed as he pushed through the front door. Work. That was what he had. And more work. And when he wasn't working, there was always work. And there were working obligations. His life was full, what with work and all. Who needed a personal, social or family life when you had work? Not Noah Tennant. That was for damned sure.

He made his way across the deserted parking lot to the big, black BMW which, five months ago, he'd started parking in the farthermost corner of the lot instead of his assigned space. The lot was well lit at its center, but grew darker at the far reaches. Too, in this corner, bushes grew thick and tall and fat. Great cover for anyone who might need it. As he did every night, Noah listened for sounds that might alert him to trouble as he approached his car. And as he had every night for the past five months, he listened for other sounds, too.

Tonight, finally, he heard what he'd been waiting for.

Instead of thumbing the key fob once to unlock the driver's-side door, Noah thumbed it twice, to unlock them all. And although he couldn't see his companion through the denseness of the bushes, he knew he wasn't alone. He never faltered in his stride as he approached his car, and not once did he offer any indication to anyone who might be watching that tonight was any different from any other.

He opened the driver's-side door at the exact same moment someone else opened one in the back, then he folded himself inside. He adjusted the rearview mirror to reflect the backseat, where he saw a lone silhouette against what little light was outside. And quietly, he said, "Hello, She-Wolf. 'Bout damned time you showed up."

CHAPTER SEVENTEEN

TWO WEEKS AFTER embarking upon her field assignment, Ellie Chandler sat down at her kitchen table to write the first of her reports for Noah, describing her progress to date. Then she decided it might be better if she fixed herself a drink first. In fact, she might need the whole bottle for this. So she padded barefoot to her wet bar—which was actually the cabinet above the kitchen sink where she stowed a single bottle of Johnnie Walker Black for occasions such as these—snagged the Scotch and a juice glass, and poured herself one neat.

Some kick-ass superspy she was turning out to be, she thought as she capped the bottle again and carried it and the drink back to her seat. Mata Hari and Emma Peel had to be shaking their heads in disappointment. Hell, even Julia Child had been better at espionage—and also poaching a chicken—than Ellie was. So here she sat in her apartment—early enough on a Monday night that she should have been out carousing with friends—all alone, dressed in baggy blue-and-white-striped pajama bottoms and a Teen Titans T-shirt, trying to put a positive spin on ways to say "I'm a menace to society."

Because Ellie finally had to admit—to herself and to OPUS—that when it came to being a spy, she sucked. Bad.

The only success she'd seen in completing her assignment had come about because of Daniel Beck. Since the night she'd told him to stay out of her life, she'd learned nothing new on her own, had identified no further contacts, had forged no creative theories about what might be going on at ChemiTech. Nor had she been able to narrow the list of suspects—except for being certain Daniel wasn't one, but she'd known that from the start. And she'd made no connections with the information she did have.

The notes from Baird's desk had been interesting, but not incriminating. The files they'd downloaded from Truman's home computer *looked* incriminating, but unless she could find something to tie them to everything else, she didn't know what to do with them. The files she'd plundered early on at ChemiTech contained a lot of information, much of it intriguing, but without the big picture, there was no way to know for sure how it all fit together. Or even *if* it all fit together. And she had no idea where the big picture lay. She only had lots of pieces, few of which connected to anything cohesive.

Ellie was stumped. She'd done everything she knew to do, had tried every trick up her kick-ass spy sleeve. But the trail OPUS had picked up, and which she'd tried to follow, had hit a brick wall. She was certain there was something on the other side of it. If she could only find the secret passage that would allow her entry.

She was lifting her drink to her lips for another sip when she heard the sound of Daniel approaching his apartment. She'd learned a long time ago to recognize his leisurely tread in the hallway, the way he jingled his keys as he searched one-handed for the right one, the whisper of paper or plastic, depending on what deli or grocery he'd hit on his way home. On the weekends, a woman's voice or laughter often accompanied his, but on weeknights, like now, he was alone. Though, come to think of it, Ellie hadn't heard him come home with a woman this past weekend. In fact, she'd heard the television going in his place on Friday and Saturday night both. Unusual for him to have a dry spell that way. Even if he didn't bring a woman home with him, he usually had plenty of invitations to go to a woman's place instead.

She'd only seen him a handful of times since the night they'd spontaneously combusted in Sebastian Baird's office. And each time had been worse than the one before it. They exchanged stilted greetings, maintained a safe distance from each other, studied each other in silence for a moment, then manufactured some reason for why they had to go. And with every new encounter, Ellie felt the gap between them widen.

She still wasn't sure what had happened that night. Other than that she'd screwed up bad. She winced when she realized her phrasing. Not just because of the pun, but because what had happened with Daniel had been a lot more than screwing and in no way bad. At least, for her. Judging by the way Sebastian Baird had reacted, though, it hadn't been any more than another night at work for Daniel.

Ellie hated it that she was now like every other woman he knew. Even if their relationship before that night hadn't been exactly what she wanted with him, she'd at least known she was special in some way to him. She hadn't been one in a string of conquests, the way the rest of the women in his life were. Now, she was. And like the other women, now that he'd had her, he would quickly lose interest.

As incredible as that night had been, Ellie wished it had never happened. Yes, she'd always wanted a sexual relationship with Daniel. But that was just it. She wanted a relationship. And she'd ruined any chance of that by having the sex first.

She waited for the sound of his front door opening and closing, but instead heard a knock at her own. Her first instinct was to ignore it and hope he'd think she wasn't home. But she knew better. Because he knew better. Over the past year, they'd become so familiar with each other's habits and behaviors, so familiar with each other, that there were times when Ellie thought they could read each other's minds. She was going to miss that. A lot.

She scooped up her drink to consume a fortifying sip on the way to answer the door. Then she inhaled a deep breath, ignored the way her skin suddenly seemed to be hot all over—gotta love that Johnnie Black—and turned the knob. Daniel was dressed in his usual work attire of baggy cargo pants and even baggier T-shirt, a faded blue jean jacket hanging open over both. He was carrying two paper bags from Panda China and wearing a very serious expression.

"We need to talk," he said by way of a greeting.

Ellie pressed her forearm against the doorjamb and held the doorknob firm with her free hand. "About what?"

"About your spy mission."

"Assignment," she corrected him. "We don't call them missions."

He uttered an impatient sound. "Well, whatever the hell it is, we need to talk about it."

She tightened her grip on the door, mostly because she wanted so badly to invite him inside and say or do whatever she had to to get them back where they were before everything fell apart. God, she'd missed him. Her entire life had felt lopsided not seeing him. She honestly hadn't realized how much she had come to take for granted the dinners and conversations they'd shared. She hadn't realized how much enjoyment of her life had involved just spending time with Daniel. Not seeing him had made her feel fractured somehow. Incomplete. Awkward.

She wasn't herself without Daniel. She wanted everything to go back to the way it had been before they had sex. Even if it meant she spent the rest of her life longing for more with him than she would ever have. Because now she would still be longing for him. And now she would know exactly what she was missing.

"I can't imagine why we need to talk about that," she said. "You're not a part of the assignment. You never should have been."

A muscled twitched in his jaw, and his mouth flattened into a tight line. "Yeah, see, that's what we need to talk about."

Ellie said nothing. Mostly because she had no idea what to say. No idea what to do. No idea what to feel. So she decided to, for once in her life, err on the side of, if not caution, with hope. She pushed the door open wide and said halfheartedly, "All right. Come on in."

He held up a paper bag as he entered. "I brought dim sum."

She managed a lukewarm smile. "Thanks. I haven't had dinner."

He nodded toward the drink in her hand as he headed for the kitchen. "Looks like you're drinking your dinner. Haven't seen you do that for a while."

She sighed without much enthusiasm. "Yeah, well, my life hasn't been this messed up for a while."

He stopped in his tracks, turned to look at her, eyeing her warily.

"With the job, I mean," she hastily clarified. No need to scare the guy by making him think she was talking about her love life. Even if she was talking about her love life.

But instead of looking relieved by her reassurance, Daniel's expression hardened. "Yeah, the job," he said. "God forbid you should ever think about anything besides that."

The icy words caught her off guard, though she knew now she probably shouldn't be surprised by them. "Daniel, I'm sorry," she said. "I didn't mean to hurt your feelings when I told you I didn't need you for the job. But I *didn't* need you," she reiterated. "And it *wasn't* your responsibility. You weren't even supposed to know what was going on. Getting involved could have put you in danger. Not to mention that the whole point to the assignment was to test my skills working solo."

He studied her for a long time in silence, then seemed to relax a little. He nodded, then covered the rest of the distance between him and the kitchen, setting the bags on the counter. "And how's that going for you?" he asked as he began to unpack them. "The working solo, I mean."

Ellie closed the door and bolted it, then joined him in the tiny kitchen. But she kept her distance, leaning back against the refrigerator, instead of moving to help him with the food. She sighed again. There was no reason to lie to him. Once she submitted her report to Noah, they'd probably be pulling her from ChemiTech, anyway, and sending in a more experienced agent who knew how the hell to do the job.

"It's not going anywhere," she said.

He did glance up at that, but instead of looking triumphant and crying, "I knew you'd be lost without me!"—which was probably what she would have done had the tables been turned—he looked sympathetic.

"I suck as a spy, Daniel," she continued morosely. And strangely, it felt kind of good to finally admit it. "Even though being an agent is the only thing I've wanted to do since I was a kid, even though I can't imagine working for any other organization, even though I have no idea what the hell I'm going to do with my life now…"

She shrugged and battled the tears she felt threatening. Kick-ass spies didn't cry, she reminded herself. Of course, dumbass spies probably cried a lot, so what was the big deal? In spite of that, she pulled herself up and repeated, "I suck. There's no way they're going to let me be an agent. If I want to keep working for OPUS—and I damned well do—then it's going to have to be as a secretary."

Daniel pulled the last of the containers out of the bag, opened her cabinet where she kept plates and glasses, and began to withdraw two of each. Without looking at her, he said, "Okay, Ellie, here's the thing. I think I found proof that Truman is your guy."

Her reaction would have been the same if he had just walked over to slap her across the face. "What?"

Still focusing on his task instead of her, he repeated, "Truman is the person who's been feeding government secrets to the bad guys. And I have proof."

Ellie set her drink on the counter, thinking she'd had enough Scotch for one night if she was hearing Daniel tell her he'd just done her job for her. "That's impossible," she said. "I checked everything I could get access to, and none of it could incriminate him. Hell, half of it was stuff OPUS already knows."

Daniel closed the cabinet and turned to look at her, but his gaze ricocheted off of hers the moment it made contact. "But, see, I sorta found some new information at Chemi-Tech," he said, crossing his arms over his chest in a way that looked at once defensive and apologetic.

She eyed him narrowly. "That's impossible," she said. "There was no new information at ChemiTech."

He lifted a hand to the back of his neck, clearly a nervous gesture. "Actually, there was," he said.

She narrowed her eyes at him suspiciously. "I looked everywhere I could for information, Daniel," Ellie told him, "and there was none to be had. How did you come by this info? Divine intervention?"

Now he did meet her gaze. "No, I went by my gut."

"Your gut," she echoed flatly.

He nodded. "For starters, yeah."

"And then what? You had an Alka-Seltzer to soothe your gut and found a secret message in the foil wrapping?"

He dropped his hand back to his side, shoved it into his pocket, removed it again. Then he crossed his arms in that defensive way once more. "No, I used my brain."

She closed her eyes, counted slowly to ten, then opened them again. Nope, she wasn't hallucinating. And her brain wasn't fuzzy enough to be affected by the Scotch. Daniel was still standing in her kitchen. And he was still looking at her like he knew what he was talking about.

"Maybe I better start at the beginning," he said.

"Maybe you should."

But instead of doing that, Daniel opened the fridge and withdrew a beer, uncapping it with a quick, wet hiss. He lifted it to his mouth to drain half of it without stopping, then lowered it again, pressing the back of his hand to his mouth. "I just couldn't let Truman off the hook," he finally said. "Especially after what we found at his place that night. I knew it was him. Why would a guy transfer from Marketing to Research and Development anyway? Aside from the prestige, I mean."

Yeah, those R & D guys were total glamorama, Ellie thought drily. A couple of them even bought their polyester pants new and sprang for prescription acne meds. And what girl wouldn't want to go out with a guy who could split atoms in his mom's basement?

"Anyway, I've just always had a bad feeling about him," Daniel continued. "So I started poking around in his office when he wasn't around to see what turned up."

Ellie shook her head. "You didn't."

He glared at her. "I just said I did, didn't I? Look, just listen, Ellie, all right? Maybe you'll learn something."

She gaped at him. "Oh, don't you dare start—"

"So while I was looking around in his office," Daniel interjected, "I found some locked files on his computer."

Ellie closed her eyes.

"And I hacked into them."

Oh, damn.

"And the stuff I found…"

"What?" she asked, opening her eyes again. "It couldn't be anything incriminating, because I checked the computers of everyone at ChemiTech who's had contact with Sebastian Baird in the last two years. Including Truman. *I* hacked into his files, too," she said. "And I didn't find anything anywhere that was in any way helpful."

Daniel set his jaw tight. "Then you weren't looking in the right places," he told her. "This stuff was buried deep in hidden files where he'd locked them up tight. I had to go in about ten times to find them. The only reason I did is because I know enough about the guy to know how he operates and what kind of security precautions he takes. You may have looked for the files, Ellie, but *I'm* the one who found them. Now do you want to know what was in them, or not?"

In spite of the way he'd gone about it, she was eager to know what he'd found. And not to put too fine a point on the whole sucky-spy thing, but she found herself wishing she'd been half as effective doing her job as Daniel had been doing her job. But if he'd found something that was indeed incriminating, how was she supposed to include it in her report? It wasn't a problem that he'd found helpful information in a way that was, at best, unethical and at worst, illegal. Since 9/11, OPUS had been moved under the jurisdiction of the Department of Homeland Security and had been awarded certain "privileges" that other government agencies didn't have. Put simply, they operated by their own rules. And most of those rules changed daily.

So the problem wasn't that they wouldn't be able to use any information Daniel might have discovered. The problem lay in the fact that it was a civilian who had done the discovering. OPUS wasn't too crazy about civilians. Even useful ones. Because civilians didn't swear an oath of fealty the way operatives and agents did. Worse, civilians tended to have families and responsibilities and obligations outside the organization, all of which might potentially be endangered. And not necessarily by the enemies of OPUS. Sometimes that danger came from OPUS itself. By virtue of having learned what he had, Daniel had thrown himself not just into her employer's spotlight, but into their headlights, too.

"Yes," she finally said. "I want to know what you found."

He reached into his jacket pocket and withdrew a memory stick. "It's all on here," he told her. "Not that I can make heads or tails of a lot of it, but I figure that's your people's jobs, right? I do understand enough of it to know this guy is doing things he shouldn't be, and he's sending information he shouldn't be sending to places he shouldn't be sending it." As Ellie closed her fingers around the memory stick, he added, "Obviously I have my uses."

He put a subtle emphasis on that last word, just enough to make Ellie take notice of it. For a second, she was confused, but when she looked at his face, she understood. "You think I used you for this assignment?" she asked incredulously.

"Well, what else would you call it?" he demanded.

"I didn't use you!" she denied. "You blackmailed me into letting you help! I didn't want you involved at all!"

"No shit!" he exclaimed. "You made it more than clear that you didn't want me around! But you oughta be damned grateful I was!"

She blew out an exasperated sound and was about to lash out at him again, when something in his expression halted her. It hit her then, like a ton of illicit memory sticks, that maybe, just maybe, Daniel wasn't mad at her because she'd dismissed him from the job. Maybe, just maybe, he was mad at her because he thought she'd dismissed him from so much more.

She chose her next words carefully. "I am grateful you're around, Daniel. I've been grateful for that since the day you moved in next door. In more ways than you know."

He seemed to go slack at her words. All the tension, all the anger, all the resentment seemed to ease right out of him. His expression opened, his body relaxed. And his voice softened when he said, "Well, you sure as hell haven't made me feel like it lately."

She hesitated only a moment before saying, "And you've never made me feel like it." There was no accusation in her voice when she said it. No resentment. No anger. It was just a simple statement of fact.

His expression turned confused. "What are you talking about? I've always been grateful for you."

"Not the way you're grateful for other women," she said.

His confusion seemed to compound at that. "I'm not grateful for other women. They're a dime a dozen. They're not like you. You're…"

"What?" she asked, a spark of hope kindling to life inside her.

"Special," he said cautiously.

She shook her head. "No, I'm not. I'm just like every other woman you know."

"How do you figure that?"

"Because I... Because we..."

"What?" he asked, the word coming out urgent and insistent.

"Because of that night in Baird's office," she finally said. "When you and I... When we..."

But she halted without finishing again, because she still didn't know how to identify what had happened that night. Actually, that wasn't true. She knew exactly what it had been for her. She just didn't know if it had been the same thing for Daniel.

"When we made love?" he finished for her.

Oh. Okay. So it had been the same thing for him. Now the hope flamed higher, melting the ice that had coated her belly since his arrival at her front door. In spite of that, she still sounded doubtful when she asked, "Is that what it was? Making love?"

"Don't you think so?"

Very slowly, she nodded. "But I didn't think you did."

He took a step toward her, then seemed to reconsider his approach and halted. "What else could it have been?"

Ellie took a step toward him, too. "The same thing it always is with you and women. Sex."

Daniel completed another step. Stopped. "What happened with you was a lot better than anything that's happened with anyone else."

Ellie strode forward one more time, something that brought their bodies very close to touching. "It was different for me, too," she said. "A lot different."

"A lot better?" he asked, hope tinting his words, too.

She nodded. "Yeah. A lot, lot, lot better."

He lifted a hand to her face, opening his palm over her jaw. Ellie tilted her head to the side to complete the fit, then covered his hand with hers. The angry heat inside her turned to a mellow warmth, then began to spread outward, warming parts of her that hadn't been warm for a while. Not since that night in Sebastian Baird's office. Not since Daniel had stopped being a part of her life.

"So what are we going to do about it?" he asked softly. He dipped his head to hers and brushed a kiss over her temple, moving his other hand to her hair. "Besides make sure it happens again, I mean."

What a loaded question, Ellie thought as she opened her hand on his chest, over his heart. Really, it could mean two different things. What were they going to do about the new direction their relationship seemed to be taking, and what were they going to do about Daniel's discoveries for OPUS? The first, she figured, would be hard to answer and easy to carry out. The second would be just the opposite. Naturally, she would hide Daniel's involvement in her assignment, but would still be honest about her own shortcomings. Getting OPUS to go along with the whole "anonymous source" thing, though, would be a feat of herculean proportions.

She pushed herself up on tiptoe and kissed him, then wove the fingers of both hands through his and dropped them to their sides. "We're going to save the you-and-me part of that equation for later," she said with a smile. "We have to finish our OPUS work first."

He looked as if he was about to object, then relented.

"Okay. I guess you're right. The OPUS thing has a specific time line and definite end in sight. And the you-and-me thing has all the time in the world and is in no way finite."

Oh, she did like the sound of that.

He kissed her again…twice…three times…four…then stepped back with obvious reluctance and returned to unpacking their dinner. "So what *are* we going to do about OPUS?" he asked.

As Ellie helped him unpack everything, she said, "It'll probably take me all night, but I need to look at the information you collected and analyze it. Try to figure out how it ties in with what OPUS already knows and what we found in Truman's computer. And I'll have to include all of it in the report I'm sending to Noah in the morning. But I won't mention you by name," she was quick to add. "I'll identify you as an anonymous source. I just hope they'll leave it at that."

"You can mention my name, Ellie, I don't mind. In fact—"

"I mind," she interrupted him. "Daniel, it could put you in danger if anyone found out you were involved. And I couldn't live with myself if anything happened to you because of me. I couldn't live with myself if anything happened to you period."

He smiled at that. "Whatever you say. You're the kick-ass spy."

She wished. But there was no reason to go into that with Daniel right now. She had too many other things to think about.

"I'll need you here with me tonight," she said. "Do you mind?"

"To clarify stuff you find in the files?" he asked.

"Well, that, too," she told him. "But mostly I just need you around tonight because I, you know, need you around tonight."

"Oh, well, in that case…"

"Thanks for bringing dinner," she added as she unpacked the last of the cartons. "Spy work makes for a ferocious appetite."

"Well, we have dim sum for starters," he told her. Then he smiled. "And maybe, if you get this report finished before dawn, we might have time for a nice dessert, too…"

ELLIE HAD KNOWN she was in it hip deep before she even received Noah's summons to his office—though she had expected that summons to take a little longer than the six hours that had passed since she turned in her report. But it wasn't until she opened the door and entered that she realized she was actually in it up to her eyeballs. Because where she'd expected the hot seat to be empty in anticipation of her own ass-chewing, instead it held Daniel Beck. And his ass didn't look any too comfortable, either.

"Daniel," she said softly, unable to stop the word before it leaped out of her mouth.

"I asked him to sit in on this meeting, too," Noah said. "Because what I have to say involves both of you. And will affect both of you."

He was using his octave-lower-than-usual, man-are-you-in-it-now voice, which didn't exactly come as a surprise. Ellie had still hoped she wouldn't hear it today. Or ever. Even more troubling than that, though, was how Noah had just implied Daniel would suffer from the consequences of her having botched the job as much as she would herself. Although she'd kept him anonymous in her report, she'd pretty much known it was a lost cause. OPUS already knew the two of them were friends. And even if OPUS hadn't known that, they would have figured it all out. They always did. Eventually.

"Of course we knew it was Beck who helped you," Noah said, as if reading her mind. "Who else would it be?" He sighed heavily. "I hate to break this to you, Ellie, but when it comes to being a field agent, you really suck."

She closed her eyes. As if she needed him to tell her that. "I'll clean out my desk immediately," she said.

"Why would you do that?" he asked.

She opened her eyes again. "Because I suck as a spy." Duh.

"I said you suck as a field agent," he corrected her. "The work you did on your report, on the other hand, was nothing short of amazing."

"Wh-what?"

He gestured toward his desk, which was littered by papers, all fanned out for maximum consideration. He lifted his chin toward Daniel. "Beck tells me you put this together last night."

She nodded. "Yeah. The report was due this morning."

Noah eyed her thoughtfully. "You assessed all this information in one evening, saw all these patterns, made all these connections, drew all these conclusions… And then you wrote it up in a clear, concise, articulate report that reads like a dream? You did all that in one night?"

She nodded again. "Yeah…"

He stood, strode leisurely around to the front of his

desk, then leaned back against it, still standing. His position should have made Ellie feel intimidated. But Noah didn't seem threatening at all. On the contrary, he seemed to be…beaming at her? Oh, surely not.

"I made copies of your report this morning and sent it out to all pertinent parties in the organization," he said. "And a few more who weren't pertinent but who I thought should know about it. All of us reviewed it at the same time, then conferred. And we are all of the opinion that never in the history of OPUS has anyone done a more thorough job or drawn more insightful conclusions, in even ten times the hours you put in on this."

Ellie arched her eyebrows at that. "Really?"

Noah nodded. "Really."

"So I don't suck in the field?" she asked hopefully.

"Oh, you suck horribly in the field," he told her enthusiastically. "Immediately into your assignment, you blew your cover. Then you enlisted the aid of a civilian—one suspected of the very crime you were investigating—to help you. Then you got caught breaking into the office of another suspect. And you didn't discover anything about the case on your own that we didn't already know."

Well, yeah, okay, when he put it that way…

"But," he added, "you are phenomenal working the other side of the team."

The other side of the team? she repeated to herself. But that was the side of the team where all the techno and computer geeks worked. All the brainiacs. The people on the other side of the team weren't kick-ass. They were… They were…

"They do kick-ass work on the other side, Ellie," Noah

said. "The field agents are the heart of this organization, but the people who work the other side are the brains. You're a member of the elite working the other side."

She narrowed her eyes at his phrasing. Was he using *you* as a universal pronoun, or a personal one? Did he mean...

"What do you mean?" she asked.

He grinned. "I mean, Ellie, that not only will you pass your training class, but we're moving you to the top of the list of graduates waiting for openings as agents. We want to put you right to work. Not in the field," he hastily clarified, "but as the brains behind the fieldwork. We want you to be the one who assimilates, evaluates and articulates the information collected by the field agent to whom you're assigned to work."

She wasn't sure what to say in response to that. Except maybe, "So then I don't have to clean out my desk?"

Noah smiled. "Only long enough to move your stuff to another one," he told her.

She was going to be an agent, after all. Okay, so maybe not the way she'd originally envisioned, but still. She had to admit she'd kind of enjoyed doing the analysis last night and writing up her report this morning. It had been interesting to see it all laid out and fascinating to find the connections and relationships of all the facts presented. Instead of finding the pieces to the puzzle, Ellie had put them together. Instead of painting the big picture, she'd interpreted it. And when she'd slipped the report into its envelope this morning, she'd been inordinately proud of herself for what she'd done. No, she wouldn't be a field agent. But she'd still be a spy. A kick-ass spy, too, according to Noah's own assessment.

So she was going to have to make a few adjustments to her career plans. So what? She'd be lying if she said she was disappointed in the new path her career had just taken. She just hoped they didn't stick her with some jerk field agent who gave her a hard time.

"We want you to start immediately," Noah said. "Tomorrow, you'll move the contents of your desk—and yourself—to a new division. And you'll be assigned to a temporary partner until your new partner completes his training."

They were pairing her with someone new? she thought. That was odd. Normally, the newbie agent was attached to a veteran for a while, to learn the ropes from someone who was familiar with the job. They must be shorthanded or something.

"So who will I be working with?" she asked. "If it's someone from my training class, why hasn't he finished yet?"

Noah glanced at Daniel, who threw another telling glance back at him. "Well, I have someone specific in mind," Noah said, "but he hasn't accepted my job offer. He hasn't declined it, though. And of course, if he does accept, he'll still have to complete the required training. Not that Mr. Beck hasn't already proved himself to be a more than effective field agent. Protocol is protocol. And by the time he finishes his agent training, Ellie, you should be pretty well seasoned to break him in as your partner."

Ellie shook her head in disbelief. They were offering Daniel a job? *Her* job? The one she'd wanted for years?

The job to which she was in no way suited? she made herself admit. Hell, she'd realized that even before Noah had. And she herself had credited Daniel with gathering the greatest amount of—and most incriminating—information about Truman. He really had proved himself to be an excellent field agent. Even without realizing what he was doing.

But now that Ellie thought about it, she had to admit that Daniel had a lot in common with the field agents of her acquaintance. He was cocky and adventurous, and he had a very high opinion of himself. But even beyond that, he was quick thinking, resourceful, courageous. And as much as he enjoyed his job at ChemiTech, she knew he wasn't quite happy with it. He loved research, for sure. But he got bored with it fast. Working as a field agent for OPUS would be a lot like doing research for ChemiTech. Except that it would be infinitely more exciting and never, ever boring. Daniel would always be challenged. It made perfect sense that he'd be interested in accepting the job.

And he was looking at Ellie now as if he was totally ready to accept Noah's offer but wanted to see how she reacted first. In that moment, she knew if she gave him the slightest indication she was disappointed by the turn of events, or that she begrudged him the job she'd wanted and didn't get, he wouldn't take it. He'd keep working at ChemiTech, a career for which he'd studied a long time, and to which he was suited well enough, and which he liked fine. But he was clearly excited by the prospect of working for OPUS. He'd enjoyed playing the role of spy, gathering information secretly, risking his safety, contributing to the downfall of a Very Bad Man. He wanted the job. Ellie could tell. But he wouldn't take it if it meant hurting her.

"He'd be perfect, Noah," she said with a smile. "And he's smart enough to accept your offer."

BY THE TIME Ellie's boss wrapped up their meeting, Daniel was barely listening to what the guy was saying. He figured he'd hear it all again once he started his training. Right now, he was way more interested in Ellie than anything some suit had to say.

She really didn't seem to mind that he'd been asked to take the job she'd wanted. And she actually seemed to be happy about working with him after he got her job. His job. Whatever. Which was good, since he was *really* happy about that himself.

He hadn't been able to stop thinking about her after that night in Sebastian's office. Making love with her had been the most incredible thing that had ever happened to him. Before that night, sex had always been a steamy, mind-scrambling event. With Ellie, it had been a steamy, mind-scrambling, *meaningful* event. Sex with her had been a million more things than just physical. She had added dimensions and textures and levels of awareness he hadn't known could exist when two people came together that way. Before Ellie, he'd always considered sex to be little more than a bodily function. Now, it was nothing less than a sharing of souls.

Working with her, he'd be seeing even more of her than he had before. It had never occurred to him to be anything other than a research chemist. Science had been his life since he was old enough to ask why the sky was blue and the grass was green. As a kid, he hadn't been able to get enough of finding the answers to those questions and a host of others that popped into his head. He'd received his first chemistry set when he was eight years old, and there had been no going back after that. Creating a new and different product from two or more very different sources had fascinated him.

But somewhere over the ensuing years, his work had ceased to be as fulfilling as he had thought it would be. New projects were exciting for a while, but then his interest began to ebb. Working with a team, inside a corporation, he wasn't the one-man show he'd been as a kid. Teamwork was fine for people who enjoyed being part of a team. But Daniel liked making discoveries on his own.

And working with Ellie on her assignment over the past couple of weeks, he'd realized there were some questions that were even more compelling than scientific discovery. Questions that had to do with human nature instead of Mother Nature. Behavioral science instead of physical science. Daniel had been completely captivated by his search for the leak. Now, he couldn't wait to finish his training and start doing it full-time.

When Noah Tennant finally dismissed them, Daniel and Ellie muttered perfunctory goodbyes and walked out together in silence. It wasn't until she thumbed the call button for the elevator at the end of the hall that one of them finally spoke.

"Congratulations," she told Daniel as she trained her gaze up at the numbers over the elevator door instead of him.

"Back atcha," he replied.

She mumbled what sounded like "Thanks," then a moment of stilted silence ensued as they *both* looked at the numbers above the elevator doors.

Finally, Daniel said, "Look, Ellie, are you sure you're not mad that they offered me the job you wanted? Or more to the point, that I accepted it?"

"Of course I'm not mad," she said. But she still wasn't

looking at him, so Daniel couldn't quite rid himself of the sensation that everything might not be okay. "I haven't completely switched gears yet," she added…still not looking at him, "and it's going to take a few days to get used to my new job description, but…" She shrugged. "Hey, I get to be a kick-ass spy. That's all I ever wanted."

"That's all?" Daniel echoed. "There's nothing else you want?"

It was only when she finally turned to look at him that he knew everything would be okay. Because the way she smiled at him then made his body heat skyrocket.

"Well, there's no *thing*," she said. "But there is some*one*."

He smiled back. "Anyone I know?"

She nodded. "You know him intimately, actually."

"Something tells me you do, too."

"Not as intimately as I intend to know him," she said. "But we've got a long time to work on that."

He lifted a hand to her hair, then skimmed it down over her cheek and jaw. "Yeah, we do," he agreed as he completed the single step that brought their bodies together. Roping his arms around her waist, he pulled her close. "And you know, Ellie," he added, "I think you and I are going to work together really well."

She looped her arms around his waist and pulled him close, too, pushing herself up on tiptoe to brush her lips lightly over his. "Better be careful, Daniel," she said softly. "You know my work is my life."

He dipped his head to hers, meeting her halfway this time. "Baby, that's what I'm counting on."

CHAPTER EIGHTEEN

MARNIE WAS SEATED on her living-room sofa with a good book and a glass of even better shiraz, and was trying to pretend she wouldn't be leaving in the dark hours of the morning to head off to God knows where, when she heard a faint rapping on her front door.

Dread uncoiled in her stomach as she looked up from the book. The last time someone had rapped faintly on her front door, it had been Noah, coming to share dinner, and more, with her. Would that he had been able to include himself in that *more*—well, other than physically—she might not be sitting on her sofa right now with a good book and a glass of even better shiraz dreading the faint knocking at her front door. Instead, she might be spending these last hours before leaving for her assignment with him.

Then she realized it doubtless *was* him at her front door. Who else could it be? Adrian Padgett wouldn't knock. He'd just silently slip in and scare the hell out of her—or worse. For nearly a month, Marnie's life had been consumed by Noah. She'd been on an indefinite leave of absence from both her jobs due to a fictional family crisis, had seen or spoken to virtually none of her friends. Ev-

erything she'd done had centered on Noah and OPUS.
Even her house felt different since his invasion of it.
Memories and reminders of him filled every room. She
wondered if there would ever be a time in her life again
when she didn't feel connected to him in some way.
Unlikely, since she'd been changed irrevocably by her experiences with him.

Sighing, she went to answer the door. Sure enough,
Noah stood on the other side of it, dressed as always in his
spy suit—well, as always except for the night they'd spent
together as something other than spies. But he wasn't
alone. Behind him, at the top of her porch stairs, with her
back to Marnie, stood a woman. And the moment Marnie
saw her, something exploded in her belly with a force
nothing short of atomic.

"Come in," she said to both of them.

The woman spun around at the summons, and Marnie
felt her knees begin to buckle. Quickly, she backed into the
house, not stopping until she felt the bump of her piano
bench against the backs of her legs. That completed the
crumpling of her body, and she sat down with a solid
thump as Noah and her sister entered. But where Noah
turned left, moving toward Marnie, Lila went right, to the
other side of the room. She turned to face Marnie fully,
however, their gazes connecting at once.

Marnie stared at her sister in silence for a long time,
telling herself she was seeing what other people saw when
they looked at her. Lila Moreau was her mirror image, on
the side of the mirror where it didn't belong. An odd Al-
ice in Wonderland sensation wound down her spine,
tumbling into her belly with an indelicate thud. Some-

thing hot and furious expanded in her chest at the same time, and the double whammy of sensation made her feel a little light-headed. She closed her eyes against the wooziness, counted slowly to five, then opened her eyes again. But she was still looking at herself outside herself, and it wasn't a comfortable place to be.

Gradually, though, she began to notice small differences. Yes, Lila Moreau's face was identical to her own, as was her size and body type. But her features seemed a little harder than Marnie's, a bit sharper, even, as if they'd been more deeply etched into her skin. Her clothing, too, was entirely different—all of it black, a color Marnie normally shunned—and all of it skintight. The spandex miniskirt hugged her hips like a second skin, as did the scoop-necked top above it. Even the black leather jacket hanging open over both somehow clung to her curves.

Marnie felt like a third-grader in her own lavender sweater and flowered skirt, her feet stuffed into well-worn clogs while Lila's sported spike-heel ankle boots. Lila wore her hair differently, too, dyed a few shades lighter and falling free to barely skim her shoulders where Marnie's longer tresses were bound at her nape. And when Lila shrugged off the jacket and tossed it into a nearby chair, Marnie saw that her body type, too, was actually different from her own. Bumps and ridges of muscle rose on Lila's upper arms—flexed as they were when she settled her hands on her waist—and elegant lines of sinew were evident in her thighs and calves. Her nails were manicured to perfection with a bloodred crimson where Marnie's were bitten down to the quick.

They were identical, she thought as her attention

returned to Lila's face. But they were absolutely nothing alike.

"Lila Moreau," Noah said, his voice seeming to come from a million miles away, "meet your sister, Marnie Lundy. Marnie, Lila."

How odd, Marnie thought, to have to be introduced to one's twin. Neither woman acknowledged the introduction, however, not verbally, not physically. It occurred to Marnie that Lila must be having thoughts similar to her own, wondering who was this stranger who looked exactly like her. It was possible she even resented Marnie. How would Marnie have felt, after all, had she been the twin who grew up disadvantaged and poor while her sister's upbringing had been warm and rosy?

She was about to speak, thinking she should probably be the one to make the first gesture—this was, after all, her house, making her the hostess—when Lila suddenly took a few broad strides across the room. She stopped a foot away, her gaze still fixed on Marnie's, her expression completely unreadable.

"I don't know about you," she said, her voice like Marnie's, yet not, "but this is some weird shit to have to take in."

For a second, Marnie had no idea what to say. Then she stood to face her sister and smiled. Then she expelled a single soft chuckle. Finally, she said, "Weird shit indeed."

That made Lila smile, too. Another moment passed where the two women only stared at each other, then Lila covered the last step separating them and drew Marnie into a hug. Not a great hug. Clearly her sister wasn't very familiar with the gesture. In fact, she hugged like a man, with a single fierce embrace and a few quick pats on the back. But it was a hug just the same. Without hesitation, Marnie wrapped her arms around her sister's shoulders and hugged her back. But no sooner had she completed the action than did Lila spring away again. Obviously she wasn't used to being hugged back, either.

Ah, well, Marnie thought. It was something they could work on.

"We have a lot to talk about," she told her sister.

"Damned straight," Lila replied.

"You're going to have to make it quick," Noah interjected.

It took a moment for her to understand what he was talking about. Such was the impact of her sister's appearance. Finally, "Oh, right," she said. She managed a nervous smile. "They've trained me to be a spy like you. Well, not like you," she hastily amended, "since I'm sure you're a lot better at being a spy than I will be. Especially since I'm supposed to be—"

She broke off there, when understanding dawned. Marnie was supposed to be posing as Lila because Lila was missing. And Lila was missing because she was supposed to have turned traitor and tried to kill someone. Now she was back. Which meant…what?

She looked at Noah, who was looking at Lila. Then she looked back at Lila to see that she was looking at Noah. And they were looking at each other in a way that made something cold and unpleasant twist in Marnie's stomach. The two of them were connecting on a level that didn't include her, and she was reminded that this wasn't the first time such a thing had happened.

Nor could she help thinking it wouldn't be the last. Now that Lila was back, would she and Noah pick up where they had left off? Even though Noah had assured Marnie that he and her sister had shared nothing more than an isolated physical coupling years ago that would never happen again, she couldn't quite bring herself to believe that was all there had been to it.

At least on Noah's side. Why else would he have been so reluctant to talk about it? And their first physical encounter had come about when Marnie had left her own mousy shell to slip into Lila's blond bombshell. He kept insisting whatever had happened with Lila was over. But time and again, she'd caught him looking at her in a way that made her think he was superimposing her sister over herself, and liking her better that way.

Would he and Lila get together again? she wondered. Did Noah still have feelings for Lila, in spite of his insistence to the contrary? And if he and Lila did take up together again, how would Marnie be able to tolerate it? A woman in love with her sister's man? Could there be a worse cliché?

"So what does all this mean?" she finally asked.

It was Noah who looked back at Marnie first. "It means OPUS has had a nice, long chat with Lila, enough so that things are starting to make sense. Though we still have a lot to go over with her. She's uncovered some new information about Sorcerer that we need to study in depth before carrying out the rest of the assignment. But Lila insisted she be able to see you first. And," he added in a softer voice, "it also means that you're being relieved of duty, Marnie."

She wasn't sure whether to feel relieved or resentful. She'd been dreading leaving in the morning, and terrified of what would happen once she arrived at her final destination to deliberately draw out a man who'd endangered her. But she'd been training for two weeks to do just that, and a part of her had actually been looking forward to the challenge, if for no other reason than to prove to herself she could step outside her normal safe life and return to it intact.

"We needed you to pose as Lila," Noah continued when she remained silent. "With Lila back, that won't be necessary. Plus, she has new information about Sorcerer that's required us to make some amendments to our original plan. The new plan will be better carried out by Lila."

Marnie told herself she should be relieved. Instead, for some reason, she felt slighted. There was no question that her sister was the better woman for the job. But then, it wasn't the job making Marnie feel the way she did.

"I see," she said quietly.

Noah frowned. "Look, I know this is coming out of nowhere. And I apologize for the abruptness of it all. You gave your entire life over to OPUS for weeks, and you've been preparing for something very dangerous. Now, suddenly, we're telling you we don't need you. We appreciate everything you've done, Marnie. We're grateful. But you can step down now and go back to living your life on your own."

OPUS was grateful, Marnie repeated to herself. OPUS appreciated her. Too bad it wasn't OPUS she'd given the past three weeks of her life to. Those had gone to Noah. Had anyone else asked her to perform the job he'd asked her to undertake, she would have stuck by her original decision not to go through with it. It was Noah who had made her feel she could do it. Noah who had made her feel needed. Noah who had made her feel, period. Falling in love with him had been infinitely more dangerous than any assignment OPUS would have asked her to complete. Because Marnie *would* have come back from her assignment intact. Of that, she was certain. She wouldn't be so lucky with her feelings for Noah. Parts of her were going to be broken forever after him.

One thing he was right about, though. She would go back to living her life on her own. No way would there ever be room in it for anyone else but him.

"Well, thank you for your consideration," she said softly.

Something shadowy darkened his eyes for the briefest of moments, then disappeared before Marnie could identify what it was. He opened his mouth to say something, evidently thought better of whatever it was, and closed it again.

So Marnie filled the awkward silence with an awkward invitation. "I have a lovely reserve pinot noir that I've been saving for a special occasion," she said. "We can have it with dinner." As she extended the invitation, she looked at Noah, to include him, too, even though she wasn't sure how he—or she, for that matter—felt about him being included.

But he started shaking his head before she even finished asking, something that suggested he was no more comfortable about the situation than she was. "I can't," he told her. "Thanks, but I have another obligation. Besides, you two don't need me horning in while you get caught up as much as you can in one evening."

Marnie wondered if his obligation was to another woman. Then she told herself it didn't matter. She had no claim on him. She never had. She never would. Whatever Noah did with his life, it wouldn't include her anymore. If indeed it had ever really included her at all.

"If it's all the same to you," Lila said, "I'd just as soon skip the wine. I don't drink. Not unless the assignment calls for it. And even then, I make it look like I'm consuming a lot more than I really am. Usually, I'm a teetotaler."

A surprised sound erupted from Noah, just loud enough that the two women both turned to look at him. He seemed faintly embarrassed at first, then shrugged. "Guess that explains how you've always been able to drink any man under the table."

Lila smiled. "You're all *such* suckers. If men didn't spend so much time looking at my ti…uh, I mean my breasts," she quickly amended with a glance at Marnie, evidently remembering she wasn't in her usual company—not that Marnie didn't wince, anyway. "I couldn't get away with half the stuff I do."

"Well, wine is rather a hobby of mine," Marnie said, "but I also have a nice selection of teas."

"Do you have lovely decaf green tea?" Lila asked.

"I do, actually."

"Perfect."

"Ladies," Noah interjected, still obviously uncomfortable, "it's been, ah, lovely, but I really should go. Marnie," he added, turning to look at her. But he hesitated, as if he wasn't quite sure what to say.

Which was kind of ironic, because there were a million things zinging through her head when she looked at him that commanded a voice. Nevertheless, she managed to silence them all.

Finally, Noah told her, "Thanks again for all your help in this matter. Even if we didn't get Sorcerer this time around, your contribution was invaluable."

Of course it was, Marnie thought. And she had a great personality, too.

"Lila," Noah said, turning then to look at her. But again, he hesitated. "It's good to have you back," he said.

Of course it was, Marnie thought. It was always better to have the real thing than a pale substitute.

She bit back the feeling of sadness that rose inside her. It wasn't her fault Noah had developed feelings for Lila a long time ago. Marnie hadn't even been around then, so it wasn't like she should even compare herself to her sister. Still, it was strange to think about the man she loved loving someone who looked just like her, but wasn't her. And her feelings for Lila were so strange and so complex and so new, she didn't need this added element of envy or jealousy or whatever it was intruding to make things even more confusing.

Bottom line, Noah didn't love Marnie. And there was nothing she could do about that. Except accept it.

"Beat it, Noah," Lila said succinctly. "Like you said, my sister and I have a lot of catching up to do."

He smiled at that, a little sadly, it seemed to Marnie. Though whether he was sad on her behalf or Lila's she couldn't have said. Then he nodded once, more confidently. "You know your agenda," he said to Lila. "And you know they've got their eye on you, so don't be even a minute late."

"Yeah, yeah, yeah," she said. "I know I've been a bad girl and I'm on probation for a while. Just don't make my curfew any earlier than midnight, 'kay, Dad? 'Cause all the cool kids at school get to stay out way later than me."

He smiled in a way that told Marnie this was old ground for him and Lila, and another little pin pricked her heart. Regardless of everything, Noah and Lila shared a history to which Marnie could never be privy. It felt strange to realize they'd both been living lives independent of hers when both had come to mean so much to her over the past few weeks. Somehow, it felt as if a part of Marnie's life was just beginning in that moment. And, she thought further, looking at Noah, a part of her life was ending then, too.

"Thank you," she told him. "For everything." There was so much more she wanted to say, but she stopped herself. Really, that was all Noah needed to know. That she was grateful to him, too. And he also had a great personality.

He smiled back in a way that was different from the smile he'd shared with Lila. That one had been playful. This one was melancholy. "You're welcome," he said. "Be on time," he told Lila again.

"I will," she promised. "Now go. Away."

"Marnie," he said by way of a farewell with a quick dip of his head. Then he turned and strode to the front door, closing it behind himself without a backward glance.

Tomorrow, Marnie promised herself. She would let herself fall apart over Noah tomorrow. Right now, she needed to keep it together for her sister. Her sister.

My sister.

How odd that two words she had never used together in her life would suddenly be a major part of it.

"So you'll be the one going off on a new assignment tomorrow instead of me," Marnie said, trying to focus on that to keep at bay all the emotions that threatened to swamp her.

"Actually, it's the same assignment I've had for a couple years now," Lila said. "Catching that bastard Sorcerer. This will just be a new direction." She smiled again. "But, hey, we've got a good twelve hours to start getting caught up. And once I put that son of a bitch in a cage where he belongs, we'll have even more time."

Marnie laughed. She couldn't help herself. Lila was just so…

"What?" Lila said.

"You're just so…" Marnie shook her head.

"What?"

"Out there," Marnie said with a smile. "I mean, you're so free-spoken. So confident. So comfortable with yourself. You're so different from me."

Lila considered her thoughtfully for a moment, nibbling her lip. "I don't know about that," she finally said. "From what I hear, you and I have a lot in common."

The comment both surprised and puzzled Marnie. "What have you heard?" she asked. More importantly, who had she heard it from? Not that she couldn't guess. And did what the two of them have in common have anything to do with him?

"Don't worry," Lila said. "Noah's not the kind to kiss and tell."

Even though Marnie had just remarked on it, Lila's frankness surprised her. "Well, evidently he told you something. How else would you know that he kissed me?"

"I didn't," Lila said with a grin. "Not until you confirmed it with that. But I speak body language as fluently as I do English. It's pretty obvious the two of you did a lot more than kiss. It's clear you and he are involved."

"We were never involved," Marnie denied. Well, Noah wasn't, anyway. "We had sex. Once." Well, one night, anyway.

She winced when she realized she had just described what had happened between her and Noah the same way he had described what had happened between him and Lila.

Lila shook her head. "No. I can tell by looking at both of you. Whatever happened between you and Noah, there was a hell of a lot more to it than just sex."

"And you and Noah?" Marnie said before she could stop herself. Then she realized she didn't want to stop herself. She needed to know. She would never be comfortable with Lila unless she knew—one way or the other—exactly where things stood between her sister and Noah. Marnie could live with it if Lila was in love with him. She could probably live with it—eventually—if Noah was in love with Lila. But she couldn't live her life wondering, not knowing for sure how things stood.

For a minute, she thought Lila was going to pretend she didn't understand the question. Then she expelled a soft sigh of resolution and said, "There's nothing between me and Noah. There never was. We had sex once, and we both knew it was a mistake immediately afterward. It was a weird situation, one that will never happen again. I don't love him. I never loved him. He's a good guy, but..." She shrugged. "He's no different from a bunch of others."

It was only half of the answer she needed. "Does he love you?"

"No," Lila said with absolute certainty.

Marnie wished she could share that certainty. She believed Lila about her own feelings. Knowing what she did of her sister, and hearing her now, Marnie didn't doubt Lila was telling the truth about how she felt herself. But there was still something inside that wouldn't quite let Marnie believe Noah felt the same way about Lila.

Not that it mattered, she tried to reassure herself. It wasn't as if she'd ever see him again.

She pushed the thought away. "Are you sure you don't want to get some rest before you leave tomorrow? I certainly understand if—"

"Waste of time," Lila interjected. "I'll sleep when I'm dead."

Marnie sobered at that, because in Lila's line of work, death could come anytime.

Lila must have realized what she was thinking, though, because she pointed out, "Yeah, and you could get hit by a bus on your way to work tomorrow. There are no guarantees for any of us, Marnie. We gotta do what we gotta do."

Even after everything she'd learned about her sister and OPUS over the past few weeks, Marnie couldn't imagine what drove Lila to do what she did, to put herself in jeopardy every single day. Yes, Marnie could get hit by a bus on her way to work tomorrow. But it wasn't likely, because she was a very careful driver, and she always looked both ways before she crossed the street. In Lila's line of work, one couldn't even tell where the streets were half the time. And all the bus drivers in her world were heavily armed.

Different, she reminded herself. They were different from each other. Just because they shared identical DNA didn't mean anything else about them was the same.

"You'll stay for dinner, yes?" Marnie asked.

"You bet," Lila told her. "But only if we order in. I don't like for anyone to have to go to any trouble for me."

Which spoke volumes, Marnie thought. Because if there was anyone who deserved to have someone take care of her for a little while, it was definitely Lila Moreau.

"I'll just go put the kettle on, then," she told her sister. "And pop the cork on a bottle of wine."

CHAPTER NINETEEN

"So Philosopher's manuscript in effect turned out to be an encrypted biography of sorts of Adrian Padgett?"

Marnie asked the question as she emptied the last of the pinot noir into her glass and set a fifth cup of tea down in front of her sister. It was just past four in the morning, but she was in no way sleepy, in spite of having consumed an entire bottle of wine over the past ten hours. She and Lila had shared dinner and countless snacks in that time, not to mention an ongoing dialogue about nearly everything that popped into their heads: Marnie's talent for music and her efforts writing it. Lila's recruitment into and experiences with OPUS. Marnie's love of wine and gardening. Lila's skill with weaponry and surveillance equipment. Marnie's annual vacations to the Outer Banks. Lila's travels all over the world.

Strangely, the one thing they *hadn't* discussed was their upbringings with their individual parents. Marnie wasn't sure if that was because the conversation simply hadn't turned naturally to the topic yet, or if both women were unconsciously—or even consciously—making sure the conversation hadn't turned to the topic. She was beginning to wonder if it ever would. Certainly not yet, since Lila was currently filling in the details of the OPUS operation to which Marnie had lent her time and alleged talents.

"Philosopher was kind of a frustrated field agent-wannabe when he was with OPUS, but he just wasn't qualified for the job. So he kind of lived vicariously through his favorite field agents, keeping really close track of his favorites."

"Like Sorcerer," Marnie guessed.

Lila chuckled. "And me. A handful of others, too."

"Has he written an encrypted *Life and Times of Lila Moreau?*" Marnie asked with a smile.

"I wouldn't be surprised. But that's how he stayed busy—and probably held on to his sanity—after his forced retirement. He had a little bit of a breakdown about five years ago," she added before Marnie had a chance to ask for clarification. "He functions well enough to live a happy life, but not at a level where he could work anymore. Especially as an archivist, because those guys have to be razor sharp, mentally. Most of them have memories bigger than a computer's. And they're privy to some very delicate information."

"Archivist?" Marnie echoed.

Lila reached for her tea, tucking her stocking feet beneath her as she leaned back. Her spike-heel boots lay next to Marnie's discarded clogs on the floor between them, and the coffee table was cluttered with the remnants of their latest nibbling—a half-empty bowl of chocolate-covered pretzels and half a bag of shelled almonds.

"Archivists keep track of every operation OPUS has ever conducted," Lila explained. "There are a dozen of them in D.C. who work for the organization. They're the ones who do the final analysis and write up the final reports. They see what was done right and what was done wrong during an operation and make a record of that, too. They send their reports to the big muckety-mucks, then they file everything away in case we have to go back and reference the case again someday. Which we've had to do a lot with Sorcerer. That bastard probably has more info stored in the archives at OPUS than anyone."

"What I find fascinating is that he was able to keep track of Padgett after he left the organization," Marnie said, alluding to Lila's earlier reports.

Lila grinned. "Yeah, he woulda made a good field agent after all. Who knew? But since he knew a lot of Sorcerer's old contacts—on both sides of the law—he was able to keep track of what Sorcerer's been doing to a big extent. Sure there are gaps in some of his analysis, but a lot of it is spot-on stuff we had no knowledge of whatsoever. That manuscript is going to be a huge help locating that son of a bitch."

Lila's language, Marnie noted, had improved some over the past ten hours. She'd used infinitely more colorful words to describe Adrian Padgett when they'd first begun to talk. Clearly Noah had been right about her sister's ability to tailor herself to any situation. Unless maybe Marnie was already having a good influence on her little sister. Lila could certainly use some buffing and smooth-ing in addition to that much-deserved tender loving care.

Then again, that last was something Marnie could use a little of herself. Having a sister suddenly turn up only reminded her how important she'd always considered family to be—regardless of how that family had included only her and her father. Until Lila's appearance, Marnie had been alone. Now her family numbered two again, and the realization of that sent a warm rush of well-being through her that she hadn't felt for a very long time.

"Somehow," Lila continued, "Sorcerer found out about Philosopher keeping tabs on him and what he was doing. Probably from one of the old contacts Philosopher used. Eventually, he found out Philosopher was living here in Cleveland and came to get the manuscript."

"But how did everyone find me?" Marnie asked. "After seeing you, I can understand why they all thought I was you. But what brought everyone to Lauderdale's that one particular night?"

Lila blew out a long sigh. "Believe it or not, sheer dumb luck. When Philosopher went shopping that night and saw you in the store, he assumed you were me and contacted OPUS, because he knew I'd been missing for five months. By then, Sorcerer was tailing him, and when he saw you, too, he concluded the same thing."

She studied Marnie in silence for a minute, her gaze riveted to Marnie's face. "Even though I knew you were my twin sister, it's so strange to see you looking exactly like me. For five months, I've been dying to contact you, but there's still a part of me that can't quite believe you're real."

"You've known about me for five months?" Marnie asked. "They only told me a few weeks ago."

"Yeah, well, they never told me about you at all, even when they knew of your existence. I had to find it out all by myself. Just like I had to find out by myself that they were training you to be me." She grinned again. "Sorcerer's not the only one who's been keeping tabs on OPUS in his absence. But that's why I finally came out of hiding. I couldn't let you go out there and risk your life for me."

"Why not?" Marnie asked.

"'Cause you're my sister," Lila said simply.

It was exactly the opening Marnie had been waiting for. "Lila?" she said softly.

"What?"

"Are we ever going to talk about our parents? I mean, we only have about another hour before you have to leave, and I don't know when we'll see each other after that. We've spent half the night talking about things that have no bearing on who we are as sisters. I think it's time for us to at least mention some of the things that do."

Lila inhaled a deep breath and released it slowly. "Just how much do you know about our parents?"

"Nothing," Marnie said, not quite able to mask the desperation she felt at having to realize and admit such a thing. "My father told me my mother died when I was a baby, and borrowed a character from a Dickens novel to model her memory on. And until a few weeks ago, I didn't even know you existed. By then, no one knew where you were, so I had no way to contact you. Had I known I had a sister out there somewhere in the world…" She let her voice trail off because, honestly, she had no idea what to say.

Lila seemed to understand, though, because she nodded. "I've known about you for almost six months," she said. "And I've known where to find you for five. But like I said, the heat on me was so strong, I couldn't risk coming out of hiding to contact you." She hesitated before adding, "And I didn't want to put you in any danger. I didn't want to lose what little family I had before I even got to meet you. But it's eaten away at me, knowing I had a sister…knowing I had *family* out there, and not being able to contact you."

Relief hit Marnie so strongly she didn't realize until then how much she had feared Lila's resentment. Yet here her sister was saying she wanted to protect her. "How did you find out about me?" she asked.

"After my…after *our* mother died," she corrected herself, "I was cleaning out her trailer, on the outside chance that there might be something somebody could use. Mostly, it was all crap. She was a real pack rat, even if hardly anything she held on to was worth keeping. But I hit a gold mine when I opened a shoe box in the back of her closet and found a few old letters from your…*our* father."

Something quick and hot sparked in Marnie's midsection. "What did they say?" she asked.

"I'll let you read them," Lila said, "but for now I have them stowed in a safe-deposit box in Vegas." She smiled sheepishly. "I've kind of been moving around a lot the last several months." Marnie was about to offer to fly out and get them herself when Lila added, "But I practically have them memorized, I read them so many times. The most important thing you need to know—at least, this was the most important thing to me—is that your…our father loved our mother. He wanted to marry her."

Something knotted tight in Marnie's stomach. "Then why didn't they marry?"

"I can only guess," Lila said. "Mom had a pretty lousy view of marriage. A pretty lousy view of men. Her parents were never married, and her dad walked when she was a baby. Not that she ever got involved with guys who were worth marrying anyway. Our father seems like the only one who had any potential."

"He had more than potential," Marnie said. "He was

wonderful. Good-hearted, good-natured, good every-thing. Loving, generous, smart, sweet, kind. The best man I ever knew."

Lila's eyebrows knitted downward, and she glanced away.

"I wish you could have known him," Marnie added. "And I wish he could have known you, too."

"How did he die?" Lila asked, still not looking at her.

"Heart failure," Marnie said. "He wasn't a young man when we were born. He was fifty-two."

"Mom was twenty-five."

"And a showgirl, I hear."

"When they met, yeah," Lila said, turning her head to gaze at Marnie again.

"And Dad taught literature." She shook her head. "The English professor and the showgirl. How on earth did they hook up?"

"We'll probably never know," Lila said. "But from his letters, it sounds like they spent the entire summer together in Vegas the year before we were born."

"So it wasn't some one-night stand," Marnie said.

"Doesn't look like it."

"Then why didn't they marry once they found out our mother was pregnant?"

Lila reached for her tea again, started to lift it to her mouth, saw that the cup was empty, and impatiently set it back on the coffee table. Then she stood and began to pace, obviously restless.

"Something you should know about Mom," she said as she strode to the fireplace and began to inspect the photos there.

"What?" Marnie asked.

"She, um, she kind of had a self-esteem problem."

"But she was a showgirl. That sounds pretty glamorous."

"Yeah, well, it wasn't," Lila said. "Not for her."

"I'm not sure I'm following you."

Now Lila moved to the bookcase, reading over the titles, pulling an occasional book from the shelf to look at its cover or flip through it. Something told Marnie she wasn't seeing any of them, however.

"Mom was a fat kid growing up," Lila said. "And her mom was poor, and her father was gone, and that made her ripe for ridicule at school. Her own mother wasn't all that helpful in shoring her up, either. Mom lost the weight when she hit adolescence, but that only made the boys give her a different reason to feel worthless. If you know what I mean."

Unfortunately, Marnie did.

Lila looked up again. "I honestly think Mom would have said no to our father's proposal because she just didn't think she was good enough for him. Or maybe she wanted to punish herself for something. Human nature's a weird-ass thing. Human brain's even weirder."

Marnie couldn't argue with that. But she still wasn't sure she understood. Maybe because no one in her life had ever tried to make her feel bad about who or what she was. Guilt began to tap at the edge of her brain again knowing she had been the twin to grow up with privilege and advantage and opportunity. Talk about sheer dumb luck.

"I'm sorry, Lila," she heard herself say before she even realized she had intended to speak. "I wish things could have been different for you. For your mom. For my dad. For all of us. I hate it that one decision changed so many lives. And I wish I knew why and how they decided to raise us separate from each other and our second parent."

By now, Lila had pulled Marnie's senior yearbook off the shelf and was riffling through the pages the way Noah had that first night in her home. She stopped on one page to study it more closely, and when Marnie stood, she saw that it was the page with the senior superlatives. Smartest. Nicest. Best Smile. Most Likely to Succeed. Marnie Lundy and Hal Peterson had been voted Most Creative. It was at their photo Lila was gazing. But where Marnie would have expected her expression to be hard, even bitter, instead, Lila was smiling.

"If I'd been in your senior class," she said, "I'd have been voted Most Likely to Kick Someone's Ass."

She looked up again, and she must have been able to tell what Marnie was thinking from her expression. She did, after all, speak body language fluently.

"For what it's worth," Lila said, "I wouldn't change any of my past, even if I could. Yeah, it sucked growing up the way I did. And no, my mom and I never got along. I won't lie to you, Marnie. I lived with a lot of bad stuff when I was a kid. It got worse when I was a teenager. But it made me who I am as an adult.

"And I like who I am as an adult," she added. "I'm not perfect. But I do good work. I'm strong. I'm smart. I can take care of myself. And I don't take shit from anybody. Maybe I'm a little lacking in social graces, and maybe I never let people get too close, but…" She lifted a shoulder and let it drop. "There are a lot of people like that who grew up in homes just like yours. A happy childhood isn't a guarantee of anything. But you know what? A lousy childhood isn't a guarantee of anything, either."

Marnie smiled, and something inside her that had been tilting a little off balance suddenly fell comfortably into place. Lila was okay, she realized. In spite of her past, in spite of her occupation, in spite of everything, she was a good person and reasonably well-adjusted. And that was saying a lot, no matter who you were.

"You're pretty amazing, Lila," she told her sister. "But I guess you already know that, don't you?"

"I do, actually," Lila agreed without an ounce of modesty. "I think it must run in the family."

Marnie chuckled at that. She considered herself to be many things, several of them quite flattering. *Amazing,* however, wasn't an adjective she would ever ascribe to herself.

"Just tell me," Marnie said, "that you won't be working alone on this assignment. I do believe I'm going to worry about you, in spite of your assurances that you can take care of yourself."

And how nice it was to have someone in her life to worry about again. Because it meant she had someone in her life to care about again. Of course, she would be worrying—not to mention caring—about Noah, too. Oh, who was she kidding? She'd be in love with him. Forever, truth be told. But he wasn't in her life anymore, was he?

"No, I had…have…a partner," Lila said. "But he's a little incapacitated right now, so I'll be assigned to work with someone else until further notice."

"I hope he wasn't injured in the line of duty," Marnie said.

Lila toddled her head back and forth. "Well, sorta. He got engaged in the line of duty."

And she considered that an injury, Marnie thought. Obviously their mother wasn't the only Moreau woman who had a dim view of marriage.

"I just have one more thing I need to do before I leave," Lila said, glancing down at her watch. "So I probably ought to get going." She looked at Marnie again. "Just know that no matter who I'm working with, I'll find Sorcerer. Between what OPUS learned from Philosopher's manuscript, and what I learned myself over the last few months, my job just got a whole lot easier. I won't rest until Sorcerer is in a cage. I promise you that, Marnie."

Marnie nodded. She believed her sister. She just hoped it was Adrian Padgett—and not Lila Moreau—who ended up in chains.

THE SUN HADN'T YET RISEN when Noah, exiting the steamy master bathroom and shrugging into his shirt, heard the sound of his front door opening and closing at the foot of the hallway stairs. The sound didn't alarm him, however. Anyone who wanted to do him harm wouldn't be audible while they broke into his home. Besides, he'd kind of been expecting his visitor.

He reached for the navy-blue trousers folded neatly over a chair and pulled them on over his boxers, fastening them beneath the still-unbuttoned white shirt. Not that his visitor would be shocked or surprised to see him half-dressed, since she'd seen him *un*dressed. Nor was it necessary to stand on ceremony with her. He didn't make an effort to greet her, though, knowing she would find him well enough. She'd only been in his house once, but even that was more than she needed to know the entire layout. Even in the dark.

He strode to the mahogany highboy that had belonged to his great-grandfather and opened the top drawer to retrieve a pair of socks. Then he moved to the matching mahogany dresser and ran a quick comb through his hair, still damp from the shower. He turned to survey the room, wondering what was taking her so long. But it looked the way it always did, save the unmade four-poster bed, which would normally be tidied: a collection of dark, heavy heirloom antiques; rich, jewel-colored Oriental rugs on gleaming hardwood floors; original Gainsborough landscapes, all of it backed by midnight-blue walls that ended in highly embellished white wainscoting.

The house had been in Noah's family for a hundred and fifty years, always inherited by the eldest grandson of whoever happened to be living in it when he died. Noah had always wondered to whom he would leave the house himself. Probably the oldest of his brothers' children, since there was little chance he'd have any of his own.

As if generated by the realization, a woman suddenly appeared in the doorway, her clothing—and expression—as dark and concealing as the hallway behind her. Her black leather jacket was half zipped over the black tank top she'd had on earlier, but she'd changed into black trousers now and added to the ensemble. Black leather gloves covered her hands, and she'd pulled a black knit cap over her hair, down to her eyebrows. She was obviously ready for the next leg of her assignment. Noah just hoped she'd be able to complete it this time.

"She-Wolf," he greeted her.

She smiled at that. "Oh, so we're not on a first-name basis anymore? When the hell did that happen?"

Actually, it would have been better if they'd never strayed from their code-name basis in the first place, he thought. He decided to ignore the question. "I'm not the one you're supposed to be reporting to," he reminded her. Of course, she already knew that.

"I needed to talk to you first."

"All right."

She completed a few cautious strides into his bedroom, stopping by the highboy, where she began to pick through the things lying upon it, inspecting them one by one. "I didn't know you wore reading glasses," she said as she lifted those and unfolded the earpieces, settling them onto her face.

"Newly acquired," he said. "Happens to everyone who hits forty."

"I wouldn't know," she replied. "I'm still a spring chick." She removed them and reached for his car keys. "Driving a BMW now. You like it better than the Merc?"

"They both have their recommendations."

She put down the keys and picked up his wallet, which she shamelessly opened to investigate the contents. "A hundred and sixty-six bucks in cash, health-insurance card, Cleveland Athletic Club ID, Triple-A membership, platinum AmEx." She looked at him again. "The wallet of a security freak. Some things never change, I guess."

Growing impatient, Noah demanded, "What do you want, Lila?"

She dropped the wallet back onto his dresser and

hooked her hands on her hips. "I want to know what your intentions are toward my sister."

It wasn't a question he'd expected to hear from her. Not just because he wasn't used to Lila having a family, but also because he wasn't used to her caring. About anyone. It didn't surprise him, though, that she suspected something had gone on between him and Marnie. Put Lila in a room with someone for more than a minute, and she could read that person like a book. What Noah found most interesting, however, was that Lila seemed to understand better than he did what he felt for her sister.

In spite of that, he said, "I think that's between me and Marnie."

Lila shifted her weight from one foot to the other. "From what I see, there isn't anything between you and Marnie."

"Then why are you asking me about my intentions toward her?"

She narrowed her eyes at him. "Because I think you want there to be something between you and Marnie. And I think she does, too."

Just what had the two of them talked about last night? he wondered. He'd assumed they'd fill the time comparing their histories and experiences and pondering the puzzle of their separation. *Had* they talked about him? And if so, what had Marnie said? Or was Lila just bluffing? And if so, why? Surely she didn't assign any more importance to the night the two of them had spent together than he did. Did she? She couldn't be thinking there was anything more to what had happened than that it was a physical response to an extreme situation. Could she?

And what if she did? he asked himself further. Would that change his feelings for her? His feelings for Marnie? Just what were his feelings for Lila and Marnie anyway?

Cautiously, he asked, "How would you feel about it if there *was* something between me and Marnie?"

"Like what kind of something?" she said.

"Like a serious kind of something," he evaded.

"Like love?" she asked frankly.

Well, he'd kind of been hoping to avoid that word because… Well, just because, that was why. And it was a damned good reason. "Like something serious," he reiterated.

She seemed to give the question some thought. Though Noah was sure she'd already given the idea all the thought she needed to give it. Lila never went off half-cocked. She didn't do anything without thinking it through to the end first. "I dunno," she finally said. "It would be a little weird, you know?"

"Why?" he asked. He decided to just cut to the chase. "Because of that one night you and I spent together? Do you wonder if there was something more to that than just the physical? If maybe there's something that connects the two of us on an emotional level, too?"

Her expression revealed nothing of what she was thinking—not that there was any surprise in that. What did surprise Noah was how quickly and affirmatively he could answer those questions himself. All this time, he'd been telling himself the reason he couldn't make a commitment to Marnie was because his feelings for Lila were too confusing. Now he realized that wasn't the problem at all. The reason he hadn't been able to make a commitment to

Marnie was because his feelings for *Marnie* were too confusing.

Or, at least, they had been before now. Because his feelings for Marnie had been tangled up with whatever he'd thought he felt for Lila. But seeing Lila again after knowing Marnie, Noah realized that whatever he might have thought he felt for Lila had been just that—thoughts. Not feelings. He hadn't had feelings for Lila since…ever. Not the kind of feelings he'd thought he might have. He knew that now, because what he had for Marnie was exactly that sort of feeling. In fact, he had lots of feelings for Marnie. Lots of, well, serious feelings. Like…love. Suddenly it was all so clear.

After a long moment of silence, Lila tilted her head to one side and said, "I don't know if there's something emotional there, Noah. But what if there is?"

It was the question he had asked himself so many times so long ago. Back then, he hadn't known how to answer it. Right now, he knew exactly how.

What he felt for Lila was affection. The same sort of affection he had for many of the people he worked with. But love? No way. And now he was wondering how he could have ever confused the two.

Probably, he told himself, because he'd never been in love before, so he'd had no idea what it was like. Now he knew. Because he was in love with Marnie. Deeply. Passionately. Irrevocably. And, strangely, it wasn't nearly as terrifying to realize that as he'd thought it would be. In fact, it was damned nice. Or would be. Once he told Marnie how he felt. And once he knew for sure she felt the same way about him.

He chose his words carefully in forming his reply to

Lila. Not because he was afraid he might say too much. But because he was afraid he might leave something important unsaid. "Look, Lila, I'll admit there was a time when I wasn't sure what I felt for you," he began. "For a long time after that night we spent together, I thought maybe there *could* be something between us that was more than physical. I don't know what," he added readily. "Neither of us is the champagne-and-roses type. But I always thought we were two of a kind in a lot of ways."

"We have hardly anything in common, Noah," she said flatly.

"We have more than you think, Lila." Not the least of which was an obvious love for and need to protect Marnie Lundy. But he wasn't ready to go there with Lila just yet. He was still getting used to the feeling himself. "And for a long time," he continued, "I wondered if maybe you and I should have explored that more."

She hesitated a moment before saying, "You're talking like you don't wonder that anymore."

"I don't," he said quickly, honestly. "And I realize now that I haven't wondered that for a while."

"Since when?"

This time he was the one to lift a shoulder and let it drop. "I guess I first started to realize it when I met your sister."

She fixed her gaze on his and asked point-blank, "Are you in love with Marnie?"

There was no way he was going to say the words to Lila before he said them to Marnie. "I don't think I need to tell you that," he sidestepped.

She ignored him. "Are you in love with Marnie?" she asked more insistently.

"Lila, I really don't want—"

"Are you in love with Marnie?" she demanded a third time.

Noah growled in frustration before finally admitting, to her and to himself, "Yes. I'm in love with Marnie."

Tears filled her eyes at his admission, and Noah felt as if she'd just kicked him in the gut. He'd never seen Lila cry. He hadn't known she was capable of it. And he certainly hadn't considered the possibility that she might have feelings for him that were strong enough to generate such a response.

"Lila, I'm sorry," he said, knowing the apology sounded lame but having no idea what else to tell her. "I had no idea you felt this way about me. I mean, I'm flattered, but… I have to be honest with you. I don't love you. I never loved you. I love Marnie. I've probably loved her since that first night I met her. And she's who I want to be with."

He hesitated before saying the rest, because he didn't want to share that with Lila before telling Marnie, either. But he needed for Lila to unequivocally understand that there was no chance he could ever have feelings for her except what he felt for his other sisters-in-law. So he told her, "I want to be with Marnie forever. If she'll have me."

She smiled at that, in a way that kicked the wind right out of Noah's lungs. Because suddenly, Lila didn't look like Lila anymore. Suddenly, Lila looked just like…

"Marnie?"

She laughed, then bit her lip, as if she was still straddling the personas of Lila and Marnie and wasn't sure how much of her happiness she should show just yet. Then she reached for the cap and pulled it off, and a mass of blond hair—darker and longer than Lila's—came tumbling down around her shoulders. "Whataya know? You were right," she said as she shook the tresses free. When she tugged off her gloves, he saw that her fingernails were short and unpainted, unlike Lila's expertly manicured and bloodred nails. "OPUS really could teach me everything I needed to know in two weeks to pass for Lila. And what can I say? I'm a quick study."

Noah stared at her in silence. Now he saw it. It was so obvious. But only moments ago, he would have sworn on his life she was Lila Moreau. She really could have completed the assignment, he thought. She was that good.

Then he realized the extent of her deception. She'd played him. Extremely well. But why? Because she wanted to know how he felt about her? Why hadn't she just asked him?

Gee, Einstein, he immediately answered himself, *maybe because you never gave her the chance?*

"Quick study," he echoed. And then, he smiled. "Must run in the family."

She smiled back, beaming. "And a good family it is, too."

Noah nodded, wondering if—and hoping that—there was room for that family to grow. He didn't care that Marnie had just played him extremely well. Because she'd done it for a reason he completely understood. She'd needed to know without doubt that he wasn't in love with Lila. She'd needed to know without doubt that he loved her. And he did. Love her. Without doubt. Without reserve. Without fear. He could only hope her feelings for him were just as strong.

For a long time, they only gazed at each other without speaking, a good six feet of floor and the corner of the bed, separating them. Unable to tolerate even that small distance, Noah took two steps forward, something that bumped his thigh against the bed. Marnie grinned and covered the rest of the distance herself, wrapping an arm around the bedpost.

"Tell me again how much you love Marnie," she said.

"I'd rather show you how much I love you."

Her eyes widened at that, her expression revealing completely what she was thinking and feeling in that moment. Oh, yeah. Marnie was definitely back. And damn, was Noah grateful.

"Then show me that," she said.

He lifted a hand to her hair and pushed it over her shoulder, then cupped her face in his hands. "I love you," he told her without hesitation.

"I love you, too," she replied just as quickly. "Now tell me how you want to be with me forever."

"I want to be with you forever," he replied.

"I want to be with you forever, too. With no deceptions. No phony identities. No secrets."

"And no clothes," he added.

She chuckled at that. "And no clothes. Well, not always."

He reached for the zipper of her jacket and tugged it the rest of the way down. The fastener hissed quietly as it opened, a sound not unlike the whisper of Marnie's jacket as it fell to the floor when he nudged it from her shoulders. That, in turn, was a sound only a tiny bit louder than his shirt as she skimmed it from his body. The rest of their clothing followed in a concert of soft sounds, leaving their bodies to join in a chorus of soft sighs.

A long time later, Noah lay in his bed with Marnie

beside him, knowing there was little chance he'd make it in to work that day. Funny thing was, he didn't care. He had everything he needed. Right here in his home.

Thoroughbred *Legacy*

Launching in June 2008

A dramatic new 12-book continuity that embodies the American Dream.

Meet the Prestons, owners of Quest Stables, a successful horse-racing and breeding empire. But the lives, loves and reputations of this hardworking family are put at risk when a breeding scandal unfolds.

Flirting with Trouble

by New York Times bestselling author

ELIZABETH BEVARLY

Eight years ago, publicist Marnie Roberts spent seven days of bliss with Australian horse trainer Daniel Whittleson. But just as quickly, he disappeared. Now Marnie is heading to Australia to finally confront the man she's never been able to forget.

The race begins in June, wherever books are sold.

REQUEST YOUR FREE BOOKS!

2 FREE NOVELS
FROM THE ROMANCE/SUSPENSE
COLLECTION PLUS 2 FREE GIFTS!

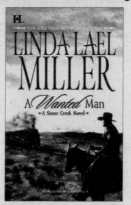

ELIZABETH BEVARLY

77276   YOU'VE GOT MALE   ___ $4.99 U.S. ___ $4.99 CAN.
                (limited quantities available)

TOTAL AMOUNT $ _____
POSTAGE & HANDLING $ _____
($1.00 FOR 1 BOOK, 50¢ for each additional)
APPLICABLE TAXES* $ _____
TOTAL PAYABLE $ _____
          (check or money order—please do not send cash)

To order, complete this form and send it, along with a check or money order for the total above, payable to HQN Books, to: **In the U.S.:** 3010 Walden Avenue, P.O. Box 9077, Buffalo, NY 14269-9077; **In Canada:** P.O. Box 636, Fort Erie, Ontario, L2A 5X3.

Name: _____
Address: _____ City: _____
State/Prov.: _____ Zip/Postal Code: _____
Account Number (if applicable): _____

075 CSAS

*New York residents remit applicable sales taxes.
*Canadian residents remit applicable GST and provincial taxes.

HQN™

We *are* romance™

www.HQNBooks.com •

PHEB0508BL